KU-310-742

THE BOOK OF SAND

MO HAYDER

WRITING AS THEO CLARE

PENGUIN BOOKS

PENGUIN BOOKS

UK | USA | Canada | Ireland | Australia
India | New Zealand | South Africa

Penguin Books is part of the Penguin Random House group of companies
whose addresses can be found at global.penguinrandomhouse.com

First published by Century in 2022
Published in Penguin Books 2022
001

Copyright © The Estate of Mo Hayder, 2022
Map © Darren Bennett, 2022

The moral right of the author has been asserted

Typeset in 10.9/16 pt Times New Roman
by Integra Software Services Pvt. Ltd, Pondicherry

Printed and bound in Great Britain by Clays Ltd, Elcograf S.p.A.

The authorised representative in the EEA is Penguin Random House Ireland,
Morrison Chambers, 32 Nassau Street, Dublin D02 YH68

A CIP catalogue record for this book is available from the British Library

ISBN: 978–1–529–15801–4

www.greenpenguin.co.uk

Penguin Random House is committed to a sustainable future for our business, our readers and our planet. This book is made from Forest Stewardship Council® certified paper.

THE

We hope you enjoy this book. Please return or
... the due date.

www.norfolk.gov.uk/libraries or
...ary app.
...one 0344 ...

S

'An utterly original novel from an extraordinarily creative mind' **Karin Slaughter**

'Unique and fearless' **Mark Billingham**

'I inhaled it! It's beautifully written and utterly compelling' **Harriet Tyce**

'Audacious, extraordinary and absolutely awesome' **Alex North**

'Fearless and compelling, lyrical and devastating by turns, the story never slackens pace. A stunning introduction to a wholly original world' **Jane Corry**

'A future classic that exists between darkness and light. I was completely entranced by it' **Christopher Fowler**

'A huge and brilliant and engaging read' **Alice Jolly**

This book, and the series, is dedicated to all those who have been affected by Motor Neurone Disease

I know I am deathless . . .

Walt Whitman, 'Song of Myself', 20

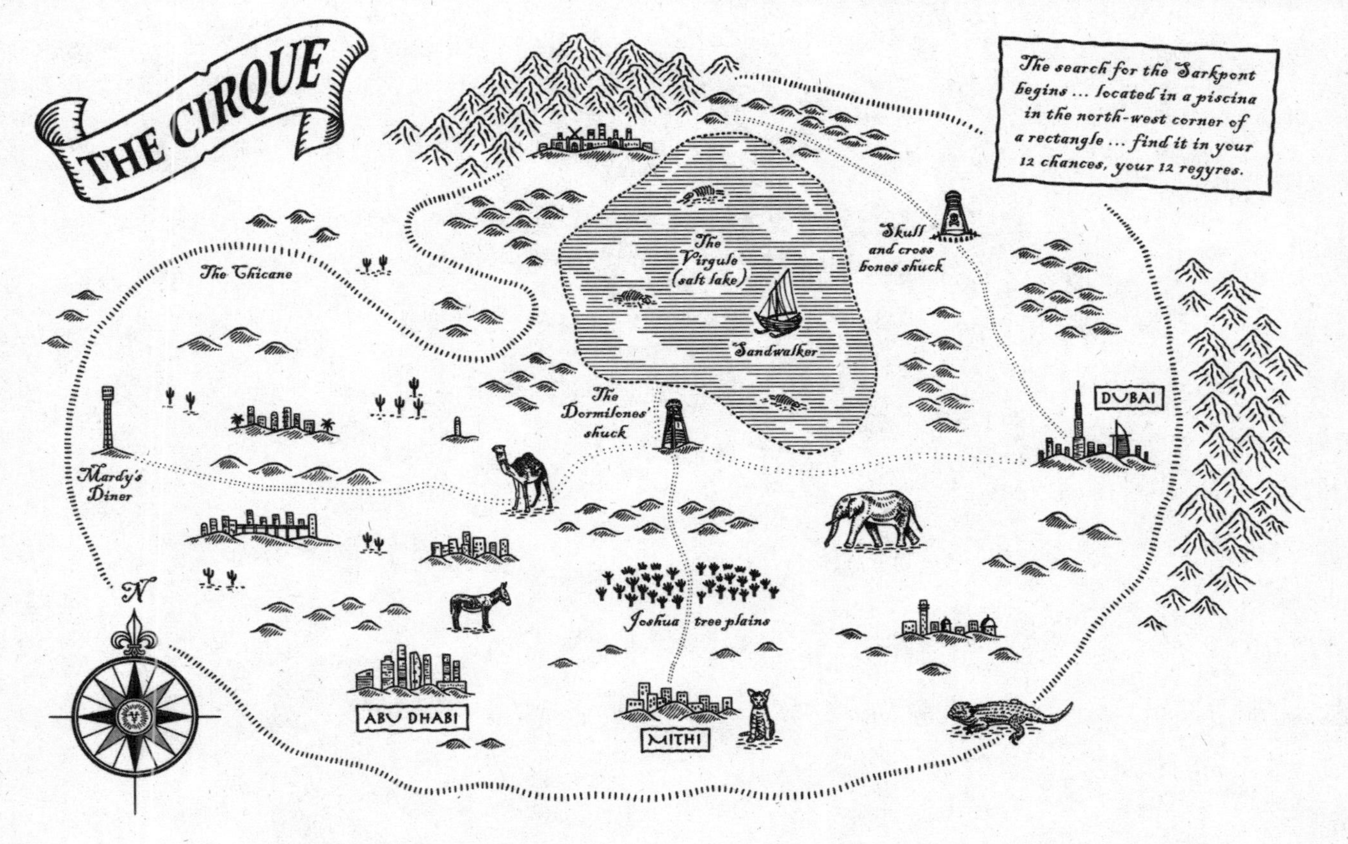
THE CIRQUE
The search for the Sarkpont begins ... located in a piscina in the north-west corner of a rectangle ... find it in your 12 chances, your 12 regyres.
The Chicane
The Virgule (salt lake)
Sandwalker
Skull and cross bones shuck
The Dormilones' shuck
DUBAI
Mardy's Diner
N
Joshua tree plains
ABU DHABI
MITHI

PART ONE

THE FAMILY

1

HERE HE IS in the furthest corner of an antique desert, just one of a string of people who move silently across the sand. The ferocious heat shimmers, although the day is on the wane and sunset isn't far. Some days this place is all Spider can remember. His skin is crusted with sweat, his tongue swollen, his feet sore, but he'll keep going, he has no choice with the sun sinking so fast.

The family are eleven in total, a raggle-taggle assortment, ranging from a child of five to a huge grey man in his sixties, and though some are able-bodied, others are less so. Spider knows that of all the family he's the strangest sight – though he stands almost two metres tall, is whip-like and healthy as a young tree, it's his clothes that set him apart: he wears desert boots, aviator goggles and a tattered woman's dress, which the slight breeze causes to flap lazily against his tanned legs. He leads the family's single camel, laden with equipment; the camel is as downcast as the family, forlorn and battered, and she drags her feet and her humps are pitifully slumped.

Next to Spider walks Amasha: squat and round-figured, moving like a regal ocean-going ship, her veils fluttering around her face. In her expression there is no urgency, no betrayal that she feels the same fear as the rest of the family.

Spider glances over his shoulder to check the family are keeping up. The little blonde-haired girl, who has been trotting bravely next to the camel for the last two hours, is crying with fear.

'Hey,' he mutters, leaning his head sideways to Amasha. 'Have you seen?'

Amasha doesn't turn back to look – she keeps her eyes fixed on the horizon. 'Of course. She's scared, but we can't stop.'

'She's crying.'

'I know, I know. But for the sake of the family, we can't stop. She has to keep up. She knows we have to get home. Don't pay attention, she will soothe herself.'

Spider wraps the camel's rope tighter around his fists and leans into the walk, putting everything he has into it. His eyes are itchy with tiredness, but he keeps going, placing one foot after the other, registering the places on his neck where his skin has burned in the last two days, the point in his boots where the leather is thin and rubbing his sole. He doesn't look up at his surroundings, the long featureless tracts of sand, up to forty clicks in every direction, the distant cities and structures of iron. Vast funnel-shaped towers, some as much as a hundred metres tall and a hundred wide. Now that the sun is setting, the structures cast shadows immense as mountains collapsed across the sand.

The little girl cries louder now. Spider stops, and the camel stops obediently next to him. He ducks under the camel's neck and bends to take the little girl in his arms, but before he can hoist her up onto his shoulders, Noor, the tall man at the head of the train, turns.

In his late twenties, he is dressed in traditional kurta pyjamas of pale gold, his hair is straight and groomed, his nose high, shoulders square and he has the natural authority of a pope. He narrows his eyes at Spider, gives his head a faint but unequivocal shake – reminding him not to disobey Amasha.

Spider lowers his arms, crouches to the little girl, who is crying hard.

'Now listen, you've got to keep walking – it's almost night. You can rest soon, but for now you've got to keep going. You hear me?'

'I don't wanna walk, I'm scared.'

'I know that. I know you don't want to, and I know you've tried your best all day long and you're totally flaxed, tired as a frickin' dog, but you got to keep going. Think of it like a competition – you and Cairo or Mahmoud. Who's gonna be home first?'

The girl rubs her eyes, and her bottom lip sticks out as she swings her sullen gaze towards Cairo and Mahmoud, the little boys at the back of the line. 'Extra pancakes if me first?'

'That could be arranged.'

She lets out a long sigh. Kicks the sand with her open-toed sandals. 'OK. Maybe.'

And so they walk on, Spider lowering his eyes against the late sun, dragging at the camel's halter.

It starts again when McKenzie hits junior year at high school.

She wakes one morning at three. She doesn't need to look at her clock, she can tell the time from the position of the constellations above her skylight, so she lies on her back blinking at them, trying to decide what woke her. There are goosebumps on her arms as if she's mid-nightmare.

She takes a deep breath, from the lower ribs, because Mom says that yoga breathing is the most calming thing you can do. The room is normal, nothing out of place, the posters of the desert on the wall, the roof windows wide open, although it's freezing. She squirms her hand down into her bed, searching for Cuddle Bunny.

She's had Bunny since she was a kid, maybe he's her best friend after India, the one she tells all her secrets to. She feels him warm against her belly, touches him, but there's no fuzzy velour. No floppy stitched-up ears. Instead a warm and scaly skin.

She gasps and Cuddle Bunny moves, squirming hard and muscular, something scratching her belly. She pushes herself off the bed and lands in a crouch, her heart racing – hands out in front of her. The quilt is moving, undulating. She backs away from the bed, half on her hands and knees, gets to the wall, trembling, and throws the light switch.

The coverlet moves, and a head appears from under it. A lizard of some sort, but like nothing McKenzie has ever seen in her life; buff in colour, it has a dinosaur-like ruff of horns around its neck.

It blinks, then ducks back under the covers, fighting with them, until it reaches the end of the bed. It drops off the bed with a thud and disappears beneath it.

She throws the door open, steps through and slams it behind her. She stands for a moment, her heart pounding, then, taking the steps two at a time, canters down the staircase to the second floor.

'Mom?' Her throat is so tight with terror the word hardly comes out. 'Mom?'

She gets to the next storey down, the long passage where, dotted along the wall, at foot height, are little flower-shaped night lights. Her brothers occupy the two bedrooms on the left – their doors are closed – and, at what seems an impossible distance, Mom and Dad's bedroom door. Closed. She's never seen Mom and Dad's door closed at night; they always leave it open.

Very, very carefully she tiptoes into the passageway, past her brothers' doors. The bathroom on the right, the door is open, a gaping hole – a triangle of mirror just visible, cut in half by a robe hanging on the towel rack.

She stands next to Mom and Dad's door, her forehead almost touching it. She raises her hand to knock, it's the polite thing to do, but changes her mind.

'Mom?' she whispers into the door crack. 'Mom? Dad? Are you awake? Mommy? Please?'

She shivers. Her feet are bare, her vest and pyjamas are thin. Can she hear scratching on the stairs above?

'Mom? Please?'

On the other side of the door she can imagine the room: large and comforting. There are family portraits on the wall, pictures of

Mom and Dad at their wedding, one of Grandpop, who was born in Shanghai and died in LA last year – that must have been a big deal. She has been back to Shanghai and seen it all: the Chinese restaurants, the hotels for the rich and famous, the long streets. There's a sofa in the corner where Mom often has her breakfast coffee and reads *The Washington Post*. The curtains are blue, printed with white tulips, and Dad wears pyjamas that smell like apple pie, when they come warm out of the laundry. His chin is always scratchy by the end of the day.

All so safe. She pushes the door a little wider, cringing at the squeak. The room is so familiar – blue moonlight from the squares of the windows. The gentle in-and-out sounds of Mom and Dad sleeping.

'Dad?'

A sharp voice from the other side of the room. Dad's voice. 'Kenz? What's happening?'

On the king-size bed Mom is sitting up, rubbing her eyes sleepily. 'Kenz? Honey?'

'Mom?'

'What's up, honey?'

'I . . . I don't know. I . . .'

'Sweetie?' Dad says sleepily. 'What's happening?'

'Mom, Dad, there's . . . I think there's something in my room. You've got to come and see.'

Sunset. Spider hates sunset. He hates the way the day seems to sag, like rotting fruit, and the familiar smell that arises, as if the ground has opened its maw. Mostly he dislikes the fact that no one in the family will remark on it, as if talking about it or naming it could give it more power than it already has.

Noor waves his arm to muster the dawdling family. 'Let's do it,' he shouts. 'We're running out of time.'

Spider leans forward, putting extra muscle into it, dragging the exhausted camel across the sand, through the cacti that surround this area, while behind him the family ramp up their efforts. The pattering and hard breathing, the subtle spatter of sand underfoot. No one wants to be out here after dark.

Half a kilometre ahead of them the family's home tower rises up against the hazy desert floor. It is enormous; with a footprint bigger than that of the Eiffel Tower, it blocks out a huge quadrant of the darkening eastern sky. Its walls are riddled with rust – the sands and the salty desert winds have driven huge holes into it. An attempt has been made to paint it, to smarten it up in desert-bloom shades of violet and pale pink, but the air has flaked and cracked the paint, so now it hangs in strips as if scabs are dropping from it.

Spider's skin is olive, though he can still burn in the relentless heat. His hair is corn-blonde and his eyes are the blue of his father's, and he struggles in this desert, always squinting, the sunlight seeming to find this special weakness in him and push its advantage. People tell him he has a fighter's face, they say he always seems to be expecting a punch from nowhere.

Nobody speaks. At the tower Spider hitches Camel to a spike on the outer wall while he helps Noor unshackle the gate. The noise of rusting metal on metal booms around the tower, causing the family to glance anxiously over their shoulders at the empty expanses of sand around them.

Spider holds the door open and waits for every member to hurry inside. Exhausted, they nod, but barely glance at him. Just as most of them are inside, the two boys at the back, Mahmoud and Cairo – always competitive, always causing trouble – dodge to the front of the line.

Tita Lily keeps her eyes on them – she half cries when she sees them moving forward. She ticks them off about their clothing and their lack of sunscreen. She worries about them not taking their hats, she worries about them showing too much skin. She is a proper worrier, Tita Lily, and cannot keep her eyes off the boys.

Cairo is trying to prove he is faster than Mahmoud – an impossibility, because the little boy, Mahmoud, is taller and stronger – but as he does so, he runs past Tita Lily. She is walking as she usually does, with her head held high, trailing her way between the cacti. She doesn't see them until it's too late. She trips over Cairo and is dragged by his momentum about a metre, against a cactus, before he stops, his hands out to her, a look of terror and guilt on his face.

'*Tang ina!*' she yells into the sand. 'You crazy son of bitches . . .'

Amasha comes back out of the tower and then, when Tita Lily doesn't jump up, the others stop and return. She is lying face down, holding down the white Grace Kelly hat over her dark hair. Her sunglasses have come off and there is a small stain of blood drifting up her white dress.

'A cactus,' Forlani says. He goes to her on his crutches, crouches as best he can, and tells her not to move. 'Did you get dragged across a cactus?'

'Yes. Get me upstairs,' she whispers.

Elk and Hugo come back and lift Tita Lily effortlessly – she is tiny and wiry – and carry her into the tower, Forlani hobbling along next to her. There is a trail of blood, Spider sees, dark-red blood, and he doesn't want to think of the scent it might leave.

He unhooks Camel and leads her into the tower, then turns and sets about slamming down the giant bars on the back of the gate. He is one of the strongest of the family, so this task comes to him – the other family members each have an allotted chore, and now they scatter in the dimly lit tower to perform them.

The older family members check all entrances to the tower are still secure, while the little girl, Splendour, joins the two boys, both shamefaced now, and they work as a gang, checking water supplies and turning on the power supply from the solar panels. Madeira, the farmer's daughter, a cigar tucked behind her ear, goes to her crops, lifting the plastic coating to confirm the irrigation system hasn't been tampered with, and reads the little thermometers. There are the animals to check on too. She dips her fingers into the water troughs and scatters grain for the chickens, four buckets of swill for the pigs.

In the middle of the disorder stands the moth-eaten camel, patient while Spider unloads their camping equipment. He hauls the bags across the sand to the lockers that are dotted around the base of the tower and throws them inside, securing each locker with a strap. He is drenched in sweat and his mouth is sour and dry from the cured rabbit meat the family have lived on for two days.

The family's home – the 'Shuck', they call it – hangs like a vast seedpod sixty metres above them, something that seems to have grown naturally like a gourd, or a tumour up in the air. The access is a spindly iron ladder to its underside, where, hazy in the dwindling light, is the giant iron lock that permits entry and exit. The two carrying Tita Lily have got to the top of the ladder and are braced there, Hugo holding her and Elk unlocking the door. Forlani is a few rungs beneath them, holding his hands across her side. His face is covered in the dark blood that weeps from her.

As Spider gets the last of the equipment stowed, he sees a slash of red high on the wall. It is the low sun throwing a single blade of light into the tower – a sign that night is upon them.

'Keep up the pace,' he yells. His voice echoes round the tower. 'Eight more minutes.'

The family's sense of urgency increases, the tasks are finished hurriedly. Splendour is crying again from fear and exhaustion, but Spider can't go to her. He lets Amasha herd her and the remaining family members towards the centre of the tower. There are thirty metres of ladder to climb, and the children are pushed to the front to get started. Spider leads Camel to her cage as, out of the corner of his eye, he sees the children make their way up, strung like vivid beads on a necklace in the late sun. Noor and Amasha bring up the rear: Noor's long, muscular shins are revealed under the gold pyjamas, while Amasha's jewelled hands and forehead glint. She hauls her bright-pink sari up above her thighs so that it rucks around her hips. There's no vanity here; she has to climb. Her arm muscles bulge fat and square with the effort, and sweat stains the silk.

Camel's cloven lip is trembling and crusted black. Smears run from her eyes. She is exhausted. Spider whips up the rope and tugs at her halter. 'Come on, girl.' He makes a soft click in his throat. 'Come on.'

She's a curmudgeonly character and needs to be coaxed, so he doesn't drag at the halter but eases her along. She needs to be in the protective cage before he can trust himself to leave her. He's made the cage with a cobbled-together arc-welder; it is thirty centimetres off the floor because somehow he thinks that will protect her. He has to ease her up the ramp.

Inside the cage he takes off her halter and rubs down her hide. Her humps are flaccid, one on either side, which should be comical if it wasn't a sign of her exhaustion. Only two days without food or water to get this bad. Her age is showing.

'Hey,' he tells her, touching her top lip. 'You've got a guard tonight. Look at this.'

In his few free hours he's been working on a screen that pulls down around Camel's sleeping cage. He will be safe in one of the Shuck pods overhead, and though the animals never suffer on the grey nights, it gnaws at him regardless that Camel has to witness what happens. He wants her protected, so he has devised a scroll-down screen. It locks first time and, when he rattles it, it stays firm.

Camel needs to drink. While she arranges herself in the cage, turning herself around to accustom herself to the new shape and dimensions, he snatches up her plastic drinking trug and makes a run for the perimeter of the tower, where the water is located. He clips open the tap and directs the head of the hose into the base of the container. It takes 180 seconds to fill, he knows this from experience, and in those moments of waiting he takes stock of his situation. Sand caked raw on his naked legs, his lips cracked and sore. Tita Lily upstairs injured, as if they don't have enough problems. And it's been another two days of searching without result. Things are shit, he thinks. Truly shit.

'Spider!'

He looks up. Thirty metres overhead, the lock to the Shuck is hanging open and in it, perched on the ladder, her legs bare, Amasha screams at him.

'Get up here.' She is holding onto the lock mechanism with one hand. With the other she beckons him, her saliva making a mist of pink in the last sunrays. 'Leave her. Get up here.'

'She needs water.' He wrenches off the water clip, flips the hose out and collects the trug handles.

'I'm telling you to leave her. She can go days without water.'

He could drop the trug and run for the ladder, but he's not going to leave Camel overnight without water, so he hefts the trug across the sand. The water tilts and laps and splashes.

'*Spider. Last chance!*'

Patiently he drags the container up the ramp into the cage. With the last of his strength he hauls it up to the hooks on the side of the cage, so Camel can reach it. She dips her head in and he takes five seconds to scratch her on the top of her head, then slams the cage and makes a run for the ladder. It creaks and groans as he scampers up it. Amasha waits, her brown arm extended out of the hole. She would rather die than leave one of the family down here at nightfall.

He makes the entrance just as the last of the sunrays leave the underside of the pod. Amasha pulls him inside, slams the lock shut while he lies on his back, breathing hard.

'Don't do that to me again. I don't ever want to know what would happen if you were left down there. I keep thinking about Nergüi.'

'None of us wants to know what would happen,' he assures her between deep breaths. 'None of us.'

The room at the top of the house is as McKenzie left it – the bed-covers pulled back, the pillow on the floor.

Her mother, Selena Strathie, shivers. 'Honey, do you ever think about closing those windows. The bills in this place are crippling.'

McKenzie doesn't answer. The thing about the windows – the reason she has them open, no curtains or blinds – goes back to before she can even remember and is one of the things they argue about all the time.

'Where did it go?' Dad asks. 'Under the bed?'

'Uh-huh.'

Dad gets down on his hands and knees and lifts the covers, peering under the bed. 'Nothing there now.'

'I did see it.'

He lifts his head and gives her a strange look. 'Didn't say you didn't, hon.' He prowls the room, checking under her desk, opening her wardrobe and checking carefully in there. From his top pocket he levers out his glasses and loops the wire frames round his ears. He gets down on his knees and feels his way along the skirting boards.

'Nothing.'

He goes into the shower room and hits the light. McKenzie and Mom come to stand together behind him and peer at the shower, the WC all gleaming in the electric light.

'It's big,' she murmurs. 'We'd see it.'

Dad opens the vanity unit and feels around under the sink, stretching to look under there. 'Nothing here.'

'Any holes it could have crawled into?'

'Nothing I can see.' After a long time of looking, Dad sits on the bathroom floor, rubbing his eyes. 'I don't know, sweetie. I just don't know. You wanna sleep with us?'

She bites her lip. 'I guess it was a nightmare. Right?'

She must have been dreaming – it happens like this, she's sure: your dreams bleed into your reality. No seams.

'I'll stay up here.'

'You want us to stay with you, for a while?'

'I guess. If you're OK with that?'

'A few minutes.'

Mom gets spare quilts and pillows out of the wardrobe and she and Dad prop themselves against the bed, wrapping the quilts around them. McKenzie lies on her side on her bed, staring into mid-air. What did she just see? A lizard?

She closes her eyes and thinks about India, her friend on the other side of the development. Neither McKenzie nor India has boyfriends; frankly, no boy has ever considered them dateable. India sometimes sleepwalks. She wakes up in sketchy places, like the car port, or once on the borders of her yard, looking down into the creek that runs way below the fall-off behind the houses. India's mom said that was the scariest.

Is that what happened to McKenzie? Has she just sleepwalked into her parents' room? Dreamed up a lizard?

'Is she asleep?' Mom murmurs to Dad, and although it's the most natural thing to open her eyes and say, '*Not yet, but don't stay*',

McKenzie keeps her eyes closed. She thinks her parents worry about her in a way they don't worry about her brothers, and she wishes she knew why.

There is a long silence. She can feel her parents' gaze on her face, but keeps breathing in and out, in and out.

'She's gone.' Dad yawns, gets to his feet. Mom, after a while, gets to her feet and seems to spend a bit of time pushing the quilt back into the wardrobe. She's a card-carrying neat-freak.

It's only when they get to the door that Mom speaks. 'Scott,' she murmurs, real sad and low. 'You don't think it's happening again, do you?'

2

SPIDER STILL DOESN'T have a clue what brought this family to the desert: all of them so disparate – from low-level incomes to the highest incomes, from South America to Sri Lanka and beyond. It's a test. Even worse, though, he knows he is not supposed to be here.

Spider is a killer, a cold and methodical killer, and he can't understand why no one has figured this out.

Tonight he goes into the main area of the Shuck where Amasha is wagging a finger at Cairo, scolding him again for his attempts to show off. Elk is in the kitchen, wearing an animal skin even in the heat. He is old, like a Viking, and his long grey hair is tied with a piece of kangaroo gut. He is the cook and the defender – the whole family could hide behind his vast bulk.

'Where's Tita Lily?'

'With Forlani – in the pod at the back. She's full of cactus spines. Take this.' Elk hands Spider a glass of thin golden alcohol. 'Make her drink it.'

Forlani, the teenager who is no larger than a child, is the medicine man in the family. Spider goes to the pod and finds Tita Lily lying on the bench with Forlani crouched over her, holding a pair of tweezers that he found in one of the cities. Her hat lies on the floor, her sunglasses are at an angle and her always-immaculate lipstick is smeared.

'Spider, no, please don't. You see me at my worst.'

'You've never seen me at my worst?'

Tita Lily is from the Philippines, born of another gender, namely that of a male. She wears her hair styled long and has implanted, helmet-shaped breasts, which she likes because of the way they fill out a dress.

Even now she is scrabbling with Forlani, trying to keep him from lifting her dress. 'I haven't shaved, damn you – I haven't shaved.'

'I have to get these spines out. Lily, I mean it. I have to do it.'

'OK, OK,' she pants. 'Just promise me. You'll shave me later? Promise me you'll do it.'

'I promise.'

Spider sits next to her and holds her hand while Forlani gets himself into the most comfortable position he can and sets about removing the spines, dabbing at the wounds, applying compresses to them. Forlani's legs were broken in five places by his uncle when he was five years old, in a mulberry orchard in Romania. He has never properly recovered, and the little girl, Splendour, sometimes looks at Spider and asks why Forlani isn't called Spider.

'After all,' she whispers quietly, 'he's the one what proper looks like a spider – not you.'

But Forlani has the gift of caring, the gift of knowing which herbs to use, the knack of standing in an abandoned hotel and knowing where the clinic is. After nearly six months in this desert he has collected whole truckloads of pills and phials and herbs and bandages. Caring for the family's health is what keeps him going, and Spider thinks he cares more about Forlani than any of them. Maybe as much as he cared about Nergüi.

Now, in spite of Tita Lily's nervy thrashing around, Forlani pushes on the places the thorns have entered, delivering five, then six cactus spines, which he places on a saucer. The last one, though, he is struggling with.

'You OK?'

'No,' Tita Lily growls, flopping her head from side to side. 'I'm not OK.'

He presses down, using the old tweezers he found. The wound bulges fat and red, but the spines don't shoot out the way the others have. 'They're too deep.'

'So what now?'

He shakes his head, stands, rubbing the back of his neck. He hates not to be able to help. 'Your body will expel them when it's time. It won't be long.'

Tita Lily dabs at her eyes with a lace handkerchief that miraculously is perfectly white.

'Hey,' Forlani says quietly. 'I can shave you now. OK?'

*

Spider is tired. He eats with the others – the children take food to Tita Lily in her sleep pod, then Spider goes to his own pod. He's been awake for almost thirty-six hours, and tonight is the end of the forty-eight-hour cycle: the night they call the 'grey night', the one after the 'white night'.

He lies for a while, the door open, lulled by the family chatting among themselves where they sleep on a platform suspended above the floor. Splendour has sunburn again, she has that pale skin, and no one – not Forlani or Amasha – can convince her to look after it.

Noor spends a short while explaining about the sand, telling everyone how they have to harden their feet up or else they're always going to complain, until eventually Madeira laughs and chides him. 'Six months we've been hearing this, dude. I mean bless you, but can you change the record?'

Spider falls asleep listening to them, but a jangling anxiety wakes him in the middle of the night. He judges, from the stars outside the window, that it is two hours before dawn. It's cold and for a moment he lies in the darkness, picking through his dreams. Did he hear anything outside? He kneels and peers out of the window, an aperture glazed with pockmarked glass. There are no lights out there. Although there are – the family estimates – maybe fifty other families in the desert, most of them don't keep their towers lit.

The Pole Star is bright in the sky, but he doesn't know how to interpret its position. The one who knows how to read the heavens, the natural navigator, is missing from the family at the moment – off on a Scouting mission – and Spider has made no headway on the timepiece he's been attempting to assemble.

His eyes travel slowly over the barren lands, hoping for a glimmer of shadow or a clue. He skips over the cities the family have explored, some with pinpricks of light, others dead and black; on he goes, past the dead Joshua-tree plains and the dunes in the south. On the western horizon is a shape that makes his pulse pick up. Quickly he finds his binoculars; they aren't perfect – he found them in Abu Dhabi under an abandoned racing car – but with a little polish and attention they serve well. With shaky fingers he focuses.

A cloud of sand on the horizon, maybe twenty clicks away.

Djinni. Or, as Amasha calls them, the *Pretas*. The hungry ghosts. Because Buddhists believe in the hungry ghosts as well.

They are swarming, but not in a direction. He's never seen that before – usually they are as swift as the wind, just a billow of sand to show where they have been, but now they seem directionless. Almost as if they are moving to and fro, considering their options, scoping the desert for a place to go.

Quickly he throws on his boots and puts his blanket over his shoulders, creeps out of his berth and down the corridor, palms on the walls as the passage gets narrower and twisty. Here, deep inside the Shuck, the family shelter seems organic; all the walls are sloping and curved, the ceilings dip and sometimes come down to within a metre or so of the floor, but there is a rigid framework beneath it, which holds them on this precarious perch tens of metres above the desert. Ridges like the segments of an orange are everywhere, and from the walls emanates a comforting smell like roasted peanut shells.

He creeps past the suspended family bed – a circular mattress where the family members who don't go to their private pods sleep together, curled like piglets. The sounds of them breathing and snuffling follow him as he tiptoes to the next floor of the Shuck. He reaches the common room, the place where the family gathers during the daytime, which he, Noor and Tita Lily designed and built.

It's a vast space, twenty metres by twenty, and stands taller than the surrounding tower, with enormous tables, cushions, sleeping mats. Along the eastern wall there is access to a series of small curved balconies; shuttered overnight and mounted atop the room, accessible only by a twisting ladder, is a polygonal lantern-shaped watchtower, glazed on all six sides by means of a clever polymer, which is strong yet soft – a person can lean into it and, though it will give slightly, it will hold one's weight.

Spider can just make out his own reflection in the dark windows as he makes his way up to the cupola. The Djinni are still there. Still hovering way beyond the sand dunes. Too far to hear them or guess what they are going to do. He crouches by the glazing, leaning his knees into it so that he is protruding dizzyingly above the drop, holds up the binoculars and adjusts them to this new angle. Before he can get the focus right, the Djinni move.

It happens so rapidly it jolts him, almost makes him lose the binoculars. The Djinni stream across the desert towards the sand dunes, moving in that familiar way, a line of sand billowing behind them, always obscuring them, so no one can see them. Heart thudding, Spider gets quickly to his feet, instinctively groping in his thigh holster for his knife.

The Djinni skirt the sand dunes and seem to be heading north towards the giant salt lake the family call the 'Virgule'. The

Djinni can cover a kilometre in a few seconds, so Spider shuffles around the lantern, following their movement across the sand. They take the easternmost route around the Joshua-tree plains and continue north, heading directly for this tower.

There is no time – no time at all. Before he can yell for the others, the Djinni are less than a click away, powerfully churning up the sand. He gets halfway to the ladder as they veer north, galloping across the long expanse of sand that lies between this Shuck and the nearest city. Spider canters down the ladder and towards the balconies, throwing open the shutters.

The night is cool, the sky black, the air smells of the sap that rises from the rough-hewn floorboards under his bare feet. He grips the knife between his teeth and stares out at the Djinni, who are disappearing towards the Virgule.

As they hit the Virgule shores, something changes. They slow, then stop abruptly, sending a spurt of sand into the air. It's too far to tell what they look like – none of the family have seen a Djinni, and even now all he gets is a brief impression of their shape: something stick-thin and white. Much, much taller than a human being.

Instantly he recoils, jerking back inside the Shuck as quickly as he came out and hurriedly refastening the shutter. Before he can drag it closed, the sand cloud is torpedoing towards the tower, a high keening voice floating up to the balcony. Sweat breaks out on Spider's neck as he struggles, trying to fit the bar across the shutters, his hands like rubber. He gets the bar in place, slides it closed and, as he does so, a deep booming echoes through the Shuck, seems to shake the foundations, rattling the plates in the kitchen.

Spider freezes, hands on the shutter. A Djinni has hit the outside shield. Spider breathes through the spike of adrenaline. And then another blow to the outside, another trembling of the Shuck. He clenches his teeth on the knife and grips the shutter closed. Never has a Djinni attacked the Shuck – it's the first time they've even come close. He cranes his neck and sees a Djinni reverse its trajectory and head back to the Virgule.

'Spider?'

He glances to his right. Noor stands there, tall and bare-chested in his Turkish trousers, his brown eyes wide. Spider doesn't trust this man.

'What the hell was that?'

Spider takes the knife out of his mouth. 'Djinni. Threw itself at the tower.'

'*What?* They can't climb it.'

'No – but one threw itself. They smelled something.'

'You were outside?'

'For a split second. I mean, what the *fuck*, man …? That's never happened – we've watched them before. They never smelled us before.'

'Tita Lily's blood?'

'There's been human blood around too – when Hugo cut himself outside the tower, and when …' He means to insert the word Nergüi, but he can't. 'It's happened before.'

From the family sleeping platform Elk appears, his long grey hair hanging over his wide bare shoulders. 'What's going on?'

Spider holds a finger up to his lip, shakes his head. 'Are the kids awake?' he hisses. 'They need to go back to sleep.'

'Sure. Amasha's with them. She'll talk them back.'

Hugo, the full-faced English guy with the mop of blonde hair, appears from his sleeping pod, scratching his stomach confusedly. He has a red web of veins across his bulbous nose, and eyes like a husky's. Then Madeira appears in white pyjamas, a cigar wedged above her ear – and eventually everyone except Forlani, Amasha and Tita Lily is in the room, whispering, shock-faced, standing at the window and trying to see what's happening outside.

'The whole place shook,' Madeira whispers, standing on her tiptoes and trying to peer out. 'Are they still there?'

It's impossible to see what is on the desert floor close to the tower; even when Spider climbs back to the lantern room and leans his weight out, he can't see. But there are no more noises and on the horizon – out towards the city with the skyscrapers, the one they haven't yet explored – a cloud of sand is rising up. The sort of cloud that comes when the Djinni have made a kill. Sometimes just one person caught out on a grey night is enough to satiate them.

Noor taps on the ladder and, when Spider looks down, he calls softly up at him. 'Let's go to the hatch. If anything happens, we need to be ready.'

Spider comes down the ladder and creeps along the narrow passageways. The light is dim in the bay, there isn't room for them all, so Spider stays crouched next to the giant door, the blanket over his head, his ear on the door, listening to the tower below, while the others gather on the level above him. Noor, meanwhile, disappears, reappearing a few moments later carrying a bow and a holdall, which he unzips. He doles out spears and knives to the family with a solemn expression. Then he comes down the few steps to Spider.

'Anything?'

Spider shakes his head. 'Doesn't mean they're not there,' he murmurs. 'Shall I open it?'

Noor stares at him, his fine nostrils twitching slightly. 'No.'

Spider thinks about this. If Noor is confident the Djinni haven't breached the tower, he shouldn't be afraid to open it, unless he thinks there's a Djinni crouched on the ladder on the other side of the door lock. It's strange to Spider that everyone in the family has so much respect for Noor, as if his natural good looks somehow endow him with authority.

'It should be safe to open it? We've done it before.'

'No,' Noor repeats. He sits cross-legged opposite Spider in the narrow margin between the metal door lock and the walls.

Spider eyes him carefully, missing Nergüi and his fighting skills.

No one likes Hugo for his privilege, his entitlement, his Britishness, his familiarity with a cricket green or an international cocktail party. It seems Hugo is unpalatable because of his grandiosity, he is always talking about high academics, whereas Noor's background is acceptable because of his looks, his ease in his own skin. But Noor hated Nergüi, for a reason that made no sense to Spider, maybe because the guy was taller than Noor, or more muscular, or whatever … In his heart Spider envies Noor, the golden child of advantage, the son of an ambassador from Pakistan who carries an air of confidence still, while all Spider can drag around is his own secret, heavy and stained.

From the holdall Noor pulls out some arrows with wooden shafts and metal heads, plus two hefty Berber swords, both found in an abandoned casbah near Ouargla. He hands one to Spider, who takes it and inspects the blade. He pulls out a hair from his head, wedges the sword between his knees and spreads the hair over it. It takes pressure to snap it.

'Blunt?' Noor asks.

'Blunt.'

Noor produces a whetstone from the bag. It's a lump of rock that contains spessartine. Spider discovered it near the shores of the Virgule, spied it glittering red in the early-morning sun and recalled an adjutant in the Foreign Legion showing him some and explaining it was 'Mandarin garnet' and made a good blade-sharpener. Spider pocketed it and later fashioned a whetstone for Noor, who is the armoury master of the family.

Spider uses nylon twine to lash arrowheads to the shafts, while Noor begins to work the blade on the whetstone. Spider glances at him from time to time, watching his technique, until Noor looks up questioningly.

'Make the angle bigger – you want about twenty degrees.'

'Like this?'

'A bit more. And as you move it, pull it from the heel to the tip.'

Noor tries but gets the action wrong.

'Here.' Spider puts down the arrows and takes the sword from him, moving it smoothly across the stone, drawing it down, then flipping it and doing the same on the other side. He breaks off from time to time to listen to the door. There is silence outside. When he has finished with the blade, he tests it with his hair again. It is as sharp as a diamond.

'Mine too,' Noor says, handing him the other sword. 'Did you see them?'

Spider pauses his work, shakes his head. 'No more than we ever have. They're too fast.'

He takes the sword and works on it for a while, always monitoring the door. He has stopped shaking now, but every time he pictures what might be on the other side of the door he feels a line of acid shoot through his veins. Camel is down there – as far as the family know, the Djinni ignore livestock, but there are never guarantees in this place.

When he's finished the sword he hands it back to Noor, who places it across his knees. Up the stairs the other family members have stopped talking – everyone is tired. The two men hold each other's eyes across the gap, their ears open, ready to respond to the tiniest movement.

They sit in silence, while above them, one by one, the exhausted family fall asleep. Soon Noor becomes drowsy. His eyes droop, sitting upright in his warrior pose with his legs wide apart, hands ready on the sword.

Spider blinks. His own eyes are tired – he is equally drained from the last two days. If the Djinni are still down there and try to batter through the tower defences, they will make enough noise to rouse him, he reasons; there will be time to wake up and ready himself. Sunrise can't be far away – it can't be long.

The last thing he thinks is that the family have been out on the balconies many times on a grey night and the Djinni have never smelled them. There has been blood here too.

Something has changed. But what? Before he can answer the question, he's asleep.

3

MCKENZIE'S ROOM IS the highest in the house because she can't sleep anywhere that doesn't have a view of the sky. Other rooms make her nervous, disorientated, like a rat in a science-lab maze. Opening her eyes the next morning, she stares up at the windows, watching the way the sun picks out the bottom branches of the live oaks, their leaves brown and limp. The trees are so high here that sometimes she wakes in the night, thinking she's been disturbed by the creak of a breaking trunk, that the next few heartbeats will see a tree crown crash through the ceiling. But she wouldn't give up this room for anything. She wonders if there will be rain today, or maybe snow. Usually she can tell, just by smelling the air.

Rain, she thinks, definitely rain, even though the sky is blue. And it's going to be crazy. A deluge. Bad as a monsoon. She sits up excited by this, sees the wardrobe door is half open and remembers last night.

The thought makes her lie back down, pulling the covers up to her neck, staring at the floor. The lizard. What *was* that in her bed? Did she really dream it? It seemed so real. And Mom, what was she talking about: *it's happening again*? Exactly *what* is happening again?

She gets out of bed and prowls around the room, checking again in all the places Dad looked. There isn't anywhere a lizard that size could hide, and nowhere it could have wriggled through. She throws back the bedcovers. Cuddle Bunny is there, lolling gawkishly, his badly stitched eyes staring at the ceiling. She picks him up, smells him. He doesn't smell of lizard – not at all – and somehow she thinks she'd know exactly how a lizard would smell. Whenever they visit the zoo she goes to the herpetarium where the reptiles are. That or the prairie dogs and the desert foxes.

Deserts are something she yearns for, places that both terrify her and excite her, all at once. She thinks about them all the time, here in tree-soaked Virginia, where the roads are wide and weary, obscured by hickory and redwood trees. She has no idea why, but her walls are decorated with posters showing desertification timelines; rainfall-per-inch graphs; and stark Ansell Adams images of the national parks. Dead Joshua trees.

The Sahara is expanding at a quarter-mile a year in every direction, and the Chinese deserts are spreading their fingers out, taking a knuckly grip on the surrounding green plains in spite of the wall of trees that the government has planted.

Pride of place is taken by the blow-up photo of a microburst – a huge natural mushroom cloud – forming above Phoenix, Arizona. She's been obsessed and half fearful of that photo since she was in second grade: it's her phone background and she can still fall into it for minutes on end, feeling her skin crawl with excitement and foreboding.

Something about it . . . Just something . . .

Dad scratches his chin and rolls his eyes in dismay at the pictures: how could he have a family like this, so dotted around and disorganised?

'*Diverse*,' Mom always corrects. '*Diverse is the word you want*.' But secretly Mom is also touchy about deserts and sand, though she'll never say why, and although McKenzie would like to challenge her, if she had the courage, she thinks she knows what Mom would do: she'd shrug and say something light about there being nothing at all to worry about, and how McKenzie is a model student and there's nothing can touch her, with her GPAs running as they are, and the *Proud Parent of an Honor Roll Student* bumper sticker that Mom gets to have on her car.

McKenzie showers, dresses, gets together all her coursework and her home study and goes downstairs, where the table is ready for breakfast – always like this, because Mom is so hyper-organised. Her brothers, Luke and Tatum, are sitting in silence, staring at Fox News, which is showing the President getting off Air Force One, cutting at the moment his comb-over threatens to gust skywards. On McKenzie's plate is a single carrot.

She stops in the doorway and looks at it, breathing carefully. It's an old joke, from her brothers. McKenzie the carrot-head.

She doesn't look like the rest of the family: Mom, with her slim limbs and gleaming dark hair. Her brothers, the same hair so slick and neat, but with Dad's musculature – sports stars, the pair of them. Then McKenzie, slim too, but with her long sheet of hair the colour of flame.

Luke and Tatum pretend they haven't seen her, but their mouths are twitching, on the verge of hysterics. Which is lame, because they are at college now – in the media programmes at George Mason University, which they only got for their lacrosse, football playing and crew – therefore evidently not old enough to have progressed in their humour.

Without a word she picks up the carrot and throws it in the rubbish bin.

'Awwww …' Tatum says. 'Wassa matter? Carrot – it's health-giving. Just wanting to help you with your vitamins.'

Luke chimes in, 'And Tatum never shoved it up his ass before putting it there, either. I promise.'

McKenzie sits down, shakes out some oats into her plate, pours herself a long glass of water. Something else weird about her – she won't drink coffee or sodas, she only drinks water. It mesmerises her. McKenzie has thought about it and thought about it, and she knows that she has the recessive gene from a sailor who made love with her great-great-grandmother and produced her great-grandmother in Shanghai. The photos of her great-grandmother had curiously round eyes and dark hair. And from her father's two recessive genes, which came together in a way that has produced her red hair.

McKenzie pours soya milk on her oats, adds honey and eats. They've had this conversation before, about how she's undateable and how the redhead gene should be eradicated. The only thing about her that bears any resemblance to Mom are her slightly sticky-out eye-teeth, which the odontologist corrected two years ago, her dark-brown eyes and raised cheekbones.

Warrior-girl cheekbones, India calls them. *You should live under a hygge bobble hat, you're so hygge.*

'Because of course breeding with redheads is completely out,' Tatum says. 'It's like keeping a gene going that has no relevance.'

'And keeping the stupidity gene going,' McKenzie says, not looking at them. 'That's helpful to the human race. I'm sure I read a paper on it when I was doing your anthropology module.'

Mom comes in the door, ready for the yoga classes that she instructs, her hair in a neat ponytail, her sneakers shiny and white. Dad is behind her, business-suited, towelling his hair. He looks stressed.

'What's going on?' Mom asks, smelling the tension instantly. 'I sense an atmosphere. You know I'm not stupid.'

None of them speak. McKenzie stares at her bowl, her face growing hotter. She doesn't want a scene.

'What's happening?'

'Nothing,' Tatum says.

Mom and Dad both narrow their eyes at their children but continue getting breakfast, putting on the coffee, filling water bottles. It's only when Mom goes to put a banana skin in the rubbish that she sees what's in there.

'A carrot,' she says, tilting her head at the boys. 'I thought we agreed we'd leave this behind in fifth grade, since that's the level of humour, or am I mistaken?'

'Mom, please.' Tatum gets down on his knees and pleads with her. He knows how to get round her. 'It's just our way of showing affection, and she *did* keep us awake all night.'

Mom cocks her head on one side. 'Is that right? All night?'

'She's got the best room in the house and we can hear everything she does up there.'

'Guys, keep it civil.'

'And you're going to let her go to Caltech? Out of state? While me and Luke stay in state.'

'Tatum …' Dad says suddenly. 'I'm telling you this conversation is at an end.'

'But it's like how insanely much is Caltech going to set you back? Like a quarter of a million bucks? How is that fair and—'

'No,' McKenzie says, suddenly angry. 'No, you're wrong.'

'How am I wrong?'

'Because I'm gonna get a scholarship.'

'Ooooohhh-woo.' Luke is delighted with the irony. He rocks his chair from side to side. 'A scholarship to, like, the most geeky college in the country. Yeah, right, that's going to happen.'

McKenzie swallows hard. 'It will happen. I'm working on it.'

'*KIDS!*'

Everyone flinches. Dad has gone the puce colour that says he's giving fair and appropriate warning he's liable to explode.

He holds up a finger – his head shakes very slightly when he speaks. 'Now I told you, and *I won't tell you again*, this conversation is at an end. Eat your breakfast. I'm going to be late for work and I will personally blame you all.'

McKenzie's brothers instantly lower their heads and concentrate on eating their oatmeal. A small smile creeps over McKenzie that they've been silenced so radically. When, after a while, Tatum glances up, she mouths across the table to him, '*I won't do your coursework for you any more* ...'

Tatum shoots a glance at Dad, who is no longer paying attention, and mouths back at her with a shit-eating grin, '*Oh, you will. You will.*'

The children are the first to wake – they begin to play-fight and squeal delightedly, and before long everyone rouses and begins to mobilise. Spider wakes with a start; his mouth is dry, his body aching and cramped from the position he's slept in next to the door lock, surprised to find he's here and not in bed. Last night comes back to him and he drags himself awake, massaging his shoulders, which have seized up.

The hatch is still closed. Noor has gone, taking the bag with him, but Spider's sword is still here on the floor next to him. He clambers up the small ladder and finds a solar-powered torch that he rigged up with Hugo's help. Morning is the end of the threat from the Djinni – even so, he is tense as he unlocks the door, straining to turn the cogs.

He peers into the opening. The light is too dim to be sure everything is undisturbed, but the smell of sleeping animals comes up to him. He leans out of the lock and lowers the torch into the vast space. The faint sounds of snoring bounce off the tower walls and he can see the animals sleeping. The tower floor is undisturbed.

He shines the beam up the side of the tower, with its steel panels bolted in place. No holes, nothing he can see to show where the creature threw itself at the tower sides.

'Hey.' He turns and looks up. Madeira and Hugo, alerted by the sound of the hatch opening, have appeared above him.

'What's happened?' Madeira asks, her teeth clenched around a cigar. 'Are the animals OK? My farm?'

'It's all good, I think.'

'My pipes?' the Englishman, Hugo, asks. Hugo is a man of few words – he keeps himself to himself, unless there is a point of classical education to comment on. He has carved out a role in the family as the plumber and is obsessed with the water supply, which comes to the Shuck from a reservoir deep under the sand that needs constant monitoring.

'Everything's the same – no break-ins. You want to see?'

Hugo climbs down, dangles out over the drop and reassures himself the tower isn't disturbed. Then he hands back the lantern to Spider, wiping his shock of blonde hair off his face. He is always sweaty and his skin is like pink marzipan, but it's always his arrogance that rules the day. 'The kids don't know a thing. We keep up the charade, OK?'

Hugo and Madeira don't speak to each other; it's only at times like this that they can bear to be in the same room. The family are bonded more deeply than anything they've known, but there are still chinks for resentment to grow: Madeira despises everything about Hugo, and in particular, his advantages. She grew up smuggling high-grade cocoa beans from Ghana to Côte d'Ivoire – and she often longs for the rain in Ghana; she chose the name Madeira in response to the children selecting different names. The shade and the smell of the sticky cocoa beans drying in the heat – they all miss something.

When the pair have gone, Spider slams the lock closed, then heads for the shower pods, where the walls are constructed from a smoother, walnut-like wood that has an oily, waterproof nature, with natural crevices where the family keep their rudimentary sheep's-milk soaps and shampoos. Hugo has been there already and has warmed and placed each man's daily washing ration in buckets at the entrance. They have to be very careful with water.

After the shower, Spider dresses. A tattered negligee and a leather combat jacket that bristles with tools and armoury, which he pulls on carefully, checking twice that all the fittings aren't disturbed. The family have long ceased to ask why Spider dresses like this – he manages to make the female clothes into battle gear, so they no longer question it. Truth is, the petticoat and fripperies give him a sense of freedom: his legs bare to the desert winds, always ready to fight to the skin. They also give him a place to hide extra tools, and a 'stuff-pocket', a hangover from the little-girl pickpockets in Paris, an extra hidey-hole to place his weaponry. He's a bad, wild boy, is Spider. There are knives, and worse, hidden under that petticoat.

In past months they've covered most of the desert accessible from this Shuck – there is just one pie-shaped segment left, and in that segment there are only two cities. One of them, from a distance, looks modern, with soaring skyscrapers; from what Hugo has told them of his travels in the Middle East in the banking industry, they think the city bears a resemblance to the Dubai skyline. The second city appears beaten and lowly, with what seems, through the telescope, to be rubbish piled in its approaches.

Spider goes up the spiral staircase, his hard desert boots clanging on the steps. He passes Madeira, who is doing pull-ups on the bottom of one of the open stairs.

'Hey.'

'Hey.'

She is dressed in cargo trousers and a white vest, her arms shining. About a third of her head is shaved and the other half is elaborate twists, all tied together and snaking down her back – she has her cigar behind her ear and wears gold earrings that make Spider cold, thinking about slashed ear lobes, should one of them catch on something.

The rest of the family is gathering in the common room – the windows are still mirrors in the dawn light, reflecting the tea lights and lamps and the sleepy faces of the family who are gathering together for breakfast. In the centre of the table is the 'Regyre fruit' – the sculpture made to represent the family's progress in the Cirque, as Mardy calls this place, the dry desert. Next to it sits a steaming bowl of cornmeal spangled with almonds and candied pineapple, surrounded with fat pottery jugs of sheep's milk, cruets of honey and chutney, and nearby a platter piled high with sliced kangaroo meat and dosas.

Elk is in the kitchen, his natural domain, the place where he alone holds sway – in his apron, grey hair tied back, sleeves rolled up to show his tattoos, his eyes blaze with the fire of a survivor.

He choreographs the procedure, handing people plates to carry to the table, ordering the children around. The gas rings, powered by the dung that Hugo collects in the vast tanks to the west of the Shuck, are lit, and Elk's gourds bubble with the daily ration of water, into which he sprinkles handfuls of the yerba-maté leaves that Madeira has arranged on the long windowsill to dry out. Yerba-maté, their answer to caffeine, grows readily here and has saved the family time and again.

'Mahmoud?' Elk peers over his glasses at the tallest child. 'You forgot pepper on those eggs. And the date juice? Is it going to walk to the table on its own?'

Hugo comes out of the kitchen bearing rows of twice-baked yams on an earthenware pot the size of a truck tyre. He stops when he sees Spider. 'Have you looked yet?' He raises a questioning eyebrow.

'Not yet – and don't say anything until then? Not until they're . . .' He nods meaningfully at the stairs, indicating where the children are usually taken before the moment when he climbs and scans the desert floor. 'Then we'll talk.'

Spider heads for the kitchen to be assigned a task by Elk, but before he can get there, one of the children – Splendour – throws her arms around his naked legs and looks up at him. She's well rested and is grinning at him with her wonky teeth, two in the front missing. She has mistletoe-grey eyes, like a steamed mirror.

'No noises, Spider. No scary stuff.'

'I know. It's good.'

'Splendour dreamed 'bout the Scouts, Knut and Yma.'

'Cool. I dreamed about them too.'

'Nice dream?'

He hesitates. 'Let's fetch the bread.' He ruffles her hair. 'Look over there at Elk. He's ready to blow a fuse. Go help him.'

Breakfast is always like this, always a chaotic event. The children are hungry and make disorderly grabs for the sweet things. Elk wants them to go slowly – to appreciate and revere the food – but his earnestness makes the other family members laugh.

'*It's just food*,' they chide.

'*It's just air*,' he replies.

Amasha and Forlani come in with Tita Lily. She is clothed, though her dress is bulkier than they are used to, as she must have bandages underneath – but she wears her usual red lipstick and her Audrey Hepburn hat, already tied under her chin. She smiles, and sits with discomfort at the table. Forlani and Amasha hover around her, getting things for her. They can't afford to lose one person – even one will be a tragedy, especially after Nergüi.

Spider eats distractedly, barely tasting the food. He wants to get going. The Sarkpont is in a piscina in a corner of a rectangle, and the Sarkpont is all they think about, day and night, day and night. When another family finds it, the end of the Regyre comes and they have to close another segment of the Regyre fruit. Ten down, two to go.

As Splendour and the two boys, Cairo and Mahmoud, get food inside them, they liven up even further. Soon there is a lot of shouting and squabbling, and more than once Amasha has to chide them, remind them to keep their energy for later. 'Do you think Tita Lily wants to hear this nonsense?'

Today Amasha wears blue silk, emblazoned with silver edging. Her eyebrows have been outlined with white jewels.

'Oh, if only the desert had monsoons,' she says, smiling, her dark kohl-lined eyes gliding to the balcony. 'Just a little rain – how we would dance! Wouldn't we, Madeira?'

'We would,' answers Madeira, lighting her cigar.

Amasha smiles. She has a lot in common with Madeira. Although they were worlds apart, they grew up in similar climates, and she often sends up long soliloquies about the tea muster-sheds and the mist that would rise up over the terraces in Sri Lanka from her family farm. She was a wealthy Sri Lankan and studied overseas before she came here.

'You need to get used to the desert,' Noor says. Today he is beautifully turned out in silvery rose kurta. 'Every day in the Thar Desert my family would run, and it worked: we survived.'

'We know all about it,' Spider says. 'You remind us all the time.'

Amasha and Elk are the 'Futatsu', which, translated from Japanese, means 'two people' – the two people counted out for restaurants and funfairs – but in this case means *The* Two People. Anywhere else they'd be called chieftains or elders, but here, in the Cirque, they are the Futatsu, and although Amasha is only in her early forties, Elk in his sixties, their decision is final. They also bear the burden of having to contact the Scouts and exchange information.

Sunrise filters milkily through the upper storeys of the Shuck, and when breakfast is finished Amasha holds out her hands in elegant arcs, linking them to her neighbours'. They settle in their seats, heads down, hands linked, except for Elk, who has come from the kitchen still in his apron. He stands behind the nearest family member – Spider in this case – places his hands on his shoulders and lowers his head to join the prayer as Amasha speaks.

'Ha'shem,' she murmurs. 'Please hear us, please today protect us all.' The morning prayers are always quick and to the point. 'Bless our Scouts in their quest, help them to listen and help us find the Sarkpont. Pray for Nergüi, pray he is safe.'

'Pray for Nergüi,' Elk echoes. 'Pray we can find the Sarkpont today. And amen.'

'Amen,' murmur the family.

Madeira and Elk clear up breakfast and a line forms in front of Tita Lily. It is her daily chore to check everyone's outfit for suitability: Tita Lily loves fabric, she hoards the sequins that Amasha loves, can summon a skirt or a shirt from the air, and nightly shaves and brushes her teeth with salt and lemons.

'Splendour, you suffered yesterday,' says Tita Lily. 'Have you got suntan lotion on?'

'Yeah,' says Splendour.

'Promise? It's your face that will burn. You understand?' Tita Lily winces. She has leaned forward too far and has to put a hand on her side. Forlani hovers near her, ready to help, but she waves him away. 'Madeira, are you really going to wear those earrings again?'

'Have I ever not worn them?'

'Those ears of yours are going to rip.'

'Then I'll make it look fierce – I can wear a little scar, don't you think?'

Tita Lily sighs. She doesn't even look at Spider, whom she has got tired of chastising. If he wants to wear a dress that will leave his legs bare to all that the desert can throw at him, if he wants blisters and bites and sand getting into places it shouldn't, that's his business.

'Don't come running to me when you've injured yourself,' she murmurs, showing the front of her buck teeth.

Now she gets to her feet with some pain and hobbles out of the room. The children follow and the moment they've gone, everyone springs into action. Spider scrambles up the ladder into the lantern. Out of the window, the stars that hung over the distant desert mounds have paled and given way to the morning's first pink hues. He's seen more than 150 sunrises here in the Cirque, and he knows the colours the sky shifts through, starting with the grey-pink of a dead rose petal, moving through orange, yellow and white to end in the clear blue of another day.

He wedges himself into the space, straddling the crossbeams so that he can rotate to every angle. He won't be able to see the area directly around the tower, as the huge walls block his view, but he can see the desert floor from about ten metres outside, and he will see where the Djinni have moved and killed.

Hugo helps him, handing Spider the telescope, which he unfurls and swivels, checking everything. The sun starts slowly – almost teasingly revealing itself, spread across the horizon. Then the beginnings of the harlequining, which is the signature of the eastern sky at sunrise. It's the most breathtaking moment – no inhabitant of the Cirque gets tired of the view – a fan-shaped luminescence like a peacock's tail, the crystals in the sky like the scales on a fish, only larger and more iridescent.

And in this brief quality of light, for approximately a minute, any object on the desert floor gets a shadow ten times its size.

Spider studies the ground in thirty-degree segments, shuffling himself round to move through the angles. He sees the distant city beyond the Virgule – the city they haven't visited because the Virgule is too dangerous – and the city they think is Dubai, and the broken-down city to the south.

'Anything?'

From the room below, Spider can feel five pairs of eyes staring up at him. He swivels again and checks once more, just to be sure. He collapses the telescope and clambers back down the ladder.

'The Djinni came from the south, skirted the Joshua-tree plains and headed towards the Virgule.' He indicates the vast, unnavigable salt lake that lies between the Shuck and the northern borders of the Cirque. 'One of them changed direction and came back here.'

'Because you tempted them,' Madeira says sullenly.

'I stood on the balcony for less than five seconds. We've all done it on a grey night – it's never had that effect before.'

'They smelled you. You've put us on their map.'

'You think we're not already on their map?'

'Hey, hey …' Amasha holds her hands up, moving the two of them apart. 'It's not for us to be arguing. Now, Spider – the desert floor? Which way can we go?'

'The kill is out towards the place you think is Dubai. But there are tracks everywhere.'

There is silence at this. Every morning after a grey night the family try to set out in a direction that will conceal the truth from the children.

Elk rests his huge hands on the table. 'Then we go south.'

'There's only one place we haven't explored south,' Noor says. 'The beat-up city. With the rubbish all piled up outside it.'

'Appearances can be deceptive, Noor,' says Spider. 'And everything is changing for us – what happened last night is a sign.'

'A sign of what?' Madeira asks through a cloud of cigar smoke.

'The Djinni have never behaved like that before. That's more aggression, more responsiveness than we've ever seen. Maybe it's a clue we need to leave this Shuck, find somewhere else to base ourselves.'

Everyone rounds to look at him accusingly. Spider opens his hands, tries to sound reasonable.

'Don't look at me like that. I know we've put a lot into this place, but most of it is transportable. Look out of the window – apart from Dubai, if it *is* Dubai, we've explored everything we can reach in twenty-four hours and we're running out of options. We move to a new shelter, put two days into the move and we'll have a completely different scope to explore. Maybe to the east.'

'No,' Madeira says. 'I can't move everything. It's been too much.'

'We could – we can take livestock, take soil, take Hugo's pipes, take some of the steel. If we find the right place we can relocate.'

Madeira stares at him across the table, her nostrils flaring. Then she shakes her head, goes to the balcony and picks up the length of pole that Spider fashioned into a javelin for her. Breathing in and out hard, she leans back and hurls the javelin as far as she can into the twinkling morning. She hurls this javelin every single day they are here. More than once, if she's angry.

The Regyre fruit is in the centre of the table – a familiar enough sight, it's been there almost since they arrived in the Shuck. Constructed by Spider and Knut from sandalwood scraps they discovered on the floor of a mosque in Abu Dhabi, it resembles a peeled orange, each of its twelve segments hinged so that it can be open or closed. At first the family thought they'd only see five, or at most six, of the segments closed before they found the Sarkpont. Now ten are closed and there are only two segments remaining.

Hugo coughs. He goes to the balcony without a word. No one looks at him. They know he is going to throw his javelin, because this is the daily routine. The challenge from Madeira is more than he can resist.

He throws. He is stronger than he looks. Afternoons spent bowling on a village green with the church bells chiming – cucumber sandwiches and Pimm's with strawberries for tea – have made his right arm strong. The javelin soars away into the air. He always throws further than Madeira, in spite of her daily workouts. That he won't cede to her, even for a moment, is another reason no one likes him.

4

DAD DRIVES THE boys to school, Mom heads to her car, a bright-orange yoga mat strapped to her back like a snail, and McKenzie gets out her rain gear, though the sun is shining. She is always riveted by the weather, by the way the clouds move, the way the sun changes places each day, albeit an infinitesimal amount. She can tell the date to within two days at sunset and sunrise, and a road crash could happen in front of her and she'd look straight past it and say, 'See those clouds? That means the front is clearing. It'll be hot tomorrow, real hot. You can take the cover off the pool.'

This morning she keeps her eyes on the sky as she hurries to the bus stop, her backpack heavy with books and notes. She trips over her long orange scarf, recovers, makes a half-hearted effort to throw it back over her shoulder, but it comes loose in her haste and she trips again.

India is standing in the cold, gloves on, watching McKenzie and laughing. 'Come here,' she tells her. 'Come right here and let me mommy you.'

India spends a little time rebuttoning McKenzie's coat and wrapping the scarf the right way, straightens her hair and wipes toothpaste off her blouse.

'How come the raincoat?'

McKenzie hasn't taken her eyes off the sky during all this. 'Rain's coming. I can smell it.'

'Well, shit, thanks for warning me. My feed says later this afternoon.'

'Maybe, but I think sooner. And it's going to be a crazy one. Don't worry, I've got another raincoat for you.'

'And anything else wrong?'

McKenzie lowers her eyes to India. 'What?'

'Something else is wrong.'

'Yeah. Yeah. It is.'

India is a great keeper of secrets, but she's a rationalist. She has a picture of Emma González on her phone and subscribes to Amnesty International. She's switched on politically, but doesn't have much time for anything that doesn't make sense. And what happened last night definitely falls into the category of not making sense.

'I'll tell you later. When we've got some time.'

The bus arrives, the panes steamed with all the kids' breath. With the exception of some of the sophomores at the back, who probably ride the bus just for the social time, India and McKenzie are the eldest on the vehicle. They both drive, but India has to pay for her own petrol, and the Strathies still haven't bought McKenzie a car because they're afraid she'll forget to watch the road and be staring so hard at a cloud formation that she'll drive into a lorry.

The door hisses as it opens. Mrs Spiliotopolous, the driver, grins at the girls as they get on the bus. She lives on the other side of Clifton – her road is known for flooding, cutting off her house. Once she nearly lost her job for leaving the kids stranded at bus stops while she struggled to make it into school.

'There's a big storm coming.' McKenzie lowers her head and whispers, so the other kids can't hear. 'It's going to be serious.'

'There's a weather warning, but it ain't till this afternoon.'

'I know, but it's going to come earlier. That gully at the end of your drive is going to flood before the afternoon.'

'You sure?'

'You know that heavy feeling in the air? It's going to be earlier. Maybe lunchtime.'

Mrs Spiliotopolous shrugs and pushes the door lever forward. 'I'll think about it.'

McKenzie and India make their way to their places in the middle of the bus. No one looks at them; the other kids simply stare in bored silence out of the windows. Outside, everything is cloaked in trees, and McKenzie has to fight the suffocating feeling they give her. She wants to be able to see for miles. It's only when they turn at the top of the dual carriageway near Manassas, and she gets a clear view of the Appalachians in the far distance, that she feels a little calmer.

India gets out her phone and fiddles with it, checking Instagram. She has 800 followers, McKenzie has 180, and she accepts follows from just about everyone. She's found that every time she posts something cool, her followers drop off by about two or three. Soon she'll be down to nothing, which will make her brothers – with their gazillion followers – howl with delight. Eventually, when she sees that India is lost in reading the comments on her latest post, McKenzie checks her page and there's a message.

She frowns. The user is 'TextbookJoe' and the photo is of Joe Marino, the guy in the college lacrosse squad whom all the girls have a crush on. He sits at the back of the bus with all the giggling sophomore girls who have manicures, wear animal-print leggings and are in drama club.

The message reads – *Hey, you've got a lovely smile. Just thought you should know that.*

She stares at the message.

Hey, you've got a lovely smile.

She doesn't dare glance over her shoulder. Instead, trembling, she nudges India, murmurs, 'Don't look round' and pushes the phone under her nose.

India reads the messages, pushes it away and sits bolt upright, her face flushing like crazy. She texts out a response.

– Whoa? Wha? That's insane.

– What am I sposed to do?

– Lemme think, lemme think …

– Well?

– Do nothing for now. Just do nothing.

A long pause, Then McKenzie types – *ok.*

*

Every moment of daylight is precious, so the family prepare for the day's expedition swiftly. Elk goes to the kitchen to wrap up boxes of cured meat and sticky dates, while Madeira checks the solar battery on the camera and Hugo prepares the vessels that he carries on the treks. Spider affixes his tool belt, makes sure his compass and his knives are all in place and that the watch fragments he's been attempting to assemble are wrapped in cloth to shield them. He loops the ropes that he carries everywhere into his backpack.

Amasha has done a lot of Tita Lily's work – she's snatched up all the keffiyeh scarves that have been drying on the balconies overnight and stands at the Shuck hatch, doling them out as the family climb out, one by one. She does a quick inventory of everyone: checks everyone is dressed properly, covered in protection and with no loose sandal straps or broken soles.

Tita Lily is helped down the ladder and Spider gets her up onto Camel, where she sits in perfect stillness, her posture rigid, her hat scarf wrapped tightly around her neck, Hugo and Madeira's javelins in front of her. Outside the sun is blinding, but they muster themselves determinedly, double-checking the equipment.

Spider wanders a short way off from the others so that he can see the sides of the tower. There is a faint glistening smear, as if a giant snail has crawled up the beaten panels in the night, but he can't see a mark where the Djinni landed.

Then he raises his eyes, and sees it. He breathes hard, his skin prickling.

'Hey.' Madeira approaches. 'What's up?'

He shakes his head. The mark is about eighteen metres up, a faint dent in the metal. He can't believe how high it is. A single leap has taken the Djinni almost a quarter of the height of the tower – which makes them how tall?

Madeira shoves her cigar between her teeth and shields her eyes to look up at the dent. 'Fuck!'

'I know. They must be six, seven metres tall.'

'You're kidding?'

'Don't tell the kids, don't breathe a word.' He hefts his backpack higher on his shoulders and tightens the strap across his chest, staring at the mark. 'Maybe Nergüi saw them coming – who knows.'

'Maybe he did.'

Spider squints. 'No real damage, it's not broken through. It's not great. Let's hope it doesn't happen again.'

'Let's hope?' She quirks an eyebrow at him. 'Sure, Spider. Let's hope, eh?' She gives the mark a lingering look and then, with a shiver, turns and, wrapping her cinnamon-brown robe over her head and shoulders, goes back to the tower, where Noor and Elk are securing the doors. 'Make sure it's proper tight,' she shouts. 'I've spent months on this farm. I don't want it destroyed now.'

Spider knows the words are meant to reach him. Madeira speaks her mind, but her bark is worse than her bite and her frustration will have evaporated in minutes.

In the absence of Yma, the navigator, Hugo attempts to read her sextant and tries his best with all his hard-won knowledge to set them on the right path across the Joshua-tree plains. The children are reluctant, they want to visit the gleaming city – something bright and shining will raise their spirits – but Noor is adamant. 'It's south,' he tells them. 'And we're already late leaving.'

The adults keep their heads high for the sake of the children, but only a hundred paces from the tower, Mahmoud stops and can't be moved.

'What is it?' Elk paces backwards, rolling up the sleeves of his cheesecloth shirt. He stands with his hands on his thighs and peers down at the sand, his grey ponytail swaying. 'What are we looking at?'

Mahmoud, who is only nine, is rigid, pointing at a gouge in the sand. 'What's that?'

The family gather round. Clearly this is the place where the Djinni have swarmed in the night. The winds haven't blown enough sand across to hide it. At least, Spider thinks, there's no blood. Many mornings after a grey night the family have happened on great crevices where violence has taken place – swirling patterns splotched with blood and intestines mapping the skirmishes where families have been taken. Once they saw a child's full scalp, blonde hair, the blood inside dried in the sun.

Elk says, 'It's nothing. Just where a lizard has been.'

Amasha falls to a squat next to the mark. She is the soothsayer, the lover of legend, the interpreter. She strokes the gouge mark with her slender hand.

'Nothing to worry about, Mahmoud,' she says. 'It's a lizard trail, where a lizard has been dancing.'

'Dancing?' Mahmoud asks, sceptical. 'Lizards don't dance.'

'Oh, I think they do.'

As if by magic, a lizard – a giant yellow and buff-coloured thing with a jagged ruff – appears a metre or so away from them. It stops when it sees the humans gathered together and raises itself on its front legs to consider them. It's a horned lizard; they are like vermin around here, used to the humans. It doesn't startle but, after some studied perusal of the family, merely lowers itself leisurely and ambles away.

'Thank you for your kind attention,' Elk calls after it. 'We consider ourselves infinitely enhanced by your fleeting company. Generous in the extreme.'

Amasha covers Mahmoud's hand. 'See, little person? The medicine animal of the desert – he means you no harm. Come along. Tell me about the aeroplane you're making. You're so clever.'

Eventually Mahmoud is cajoled away, but he is unconvinced and can't help glancing back at the marks as they walk off in their train. The boys can be nightmares, always at each other's throats. Cairo, born in Tripoli, is envious of Mahmoud, who not only came from Egypt but has longer legs and a broader chest; and when they chose their names early in their time here, Cairo dumped his name, Tareq, and chose the name of Mahmoud's home town as an affront. Mahmoud said nothing. Cairo is small and sly – Spider sometimes suspects there is a bushy red tail he's hiding somewhere – but he's still childlike and his anxieties are real.

The giant shining city on their right gets larger and more prominent, while the city they are heading towards seems to be resolutely small on the horizon. The breeze plays lazily with the skirt of Spider's petticoat, ruffling it against his bare legs. At midday the family stop for lunch in a dried-out cactus grove. Elk unpacks the provisions, Hugo logs their position with the sextant and Spider helps Tita Lily off Camel and assembles the sun-guard.

The family sit under it in a circle, back-to-back, each chewing dates or kangaroo meat, each gazing out at the desert. Lost in their contemplation and tiredness. Forlani checks Tita Lily's bandages, her back to the family, while Camel gets onto her knees and rests her chin gloomily on the desert floor.

They eat and then take a few moments to rest. Splendour plays with her patchwork doll, walking it in circles around a cactus, while Madeira unpacks the trowel she takes everywhere and kneels in the sand, digging ruminatively to check on the sand conditions. Forlani practises with the new crutches he's brought out today. He and Spider made them with wood Hugo supplied from the depleted stores in the tower, and today is his first day with them.

'What do you think?'

He shows off for a bit, racing in ten-metre stretches along the sand, to the delight of the children. He executes an ornate turn, using the padded armrests to twist himself around, and the pouch he carries around his waist, full of herbs and ointments, flies gaily around like a flag.

The children giggle at Forlani. His legs have about one-tenth of the strength that Spider's do.

'Are the handholds good?' Spider asks. He takes one of the crutches and inspects it. Then he holds out his hand for Forlani's. Forlani opens his palm for Spider to see. There is a red-raw area between the thumb and forefinger. 'That hurt?'

'Not at all.'

'It's been bleeding.'

'It always bleeds.' Forlani, embarrassed, lowers his voice and gets a little closer to Spider. 'Today it's bleeding less than ever, thanks to your new crutches. What do you call them? *Bequilles*?'

Spider rubs his fingertips across the groove on the grip of the *bequilles*. There is a small section of splintered wood. 'If I sand them down more, they'll be comfortable.'

'They are comfortable now, brother. You have no idea how comfortable.' Forlani lifts his disjointed face to the sun and smiles. 'Everything here is more comfortable than before.'

Science lab has the usual joyless atmosphere. All the animals in the experimental micro-environments dotted around the place are dying – helpless newts and fish that the students were supposed to have kept alive. It's heartbreaking, McKenzie thinks, all these dead animals, daily netted out and put into the rubbish.

This is the honours class, so Joe Marino and his squad never come near; in fact she never sees him at school except occasionally in the locker bay, but she's still twitchy and keeps checking her phone, still confused by the message. That he has noticed her at all makes her flush with colour at least five times an hour, but then she pictures speaking to him and knows she can't, knows she will make an idiot of herself.

McKenzie imagines herself as a very small member of a theatre audience, in the back row of the auditorium, straining to see the players on the stage, so small, stiff and distant they bear no relation to humans and yet are washed with the suggestion that they represent life lived the way it should be, reminding her that she has no idea how to behave.

Outside the window the clouds are getting darker and heavier by the minute; she glances at her phone – almost half-eleven. The weather app has brought forward its prediction of rain to 1 p.m., but she still thinks it's going to be sooner.

To the east of DC is the ocean. She imagines a ship, or an aeroplane, skipping over the blue. Or a girl, running in an inflatable bubble like a hamster wheel – someone tried that recently. She would land in … in Africa. Yes, Africa. Why Africa? What does it mean? In the Sahara are ancient Egyptian treasures and Second World War aeroplanes missing for decades, their crew skeletonised and picked clean by vultures. She closes her eyes and she's there, running in the sand. The slatey dryness of the air, the silicate scratch on her skin. Sand in her sandals. The rusting remains of machinery in the desert.

'McKenzie Strathie?'

She opens her eyes. The teacher is frowning at her.

'Thank you,' she says in her slow southern accent. 'And now I have all your attention, let me tell you – I know it's early to be thinking about college, but the NOVA Science Fair is a big, big deal. It's the sort of place to be making your mark: lots of professors from colleges all over the country will be there. Now have any of ya'll got something planned?'

India grabs McKenzie's arm and throws it up in the air. 'Kenzie has. It's awesome.'

'Cool, McKenzie. You wanna go ahead and tell us all about it?'

McKenzie's been thinking about this since she saw the flyer two weeks ago. On the list of delegates one sentence jumped out at her: *Faculty members from the Californian Institute of Atmospheric Science.* She's read that Professor Armitage from Caltech avoids teaching with dry theory and is a fan of the visual representations of weather phenomena, so she plans to give life to the extraordinary sand formations that wind alone could carve.

'Not really,' she mutters, embarrassed.

'Yes, she does,' says India. 'She's going to get glass tanks and fill them with sand and use them to show how different sand-dune formations are made.'

The teacher crosses her arms and leans back against the desk, smiling with her head on one side. Her teeth are very small and bright white. 'I'm intrigued. It sounds like a great idea – the places that major in climate sciences and geology will be very interested. Kinda expensive, though? Glass tanks? Sand? Are your parents helping fund it?'

'Um …' McKenzie opens her mouth and closes it. She can feel about ten pairs of eyes on her. All the students in the room who pay her to do their homework on Firefly. Though it still matters how much she gets teased about her hair and her clothes, how much they laugh at her because she can't walk in a straight line without being distracted, somehow taking their money gives her the smallest sense of power in a world where she has no other power. She has almost a thousand bucks in her account. 'Yeah, like, my parents'll help me figure it out.'

'Great, cos it sounds so promising.'

Outside the rain starts. Very suddenly, seemingly out of nowhere. The noise is so loud on the roof that several of the students actually flinch in shock. One or two involuntarily raise their hands to protect their heads, before laughing nervously and carrying on, embarrassed at their highly strung nerves.

India rolls her eyes and shakes her head at McKenzie. 'Are you ever wrong?'

The rain goes on for hours, until the tarmac is deep in water, like a river. At let-out, the students run squealing from the school buildings to the bus bays, pelted with monsoon-like rain. McKenzie thrusts a raincoat at India, zips her phone in her backpack and together they go to the door, push it open and step outside.

The bus bay and parking lot are jumping with rain, the size and speed of bullets. Giant lashing exclamation marks, mud flying as the water hits. Unlike the other panicking students, McKenzie turns her face to the sky. It isn't icy rain; it's soft, like warm rubber against her face – she closes her eyes and breathes it in. It's from the South Atlantic, full of salt and heat. Almost fishy.

Their bus is there, at the end of the bay, Mrs Spiliotopolous at the helm, counting the students in. McKenzie and India clatter on, spattering rain on the floor. Their clothes smell of mould and stale baking. Mrs Spiliotopolous stops McKenzie before she goes to the back of the bus. 'You told me it was gonna rain and you were right.'

'Yeah,' she says shyly, aware that Joe Marino is at the back of the bus already, grinning, his arms spread across the backs of the seats, four girls around him. 'It's kind of my thing. You know.'

'I got the car out, cos you warned me. And my dog and my toothbrush and my nightdress. I'm staying at my sister's tonight till the gully drains. Thank you.'

McKenzie smiles and takes her place next to India, her back to Joe, conscious of the gabble of conversation the girls are having:

'*I wish I could be Kim Kardashian, she's totally everything goals.*'

'*No, Kylie. I'd like to be Kylie.*'

McKenzie opens her phone. Nothing. Not a single message, or like or follow. She scratches her wrist and leans her head back on the seat, staring out of the window.

As the bus rattles away she pulls off her orange scarf and spreads it over her knees to dry. She tries smiling to herself, testing the way it makes her mouth feel. She's got nice teeth, it's one of the few things she's confident about, but the rest of her? No boy has ever looked at her. The message has to be Joe yanking her chain – it has to be.

'So-o-o-o …' India murmurs, dropping her chin and sidling up closer to McKenzie. 'Are we gonna chat?'

'About what?'

'About the dude five seats behind us. And NO! Do NOT look over your shoulder – he'll know we're talking about him. Wait till he texts again, then consult me: your sleuth sistah. My brother says don't trust him.'

McKenzie is silent for a moment. The trees whip past the window, the storm drains throw up giant brown spumes, and every raindrop pistoning down on the bus roof sounds like a bullet exploding.

'Kenz, you were weird this morning too, before the text. You said you'd tell me.'

'It's nothing.'

'Well, it wasn't nothing, was it?'

McKenzie picks at the wool on her scarf where it bobbles. How come no one else's scarves or sweaters bobble the way hers do, and how come she doesn't really know what colours to choose – '*Orange, so bold,*' Mom once said about the scarf. '*With your hair, it's kind of … Sort of … No – it doesn't jar. Really it doesn't. In fact I think it's a brave choice. Yes, brave.*'

'I dunno,' she says eventually. 'It's like, Mom kinda said something I wasn't s'posed to hear. I had a nightmare and Mom asked Dad if he thought "it" was happening again.'

India frowns 'It?'

'Yeah – she didn't say what. It's like there's a giant secret in our family that no one will talk about, and mostly I'm the centre of the secret.'

'That's fairly freaky.'

McKenzie's phone pings. It's Joe again.

– what are you two whispering about?

She nudges India, shows it to her.

'Ignore it,' she hisses. 'I'm going to ask my brother about him. Leave it to me.'

McKenzie sighs and shoves the phone in her pocket. The bus is passing the shopping mall, and the man who is paid to dress as the Statue of Liberty and wave at the passing traffic every day, advertising an insurance company, is so wet his grey-green make-up is running. Still he manages to raise a hand to wave.

Inexplicably sad, McKenzie raises her hand and waves back. The rain is exciting, but it's scary too. What would it take to wash all of this away and dump it in the Occoquan Reservoir?

Something in her world has shifted. She can feel it as clearly as if a bone in her back has just moved position.

5

EVERYTHING HERE IS more comfortable than before …

Spider thinks about Forlani's comment as he kicks away the traces of sand that the crutches have disturbed, as the family gather up their belongings and continue on into the blazing sun. Though none of them has ever verbalised why they think they were chosen for this task, it's true: this place is the chance they all thought they would never have.

It's almost six months since they met – almost sixty kilometres west of here, one morning. All of them tired and filled with curiosity.

Spider found himself looking out at a ferocious desert. He was crouched, one knee down, and saw the whole thing in a blink. He was born in Paris, but knows how to live in a desert. It was sand as far as he could see – the sun was coming up in the east, lighting the various exhausted cities, all of them blackened as if they'd been abandoned. The smell of rust and dried rubber filled the air.

He heard voices behind him and turned.

There were thirteen other people – all staring at him.

Spider stood up, wiped his hands on his skirt. They were standing on a platform that must have been almost a thousand metres high. Around him, nothing except a locked hatch in the centre of the platform and these thirteen people.

'Do I know you?' Spider asked.

Forlani was dressed in oversized jeans and a football jersey, no crutches, his broken legs forcing him to sit. 'I've met you somewhere,' he said.

'And I've met you.'

'Where?'

'I don't know.'

Spider looked at Yma, who stood uncertainly – glancing in bewilderment at the others as if this was a joke. Her long hair was plaited down her side, she was dressed simply in brown dungarees, the sort an American farmhand might wear, and she was barefoot, her arms tanned and supple. Elk, with his broad Boer shoulders, his long grey hair in a ponytail – even he was familiar. And Amasha too: so short and female, so glistening of hair and skin.

Splendour skulked in the centre of the platform, her knuckles jammed in her mouth, her big mistletoe-grey eyes flicking nervously across everyone, while Cairo and Mahmoud stood slightly embarrassed, staring at their feet. There was Nergüi, the Mongolian man, tall – a fighter with a grim expression; and Noor, standing a little aside from the group, staring at the desert. He was good-looking, in the way a Bollywood film star was gorgeous – so straight and gleaming, the wind just wafting the silver pyjamas he wore against his lean stomach.

'Hey,' Spider said.

Noor turned. 'Hey,' he said. 'It looks like my home, this place – it looks like the Thar Desert.' Then Noor looked over the other people in the group. Especially he took in Yma, ran his eyes up and down her body. Spider saw that. He saw the attraction, saw her meet Noor's eyes.

'Hey,' Spider said to his neighbour. 'I'm Spider.'

The man shook his hand, his pink fingers soft and slightly sweaty. 'Hugo. I'm from England.'

'I'm from Paris.'

'Yes.' Hugo let his eyes go up and down Spider's outlandish outfit. 'I see.'

'You know why we're here?'

He shook his head. 'I imagine it's something to do with that.' He nodded at the desert. 'Though I can't think what.'

Everyone turned and looked at the desert. It seemed limitless and imponderable.

Spider took a walk to the edge of the platform – he wasn't afraid of heights, had never been afraid of them. What would save you at heights was what was close, and not focusing on what was below.

He peered over the edge, down the incredible rusting frame that they stood on. It seemed to go on forever. Everywhere, less than a metre down, were girders poking out about ten metres above the drop. He moved a few centimetres and studied the fall, but then felt a soft hand on his arm.

He turned. It was Amasha, gazing up at him with her treacle-brown eyes. 'Please. Be careful.'

'I am careful. I do understand heights, I really do. I've lived with them all my life.'

'Really?'

'Really.'

He moved on then, rounding the platform, gazing out at the desert, cataloguing everything he saw: the dunes and the cities, the distant clouds.

When he got to the third side he saw, sitting on the end of a girder, her back to him, an overweight woman in what appeared to be a badly washed dress of pale pink.

'Guys,' he whispered, beckoning to the others.

The woman was slouched over the impossible drop. She seemed to be launching paper aeroplanes at the void.

'Hey – you? Are you one of us?'

'Hey – lady?'

She didn't respond, so they continued shouting. She ignored them all.

'Here.' One of the boys, Mahmoud, scraped up a little of the flooring material on the top of the crane. He distributed it amongst the others. They all stood on the third side and took aim.

'Hey,' called Spider. 'We're going to throw shit at you if you don't respond.'

She didn't turn. Just continued throwing paper planes into the air, apparently not caring to watch where they went.

Mahmoud was the first to throw something. A tiny pebble, which pinged off her back, eliciting not a single reaction. Spider and Noor threw more, with the women shyly joining in later.

Soon the pink lady had been pebbled with missiles, but hadn't reacted. Spider knew it was up to him.

He lowered himself to the girder, ignoring Amasha and the others who were telling him to be careful. He dropped onto it, felt his feet solid in his boots and began the walk across the impossible drop.

His trick was to look at what was near to you – not at the air below. It always worked.

He got close to the woman, and reached out a finger. He prodded her in the back.

She turned, and it was Spider who took a step back on the centimetre-thin girder.

She was old and raggle-taggle, dressed as a waitress, he guessed, though she seemed too old to be one. She wore a greying caterer's cap and dishevelled apron, rings on her fingers and a badge on her chest that said 'Mardy'. Her skirt was short – very short.

But it was her eyes – her eyes that seemed to take in everything: everything about him, about the situation.

'What?' he said as he backtracked to the platform. 'Why are you looking at me like that?'

She sighed, said nothing. She took a moment to look up at all the people on the platform. Then she smoothed down her outfit and stood.

Spider got back onto the platform – he was shocked by her nimbleness at height. She didn't look below, though she was neither delicate nor supple. She had chewed fingernails, and the pins holding her hat in place couldn't disguise the greying roots of her hair. She had very fat ankles in wrinkled stockings, there was a worn pair of carpet slippers on her feet and she shuffled arthritically.

'Who are you?' Spider said.

She smiled, showing long horse's teeth. 'Why, I'm Mardy. See?' She underlined her name tag with her finger. 'Can't you read?'

'I can read.' He narrowed his eyes. 'Why are we here?'

'Give me a moment. Would you help me up to the platform. I have arthritis, you see.'

He reached down for her, pulling her, with Elk's help, up onto the platform. She stood, straightening her weird uniform, her legs bloated and massive, in a skirt far shorter than it should be.

'Are you going to stop staring?' she said eventually, not looking up at them. 'You keep your mouths open like that and a fish will jump in.'

Splendour clamped her hand over her mouth and stared at Mahmoud, who gasped, half smiled.

Mardy looked up, frowning. 'Is that behaviour appropriate to your situation?' she demanded. 'You can keep your gasps and your laughter until you have something to laugh about.'

Mahmoud closed his mouth abruptly. 'Who are you?'

'I just told you – I'm Mardy.'

'What's that supposed to tell us?' said Noor.

She smiled again, a glimpse of yellow between her lips. 'Look around you.'

Everyone did, exactly as she told them. At the desert with no boundaries.

'Except there *are* boundaries, but you have to find them,' she said. 'It's an assessment – an exam of how you will cope. Each one of you has been selected.'

Spider frowned. Of all people, he should not have been selected. He'd committed murder in the slowest way imaginable. 'When did you do that?'

'Don't interrupt, please. You've been selected and that's all there is to it. And dear though you are, and very pretty ...' She glowed at Splendour. 'You can take the name of the Dormilones family, after a shy little mimosa flower. Shy but beautiful – rather suits you all, but importantly, do any of you know how to cope in an environment like this?'

Only Noor spoke. 'It's like my homeland. I'll be fine here.'

She raised her eyebrows at him. 'And you'll find shelter out there?'

'Maybe.' He lowered his eyes.

'Because it's not as easy as it looks. Lots of dangers out there in the desert – or the Cirque, as you will come to call it. It's not as endless as it looks.'

'Meaning?' said Spider.

'You'll figure it out.' She looked at them all then, weighing up each of them. 'You have to work as a unit. You are family now, and you use each of your skills. And you treat each other like family.'

'Family? But we're—'

'Yes.' She held Spider's eyes sternly. 'You are family, do you understand?' She held up a finger and pointed it meaningfully from one face to the next, taking special time to linger on the men. It seemed to Spider that she held his gaze in particular. 'You know what I am saying. Don't you?' She whipped back round to Spider. 'Don't you know? How to treat brethren like brethren?'

Spider cleared his throat and lowered his face, pretending to scratch his nose, glancing sideways, trying to keep his eyes to himself. He had already figured out that Elk had chosen Amasha for the curves of her body. He'd noted Yma too. He knew what Mardy was saying: keep your eyes to yourselves, these women are your sisters.

'Brothers and *sisters*. You remain vigilant for each other, just as a brother would for a sister – understand, you Parisian drain-pipe rat?'

Spider opened his mouth to object, but Mardy shrugged him away. She went to the locked hatch and produced a key. She unlocked the hatch and climbed down. It took a moment for the family to realise they were expected to follow.

They went down hurriedly, glad to be free of the vertiginous platform, the wide blue sky. Forlani was crawling until Spider picked him up and carried him down – his first time. He weighed less than a child.

At the bottom of the stairs was an odd-shaped bar, made of gleaming metal tubes. There were low-hanging tube lights and the windows had been covered in pictures of deserts. A creaky great silver monster of a machine seemed to be blowing out cold air.

'It's a diner,' said Mahmoud, opening his arms and turning round and round. 'Wow! My first time in a diner.'

Mardy had gone behind the bar and was fussing around. Mounted above a steel hood was an enormous battered book with a crumbling leather spine and gold-tooled writing on it. There were industrial-sized catering trays under the hot lamps at the end of the bar. The trays didn't contain food, but clothes and equipment.

Noor, the most confident, sauntered over and sat on a stool at the bar. Mardy was standing behind the bar, wiping down the sweating metal pumps. Slowly the fourteen new arrivals gathered around the bar. They stood there for a long time while Mardy began her preparations, setting a glass pot of coffee on to heat, using a bucket to load ice out of an ice-chest, pulling napkins out and placing them on the bar. Fourteen in all. One each.

Spider watched Mardy carefully. Was it just him, or was everyone aware of what happened when her uniform moved. There were bumps on her skin where the sleeves shifted. It reminded him of a chick that was fledging – tiny bumps as if feathers were about to spring out.

'Now, do you want a soda or not?'

'Sure,' the other boy, Cairo, chimed. 'Two, please.'

Mardy arranged the sodas on the bar. The kids drank theirs straight down, while the adults sniffed and sipped the freezing lemonade.

'Basic instructions. That book there is the *Metse'haf*. You won't read it until near the end. What you need to do – what you need to find – is the Sarkpont. You'll have twelve chances, twelve Regyres.'

'What's a Sarkpont?' Madeira wanted to know. She had been sitting at the end of the bar, refusing to drink from her brimming glass. Even then, she had found a cigar from somewhere and was wreathed in the smoke. 'What's a Regyre? All these words – we're supposed to remember them all?'

'You'll remember them, that I can promise, little farm girl.'

'No shame in being a farm girl.'

'No shame in being a waitress.'

'At least my arms are strong.'

'Oh, my arms are strong,' smiled Mardy. 'I just choose the times to use them, and now isn't one of them. Now I would drink your soda, if I were you. You'll miss soda, I promise you.'

Eventually Madeira took the soda and drank it down in one, putting the glass challengingly on the counter. Mardy didn't react, but continued cleaning the bar, checking the temperature on the coffee, while the ice-maker clunked and shuddered.

Spider sipped at the drink. It was good – bitter like lemons, but sweet too. It might have been the best thing he'd ever drunk. He finished it and set the glass down. 'I think,' he said, 'you need to tell us what the Sarkpont is.' He could feel Yma and the others watching him. 'Don't you? If you're going to assess us, you'll need to tell us at least that.'

Mardy sat down on a chair behind the bar, puffing hard, and with effort lifted her massive left leg onto the bench. She pulled off her slipper and began massaging her foot, pressing the bloated toes down to relieve the pressure.

'You will remember the name the Sarkpont, young man, because it will become all you think about. It's a Hungarian word, I believe, and it means pivot. The Sarkpont is located in a piscina in the north-west corner of a rectangle, and I promise by the end of this you will be able to say it backwards to yourself in your dreams.'

'What sort of rectangle?' Elk asked.

'And what's a piscina?'

'You will learn. That is part of the test.'

'But why us?' Elk said, glancing from face to face. 'We don't know each other. At least – not obviously.'

Mardy bowed her head to Elk as if he was insufferably rude, but she was prepared to be civil to him. 'You'll end up knowing each other better than you know yourself. But you can't lose more than two family members, because that will send you straight to the beginning of your time here and you will forfeit your chance to find the Sarkpont – and you don't want to know what that means. You hear?'

Everyone nodded. *No more than two.*

'And when you find the Sarkpont, there will be more soda. Plenty of soda.'

'With ice cream? Splendour likes ice cream.'

'Oh, I think we could stretch to a little ice cream. Vanilla or chocolate, or something else?'

'Chocolate.'

'Good, now go to those trays and take supplies.'

'No, no, no …' said Noor. 'You haven't explained.'

'There is nothing more to explain. Except …' She pointed at Elk and Amasha. 'I want you two to stay.'

'Why?'

'You are the Futatsu – you are the leaders. Everyone else, hurry up.' She glanced at her watch as if they were wasting her time. 'Get your kit together and get out of here.'

Noor held Mardy's eyes. Then he shook his head, sighed and held up his hands in surrender. 'OK. Whatever your heart desires.

Let's get this thing under our belts.' He picked up a backpack and, because he'd always had a gravitas about him, soon everyone followed his lead and filed to the trays. There was a water canteen for each and a packet of mango wrapped in splotchy greaseproof paper. Also suntan lotion and rope.

'I know who you are,' the Englishman, Hugo, said suddenly. He was loaded up with equipment and his blue eyes, like a snow dog, were grave. 'I know you.'

He leaned across the trays and tried to grab Mardy's hand.

She snatched it from him with a sharp, 'Impertinent! I'd rather that wasn't your approach. *Noli me tangere*, please.'

'But I do know who you are.'

'I doubt that.'

'And I think I do too,' Forlani said warily. 'At least I think I know what you represent.'

'That's quite enough now, I'm growing very weary of you all. Now off with you. There's the door. You have a week to find a shelter, then it starts for real.'

She ushered them all to the door, silencing their questions with her palm, then pushed them out with the demeanour of an impatient bar keeper. 'Go on, and good luck.' She looked at Spider. 'Bring me back a Desert Rose, will you?'

The family found themselves on a spindly steel fire-escape-type ladder, which led down and down.

Spider had got almost to the bottom when something made him change his mind. He stopped, let the others go on ahead and turned to climb back up the ladder. It was hot and he needed water halfway up.

In the diner Mardy was wiping the countertops and slotting the glasses into a dishwasher. But something had happened. Elk was standing at the sink, where he had vomited, and Amasha was sitting at a table, wiping away tears.

'What's wrong?'

Mardy turned to look at him. 'What do you want, Spider? You need me to give you special dispensation.'

'What's going on? And yes, I came back because I want that book.'

She laughed. 'Yes, everyone wants that book. But you can't have it. You will learn – that's part of the joy.'

'And is part of the joy understanding what you've been talking about?'

'Nothing,' said Elk, though clearly he was lying.

Spider thought of the man he'd murdered in Paris. Not an enemy in the Foreign Legion, but a high-up official – someone close to the then President of the Senate. A brief flash of the man's last hours. A tank. A tube.

Eventually he filled up the water gourd with more water and turned for the ladder. No joy with Mardy – whoever she was.

Elk and Amasha were silent for the rest of that day. The family found a place to shelter, in a city that had giant roads on top of pillars. They lit a fire and soon the children fell asleep. Back then Nergüi was still with them. His name meant 'nameless' in Mongolian and he was a fighter and a warrior; he knew how to deal with the sand, and for a while he was Spider's best buddy.

'Are you going to tell us what happened back there?' Spider asked the Futatsu.

Elk glanced at Amasha. She closed her eyes, put her fingers against the lids.

'Two things to worry about,' Elk said eventually, his voice a deep bass. 'When we have found a shelter, we need to be secure inside it at the end of every second night. The second night is the grey night and we need to be enclosed safely.'

Amasha dropped her hand. 'And really – we have to be safe. Please understand this, please don't argue with it. We don't need to tell the children.'

'And what made you throw up?' Spider said. 'What made you cry?'

Both of them looked at each other. Amasha curled her lip as if it was an unpleasant memory. 'We saw what would happen if we didn't find the Sarkpont after twelve chances.'

'And?'

There was a long silence.

Then Elk said, 'You don't need to know. You just need to take it very, very seriously.'

6

THE BUS PULLS into McKenzie's development. It's a wide road, the houses spaced out well on two-acre lots, and this afternoon it's gloomy, the trees getting skinny, leaves swept up into piles at the ends of the driveways. Some of the electric pumpkins already glow on the porches, though it's not yet 3 p.m. Number 1,107 has an illuminated graveyard where two of the gravestones have shorted out in the rain.

India and McKenzie get off, say their quick goodbyes and then, hoods up, separate and head off towards their own houses. The rain hammers down on McKenzie, like nothing she's known. The door to the verandah at the back is open and she clatters in, past the fake glittery cobwebs and hanging skeletons. Mom's home – no yoga classes in the afternoon, something about her diurnal rhythms – so she's in, laying down recording workouts for her YouTube channel.

'Don't slam the door, Kenz,' she calls. 'I don't want my paintings coming off the wall, I've told you. And how many times do I have to tell you to take your shoes off in the house? I will kill you.'

In the kitchen McKenzie fills a pan with water and puts it on the heat. She's got hold of a hot-water bottle from eBay, an old-fashioned rubber thing like the British use in those Netflix box sets. She'll take it upstairs and wrap herself in the quilt, then open the window and listen to the storm cantering across the lowlands and the trees and the shopping malls. She'll figure out what to say to Joe, and how she's going to get her project for the Science Fair to really catch the attention of the Caltech professors.

A scratchy wriggling sound behind her, like sand being thrown at glass. She turns, her mouth open, in time to see water splash from the pan and land on the hot plate, as if something has dropped into it. The pan rocks to and fro, little colourless balls of water hissing on the ceramic hob. Something heavy has landed in the pan and is struggling.

'Mom?' she calls over her shoulder, not daring to take her eyes off the pan. '*Mom?*'

She snatches up the oven mitt and Mom's favourite painted porcelain ladle and shakily approaches the pan. Now it's rocking violently from side to side and appears about to fall off the hot plate.

'MOM!'

With her face half averted, prepared for something to jump at her, she takes another step forward and, trembling, leans over just enough to peep over the edge of the pan. The water froths and bubbles, and struggling in the bottom of the pan is the creature from her nightmare – the lizard.

Her instinct to scream is overtaken by her instinct to save the animal from the boiling water. She grabs the pan and races it to the sink, tips out the lizard and runs the cold-water tap on it. The lizard is completely still.

'No, no, no,' she begs. 'Don't die, please don't die.' She shoves the pan under the nozzle of the ice-maker, fills it, then chucks the whole panful of ice into the sink. The lizard begins to move. Sluggishly at first, and then suddenly rapidly. It raises its peculiar ruff-like neck, the bark-like eyelids open and close, then before McKenzie can do anything, it has canted itself back woodenly on its hind limbs and magically propels itself out of the sink and scurries across the worktop.

'Mom, come now!'

Footsteps on the stairs. The lizard is heavy as it skitters along, knocking over the smoothie-maker and sending Dad's granola jar flying. It runs straight off the edge of the worktop and lands with a meaty thud on the floor. McKenzie put her hands over her face, sure it's dead, but instantly it seems to recover and, with a click of claws on wood, reverses its trajectory and scampers in front of her, finding, in its terror, the tiniest gap where the door under the kitchen sink is slightly ajar.

In a flash of brown, it levers itself through the door just as Mom appears at the top of the basement stairs, shock-faced and bewildered.

'Hon?'

'In the cupboard,' McKenzie mouths, as if the lizard could understand. 'It's in there.'

'What's in there?'

'The lizard.'

Mom's face falls. 'Really? All this jumping around? Really?'

'It's the one I saw last night and it's huge.'

Mom frowns, but goes to the sink, throws open the doors, drops to her haunches and peers into the gap. She's still in her yoga pants and neat turquoise pumps, her hair held back in an Alice band. She's silent for a moment, her head drooping sadly. 'Honey, it's not here now.'

McKenzie drops her hands from her face and leans over. The cupboard is, as Mom says, empty, save for the few items of household cleaner, rubber gloves and a tin of dishwashing tablets. 'I don't …' She puts her hands on her thighs and leans in closer. The sink overflow disappears into a hole cut in the chipboard. 'There,' McKenzie says. 'It must have gone down there.'

A moment's silence. Both of them stare at the hole in the board, expecting to see a head or a tail. Even a rustle of movement. But nothing happens. Mom straightens.

'Well, it's not there now. Shall we forget this happened?'

'We can't leave it there.'

'Yes, we can,' Mom snaps. 'Now please forget all about this. I'm in the middle of recording – I'll have to start from scratch again.'

She turns on a heel and stomps back down the stairs. McKenzie watches her, deflated. She goes to the cooker hood and peers up into it. There isn't a place in the hood that the lizard could have squeezed through. She goes to the laundry room and pokes a broom handle up into the laundry chute, lifts the lid on the old top-loading washing machine and gets down on her hands and knees to check the backs for any cracks or holes in the plaster.

When she's searched everywhere, she goes to her bedroom and lies on the bed, staring at the rain running down the windows. What would India say? What would she do? McKenzie pulls out her phone, takes a photo on Snapchat and types out – *CALL ME*.

India FaceTimes her instantly. 'S'up?'

'OK, you gotta be reasonable about this, OK?'

'Is it Joe?'

'Nope, it's the nightmare I had last night.'

'Okayyy …' India says cautiously. 'Fire!'

'Right – I wake up in bed and there's a lizard next to me.'

India snorts. 'Did he look like Joe Marino?'

'Please, India – listen, this is serious. It's really big, like two feet long, and it runs away and when Mom and Dad came to look for it, it was gone.'

'OK, sounds like your routine Freudian dream. You need to masturbate more often. I keep telling you, the joy of the vibrator.'

'Jeez, India, please, will you just listen? So after we got off the bus, I come in and I'm boiling water, right, and the lizard drops out of the cooker hood into the water.'

'Fuck! Dead?'

'No. It gets up and runs away. Mom comes in and doesn't see it, and now she's being weird, like y'know, McKenzie's definitely losing it.'

There is a long silence. Then India says, hesitantly, ‘So there’s a way it came to be in the cooker hood, right?’

‘Ummm …’

‘Kenz … ?’

She rubs her eyes tiredly. She hadn’t realised how wet and cold her clothes are. ‘You know what?’ she says. ‘I think I imagined it. Let’s talk tomorrow.’

She hangs up on India’s protests and lies on her bed, biting her nails. After ten minutes she responds to Joe Marino’s message.

– *We were talking about science class. Why?*

The reply is instantaneous.

– *Hey, I thought you were blocking me!*

– *No.*

– *Send me a pic of ur smile.*

McKenzie frowns. She switches her phone off, buries it under her pillow and lies, face down, her head thudding. She knows not to send a photo. Not yet, not until she’s confident about him …

Spider is always thinking about the man in Paris, and how it slipped by when the selection process was happening. He can smell it sometimes, the rainy drains outside, the scent of fear, the gas lights in the attic. And his own achievement, the watertight tank. The man inside it.

But all in all, he thinks about the Sarkpont more. It has become second nature to the family – as have other words for objects and instructions – all in a mixture of Slavic, Chinese and Romance languages. Hugo and Tita Lily are the best linguists, but the term ‘piscina’ foxes them.

What would a swimming pool be doing in the middle of a desert city? they wonder. Does it have another meaning that they don't understand? They argue incessantly about Mardy's cryptic sentence, spoken when they were not fully concentrating. What sort of rectangle, they debate? It could be a city square, it could be the boundaries of a wall, it could be a garden or a room. They're sure it will only be with the aid of the Scouts and their 'altivoyance' – their unique ability to view the cities from a totally different perspective – that they will find the Sarkpont and be released.

From time to time Spider shoots a look at Tita Lily. He needs to know she is safe. They have already lost one of their number – by sheer fluke, or was it Noor's retribution: he doesn't trust Noor. Nergüi, the Mongolian, lost one day to the Djinni. The pounding on the outside of the tower, the yells and screams when he realised he was locked out. And Noor the one who did it.

They reach the shambolic city. It is called Mithi. It's Amasha who reads the word, written in Arabic and in old Sanskrit, the Brahmi faded and barely legible. She's a canny woman, curvaceous and nurturing, yet with the brain of a fox.

'Mithi.' She runs her fingers over the carved words and places her palm flat against them as if to feel the vibrations of the stone. 'It's a city in Pakistan. My parents told me about it. It's both Muslim and Hindu.'

'Did you ever go there?' Elk asks her.

'No.'

That seems to surprise him. He wobbles slightly, exaggerating his disbelief, to which Amasha only raises a slight brow.

'Well,' Elk asks, with gnarly eyebrows raised, 'if our most worldly of members hasn't been to this place before, have *any one* of us visited this place?' He looks at Noor, who shakes his head. Then at the rest of the family, who all shrug. 'Anyone even heard of it? Read about it?'

No one speaks. Elk gives a long, resigned sigh. Sometimes he walks crookedly, and for the first time Spider realises the big man is weary. Under his bulk is muscle, but he carries fat, and his hair is greying. Spider would help, but Elk is too proud for that – he grits down on the pain and exhaustion and keeps going, the thin, fierce Afrikaner blood in his veins pushing him on. 'OK,' he says. 'OK, so we start at the beginning then.'

There are still three hours before sunset, and Mithi, with its badly painted signs and colourful rubbish on the streets, like piled-up dead flowers, seems very small. Storks have been here, leaving derelict nests the size of tractor wheels. Their droppings coat the streets.

The family quickly reach the centre, where there is a small red hill crowned by a gold-and-green-tiled temple. They get to the monument and Spider lifts Tita Lily off Camel, into a dark corner where she can lie, then sits Splendour down with the others to drink some water from the gourds. Soon they'll separate out to search the city, but first he wants to see what lies beyond it. He goes into the temple, climbs the internal steps that smell of moss and dirty water to the top floor, where he finds a vantage point and focuses his binoculars on the horizon.

Mithi is the greenest city he's seen in the Cirque; each reddish-brown house has verdant hedges and trees. No one in the

Cirque knows what happened to the inhabitants of the cities – the family's become accustomed to the randomness of the desolation: some places are buried beneath tens of metres of sand, while others appear only just abandoned, with taps that produce water and lights that still glow. Once, in Abu Dhabi, Spider stumbled on a fridge full of edible cut pineapple and a stash of Hansen's black-cherry soda. There are no rules of physics that can be applied here.

Spider scans the desert beyond the city, examining the contours of the land. He's looking for anything, a lump or a bump, the tiniest anomaly that could warrant his attention. On white nights like today, if they don't find the Sarkpont in the city he will walk all night, trying to get as far into the desert as he can. He's not always alone – Hugo has done a few journeys and is usually willing; Noor also. They follow him all night, often only to discover that the promising bump on the horizon is a tree or an oddly shaped dune. Once it was the carcass of an elephant.

There is nothing to the west, so he slowly turns the eyeglasses towards the north. The Shuck is immediately visible – small and slighter from this unfamiliar angle; most people would see it only as a small discrepancy in the smooth dunes – and beyond it is the Virgule, the immense salt lake.

He moves further east and south, past the glinting, imperious skyscrapers of what they believe is Dubai, swinging all the way south, but no matter how hard he makes it work, there is not a solitary notch on the smooth horizon, except the places they've explored already.

'Spider.'

He turns. Amasha is there. Her blue-and-silver sari is stained from sweat and the soil of this place. Most of the diamonds on her eyebrows have fallen off, but she retains her haughty beauty. No wonder she was chosen as Futatsu.

'If there's nowhere to explore, then don't. Stay with us tonight and rest.'

'I've got to. We're running out of places.'

She lets out a long, tolerant sigh. '*Pætiyo*, my sweetie, aren't you human like us all? You don't have to flail yourself every white night, boy. If you kill yourself, the rest of us will suffer beyond our imaginations. We'll die too.' She puts her hand on his chest and closes her eyes. This is Amasha's way of reading the way that her family are feeling. 'And anyway …' She opens her eyes and touches his face. 'You're exhausted. Give yourself a break tonight.'

7

INDIA, IT TURNS out, really is the best friend of all best friends. It takes her a while to stomach the notion of a lizard loose in the house that no one but McKenzie has seen, but she soon steps up to the plate. That weekend she finds an old skunk trap in her parents' garage, cleans it up and brings it round to set up in McKenzie's bedroom. Then she drives McKenzie to Fair Oaks Mall to find glass fish-tanks and about twenty gallons of hobby sand in rainbow colours.

'He's called Mr Blonde,' McKenzie confides as they carry all the sacks of sand up to the bedroom. 'Because of the colour – sort of sandy, not like the green-and-brown tiddlers you see round here usually. I think he's a horned lizard, which isn't native to Virginia, so he must be a pet that's escaped.'

'He? Mr?' India says, dumping all the sand on the bedroom floor. 'How do you know it's a dude?'

'I don't. It's almost impossible to sex a reptile unless they're mating.'

'Well, that's a phenomenon neither of us is likely to witness, are we?' India pushes the bags of sand into the corner. 'And on that subject, anything else from Joe?'

'Nope – I didn't send him a picture, so he's gone quiet.'

'Good girl. You don't send him a single pic, especially if he asks for booty. You hear me: he's up to something. My brother's working on it.'

McKenzie sighs. It's not her imagination. Even her best friend thinks Joe Marino cannot be interested in her if there isn't a hidden agenda.

'And, biatch, you're wearing odd socks.'

McKenzie grabs at her jeans and pulls them up. India's right: one sock is white, the other is blue. She smoothes down her jeans. Life feels very heavy and indissoluble at the moment.

The week passes slowly. Four days in a row Joe isn't on the bus, and India murmurs something sinister about him being suspended, but then on the last day he appears at the back of the bus, surrounded by gossiping girls. He winks broadly at McKenzie, runs his tongue across his lower lip. She sits down hurriedly, scowling.

'He's trouble, Kenz,' India tells her over and over again. 'I'm going to get you proof. You believe me, don't you?'

McKenzie doesn't have an answer for that. She has no answers for the way her stomach twitches and rolls when she sees him – none at all. In the nights she lies awake, checking her phone and rereading his messages. Then, when she's composed a hundred texts to send back, deleted them all, recomposed them and deleted those too, she lies on her back and listens to the walls.

Dad says he lost a hamster as a child and it turned up in a wall cavity – but the house is silent, and McKenzie is worried Mr Blonde might be so injured by the hot water that he's crawled away to die, and the first they'll know about his location will be the smell. They'll dig him out and he'll be covered in bits of fluff and maggots. How sad would that be? India's skunk trap is gathering dust amid odd pieces of laundry that needed airing.

She's been working on the science project, partitioning the two glass tanks with specialist aquarium dividers, making four separate sections, and has made the craft sand into ice-cream colours of pistachio, strawberry, melon and lemon. She has to find a way to get a supply of air to mimic the wind and create Aeolian dunes, but so far she's lucked out. Maybe the answer is to use water to replicate the action – it's not such a leap; after all, the sandy bottoms of the oceans often bear similar patterns to Aeolian land-based sand dunes, and by fixing a hose up to the side of the tank she might be able to reproduce crescentic, linear, lunette and parabolic dunes, which will mimic dunes produced by the wind.

'If the lizard does exist – I mean, outside her freaky brain, that is – then it's already starved to death for sure,' Luke says at the dinner table one night. He and Tatum have made no secret that they resent their parents humouring McKenzie.

'Yup. As of its fifth day *in situ*, India's skunk cage does appear, to all intents and purposes, to be empty. Again.'

'Stop it, Tatum,' Dad says, spooning vegetables onto his plate. 'Leave her alone.'

'One of the guys in fifth grade had this gecko.' Luke is forking sweet-potato fries into his mouth. His hair, wet from the shower, is dripping on his grey college T-shirt. 'It bit the dude's finger and he's like that' – Luke flicks one hand in the air. 'So the lizard's let go and it's flying across the kitchen and hits the wall and slides down it, and the dude's hysterical and is like, "Oh no, my little scaly baby, I didn't mean to hurt you." But the lizard just picks itself up and disappears down some hole or something.' Luke gets up, opens the refrigerator and pulls out a San Pellegrino. He sits down and pops the can, fisting it like it's a beer. 'The guy has to try every trick in the book: turns out all the lights, puts out a heating pad in the middle of the room, covers every wall in bubble wrap so the damned thing will make a noise. He leaves out mealworms, tin foil covered in flour, but the gecko is history. The mealworms all escape, the flour gets trampled all over the house and the guy's mom is so mad – you can imagine, right?'

'I doubt this lizard is your friend's gecko.' Dad pushes his glasses up his nose and twists to regard his son. 'Unless it was possessed of extraordinary powers and able to hitch a lift or get an Uber.'

'It was albino, if that counts, and they've got some magic superpowers. Its name was "Polar", cos it was white. So when it never made a reappearance, all the kids called it "bye"-Polar and wrote it on the chalkboard, but that made the dude cry, so the parents came to see the principal and you can guess the rest.'

'Lovely,' Dad says. 'Thank you for sharing that with us.'

Quietly McKenzie puts down her fork. She's lost her appetite. Luke has done this for as long as she can remember – always doubting her, always questioning her. Once he challenged her to do an IQ test with him; she was in fifth grade and he was a high-school freshman. Sitting on the other side of the table from her, with Dad acting as reluctant adjudicator using his phone as a stopwatch, Luke had laughed all the way through it, stuck out his tongue, shoved his finger up his nose, made monkey-faces when Dad wasn't looking. McKenzie scored 15 per cent higher than Luke. He's never referred to the test again.

'Most girls will be like "*I'm proper having a wet dream about Justin Bieber*",' Tatum offers. 'But my sister? No. My sister will be like "*The wind is going to reach a hundred miles an hour in Antarctica today. Isn't that lit? And while you're at it, I've lost my lizard friend, which I only associate with because I'm dysfunctional.*" And if you're asking me – personally I'm forming a relationship with the live ants in the fridge.'

'He has to eat something when he comes out,' McKenzie murmurs. 'If he comes out and he's hungry – what then?'

'That's enough!' Mom gets up and begins shuffling sweet-potato fries onto any available plate, as if that might help the atmosphere. 'This is not the way our meal is meant to be going. This is all a mistake, so let's start again. We do not talk about the lizard.'

'What lizard?' Tatum says, innocent.

Mom dumps the casserole in the sink and turns on the tap. Her usually jaunty little ponytail has slumped onto her nut-brown shoulders. 'Boys – go to your room. McKenzie, Dad and I need to talk to you.'

'Oooooh,' her brothers chorus. 'She's in the highchair. Let's pray for her, bro.'

'One more word …' Dad threatens as they slide back their chairs and leave the room, Luke stopping to jettison a can into the rubbish bin from the kitchen doorway. 'One more word.'

'Close the door, Selena.' Dad wipes his mouth with his serviette and puts down his knife, twitching it from side to side thoughtfully, as if he's deciding how to arrange his words. 'Have they gone now?'

She nods, looking at the ceiling, listening to her sons thumping around up there. Then she pours herself a glass of water and sets it on the table, sitting down opposite McKenzie.

'What is it? What's going on?'

Mom reaches across the table and covers her hand. 'Sweetheart – does your school counsellor have access to a professional?'

'A professional what?'

'A psychiatrist. Someone you can talk to if you're under stress.'

McKenzie jerks her hand away. 'I'm not under stress. What're you talking about?'

'You might be and not realise it.'

'Only with the science project. I want to impress the Caltech professors. There are going to be two at the Science Fair.'

Mom sucks in a breath. 'About the project. I saw all that sand in your room – why don't you tell us about the project, honey? Give us the outline.'

'Why?'

'Because your parents are interested.'

'It's about wind in the desert . . .' She trails off. Mom and Dad's faces are stiff. 'Why do you need to know?'

Mom takes a long deep breath. She lowers her chin and begins to play casually with her ponytail. The way she always does when there's something she doesn't want to say.

'What?'

Mom shrugs. 'Oh, I dunno. Just thinking – does it have to be sand?'

'It's the easiest medium. It's light – gets carried in ways soil doesn't.'

Mom passes a quick, panicked glance across the table to Dad. It's fleeting, and she covers it quickly with a smile, but not quickly enough.

'Is there a problem with sand? I'll vacuum. I promise not to get any on the rugs.'

'It's fine. Don't worry about it.'

'Absolutely fine, honey, you do what you want to do . . .'

But they sound as false as soap-star parents.

'What, then? *What?* Mom? Dad?'

Mom's movements are suddenly precise, her dance training in evidence. She picks up the glass of water and drinks to cover her confusion. McKenzie stares at her throat, at the way it moves when the water goes down.

Mom stops drinking. She slams down the glass, suddenly flushed with anger. 'For the love of God, why do you always stare at me when I'm drinking water?'

'I wasn't staring.'

'You were – you always do. What is *wrong* with you?'

'Selena, hon, please, let's keep this nice.'

Mom sighs and pushes her hands between her thighs, staring sideways so she doesn't have to engage with her daughter. Dad pulls up his chair and puts his arm around McKenzie. 'Honey, just an idea, but do you think it's time to forget this lizard? Maybe tell ourselves it really doesn't exist.'

McKenzie lowers her eyes, stares at her hands. 'He does exist – I've seen him.'

'And is this something you would like to talk with a counsellor about? You know, the fact that your brothers don't really believe there is a lizard.'

'You think I've dreamed it or that I'm half crazy. And it's happened before, hasn't it? Maybe years ago, when I don't remember?'

'Don't talk insane stuff. That's not what we said – not what either of us said. We simply want you to speak to a professional as soon as possible. We think you're stressed.'

'I'm not stressed,' McKenzie says, her voice thick. 'And there IS a lizard in this house.'

The Dormilones family separate out to search Mithi: Elk partners Noor, and while Hugo, Madeira and Splendour go as a three-hander, Amasha is with Mahmoud. Spider is paired with Forlani, which Splendour finds hard to accept. She hangs onto Spider's legs as Madeira stands patiently on the path down to the city, waiting to take her into the search.

'Spider?' Splendour thumps his naked knee with her small fist to get his attention. 'I don't want to go.'

'I know. But we have to search.'

'We're always searching. We never find it.'

'But one day we will.'

'One day,' she says wonderingly. 'Is it going to be today? Are we going to find it today?'

He starts to talk, then stops himself. He doesn't want to give her hope. 'I don't know.' He puts a restrained hand on her head but doesn't crouch to look at her. 'Now go with Madeira and Hugo.'

She needs a little more coaxing, but eventually she trots off sullenly and takes Madeira's hand. Spider watches her go. What is going to happen to her? He and the other adults – he can accept they have an unimaginable fate. But Cairo, Mahmoud and Splendour? Little children? And Forlani? And Camel?

He glances up at Camel's crusting nostrils, her humps already beginning to sag a little. The family inherited Camel when they arrived in the Cirque. She was wandering around near the northern borders, aimless, and was pathetically easy to catch. Maybe her previous family had abandoned her when they found the Sarkpont. Attached to her saddle, bumping at her side, was a dummy baby camel. It turned out to be the ancient skin of her own calf stuffed with sawdust, the smell of which was intended to keep her producing milk. The first thing Spider did was to get rid of the wretched dead baby – Camel has never been milked by this family, and never will be.

'Are you ready?' Forlani asks at that moment, jolting him out of his thoughts. His misshapen jaw always shows its tendons straining like agonised cables into his neck. Forlani squints when he speaks, and it took Spider a long while to realise it's because his crooked legs mean he's lower than other people and always has to raise his face to the relentless sunshine. 'Tita Lily is OK – she's asleep, I gave her some medication, but …' He rubs his hands, smiling. 'I want to search this place.'

Spider ties Camel to the monument door and opens a water gourd for Tita Lily, then he and Forlani head down the edge of the little red hill towards the city. They have established a method of searching, using the rudimentary compasses that Yma constructed for the family. Forlani has a native instinct for where to look, so they move swiftly, eliminating buildings and roads in quick sweeps.

Mithi has flat, wide streets of beaten soil, the houses are of adobe and low corrugated-iron roofs, with rusting metal spikes on the outside walls of the larger houses, while others are separated from the street by corrugated iron painted blue. Like most of the cities in the Cirque, the sand has blown into the abandoned buildings. Twice Spider and Forlani stop and use a spade to remove it from the small yard of a dwelling, but each time the north-west corner reveals nothing more interesting than the skeleton of a bird or bailed chicken wire.

In their idle moments the family talk endlessly about how they picture the Sarkpont: Amasha thinks it will be an ornate alabaster bowl in the corner of a musical chamber, a single harp sitting in the centre of the room, while Elk thinks the piscina will be huge, and floating in it a monstrous boat with a pointed prow. Madeira pictures a white bull standing in a shallow pond, and Splendour once told Spider that the Sarkpont was going to be the drinking trough for a stable full of unicorns – that Mardy would be waiting for them when they found it, holding chocolate ice-cream sodas.

Spider's decided he hasn't got an imagination, not like the others, because he can't summon up any images – except a racing mountain stream with the sweetest, coldest water. Water is gold in the desert. Pure, fresh gold.

He and Forlani stop and drink from the mouldy-tasting drinking bladders, then continue on down the street, Forlani checking every crevice for plants. He's always collecting new leaves and medicines to filter down – he has collected almost everything – but there are still two holy grails he hasn't discovered in the Cirque: a willow tree, nature's greatest painkiller, he claims; and *Hamamelis* or witch hazel, which can also be applied to Tita Lily's wounds. Neither is suited to desert conditions, and though there is water in Mithi – the green weeds are evidence of an underwater supply – Forlani fails to find anything more than a few cacti, which he de-thorns and shovels into his pack.

Spider scrutinises the street. Everywhere are abandoned cars, all Japanese. In the next street he can see a minaret built in white brick, beaten zinc tiles on the roofs.

'Come on.' He ties his spade to his tool belt and they head on, poking their noses into every house, every shop. After a while they cross a dried river bed where washing has been abandoned on stones, dried out and stiff with dust, and discover on the far bank a monument to Hindu gods, an effigy of a man painted blue, wearing his black hair piled on top of his head, brandishing a rearing cobra in one hand. Until he was brought into the Cirque,

Spider had never seen a place of worship that wasn't Christian, Jewish or Muslim. These odd, black-eyed icons, always with a hand raised, sometimes contain so much wisdom in their distant eyes that he wants to weep, looking at them.

Everywhere are ragged, worn-out cats. They sit in the doorways of abandoned buildings and stare at the two men in timid fascination.

'Cats,' Spider says as they walk. 'That's a first.'

It's not the first time they've seen live animals in the Cirque. They've seen camels and horses that canter away in clouds of sand, and there are the sheep they've taken back to the Shuck to milk and shave. Once they found five donkeys, mummified where they stood in their stalls by the tonnes of sand that had drifted over them. The donkeys made Mahmoud cry – he said he had a donkey in Egypt and regrets he didn't treat it well.

'When I was a kid, my mother had a dog,' Forlani says. 'In Buzau. Our house was on the edge of a road, and one day our dog got hit by a car. I was two – but I remember it happening. I remember the squealing, the way the dog spun herself in the gravel, trying to get at the wound. The neighbours said we should have shot her, but my mother didn't. She waited to see what would happen.'

'And what happened?'

'The dog lived. Its back end was numb and useless, but its front end was strong.' To demonstrate, Forlani executes two turns on the crutches Spider made him. 'Just like me. And what the dog discovers, after some months, is that she is fed more. People pity her, dragging herself across the street. They give her titbits and she gets fat. Then one day the dog's sister, which has been watching her getting all the attention, learns how to pull her back legs along, like she's injured. She goes into town like that, and the place happens to be full of tourists who throw her meat and treats. From that day on, she walks like a cripple.'

After a long, contemplative silence, Spider speaks. 'Are you trying to tell me that you chose to be a cripple?'

Forlani laughs uncontrollably. 'No,' he says eventually. 'I'm trying to tell you that dogs are smart. Smarter than cats.'

'I had a cat once, back in Paris. The cat worked out there were wires going over the street from one rooftop to another. It never had to cross the street. Never had to drag its legs to get by.'

'Cats versus dogs? It's one of those arguments that never gets boring.'

Spider laughs. Forlani has the ability to make him smile, even at the worst of times.

'Come on,' he says. 'Let's find this pool.'

At the end of the street they come to a T-junction in front of which rises a building that seems carved from the sand itself, as if a giant toddler has created a sandcastle with her fingers. There is storey after storey of columned balconies, great intricacies of design going on and on. On the top is a tower from which rises the flag of Pakistan.

'Well, fuck,' mutters Forlani. 'That's a monstrosity.'

Spider walks around the base, peering up at it. There are ventilation or water holes in a zigzaggy formation leading up to the first row of columns. He puts his head on one side and makes a long, experienced study of them.

'No,' Forlani says. 'You're not going to.'

'But climbing's my skill. Didn't get called Spider for any other reason.'

'And you never stop reminding me of it. But I will never stop reminding you of the rules: clear, from Elk and Amasha. No separating. We stick together – it's too dangerous to do things on your own and you can already guess, by my swag way of standing, that I'm not going to be climbing no walls today.'

'The Sarkpont could be on the other side of this wall.'

Forlani stretches his misshapen jaw out further, narrows his eyes and examines Spider's expression. Then he makes a cluck of disgust. 'No arguing with you, I should have learned that several Regyres ago.' He shakes his head. 'I thought I saw some lavender in a yard back down that street. I'd better go back and inspect it again – it could be important.'

Forlani's need to help the family preoccupies him day and night. Once, in a ritzy hotel in a city Spider can't even remember the name of, he found phials of what he thinks are IV antibiotics, though no syringes. For now, the medicine is useless, but Forlani guards it anyway, buried in a box under the sand in the tower – dark and cool, a secret unmarked place. He's always on the prowl, always hoping for something new.

He hobbles away, leaving Spider in the middle of the road, watching him go. Forlani is canny as a snake, loyal as a dog. The best brother a man could hope for.

Spider drags out the bandages he keeps in his tool kit and wraps them carefully round his bare knees. He crouches and places his hands against the bottom of the wall – it's sandy and absorbs some of the grease and moisture – then wraps more bandages around his palms. He reverses the cap he wears so that the peak covers his neck, checks all his belts and tools are strapped to his body and begins to climb.

Climbing is when he is most at ease, most free. Paris cured him early of any fear of heights – he has a million mind-tricks to call on and is never troubled by the drops – so with fear buttoned away, he is free to concentrate on his technique. He was never formally taught; everything he knows he learned by trial and error when he used to live among the rooftops and swing onto the balconies of the pretty girls near the Gare d'Austerlitz – shinning down drainpipes like the rat that Mardy called him.

Once he asked the family if they'd noticed the incipient feathers in her skin, and they'd all looked at him as if he was crazy. So it was he, and he alone, who had noticed. And then the rest … the stuff he has to hide from the remainder of the family. The man in the immersion tank. Spider waiting and waiting. Smoking Gauloises, crunching the butts under his heel. The smell of rust. The rasp of the man breathing.

The handholds are the perfect size, the stone doesn't crumble and the climb is so easy and natural – every hair on his body seems to stand up in the air, as if some wolfish instinct is shaking alive inside him, and within a few short minutes he has reached the first row of columns. They are close together, the space no wider than a man, and he drags himself up to the platform and sits, unwinding and readjusting his bandages.

Behind him, Mithi lies low and dusty red, the streets a maze meandering around. Forlani has disappeared, maybe into one of the buildings.

Spider gets up and crawls to the inner side of the landing, peering over. The building is enormous inside – open to the skies and deep – consisting of a series of rooms arranged around a rectangular courtyard maybe twenty metres below him. The centrepiece is a dried-out pool, the green-and-white tiles cracked and discoloured, and past it another wall with a single, blocked doorway. Beyond that wall he can see the top of an iron structure, which seems curiously out of place in a city like this.

Frowning, he stands and tries to get up high enough to see it, but standing on tiptoe isn't enough and the columns are too smooth to climb. He lies on his front and peers down at the wall that extends from this place: a long drop, with no visible handholds; no natural chinks, like on the outside wall, and no weeds sprouting from the mortar. The opposite wall is similarly smooth.

It's too far to drop – he's agile, but not that stupid – so he unwinds the rope that hangs from the back of his tool belt. It's a wonderful thing, this rope; he found it in Ouargla, dangling from a rusting construction crane, as translucent as gossamer, no thicker than Splendour's little finger and seemingly impossible to tangle, no matter what contortions he puts it through – it carries his weight, and more. He's had Noor, Elk and Madeira tethered to one strand of the stuff, hanging under the Shuck, and has dragged them several metres up from the bottom of the tower and kept them dangling in mid-air, until Madeira lost her sense of humour about being suspended in space and demanded that he let them down.

He wraps this bizarre material round a column and ties it in a good, solid bowline knot, then tests his weight against the column. It holds and allows him to abseil down the wall to the floor of the courtyard, which is cool and shaded, with the smell of dying vegetation. Everywhere grow small plants, about knee-high, which produce large flat leaves, as waxy green as if they are on a forest floor.

He passes a stack of plastic bottles made milky by the sunlight, skirts the pool and comes to the doorway. Something comes to him then – a smell or a sense – forcing adrenaline into his system, making his throat tight, his mouth bitter. What, he thinks as he pushes the door open, what is creeping him out hardcore like this?

The door creaks, a few cockroaches scatter at his feet and he steps through.

Another courtyard, as dank as the last, the same shadows and plants. In the centre, though, suspended from thick wires bolted into every wall, dangles a steel box the size of a Greyhound bus.

He shrinks instinctively back into the first courtyard, his hand going to his knife, and stands with his back against the wall, breathing hard. It's a Shuck – he's sure of it – and maybe another family here. There have been other families – but all at a distance, and he's never been within more than half a kilometre of them. Everyone here is shy, they all hide what they know.

He tips his head back and stares up at the roof of the temple, so far away, its rafters cracked and blistered, covered in birds' nests. How far is it from here to the distant wall – and how long would it take to clamber up the rope? He'll call to Forlani and ... and ...

He shakes himself. If anyone has heard him approaching, they've had ample time to react, and how does he know they will be aggressive?

He scrunches his eyes closed, forces up some of his old Legion training. What did he *see*? What specifically did he see there, and how can it help him?

Weeds. The smell – he thinks that's what alerted him – of decay. Plant matter maybe, or food: something going bad. And rust. The Shuck is rusting around the windowpanes and there is a wind-torn flag on top of it. It is stained and battered. If a family are here, they are weak and have stopped taking care of the Shuck. Or maybe they're gone.

There is a piece of rebar lying amongst the plastic bottles. Stealthily Spider retraces his steps, taking care not to make any noise, snatches it up and retreats to the wall, licking his lips. There's a ladder going up to the Shuck, and a piece that protrudes from the top like a turret – a lookout tower exactly like the one the Dormilones made.

He takes a deep breath and uses the rebar to push the door. It creaks deafeningly, but opens a short way. He lowers his head slightly and twists just enough to give himself sight of the courtyard, then shrinks back.

So, an inventory:

– animal pens to the right (open, doors wide)

– earth ridges (an attempt to cultivate crops perhaps, but anything planted is dead)

– a door open, lolling on its hinges

– windows cracked.

It's abandoned. Has to be abandoned.

He pushes the door wider. There is no sound, only the flapping of a startled bird rising from a nest on top of the Shuck. This time Spider doesn't recoil, but stands still and watches – taking in the entire courtyard, from the sandstone colonnades four storeys above floor level, to the broken ladder.

The Shuck reminds him of the Airstream towing homes he encountered on a Scout mission three Regyres ago – it is smooth, with recessed windows that have protective meshes mounted over them. Rust rivers run down it and there is a huge hole in the bottom, through which he can see a plastic-covered seat, lemon-yellow with what must once have been a cheerful pink daisy-print scattered across the cushions. A pair of boots hang from a hook above them and there is a nest of some description on the table.

He lets out a breath, wipes his forehead. He saw lots of Shucks in the first week, when they were labouring to find the right place to settle; either they were clearly inhabited or – like this – abandoned back to nature. Carefully he goes to the wire that stretches from the lower corner to the wall and tests it. It is solid, has no rust or give, though where it is bolted to the wall it looks clumsy – as if done in a hurry with makeshift tools.

So far all the shelters have been outside cities, but this one seems to have flourished once. The livestock pens are of various sizes, each has a water trough of beaten metal, a separate food net and evidence of sliding screens to protect the animals. There are also pipes leading down and trellises too, though nothing growing on them.

He goes to the ladder and climbs carefully. The door is open and inside is a living area, full of sand and debris, sleeping bags suspended on a line above a rusty sink. There is a gas stove of sorts – nothing like the one Elk has installed at the Dormilones' Shuck, but adequate, and a coolbox, open and empty. The cupboards also stand open, and the meshes that guard most of the windows are picked away at. Someone has come after the original occupants of this place, has ravaged it and taken everything useful.

There is a silted-up door that he pushes open, to find a sand-filled corridor leading to the sleeping quarters. It takes a while to get the doors open but when he does, he finds each one has evidence of its occupants – pencil drawings on the walls of cacti, dogs and stars. An image of a fountain and a waterfall, as if someone was dreaming of a world where water was everywhere. A row of shells on a bedhead and, in a pillowcase, a heart embroidered with cotton strands from torn-up T-shirts.

Spider's mother used to sew hearts whenever she could – using whatever materials she could find. She didn't teach him about Aesop's fables or the things that Hugo understands, but she taught him the simple stuff, like how to show appreciation and how to be honest. He has to turn the pillow to face the wall, thinking about his mother. She never really had a chance, never had a chance.

He moves on down the Shuck – finds showers and lavatories, clean apart from the inevitable creep of the desert, self-seeded air plants and cacti; and at the other end of the Shuck an entire raft of maps scribbled using a thick charcoal. He sorts through them, recognising that the Dormilones have crafted far more finely honed charcoal pencils, and Spider has a momentary lift of pride thinking of Knut's maps, shaded and nuanced, with neat annotations, so skilled compared to this sketchy mess.

There are empty jars unlike any he's seen in the Cirque before, stained as if they contained a pigment. Also, scattered around, a few pieces of looped metal he can't comprehend: about the length of his forearm, and shaped like a teardrop with a hole in the centre. He studies these for a long time, tries to bend them – they are rigid; tries to chip at them – they resist. He goes into the kitchen and holds them up to the refrigerator door and they bind with a loud clap. Magnetic then, he thinks, turning them over and over, but can't imagine their use. He places two in the bottom of his rucksack, then on top of them places some of the more-complete maps, a flexible ruler with illegible words scrawled on it, and a chunk of dates wrapped in some murky cellophane.

He pauses. On the floor under the table is a scruffy book: a cheap children's jotter, and scrawled on the front the words 'PLEASE READ'. Frowning, he picks it up – opens it to the first page. Written inside the cover are the words: *If you find this, please read and learn from our mistakes. The Dulyeowos.*

The first page starts: *We are a happy enough family, though apparently our name means 'Fearful'. We've never met before, but it feels already as if we have known each other all our lives. This is our first Regyre, and we have been lucky enough to find a shelter almost immediately in a beautiful city …*

Spider sits down and reads on, scarcely breathing as the history of the family progresses. Outside, the shadows grow higher up the walls, the entire temple falls into shadow, but on he reads, the sinews at the back of his neck growing tight and sore with dismay.

When he has finished the last page he does nothing for a long time. He breathes slowly, staring at the final page, feeling the ticking of his pulse and the ticking of time.

8

IN THE RUN-UP to the fair McKenzie's sleep is disturbed. She often wakes with a jerk in the night, her head pounding, consumed with thirst. Her vision is disturbed, and it seems that on her retina a giant clouded image is imprinted – sand dunes, reaching as far as the eye can see.

On the one hand, she's concerned that her project isn't attention-grabbing enough for a faculty member of the world's foremost atmospheric-sciences college; on the other hand, she thinks with its colourful dunes it's a little childish. Even for a junior, and even with the hard science of it backed up on the display board, she's followed a plodding format given her in seventh grade, with boxes labelled 'hypothesis', 'abstract', 'conclusion' – hoping it'll keep the science nerds at bay, with all the citations of angle and wavelength and sand-transport saturation rate. But outside that, isn't the project a little ordinary?

The night before the fair she drinks two entire pints of water and spends half the night thinking up hashtags for her Science Fair posts. She decides on #dreamsofdesert and #sandformations and #aeoliansandforms. She eventually sleeps at 3 a.m. and is woken four hours later by a sound. Lying there in the first light of dawn, she hears a faint skittery sound coming from the bathroom door.

She rubs her eyes blearily, her head tight and hot. The room is quite clear, lit by the oblique early-morning sun. Her clock says 7 a.m. And then, again, the sound. Unmistakably the noise of sly, secretive lizard nails on bathroom tiles.

And then, as if by magic, Mr Blonde appears on the carpet divider between the bathroom and her room, braced up fiercely on his forelegs to all of four inches high, his head cocked on one side.

'Shit,' she murmurs, struggling up to a sitting position, awed. 'You're alive.'

Mr Blonde blinks at her twice but otherwise shows no signs of fear. She considers yelling for Dad, but that'll startle Mr Blonde. Tentatively she gets out of bed. She expects him to skeeter away, but he doesn't; he cocks his head to one side and studies her. 'You're beautiful,' McKenzie breathes. He seems to shine in the thin sunlight, the warty ruff around his neck like the mixed browns and beiges of autumn leaves.

Grabbing the ant jar, she swings her legs out of bed and takes a few hesitant steps towards the bathroom. She squats down and holds out her finger. The lizard ignores her finger, rotates his head to one side, but doesn't run away.

'Wow! Do you want some ants?'

Mr Blonde doesn't flinch or move. She tips a few ants into a matchbox – not too many, as her reading makes it clear that harvester ants can gang up on even a healthy lizard – and nudges them close to Mr Blonde. One or two of them swarm up the side of the box and make a bid for freedom, but Mr Blonde uses his long tongue to scoop up the ants. It's so quick: he whisks them back into his mouth, swallows, then shoots out his tongue again to catch the next two escapees.

Awed, McKenzie dares to get up and tiptoe back to her desk, keeping her eyes on Mr Blonde as she goes. He appears content to continue scooping ants from the matchbox. She gets the eye-dropper and the mister spray that she's kept on hand for this occasion, goes back and crouches carefully next to Mr Blonde. 'OK,' she says, shuffling herself forward on her haunches. 'Don't freak out, but I've got to use this. Just to hydrate you.'

She raises the spray and gives it a puff. Far from being alarmed, the lizard seems to welcome the fine mist of water. He doesn't stop eating, but arches his body upwards as if he's enjoying the sensation, almost wriggling with pleasure.

'You like that?' She squeezes the bottle again. 'You do. You like that.'

She leans in a little nearer and inspects Mr Blonde while he vacuums up the ants. The last two weeks, in between working on the project, she's learned a lot about horned lizards – or horned toads, as they're called colloquially. He looks healthy, considering he's been hiding for almost two weeks. They don't need much water, as apparently they get a lot of it from the formic acid in ants, but this one maybe hasn't eaten in days. And yet it looks like the comparison photos she has on her phone. No folds, no discoloration, not scared.

McKenzie gets up and goes to the door, opens it and is about to yell down the stairs, 'Hey, Tatum, my lizard's here' when something occurs to her. She turns and looks back at the rainbow-coloured sand in the tanks.

The project. Lacking.

What would Mr Blonde look like, running up and down those sand gullies?

She closes the door, goes back to the lizard and crouches. 'Hey,' she says gently. 'Do you feel like an adventure?'

Surprisingly the lizard doesn't resist when she picks it up. It sits in her hands, its chest up, its huge warty head moving slowly from side to side. She carries him across to the tanks, rests him on the miniature sand dunes. He is very still for a moment, then he tiptoes his way across them with the poise and delicacy of a ballerina. He makes the dunes look vibrant – he somehow highlights the incredible contours and variations. The glue holds the formations in place and when, after five minutes, she lifts him out, there are only a few tiny grains of sand clinging to his claws and the dunes are totally undisturbed.

Her phone is on the bedstand – she snatches it up to Snapchat India, but there's a Snap from Joe. His face, looking sad.

– hey you ignoring me? wanted 2 wish u luck at the Science Fair, i'm gonna be there will stop by and say hi if that's OK

She stares at the screen, her eyes on stalks, goosebumps on her arms.

– sure, that'd be great

She waits a few moments, but he must still be asleep because he hasn't read her reply, so she texts India.

– OMGOMGOMG You awake?

– I wasn't but I am now thanks

– The lizard turned up. I'm gonna take him to the Science Fair in the tanks

– kewl – u r the shit

– true dat (ha-ha)

There is a long pause, then India types out:

– Kenz …

– Yeah?

– You haven't spoken to that shitbag joe have you?

– Nooooo

– Truth?

– True. Why?

– i got proof. he's a dick

McKenzie hesitates, then types:

– what?

– just trust me

– i wanna know – come on.

– I was gonna tell you this after you slayed the Science Fair, but he might be there, might try and use it as a chance to chat to you, pls pls DON'T. k?

– just tell me ffx

– It's a wind-up, you're on his radar

McKenzie's heart thuds, fills her ears and her head.

– i don't believe you …

– Aww Kenz, please

– I don't. Where's the proof?

– you don't wanna see it

– i do

A long, long silence.

Then her phone pings with a screen grab from maybe India's brother's phone. She studies it, then drops her phone and lies back on the pillow, staring at the sky.

Eventually, in the dusty Shuck, Spider wipes his eyes, puts the journal on top of the backpack, gets to his feet and pulls his hands down his face to clear his head. Outside the temple the sky is pre-twilight blue – and the gentle click-click-click of cicadas floats up from somewhere. Cicadas only exist in the cities that have water, and the sound of them comforts him as he makes his way back to the rope, thinking of how it might have comforted the Dulyeowos.

At the rope he gets the backpack positioned right, checks the bandages on his hands and grabs the rope. Five steps up, it pings lightly and drops him a metre. He lands well, weight equally placed on both feet, and tips onto his back – but instantly sees his mistake, because coming down like a mountain is the stone column that the rope was belayed to.

'*Shit!*'

He rolls sideways over his backpack, arms coming up over his face, and curls into a foetal position, feeling rock slam into the ground behind him. Something grazes him, sends pain into his ribs and he scrambles further away. Eventually silence comes and all that is left is his breathing, echoing off the courtyard walls.

When his heart has slowed a little he sits, stares up at the wall. No more rockfalls; the rope lies at his side, still attached to the crumbling slabs of stone. A fault line in the grain of the stone: a beginner's mistake. Tentatively he touches his back, feels the adhesion of his palm against the skin, brings his hand back and sees blood – tacky and dark.

Blood in this place is not good; it doesn't happen often, and always Forlani has the right poultice or covering. Spider wipes his hand clean on the plants and tries again, and this time there is less blood on his palm – he's probably got away with it. Shakily he gets up and goes to the wall, pressing his hands against it, and peers up at the platform. There aren't any handholds in the wall – no way of clambering back up.

He sorts through the fallen masonry until he finds a good chunk, which he attaches to the end of the rope. Then he coils the rope into a loose lasso under his arm, wipes the sweat from his forehead, reverses his cap again and leans back to aim the rock at the columns. It's a good throw and streams up into the evening air towards the gap left by the fallen column.

But the rock bounces off the neighbouring column and plummets back down, nearly hitting him in the face. He tries again – this time the stone goes through the gap and out the other side, but clings to nothing, and when he pulls, it comes skittering back down in a series of jerks.

Spider throws it ten or more times, and each time it misses. He wonders if Forlani is on the other side, laughing at him; and thinks that if he called now, he could get Forlani to catch the rope and secure it to a post or a window strut in the street. He clears his throat, puts his head back – but stops. Forlani won't find it amusing, he will forever repeat, 'I told you not to go …'

Spider turns and studies the walls in this courtyard. There's nothing he can climb – not a single ingress anywhere. He goes back into the second courtyard and examines the line that anchors the Shuck at its lower end. It can't be that difficult, he thinks, taking it in both hands and allowing it to bear his weight.

He swings for a while gently, to and fro, his legs bent, listening to the metal strands adjusting. When they have stopped making a noise he checks his equipment, then hauls himself onto the line, hands and knees gripped around it, and shuffles himself like a monkey along it until he gets to the Shuck. He climbs the side; the metal is still hot from the day and he has to move fast in his thin sandals to stop it frying his feet. On the top he races across to a higher line that leads to a place nearer the top of the wall. Just as he leaps onto it, he sees in the surface of the Shuck a mark that is eerily familiar.

A dent the same shape and height as the one on their own Shuck. He swings on the rope in silence, digesting this, again trying to picture a creature that could reach so high. Eventually, his heart heavy, he shuffles his way up the line to where the steel wire is tensioned. He's about three metres short of the landing.

Morocco, he thinks, the time the 4th Infantry Regiment was in a blockhouse besieged by Moroccans and he had to scramble up a wall as if by magic. How did he achieve that? By sheer force of will, because he was panicked? Or a residual skill?

'Both,' he says. 'Both.'

He closes his eyes and imagines the Djinni in the Shuck – tries to picture them making that hole, leaping to that height. For once, his imagination works and he finds the adrenaline to throw himself at the wall, finding handholds where none should exist, balancing his weight on his toes and fingertips, the Parisian streets coming back to him – a taste of sewage and absinthe and sex – his muscles boiling and shaking, until at last he's crouching on the top of the building, holding it, panting, as if his life depended on it.

So much for his judgement. He should have listened, should have listened. Just like his mama told him once – it seems lifetimes ago – *Listen carefully, child, and stop thinking you know best.*

The sun is low now, merely a red bruise across the top of the roofs, and when he makes his way back along the colonnaded platform to the place where he climbed, there is no Forlani waiting in the street below. He clambers down and goes looking in the abandoned buildings. For a while he thinks he's been deserted, then he finds Forlani crouched in a filthy kitchen, fingering his way through the packets in the drawers.

Spider licks his fingers and tries to clean the worst of the dirt off his face. He pushes his hair back and makes sure his petticoat is straight, no blood or dirt on it.

'Hey,' he says casually. At first he thinks Forlani hasn't heard him, so he repeats it. 'Hey, you cool?'

'Yeah, cool,' Forlani says, not looking up. 'I mean, I think I found some witch hazel.' He turns and smiles at Spider. 'Which is awesome and . . .' His smile fades. 'Oh, fuck, dude. What happened?'

*

So Joe Marino and his bros have got a WhatsApp group called *Nekkid Nerds* in which they convince the geekiest girls in the school to send them naked pics. They bet each other over who will give it up, and McKenzie has a 200-dollar price on her head. That's the only reason Joe's going to the Science Fair – there must be other girls with prices on their heads and where better to net them than at the bonanza festival of nerds, the livestock show of geekiness. The Science Fair.

When she has to be, McKenzie is ruthlessly rational. Usually she can strap down those thoughts – relegate them to a secret area of the brain where she can choose to keep them, or to unwrap them – but the Joe Marino thoughts take more handling than usual and she's still shaking like a leaf when it comes time to go to the Fair.

'What's up?' Dad asks.

'Nerves.'

'Yeah, well, it's a biggie. But we're all going to be there for you.'

Her brothers are only coming along so that they can gawp at the senior girls and maybe laugh at the teachers who used to give them detentions, while Mom and Dad are coming because it's the right thing to do. Dad helps McKenzie carry the glass case down the stairs; it's covered in a throw, but all the way down she expects Mr Blonde to move. He doesn't, maybe from fear, and Dad loads it into the trunk of the Duster, plus the little kindergarten handcart that she and her brothers used to play on, which Dad has cleaned off, and a display board with all her notes and workings.

All the way to George Mason University she's thinking about Joe Marino and what she'll say to him, if she sees him today. He texted her an hour ago, saying he was looking forward to seeing her and would she send him a photo? She hasn't replied. Maybe when her stall is crowded with people – and she's sure it will be, because who can resist a live display – maybe then she'll shrug and say something cutting. Or she'll send his phone that code which shuts it down, or she'll offer to do his Firefly assessments and screw them, or she'll go to the school counsellor and explain what's happening, or she'll …

'We're here.'

She looks up. They are outside the Patriot Center arena, where a massive banner reads: NOVA HIGH-SCHOOL SCIENCE FAIR WELCOMES THE COUNTRY'S FUTURE WORLD-CLASS SCIENTISTS!

In the foyer, under the sign that reads: CHECK-IN 11TH-GRADE COMPETITORS, is a security guard with close-cropped hair and lots of badges.

McKenzie glances anxiously down at the kids' cart, the glass tank covered with a throw. 'You guys go ahead,' she tells the family. Dad locks the car and they wander into the centre. McKenzie straightens her shoulders and marches up to the security guard, wheeling the cart behind her.

'Name and section?'

'McKenzie Strathie. Earth and Environmental Sciences. Harbinson High School.'

'McKenzie Strathie, Robin … Uh, hang on, Harbinson?'

'Yeah, Harbinson. I know, it's OK you've never heard of us – we don't have many entries.'

'Found you. You're the only one from your school in this category. Don't kids in your school like science?'

'No. Not even a little bit.'

'Shame.' He pulls back the cover of the glass tank and peers at it, frowning.

McKenzie holds her breath. Mr Blonde rolls his eyes to the guard, then slowly raises himself, pushing his weight into his front legs as if meeting the aggression.

'It's important I bring this in.'

The guard gives her a strange look. 'Yeah, sure it is.' He ticks her name off. 'Enjoy the fair.'

She waits for a moment, not sure what to do. He frowns and jerks his head to tell her to go in, then extends a smile to the person in the queue behind her.

She swallows and walks through tentatively. The place is overwhelming – so many people, so many other students, all smiling and showing their immaculately presented projects. Everyone seems to have someone to speak to, and to know what they're doing, talking excitedly, exuding that focused, confident air she envies. Teachers and parents are going from stand to stand; professors and bursars from universities wander around, speaking into their phones; there's a kid on a stall showing off a hat that has dancing lights on the peak; another girl is demonstrating a homing device on a credit card.

She can see Mom has been drawn to the place where the banner declares MEDICINE AND HEALTH-SCIENCES DIVISION, where other yoga moms greet her with squeals. Dad, Luke and Tatum have migrated to the sports-science stalls, where they're intrigued by a grip-strength monitor. Next to the drinks machines a bunch of kids are talking loudly in Mandarin. Is that how it will be at California Tech? Will everyone talk a hundred different languages and hold conversations in Mandarin about quadratic equations?

'Hey,' India appears at McKenzie's side, a worried expression on her face. She's wearing a smart black turtle-neck that must be her brainy sweater, because it looks all wrong. 'You OK?'

'Is he here?'

'I haven't seen him.' India puts an arm round her and kisses her cheek. 'You've got this, gal. You can do this.'

On the other side of the hall, Mom, oblivious to her daughter's dread and excitement, has joined Dad and the boys and is squealing and giggling at Luke's record-smashing attempts on the grip monitor. McKenzie's future could be right here in Virginia, maybe working in a bank, waiting for a jock like Joe Marino to take her seriously, then going to ball games and trying to keep up with school-bake sales and always feeling like a fish on its side, gasping for breath.

At that very moment Professor Armitage, the faculty representative from the Atmospheric Science Institute at Caltech, walks within a few feet of her. He's very tall, with a herringbone jacket and dusty pink jeans, and has a slight stoop as he studies his name on the lanyard around his neck. He's flanked by two girls, smiling up at him intensely, talking fast and loud. Both are dressed in sensible trouser suits, little bows on their blouses like secretaries; almost certainly they're seniors from Jefferson, the local Advanced Placement science school, where every senior gets their first choice of university.

'Shit,' McKenzie murmurs, staring at him. 'He's the one I've got to impress.'

'Then do it. You're gonna be dope. I'm going to rustle up some enthusiasm with the crowds, OK?'

India heads off, while the assistants direct McKenzie to a three-sided room – a curtain hangs on the far wall, closing her off from the main hall so that she can set up in private. Above the central table, suspended from the ceiling, hangs a screen that shows her name, her school, the title of the project – WIND AND SAND FORMATIONS – and her time slot: 11 a.m. Just five more minutes.

She sets up the display board under the spotlight and carefully lifts the tanks onto the table, taking the opportunity to check that Mr Blonde is OK. He's alert but calm, and the box of ants she left in there is empty.

'*You stay there. It won't be long.*'

He blinks at her slowly, almost as if he's saying, *I understand, I won't let you down*. Will he panic when the cover comes off? With all the lights and the attention?

The curtains twitch and India comes through, excited. She's followed by a blonde girl, who looks about twelve and wears mom-jeans, a Science Fair baseball cap and a Facebook-logo sweatshirt. She's got a huge camera on her shoulder.

'Hi. I'm Maisie.' She flashes a row full of braces and holds up her hand to McKenzie. 'Jefferson High.'

'Hi. I'm McKenzie. Harbinson.'

'Not many students from your school.'

'No. And lots from yours.'

Maisie screws up her face happily. 'We're the geeks. I'm doing the live-feed.' She taps her Facebook sweatshirt. 'Right now I'm recceing for students I'll feature in the next time-slot. What have you got here, and before you answer, I'm just saying: I can cover max eight projects in one hour and they gotta be, like, *outstanding*.'

The Facebook live-feed is being relayed to the monitors above the huge hall, and the numbers of people watching keep getting bigger and bigger – since McKenzie's arrived, it's jumped from 580 to more than 1,000. The hearts and likes and comments are now scrolling, instead of spotting around.

'OK.' She licks her lips feverishly, trying to ignore the thirst that has sprung up out of nowhere. 'What I am showing here,' she gestures to the board, 'is the effect of wind on sand dunes. Desertification is a big problem in developing nations, and this study aims to identify optimum locations for vegetation banking.'

Maisie stares back leadenly, unimpressed. 'Yeah, OK. And what's under the cover?'

McKenzie puts her fingers on the throw-side of the cloth, is about to pull it back, but stops.

Maisie raises her eyebrows questioningly.

'The cover,' India comes to McKenzie's rescue, 'the cover is the *real* reason you should focus on McKenzie's project. Sadly, we can't show you right now what is underneath it.'

'No, we can't,' McKenzie agrees.

'Because we don't want to give the game away.'

'I can't put you in the webinar if you won't tell me what's there.'

'She has to be very careful. Because it's alive.'

Maisie's bored expression changes. Her eyebrows rise a little. 'Alive?'

'That's right. And it's the last thing you'd expect.'

Maisie hesitates. Then she gives a long, slow smile, acting like she's ten years older than India and McKenzie. 'I like you. You can be at the head of the feed. Six minutes at eleven a.m., which is in – uh – one hundred and eighteen seconds.'

9

THE DAY GETS long and drawn-out. Forlani checks and dresses Spider's head wound, then they take some time to collect mimosa branches from the gardens around the foot of the hill. They trudge back up to the temple, passing telephone poles improvised from trees, washing lines with garments sun-bleached. Above them the rest of the family have already gathered in clumps, and the nearer he gets, the more sombre Spider feels, because he recognises their defeated expressions. No one has found the Sarkpont.

Inside the temple they are attending to night-time chores: Madeira and Hugo are both working as fast as they can – neither wants to be the last to finish – then they will throw their javelins. Elk is unpacking food, while Splendour helps Amasha unroll the night's bed-rolls. Tita Lily is still asleep and her legs, which used to have muscle, are yellow and gristly. Forlani checks her temperature, wakes her and gives her another two pills.

No one speaks. It's another fruitless search. Another day wasted. Outside the temple Spider throws down his tool bag and stands in the sand, his feet planted wide, his hands pressed against his temples, jaw gritted, as if he has a sudden and intolerable headache. It is impossible, impossible. *Another day*.

'Hey …' Amasha comes to where he stands, puts her hands on his shoulders.

He doesn't move, but continues to stare at the city, willing it to be other than what it is: just a city. A lump of houses and fences and buildings together.

'Don't, please. The children are watching.'

He dips his chin slightly to look, and sees she's right. Splendour, Cairo and Mahmoud are on the steps of the monument – Cairo playing with a toy helicopter. It's one that Mahmoud has bolted together from rusted-away chunks of metal, but he allows Cairo to play with it and watches him holding the aircraft above his head and spinning the rotor blades. Occasionally he gives gruff instructions about how to fly it, but he keeps throwing the adults glances. No one doubts that Mahmoud is the more mature of the two.

'Meeting,' Spider murmurs. 'Adults only. Five minutes. Inside. OK?'

Amasha frowns. 'OK. Inside.'

When she's gone, he clicks in the back of his throat to summon Forlani, who nods, tucks the scruffy jotter under his arm and goes inside. Spider finds Noor at the side of the temple, practising with his bow and arrow – he does this each day, takes himself somewhere private because he doesn't want the family to know that hunting's not natural to him. His problem, Spider thinks, is that he's not relaxing the bow-holding arm, so the bowstring clips his arm slightly on release. Spider itches to correct him.

This time Noor turns the arrow directly at Spider. Spider freezes – confused. He misses Nergüi at this moment, who was always in his corner. Noor eyes him carefully through the sight and Spider raises his hands.

'Not smart,' he says. 'Not smart.'

'Why not?'

'You could lose control of the bow.'

'But I never hit my mark, so what is it? Are you in danger?'

Spider stands quite still, breathing carefully through his nose. He doesn't understand this – not at all. What does Noor want?

Eventually Noor lowers the bow.

'I'm joking, man. You're not in danger. Not from me.'

Spider holds his eyes. Not in danger from *me*. He licks his lips. 'Inside. Important.'

In the temple, in as much silence as they can muster, the adults gather around Spider and Forlani. Forlani opens the notebook and hands it to Noor. The others gather around him, squinting and standing on tiptoe to read it.

The writer was a woman in her twenties. Disciplined enough not to discuss her own feelings, focused enough to log the family's mission in clear detail, she wrote with clarity and precision. The words are etched in Forlani's head, and he can tell from his own family's expressions which part of her narrative they have reached.

We are now in the ninth Regyre, she wrote, three-quarters of the way through the book. *And it's looking desperate. The family's divided about what next. I suggested we should move to a new shelter, one with access to other places, but I was voted down by seven to three …*

And later: *The eleventh Regyre. Last night the Djinni came closer than they ever have. It's as if they can smell our fear. Or as if they know we are getting close to our end …*

This morning the Futatsu admitted I was right and we should have gone to a new Shuck. There are no more cities to explore. Sometimes I think I can reach out and touch the Sarkpont – I dream about it, about freedom, about cold water and sodas. We are going to leave tomorrow … we will go west, past Abu Dhabi – we saw a Shuck there and maybe we can get to it.

Amasha presses her thumb and forefinger into the corners of her eyes to stem the tears. She is getting near the end of the book, and he knows what she's seeing. *The last Regyre:*

What can I say? We didn't get to Abu Dhabi before the Regyre ended, before another family found the Sarkpont. What will happen now, none of us dare to think – we don't talk about it. The water supply is suddenly low, we don't know why, but we've stopped washing and we're limiting how much water we can drink. There isn't enough to give to the animals, so we're slaughtering them and salting them …

'There was food?' Elk hisses. 'In this Shuck you saw food?'

'No. There have been other people since, and everything was gone except a packet of dates. No water, either. Read on.'

This morning I got up before the others and I let go the little sheep I call Jasmine. When I opened the pen she didn't run, but seemed instead to expect me to pet her, or give her the alfalfa from the farm. I didn't look into her eyes, I found a stick and beat her until she ran. She cried as she ran and it wasn't from pain, it was confusion. She stopped once and turned to look back at me. I will never forget that look . . .

Madeira puts out her cigar. She takes out a handkerchief and presses it to her face.

Another family have found the Sarkpont. The birds are flying west; we know it's the end. We don't know whether to go back to the Shuck or wait here in the open for whatever will happen . . . To be truthful, we are all so thirsty – so dehydrated – our will to survive has gone . . .

Back now in the Shuck at Mithi . . . The men are at the window clutching their bows and arrows. Twenty minutes ago, in the desert, on the outskirts of the town, the Djinni took two of us and forced the rest of us to watch. It was unspeakable and I won't write about what they did. Nor can I try to describe them – their unreal height, their proportions. We have been told to make our peace now, because the Djinni will come for us all when the sun sets.

Pray for us, whoever is reading this. Please pray.

There is a long silence when the family have finished reading. No one meets anyone's eyes. Spider folds his arms and presses his mouth together with his forefinger and thumb, waiting for a response. He can feel Noor staring at him – as if he's angry with this revelation. Eventually Amasha shakes her head, holds up her hand to say it's too much. Spider has never forgotten the look on her face when he came back up to the canteen: the fear, the tears.

Some of the family break off and go away into the recesses of the temple, their hands tucked into their armpits, bent over. Elk is crying openly, rubbing at his face with his knuckles.

'We had to see it,' he tells Spider, hugging him. 'We had to.'

McKenzie cannot remember ever having been so nervous in her life. Her mouth becomes so dry that her tongue is like glue. Mom, Dad and her brothers have arrived and are gathered in the little booth – Luke and Tatum wearing bored expressions, while Mom and Dad have those brave, bemused smiles they always wear: as if they're happy to humour her in whatever difficult phase she's going through, just so long as it doesn't last forever.

As the overhead monitor clicks to 10:59:40 India slides through the curtains into the booth from outside. 'You won't believe it! Maisie is there, and Professor Armitage is too.'

'Jesus, Jesus, Jesus,' McKenzie mutters under her breath. 'Jesus. Joe?'

'*Nada*.'

'Thank God.'

'Eleven a.m. projects,' comes a voice over the sound system, 'you are live in three, two, one.'

The curtain is opened by an assistant and McKenzie can see the entire hall. A small group of people stand in front of her kiosk, attracted, she assumes, by the fact that Maisie is there with her camera. Professor Armitage too.

She takes a deep breath – a yoga breath – and unsticks her tongue from the roof of her mouth. 'In light … in light of what happened to China's famous failed "green Wall", I have … I have been considering ways to optimise the location of vegetation banks globally.'

Professor Armitage folds his arms, frowning as if he's interested. Her heartbeat picks up a notch further.

'The key lies in analysing the way the wind blows. Allow me.'

Heart in her throat, McKenzie tugs back the throw. With the downlighters, the pastel colours in the two tanks blaze like neon. In the tank at the front, Mr Blonde lifts himself defensively onto his front legs. She holds her breath, waiting to see what he'll do.

'Wind speed and direction and intensity,' she continues in a tiny voice, not daring to take her eyes off Mr Blonde, 'can depend on many geographical features. And look at the astonishing shapes that wind alone can create in the sand.'

No one speaks. Everyone's gazes are fixed on the tanks. Mr Blonde blinks.

'Let me introduce you to Mr Blonde,' she says. And then, catching the curious frowns on the audience's faces, she explains, 'He's a horned lizard. His natural habitat is the desert, usually in the south-western states and down into the Mexican isthmus. He's very at home here in the sand. See? He's relaxed.'

Indeed Mr Blonde, to her amazement, is totally chilled and, as if on cue, he begins to walk calmly up and down the dunes, as if he's been choreographed. India hitches in a breath, but it doesn't put him off; he does a short tour of the crescentic dunes, then lumbers to the top of the parabolic mound and stops. With near-miraculous good timing, he bends and straightens his front legs three times very deliberately and slowly.

'Lizard push-ups,' McKenzie smiles.

'Kenz?' India says quietly at her side. 'Kenz …'

But McKenzie continues. 'It's his way of thermoregulating.' She smiles at Professor Armitage, who's wearing a perplexed expression. 'That means he's cooling himself off by increasing the vascular flow to the surface of his skin and—'

'*McKenzie!*' This time the word is short and sharp. India is shaking her head. '*McKenzie, stop this.*'

'I haven't finished. I was saying that the area of skin exposed has to be directly proportionate to—'

'*McKenzie, stop this,*' India hisses. '*Just stop it.*'

It's then that McKenzie registers the shocked, pitying faces; Professor Armitage's look of embarrassment – or compassion, maybe. The crowd that earlier was watching her in anticipation has got bigger. They're not looking at the tanks, but at her. Mom steps forward, pushing Maisie out of the way and drawing the curtain across the booth, ushering the spectators to leave.

'What?' McKenzie says in a thick voice, feeling the headache take a grip around the top of her skull. 'What is it?'

India is silent, looking at the floor. Tatum and Luke are frowning, not smiling. Dad's face is red.

'Everyone out,' he says, grabbing the cover and throwing it over the glass tanks. 'Everyone out. We're going home.'

10

AFTER THEY'VE READ the book Spider leaves the family in the temple and goes outside to breathe. Splendour, Mahmoud and Cairo are sitting on the steps, cowed expressions on their faces, sensing some big change in the air.

He passes them and heads down the steps to feed mimosa to Camel, who is tethered to a cleat buried in the ground. She is such a lugubrious and unflustered creature, just watching her prehensile upper lip navigate its way around the leaves calms him a little. A crowd of mangy cats watch him shyly from the shadow of the monument wall. He observes them as he works, filling Camel's water from the family's supply, though he knows he will catch Amasha's wrath if she sees him. Next, he uses a finger moistened with spit to clean his boots, then he unpicks dust and sand from his petticoat. He likes cats. Later he'll go and befriend them.

The evening meal is taken sombrely. The small, shy crowd of cats appears at the edge of the group, where the firelight bleeds into darkness. Elk spoons out food for everyone, Hugo pours them their nightly ration of water. When Madeira sits down, cross-legged, with her own bowl, she is still for a moment. Then she puts it down and looks up balefully at Spider.

'I miss the shade of the banana trees. I miss the smell of the cocoa flesh drying. I miss the smell of water. All the time I do.'

'We all miss something. I miss bathtubs and French coffee.' Spider lowers his fork and frowns at her. 'What are you trying to tell me?'

She is silent for a while. Then she leans forward and whispers quietly, 'We are not them. We are better.'

'Not who?'

'That family. We don't need to leave the Shuck. This isn't the beginning of the end.'

'We do need to leave it; we've got to face facts. There isn't anywhere else to explore and you've seen what the Djinni are doing.'

'Because you tempted them.'

'No – because we're near the end.'

'You think I'm going to root out all my crops and take them somewhere else? When I've spent day after day measuring the sunrays, measuring the little water we have – making it into the best it can possibly be.' Madeira strikes her fork on her bowl to get everyone's attention. 'You all need to know – I can't just pick up and go. The farming system is not transportable.'

'We need to move to another Shuck. We're out of space in this one – there's nothing to—'

'Uhh!' Amasha raises a hand to silence him. 'We're going to talk about this when we get back. Not now.' She gives them both a fierce look, ticks her head to the side to indicate the children. 'And besides, Elk and I need to think about it.'

'Think about what?' Cairo asks, but Amasha shakes her head.

'Nothing, *Pœtiyo*, absolutely nothing. Eat your bread. Come on now, do you want me to feed you like a baby in a high chair, eh?'

The rest of the meal is subdued, no one meeting anyone else's eyes, and when it's over Amasha insists that everyone holds hand to pray. 'Ha'shem,' she intones, because that is the name they have given it – because it is Hebrew for *the nameless God* and they composed it in the first few days of their lives in the Cirque. 'We want to thank you for your bounty, for our food, for watching us today. We are grateful for every day that passes.'

Spider lowers his head and prays alongside the others. It's automatic, because it's a prayer the family wrote together. They chose it during the long trek across the desert to the tower, when the family were fresher than peppermint and awed by the way they'd been placed together. When they were getting to know each other, simultaneously wonder-struck by how much they already knew – by faces that should be new, but were recognisable from long-ago dreams; by sentences on each other's lips that had been bubbling in their heads, unspoken, for years.

They did so much talking. They chose their names, Spider taking on the tag he'd had in Paris: *araignée*, the climber; Elk choosing to be named after the animal he most admired. Meanwhile others, like Amasha, kept their original names.

'Thank you for the abundance of food.'

'And to the kings of beasts,' Elk says. His voice makes the walls tremble, it is so low and resonant. 'Thank you to the rabbits and the kangaroos, for giving their lives.'

'Thank you,' the others join. 'To the beasts for giving their lives.'

'And to Camel,' Amasha continues. 'For devoting herself to us. Thank you also for the white nights and for the water under our Shuck … Amen.'

Everyone is silent for a short time, looking at their laps, musing on the day's events. Spider thinks about the Dulyeowos and wonders if they had a similar prayer. And if they said it when they were being taken by the Djinni.

'OK.' Elk stands and stretches. 'There is food here that will spoil. Mahmoud? Cairo? Splendour – I suppose you want to feed the cats?'

'Yes!' Mahmoud shoots his hand up. 'Yes.'

Splendour jumps up and grabs a bowl to gather up the slight remnants of food.

'Really, Elk? Really?'

'Yes, really. But keep it away from us.' He ushers them to move down the side of the hill. 'And no water for them – they can live on the moisture from the food, so don't give them water. Have you got any brains between the pair of you?'

Spider rarely has the chance to spend a white evening with the kids, so while the adults prepare the sleeping arrangements, he follows the children a short way down the hill and helps them scrape the food off the dried-gourd plates. The cats crowd around to watch, timidly waiting to see what will happen.

While the children occupy themselves with the cats, Spider takes from his backpack the cloth of watch-pieces and carefully unrolls it on his knees, gently lifting the mechanism and studying it. He wonders why he is still trying so hard with this – yes, in Paris he understood well the logistics of a watch or a clock, his fingers are nimble and he can tell in a breath which parts should go where, but he's made a tortured spring that should work, but something – maybe the desert air – keeps moving it out of true. It's lucky for him the skies are so clear and they can see the movement of the stars and the sun to keep them on track.

The cats sit in a formal circle, blinking at him as he works. Then one of them, a wiry creature with enormous ears, breaks ranks. It executes a leisurely circle, as if its only intention is to stretch its legs, then sits and begins to coolly groom its flank. In this casual way it has positioned itself a few centimetres nearer the food.

Spider smiles. If Forlani was here now, they'd be arguing about the virtues of cats. Their manners and their stealth. He puts away the timepiece and puts some food on his finger, holding it out to the cat. It raises its head to look at him, lowers its eyes and takes a calm step closer to the food. Then another. In a smooth movement it darts its head out and snatches the food, dragging it backwards until it can break into a run and escape out into the darkness. The other cats watch the humans' reactions and, when they realise they aren't going to be attacked, one by one they begin to make rushes for the food. Before long all the cats have something to eat and are contentedly hunched over, gnawing at their spoils.

'Can I touch them?' Cairo asks. He's a sullen child and has never trusted Spider, but on occasions like this he defers to Spider's age. 'Are they safe?'

Spider shrugs. 'I don't know. I think so.'

Cairo and Mahmoud have just enough curiosity to approach the cats, and slowly Splendour follows their lead. One cat in particular takes a liking to them, a scrawny ginger-and-white scrap of bone with a cloudy eye. It accepts more titbits from Splendour, delicately licking them from her fingertips as if it has been schooled in the finest manners, which to Spider's mind equals another notch-up in the competition with Forlani.

Soon there is a whole host of cats rubbing against their legs, and a kitten lies on its back to allow Splendour to scratch its belly. Even Spider finds himself sucked in, sitting on the ground so that a tabby with a scabbed spine can perch on his knees. He scratches it under its chin, wondering whether it's in pain with the sores on its back.

'We should take them back to the Shuck.' Splendour has picked up her cat to kiss. It allows her to flip it onto its back like a baby and she sits with it snuggled against her stomach, grinning happily. It uses its head to butt gently at her finger. 'They can live with the chickens. Cuddly.'

'You want Elk to find a way of cooking them?'

'Do we have to eat all the animals? Can't we have some animals just because they're pretty?'

Spider doesn't answer that, because there is no answer. His tabby is now licking his fingers ferociously, the little barbs of its tongue scraping against his skin.

'Hey,' he says. 'You looking forward to going back to the Shuck tomorrow? Nice to be home, won't it?'

Splendour is silent. She traces her finger in the sand. She's wearing a sweater that Tita Lily knitted from their own sheep's wool. Today she hasn't been vigilant about keeping her pale skin under a hat, because her small nose has a cherry-blush stripe over it and her cheeks look hot. 'Spider,' she says eventually, 'why don't we ever find it?'

He sighs. She always asks the most difficult questions. 'Because … because I guess it's not our time yet.'

'Amasha says you speak in riddles.'

'Does she? Well, she should know.'

Splendour tries to smile. But the effort is too much.

'What happens to the families that don't make it?'

Spider has to take his time trying to find a reply, because he doesn't know the answer – only that it's bad.

'I guess they start up all over again,' he says eventually. 'I guess they get recycled and start all fresh.'

'With a different family?'

'Maybe.'

'I don't want to ever be part of another family. I like the one I got.'

'Me too.'

'*Ow!*' Cairo stands suddenly, shaking his hand. The cat he was holding falls to the floor. 'It bit me.'

Before Spider can react, his own cat bites him viciously. '*Merde*.' He jumps up, shocked, and shakes it away. It runs off into the shadows.

'Hey, kids, let's go, come on. Let's go.'

He takes the kittens from the protesting Splendour and drags the children up to the temple, casting glances back down the hill, to where the cats have scattered into the shadows. He doesn't like the way two animals bit simultaneously, as if programmed.

On the ground floor of the monument, inside the large doorway, the bed-rolls are arranged in their usual cluster: all wedged into each other, so that the family can be together. Spider has slept in the past with the family, but he is still wary at times, still the outsider. Madeira and Amasha are arranging the sacking, Forlani is in deep conversation with Tita Lily, touching her wounds, while Hugo is just outside the monument, setting out his pots for the night.

'I've looked at the maps,' he tells Spider. 'The ones you found in the Shuck belonging to the other family.'

'Yeah?'

'They're no better than Knut's. In fact, not even close. We've already done more than they did.'

Hugo calls himself the 'brass boy' since he came here, because although he was a banker in England, now he finds himself demoted to the lowliest role – dealing with the fertiliser, the night soil from the animals in the Shuck, and the family. If anyone in the family needs the bathroom while they are away from the Shuck, they do it in Hugo's collection units, and he also provides fresh water to the Shuck by means of a tank under the sand. Spider could have helped him make the tank – he has experience from Paris – but he didn't offer. Hugo has never complained about his role and this further perplexes Spider, because Noor does nothing as helpful, and yet he is liked more.

'OK,' Spider says. 'I guess that's reassuring.'

While Hugo makes his arrangements, Amasha is in the corner acting like a fussy mother, making sure everyone brushes their teeth, chastising Splendour for not wearing enough sun cream: '*You're as white as a drink of milk, how do you expect to be out in this sun without burning – huh?*' Meanwhile Forlani moves on from Tita Lily to inspect Cairo's cat bites. Tonight there is no one to check their shoes for holes, their clothes for rips, because Tita Lily is in too much pain and lies in the corner, not speaking.

Spider takes a little time to bring Camel round to the entrance and gets her tethered for the night, another cluster of mimosa within easy reach. She gets to her knees, kneeling with her eyes closed, her chin resting on the floor; and it has always seemed to Spider, city boy that he is, such an uncomfortable position for her that often he has shuffled up close and tried to adjust her head, so it is resting on its side, on his legs maybe. Each time she resists, or complies for a while with a deep sigh, only later – when she's sure she's made Spider happy – lifting her head and dropping her chin back into the sand.

Satisfied that she's settled, Spider drags up sheets of beaten tin and arranges them around the entrance to the temple while everyone climbs into their sleep-sacks. Forlani jams his crutches in the earth floor, crossed over his bed-roll like some soldier memorial, and curls up under them. Spider gets onto his mat, still wearing his boots and with his knife strapped to his leg, while Splendour wriggles her way across the group bed, ducking under a startled Hugo, jamming her foot in Madeira's stomach and generally causing chaos until she reaches Spider. She squirrels her way up into his arms, so that her face is opposite him. Her breath smells of lemon and her eyes are so bright and trusting, it scares him.

'Spider?'

'What?'

'Are you staying here? In here with us?'

'I am.'

'You're not going out there?'

'Not tonight.'

'Really?'

'There's nowhere to look.' He puts his arms around her and she rests her head on his chest. 'So I decided instead I'm gonna stay here and tickle your feet.'

She giggles and squirms, tucking her feet up underneath her. 'I ain't gonna let you.'

'Well, that's good. Sounds like you're learning something, at least.'

Spider finds her keffiyeh and drapes it across her eyes. The keffiyehs are a good distraction from the smells of the desert; they protect from the blown sand, and they are useful at night too, as a shield for the eyes. Amasha douses the flame from the oil lamp, then she and Elk adjust themselves into the places where they sleep, always slightly apart from the rest of the family, always near the exit. Some nights, when they think everyone is fast asleep, Spider has seen them lying awake, about a metre apart, wide-eyed, staring at each other. He thinks they are in love – but love in the family has to be familial, so it cannot be the love that a man feels for a woman or vice versa. *If only* . . . he thinks. *If only.*

Splendour falls asleep instantly, lying against his chest, within moments sleeping so deeply that her mouth is open and her face crushed against her raised arm. But Spider can't relax. Gently he tilts Splendour's head to one side, so that he can shift onto his back and stare up at the ceiling of the monument, the rendered struts of the ceiling. The Dulyeowos, encircled by the Djinni, like a herd of antelopes reaching its end – the sick and the injured maybe going first. And the writer, unable to bring herself to describe how the Djinni attacked.

Slowly the exhalations and smells of sleep begin, a soft timpani: Elk's big, granite-like snore, Amasha's stomach gurgling, all laced around with the soft whimpering of children beginning to dream. Spider stays in this uncomfortable position for a long time. The minutes pass, maybe the hours too, and eventually, lulled by Splendour's warmth, her slow, trusting breathing against his side, he closes his eyes and sends his mind like a tendril in silence, crawling out from the monument, down the slopes of the hill, and slowly, tentatively, under the shadow of darkness, he hunts among the ruins of the Cirque for the Sarkpont. Hoping to happen on something remarkable, an alley that hasn't yet been explored. A swimming pool, or a harp. Or a unicorn stable.

Unicorns would be peaceful, he thinks. Unicorns with gentle eyes, ready to carry them all away from this desert.

11

THE STRATHIES' DEVELOPMENT was built in the 1970s when Fairfax zoners weren't thinking about the higher-density counties surrounding them and how it would create bottlenecks for the traffic trying to get to DC. Concerned about the run-off into the local reservoirs, they plotted the houses out on two-acre lots, which they overplanted with oaks – the trees have long ago outgrown the houses they were intended to complement and now tower over the buildings. All the residents seem to do at weekends is take down trees, and the air is perpetually buzzing with the sound of chainsaws and the sticky scent of wood-sap.

Today the noise of trimming and cutting and pruning washes over the Strathie house, into the kitchen where McKenzie sits at the table with her parents, her head lowered. Mom has made some lemonade and Dad has sent the boys off to the movies, telling them to come back late. The house is strangely hushed, as if a close relative had died.

'I saw him.' She sits at the head of the table next to the ornate silk-flower centrepiece Mom keeps there. Her sleeves are pulled down over her hands. 'I held him. I touched him.'

'We know you think you did.'

'I'm going mad, aren't I?'

Dad's hands are on the table. They have a whitish tinge to them.

'One more time, tell me truthfully, not cos we'll be mad, but so we can help – no drugs? Nothing you want to tell us about?'

'No drugs – nothing.'

'Then you understand we'll have to get a professional, don't you?'

She bites her lip, looks out of the window. The sun is already sinking into the trees. Everything out there looks the same – the yard, the old swing set that Dad still hasn't got rid of, even though she is way too old for it. Everything's the same, but actually everything's so different. As if she's grown a different skin.

'McKenzie?' Dad pushes. 'Do you understand?'

'I do.'

'We've found someone already. The exact fit. You'll like her.'

Mom reaches over and covers McKenzie's hand. She's been crying this afternoon and her nose is still thick and blocked. 'You don't have to go to school on Monday – you can have a day or two off.'

'No. I'll go back. If I don't, they'll think I'm a coward.' She sniffs up the tears and blots her face with the sleeve of her sweat. 'Mom? Dad? What's happening to me?'

Dad gets up and hugs her. She leans her face into his chest, smelling the familiar cologne and the roughness of his chin and shirt. 'Daddy?'

'It's going to be OK, it really is. We're going to get you the care you need.'

Later that evening she climbs out of her bedroom window to a place where she can lodge herself on the roof behind the chimney. Her parents don't know she sometimes does this when she's upset; it's a private little place where she can cry, and no one – not her brothers or her parents – will hear.

She takes Cuddle Bunny and sits with him pressed to her nose, so she can suck up all his comfort. It's cold today, there is snow in the air, and the view across the neighbour's chimney and the coppice to the right of Burke Lake is so familiar – she knows the dip where the mighty power lines run, the sugar-white tower of the Korean church. It has always seemed to promise something to her: an escape or a freedom in her future, except that now her future is madness and brain scans, and medication and doctors trying to figure out why she hallucinates.

She takes a deep breath and pulls out her phone. The screen is dark, but she knows what it will look like when she switches it on. It's a kind of self-torture, but she logs on anyway. Her Instagram feed is full of follow requests, and her Snapchat icon has the number forty-seven hovering over it; WhatsApp has messages and friend requests. She's been tagged over and over again. People are using every single social-media outlet to get in touch with her. What do they want?

She scrolls through the messages, trying not to read any of them – they all seem to have laughing emojis, lots of memes she doesn't want to read, until she finds India.

– girl what's happening? Are the parents on your case? Call me. I love you, nothing's gonna change that. you hear me?

Fist in her mouth, McKenzie taps out a message.

– sorry, dad made me leave straight away. I dunno what's happening to me. Scared, tbh, gotta see a head doctor. You can guess.

She shivers, hugging herself while she waits for India to pick up the message. She thinks of that over-lit booth – thinks of herself pale, nervous, but gauchely excited, her hair flaring bright orange under the spotlights. What happened? Mr Blonde was *so* real, *so* tangible, she felt him on her hand, she saw him whip out his tongue to lasso the ants, she can almost smell him now, even in this tart-tasting iceberg of a night.

But her room, which she checked on her return, was crawling with carpenter ants and there was no trace that a lizard had ever been there. No dung on the floor, no scratch marks, nothing behind the vanity-unit panel. Nor was there a place he could have entered the shower room – it's as if he's left no trace at all, as if he's never been there.

She dares to look at her phone again, dares to read some of the comments. Every one of them is sarcastic. One of the drama girls has posted a picture of the sand dunes in the tanks, edited to make the linear Aeolian formations look like a penis. #dickdune and #invisiblelizard are trending locally and it's properly open season on any of her posts. Her own hashtag #dreamsofdesert is circulating too, with snide comments about drug use and whether lack of sex makes a person hallucinate. Someone, @Newtin-Seattle, has left a message saying:

– *I saw it too. Don't be afraid. DM me.*

Everyone is laughing at her; she's a minor celeb in the way no one wants to be a minor celeb. This is bad fame, not good fame, and Professor Armitage was witness to it all. Her dreams of Caltech are over.

The screen lights up. It's India FaceTiming.

'You OK?'

McKenzie wipes her nose, sniffs. 'Yeah – I mean the world's been laughing at me since, what, forever?'

'You really saw him, though, didn't you? Mr Blonde – you really saw him?'

McKenzie starts to answer, but she can't. She can't explain to India how it feels: to know that the only thing she's ever had a moderate faith in – her brains – are draining away into a place she can't chase them.

India is silent for a moment. 'I've been thinking,' she says in a whisper. 'Maybe you have to think about whether something happened in your past to make you see the things you're seeing.'

'How do I know where to start? I'm seeing images of the desert – how do I explain that?'

'I don't know. I suppose, with your dad's job, you've got a lot of excavating to do.'

McKenzie is about to speak, when the significance of India's comment sinks in.

'With Dad's job?'

'Yeah. I bet there's all sorts of things he's talked about over the years, places he's been – you maybe saw a photo or overheard something.'

McKenzie drags her coat closer around her shoulders. She feels so cold, so very cold. 'Why would Dad's job be important? He works for the State Department.'

'Yeah – the "State Department". And we all know what that's code for.'

McKenzie's confused. 'No, I . . . I don't know. What is it code for?'

'Don't you know? *Really*, don't you know? It's what everyone in the CIA tells their friends: I'm State Department. Let's not talk about it now, but have a little think. Maybe you saw something you shouldn't have, maybe this is PTSD. Either way, you have to be careful – be really careful. I'm going to be your shadow from now on.'

For the next few days McKenzie cannot look at her father. At mealtimes she stares at her cereal, the conversation with India on a rotating drum in her head. Luckily everyone is too subdued by the events over the weekend to speak much, so no one thinks it's weird; from time to time she glances up, trying to see Dad's face more clearly, listening hard to the things he says. His hands, always so clean and fresh, the nails perfectly manicured; his hair, cut so short it's almost military, like the other dads who live around here.

When she was little, Dad used to go away a lot. Mom always said it was 'just business', and on some occasions the kids went with him. She doesn't remember the trips, but she knows they happened, from the photos on Mom's screensaver – a week in

Hawaii, Mexico and Nevada. There's a picture of her brothers, dressed in shorts, and her as a one-year-old, dimpled legs, sitting next to Lake Tahoe, squinting at the camera.

She has no memory of it.

India seems to be constantly calling and texting. 'I'm not going to kill myself,' McKenzie tells her. 'And I'm not plotting to shoot up the entire freshman year. You can relax.'

'I am relaxed. I just want you to have someone next to you.'

And so McKenzie has a shadow, an apologetic, smiling shadow who insists on straightening her collar and suggesting ways that she can pretend her performance at the Science Fair was all planned. 'Like, has anyone in this school got this many follow requests? Like ever?'

Her phone keeps filling up with comments, to the point where she has to offload some of the apps and reinstall them. @Newtin-Seattle has sent about twenty requests to her Insta account, begging her to accept him as a follower, and many more to her Snapchat – *I CAN HELP!* says one. McKenzie doubts that. She deletes them all.

Mom and Dad get an appointment with the doctor on the Monday after school, and although Mom begs her again not to go to school, McKenzie is still determined. The first hurdle, the bus, is easier than she expects – Joe Marino isn't on the bus, and if anyone is aware of anything, they don't say a word or giggle. Maybe the smartphones are twitching behind the seat backs, waiting to video her; and maybe Mrs Spiliotopolous is on to them, because she keeps barking at the other kids, telling them to get back to their places.

McKenzie breathes steadily, keeping her eyes on the road, on the poor dude in the Liberty costume waving at the passing traffic. It's only when she gets off the bus that she sees one of the ninth-graders staring at her with a kind of fear in his eyes that shakes her.

'Are they afraid of me?' she whispers to India.

'No. They're confused, because they're stupid and naive. Remember that. And keep your head high.'

The school counsellor is like a homing missile – he catches her before first period, extracting a promise that McKenzie will meet with him at lunch, and in science class the teacher is at such great pains to be kind to her that it's clear she saw the whole thing. More than once McKenzie catches one of the other students staring, then colouring and looking away, pretending to chew their pen or be looking at the screen. She's the open secret no one wants to talk about.

At recess India guides her back to the locker bay. 'Different classes – I've got to leave you. You going to be OK?'

McKenzie eyes the other students. She catches one or two faces that were staring; they look away hurriedly and pretend to be rummaging in their lockers.

'I guess.'

'I'll meet you straight after this period. Here, let me tie your laces, you're going to trip.'

India ties the laces and McKenzie has a brief flash of a life that might await her – people attending to her needs while she stares off into outer space, letting them wipe the dribble off her chin.

'I can do that,' she says.

'Sure.'

India grabs her books and heads off into the stream of students that moves down the wide passageway. McKenzie finishes tying the laces, feeling the attention of a dozen students boring into the top of her head. She takes a few deep yoga breaths, straightens and, without looking at anyone, grabs her books and heads into the crowd of students, her head up, eyes not focused.

'Oh, babe,' says a voice close by. She looks up. Joe Marino stands a few feet away, wearing a skinny T-shirt and low-slung jeans. He's got a little vest over the top, with pockets that she thinks might be against school rules, since it looks like a hunter's waistcoat, and he's smiling the sort of smile that says, '*I know what you're thinking, and I can use it to help you or to crucify you. Which is it going to be?*'

She stares at the vest, not making eye contact. He comes a little closer. She can see the dark hairs at the neckline of his T-shirt.

'You OK, McKenzie Strathie?'

'Yes. Why wouldn't I be?'

'There are some pretty shitty things being said about you.'

She can sense about a dozen other students stopping to watch this exchange. Some are seniors, she's sure. She really is the village idiot. 'Like what?'

'Like how you're going to hear voices telling you to shoot the principal.'

'Right. Well, my family don't carry guns, so that's not going to happen, is it?'

'Maybe – but where there's smoke …' He grins. 'Lucky you know someone who can help.'

'Like who? You?'

'Of course. I can make it worse or I can make it a hundred times better.'

'And the price?'

Joe takes another step towards her and lowers his face. She can smell cologne and something sharp, maybe tobacco or wood smoke on his clothes, she isn't sure. 'Just a cute little pic,' he whispers, lifting his head to check none of the onlookers can hear. 'That's all.'

'What sort of pic?'

'Of all the places you shave.' He gives a small hiccupping laugh. 'By which I mean all the places you really oughta shave. OK?'

She stares at the pockets on the little vest, the zips and buttons, and rewinds through all the ways she's thought to get at him. The hacker code, the screenshot of the WhatsApp thread to the principal, the homework. But in the end all she does is nod. 'I'll see what I can do,' she says quietly.

'Good. I knew we'd have an understanding. You're a good girl, and I do still love that smile of yours.' He pushes a piece of her hair out of her face. 'As explicit as poss, OK?'

He turns and heads off in the opposite direction, accompanied by a low whistle from the onlookers, sarcastic giggles, whispers. McKenzie doesn't look at them, but heads towards her class, her head thudding, the insane thirst clawing at her throat.

She's gone about thirty paces when she spins on her heel and heads off in the direction that Joe Marino went. The small crowd has already dispersed and the corridor is almost empty, but as she passes one of the branch passages, she catches sight of Joe disappearing into the men's room. She goes fast down the corridor, pushes the door open.

The room is glistening white, smells of bleach and drains, and there's a mirror just like in the girls' room except that it's chipped and smeared. A few guys stand with their backs to her at the urinals and don't even look up as she comes in. Joe also has his back to her, is unzipping, one hand on the tiles. She unwinds her scarf as one of the guys turns to glance over his shoulder. He lets out a small yelp, but it's not enough to warn Joe. She throws the scarf around Joe's neck and pulls him back. His arms cartwheel helplessly and he staggers into her, trying to right himself and grab at the scarf at the same time.

Someone starts shouting, but McKenzie is down, on top of Joe, the stench of smoke and urine full in her nose, her throat so tight she thinks she can't breathe.

'Don't you ever do that again, or the person I will gun down will be you, you turd. Get it?' She tightens the scarf and tugs it harder. 'You hear?'

He nods, still scrambling for her hands around his neck.

'Good.'

She releases the scarf and shuffles herself back to the wall, sitting against the stinking tiles, her hands on her knees, breathing hard.

'OK,' she says to the shocked faces. 'Now you can go ahead and call security.'

Spider jolts awake. At first he's disorientated, in darkness. Around him there is merely the soft snuffling and breathing of the family asleep, above him the red-brown ceiling of the monument. He must have been asleep for a long time, judging by the cramp in his legs, and he still lies on his back, Splendour's head on his chest.

He tries to think what woke him. Gently he shifts Splendour's sleeping body to one side, lifts himself up on his elbows and looks at the door. Beyond the arched door the moon has risen blue and full, and sitting on the beaten metal shields is one of the cats.

He rolls onto his front and extracts himself carefully from under Splendour, tiptoes between the bodies. The cat watches him with scared eyes and when he comes close, it mews piteously.

'Fuck off,' he hisses at it. 'You bit us.'

The cat cringes from him. He flips a hand at it and it turns, drops from the barrier and scampers away down the hill, where it slinks under a tree. There are other cats there, the moonlight picking out their eyes like tiny headlights, all staring up at him.

'You are bang sketchy, you know that?' he murmurs, watching them. The cats don't move, just stare. Eventually he goes back into the temple and lies down, poker-straight on his back – as if he's in his coffin – listening and staring at the barrier in case they come back. He imagines the sheep, Jasmine, wandering the desert. Maybe only her ghost now.

He's still awake, listening to the night, when the light begins to change and dawn comes, pink and crystalline. The wind rises and makes the cooking pot above the dead fire clank gently, lifting a few soft ashes into the air. There is more than enough time to get back to the Shuck, so he won't wake the rest of the family. He stands carefully, lifts his tool belt and picks his way across the sleeping bodies.

Outside there is a cool breeze and the sky is already a peachy blue. Cloudless. Camel grunts, opens an eye and, realising it's not breakfast yet, closes it, settling her chin back on the ground with a sigh. Spider makes his way past the tin barricade. Under a tree down the side of the hill, the cats are asleep in a herd, exactly the way the humans have been sleeping. One or two wake. They lift their heads and watch him pull aside his petticoat and pee into one of Hugo's pots. He thinks of how they worked in such unison last night. They are nothing like the cats back in Paris, gleefully stealing food and tightroping their way high over the streets. These cats are strange and cowed – they look as if they haven't eaten in weeks.

He pulls his binoculars from his jacket and trains them on the horizon, watching the silent sunrise, the distant dunes and cloudless sky. Studying the familiar outlines, he realises that Mithi is a long way east, because from this angle the city they think is Dubai looks very different. More skyscrapers are visible at this angle, the skyline is ornate and elaborate, The Shuck must be facing the range of buildings nose-on – and they've never recognised that the city goes a long way back to the east.

He swings the glasses round to the west, the entrance point for all families. The Dormilones' first instinct was to get as far away as possible from the noise and unpredictable skies of the west – they sensed the further they got from Mardy's diner, the better. They didn't have Camel then, so they all went on foot, having to go as slowly as the slowest member, which was often Forlani or Splendour. Though generally Spider, Elk and Knut could carry the children, Forlani wore himself to a shadow trying to keep up and not slow the family down. He still feels guilt that he prevented them penetrating as far into the Cirque as they could.

In those days it had seemed as if the Cirque went on forever. It was Spider who walked headlong into 'the Chicane', about 330 degrees north-west of here.

He was in the front of the group and had been walking steadily when something slammed into his face. Shocked, he toppled backwards, barely keeping his balance, pressing his hand against his face, unable to believe how easily he'd collided with something invisible. Mardy was right: the desert has its limits.

The family gathered round and began prodding the substance he'd hit. A flexible, yet impenetrable wall, completely invisible. They began to feel their way along it, discovering that for a long time it had been within metres of them and they hadn't noticed. Later Yma would say she'd thought it odd there'd been no wind or air on that side of her face – she was sensitive to changes in the atmosphere – but she hadn't given it much thought. Ultimately, as they examined the pliable, yet completely imperceptible wall, they realised the distances that they'd thought were to their left were actually artifice, a visually manipulated border.

They'd reached the end of the Cirque, and the name they've given the barrier is 'the Chicane'.

In some places the Chicane bounds the Cirque tightly – at its narrowest point the desert is less than ten clicks wide, Knut has estimated. Those places are easy to understand, but the parts the family understand less are beyond the gaps in the Chicane, from which the desert could tentacle and branch off for hundreds of kilometres. There could be vast cities and civilisations on the other side of the Chicane and they'd never know, presented as they are with distant vistas.

He is about to return the binoculars to the pouch when a movement further behind the family's own Shuck catches his attention. The haze near the start of the northern Chicane is broken in one place. He refocuses the crude binoculars and tries to decipher what he's seeing: a series of small moving dots shimmers on the horizon. Spider is well versed in the optical tricks of the desert. He thinks it's another family trekking through the sand.

They appear to be maybe ten kilometres beyond the Shuck, very close to the Chicane, not far from the Virgule, which instantly strikes him as strange. He squints, trying to count the dots. It's impossible – the people are too far away to be sure. But what he can see is how fast they're moving. So fast. There's usually only one reason a family would be moving that fast: if they knew where the Sarkpont was and were heading directly for it. His instinct is to tell Amasha immediately. But something is wrong – what would a family be doing out near the Chicane?

'OK?'

He turns.

Noor is standing there in only his boxers, rubbing his eyes sleepily. 'What you looking at?'

Spider hands him the binoculars. 'Out beyond the Virgule. Past the Shuck. See them?'

'What am I looking for?'

'Another family. Just dots.'

Noor frowns, fiddles with the focus. 'Where? No. I can't see anything.'

'Here – let me look.' Noor hands over the glasses, and Spider refocuses. The dots are moving very fast now and must be on the spit of sand between the salt lake and the Chicane. 'Yeah – right there.'

He hands the binoculars to Noor and stands behind him, aiming the glasses at the Virgule.

'See?'

But still Noor can't, or *won't*, see them. 'You sure?'

'Yes, I'm sure.'

He takes the binoculars and looks again. This time the family have gone – they must have moved directly north and disappeared from view below the horizon. Did he imagine it? He refocuses the glasses and squints again, but the dots have disappeared.

Noor takes the eyeglasses and focuses them on the city they believe to be Dubai. He is silent for a while, frowning. 'Hey, have you seen this?'

'The skyline?'

'It's different. You know, I think Hugo's right – it's Dubai. I recognise that sail-shape thing.' He tilts his head to one side, shifts the binoculars. The sinews in his neck tighten, show the definition of his shoulders and clavicle. He's so damned good-looking, with his thick black hair and a reticence about the eyes that must be catnip to women. 'Yeah, it is – my parents took me there once: dinner with a sheikh who had seven Rolls-Royces, one in each colour of the rainbow. Now that is one hell of a city: water all over the place. It's full of pools, ponds, fountains. Why didn't we think about it before – the Sarkpont could be in every single building in Dubai.' He hands Spider the binoculars and turns for the temple. 'That'll be our next target.'

Reluctantly Spider takes the binoculars, tucks them in his belt and makes his way back up the slopes with Noor, feeling like he's just been slapped down. Madeira and Hugo have already been out and thrown their javelins – down the street that runs from the temple. Again Madeira's shot is short, but she says nothing and is building the fire.

Tita Lily lies in the corner, not speaking, staring at Spider, who helps Madeira heat water for the yerba, listening to her chit-chat about what plants she has discovered out here in Mithi that she can take back and propagate in the Shuck farm.

Amasha comes and sits next to him. She licks her fingers and says, lightly, 'How grateful are we for what Elk makes us. And yet . . .' She smiles slightly, tilts her head. 'And yet don't you miss a few things? What did you eat in France? Croissants.'

'Sometimes. But only when we were hating foreigners.'

Amasha laughs. 'And when we were hating foreigners, we ate *idiyapaam*. String-hoppers.'

'What?'

She shrugs. 'I can't explain them to you. Maybe Elk will make them one day, if we find coconut. But you have to have grown up with them. In the morning, when there is mist rising on the terraces. And a good pot of tea too.'

Spider thinks of his mornings in Paris, sometimes so cold he'd have to heat ice for his morning coffee. And sometimes like a kind of heaven, the sun picking out the spires and the cold, white slab of Sacré-Coeur. He thinks he should tell Amasha about the family on the far side of the Virgule.

'I had a husband,' she says, almost inaudibly.

'You loved him?'

'I thought I did. I thought I did.'

Splendour appears, shyly sucking her finger, reaching out and tugging Spider's petticoat.

'Need potty,' she says. 'Need caca.'

Both Amasha and Spider sigh. Hugo's waste pots must be returned to the Shuck, and there are few things worse than having to carry one's own waste across a hot desert: most of the family have trained their bowels to play the game and wait until they are back at the Shuck. Not Splendour, though.

Amasha takes her hand and bends down to address her. 'Splendour, you must learn to use the pots here, right here, like the rest of us. We're family, there's no shame. And we don't like leaving traces.'

The little girl lowers her face, scowling. She hates to go in the pots and would rather sneak away somewhere private and bring her own droppings back to give to Hugo, wrapped in leaves and sand, if necessary.

'You have the makings of a prima donna,' Amasha laughs. 'One day we'll wean you off this.'

'Spider come with me.'

'It's really my job to take you, darling. It's proper that I should accompany you.'

'No. Spider.'

Amasha rolls her eyes heavenwards. 'Ha'shem, please bless this child and cure her of her vanity. And make sure you dig it down deep.'

Spider finds his small spade and Splendour nods and trots away in the direction he points. Down the hill they go – if they kept walking, it would take them eventually to Dubai – the little girl in her oversized sweater and thong sandals winding her way through the derelict buildings and the drifts of sand. Spider follows a metre or so away; she wants his presence, but she wants her privacy too.

She's a strange little thing, Splendour: she loves the stars and the moon, and though she has a grasp on the physics of what happens in the heavens, she also believes fervently in horoscopes and the importance of lunar cycles and moon phases; her head is full of myths and legends.

'Spider, stay there.' She darts her head out from a lane between two buildings and points a bossy finger at his feet. It means she's found a place she feels safe. 'Don't move.'

He grins, salutes and turns away. 'Dig in the sand first,' he yells over his shoulder. 'Make sure it's covered when you're done.' A moment's silence, then he repeats, 'You hear me? Make a hole.'

He stands for a bit longer, his arms crossed, and monitors the horizon. The family he saw could have been a fake exploration. One of the tricks the families in the Cirque play is to lay false trails for other families. Like everyone in the Cirque, they are trying to survive, and if they think they are getting close to the Sarkpont, they will do everything they can to lie about their movements.

Behind him a scream. He turns. Splendour is running up the alley towards him, pulling up her breeches, her face bleached with fear. '*Come quick, Spider. Come quick.*'

12

MOM HAS TO cancel her yoga classes to come and get McKenzie from the school counsellor's office.

'That,' Mom says in a tight voice as they drive into DC, 'is the most humiliated I've been since—' She stops, closes her mouth, hitting the indicator with unusual force.

'Since what?' McKenzie asks. 'Since the Science Fair?'

Mom sucks in a breath. 'It doesn't matter how much of a jerk Joe Marino is – you don't take the law into your own hands. Dad and I are going to have to work very hard to get the principal to review your suspension.'

'Joe Marino is an asshole and a racist.'

'I don't care,' Mom says, suddenly explosive, hitting her hand on the steering wheel. 'I don't care. You DO NOT behave like that. You hear?'

McKenzie says nothing. She watches the houses and the trees going past. Mom hates driving into DC, but the fact that she drives all the way to the doctor's offices in Georgetown is testament to how concerned she is. McKenzie, meanwhile, has already diagnosed herself – there are only two possible explanations for her hallucinations, her loss of control, and she doesn't much want to give either of them too much consideration.

Dr Maria Shreve's offices are in a narrow terraced house in Georgetown, on the second floor, not far from the Grace Street coffee shop. Georgetown seems a world away from Fairfax, and it occurs to McKenzie that this must be costing her parents a lot of money. The reception room has very tall oil paintings of arum lilies on the walls, the floors are painted white and covered in deep-red rugs that look as if they came from expensive parts of the world. The receptionist has a strong New York accent and pencil-thin legs in jeans.

Dr Shreve herself is less tidy, with a barrel-like torso, her breasts a wide, precarious shelf perched on top of her wide ribcage. She wears a printed scarf and her dark hair is curled around her red-framed spectacles, getting tangled in the hinges.

'It's nice to see you both together,' she says, ushering them into the room that has a view of the Potomac out of tall windows. It smells of incense and there is an elegant box of Kleenex on the glass table, which is wedged between two chairs. 'Why don't you and your mom sit down? We've got two hours, and I thought it would be good to have a chat with Mom and you together. Then, Selena, I'll ask you to leave the room, so I can be alone with McKenzie.'

'Sure,' Mom says. She takes a seat and, after a moment's hesitation, McKenzie does the same, unwinding her scarf. The room is weird, she thinks, with pictures of flowers in bright yellows and blues. Dr Shreve smiles and sits opposite them and crosses her legs. Her calves and ankles are very thick in their opaque red tights, her shoes very narrow, as if they have been surgically attached to her feet. She has a small pad on the table at her side, and a red enamel pen that she picks up and toys with.

'Sometimes,' Dr Shreve smiles, 'I find it useful to tell you what I already know, and then you can tell me what you'd like to add. So . . . I heard what happened today at school. I spoke to the principal and I can tell you that, firstly, whatever we talk about here will never, ever get back to him – OK? If I speak to him, it will be purely about your improvement and your fitness to re-attend Harbinson.'

'He's considering letting her back?' Mom asks.

'I'm coming to that. The principal has a very open mind, I'm pleased to say. There are going to be some hoops to jump through – a lot of due process – but it sounds as if he feels there are extenuating circumstances, that your "victim" had made some serious errors himself over the months and years. Apparently there's a WhatsApp group that the principal now has access to.'

'He knows?' McKenzie says.

'Yes. He was shown it this afternoon by one of the junior girls, he tells me. Now I'm not condoning what you did, but this boy you attacked – he's been on several disciplinary measures already. Plus, apparently, you're a model student.'

'Was,' Mom says. 'Straight A grades. I can assure you she doesn't get it from me.'

'So, as I see it, if you work with me,' Dr Shreve looks directly at McKenzie, 'and you actually *want* to go back to Harbinson, I think there's a path to that. Our first step is to get to the bottom of what is happening to you? OK?' She opens the book and makes a few notes, underlines something. 'Now, Selena. You said that before we start you wanted to talk to McKenzie with me here, so that she can get some insight into what's been going on. Am I right?'

McKenzie shoots her mother a look. Selena is looking down at her hands and her mouth is trembling a little. She nods. 'I'd … I'd like that. I want to clear the air.'

McKenzie stares at Mom, her thoughts racing. What is she going to say? That she's adopted? That Dad really is CIA, and she has somehow been affected by it?

'It started when you were less than a year old, and we knew that somehow you were different.'

'Adopted? Is that why the boys ride me all the time?'

Selena smiles sadly. 'Honey, not adopted. You're ours totally – red hair and all. Look at my eyes and cheekbones: you're so similar to me. But you have always been … unexpected. We haven't talked about it because as you grew up, you grew out of it, but …' Mom takes a moment to collect herself. She swallows, then begins to talk in a low, guarded tone. 'When you were little, we were so worried about you. You didn't speak at all – not a word – for the first twenty-four months, and you had this uncontrollable rage. Physical. Once you threw a chair at a door, cracked it. Can you imagine?'

'Feisty?' Dr Shreve asks.

'More than feisty. She was … Put it this way: what happened today, that was the sort of rage McKenzie had as a toddler. We didn't know you were going to be an egghead, Kenz; in fact the opposite, and all the time we were waiting for some well-intentioned nurse or friend to tell us it was time to have the paediatrician run tests. But then, just as we were ready to take it seriously, there was Nevada.'

'Nevada?'

'We went to visit Dad's friends. The Petersons.'

'Near Lake Tahoe? The place we had that photo taken? Me, Luke and Tatum.'

'Sure. The Petersons were working for FEMA and had a short posting there, but they didn't have children, so it was weird – I mean, us with our tribe. But one evening the boys were out playing on go-karts, and Dad and I got caught up cooking and chatting, and we turned round and you were gone.' Mom has a scared, furtive expression, as if this is a subject she finds hard to articulate. McKenzie looks away, stares at Dr Shreve's red-clad ankles while she listens.

'It was a hell of a day – in the high nineties, and Nancy was fretting about the chocolate frosting on this cake she'd made: in the heat it was going to run all over the cake base, so I was with her in the kitchen, helping her with a spatula, then I went out onto the deck. Dad was at the barbecue with Mr Peterson, his back to me, drinking a beer – there were steaks and frankfurters on the grill – but you weren't with him. The boys were up on the top acre, and they'd got hold of a white leather jacket and a megaphone. Man, they were yelling like crazy, but you weren't next to the go-kart track, either.'

'You're going to tell me I was abducted by aliens.'

Mom smiles. 'Well, now you say it, it wasn't that far from Area Fifty-One. So, you know, let's keep an open mind.'

McKenzie tries to smile, but can't. Dr Shreve gives a short laugh, then puts her mouth straight back in the neutral position. 'But seriously, Selena. What happened?'

'OK – well, the steps from the deck went down into the desert, and there were jackals and rattlers and God-knows-what out there in the evening, but McKenzie was wearing cherry-pink half leggings and a Hello Kitty vest top and a pink sun visor, so I knew she was going to be easy to spot. All of us adults dropped everything and went running in different directions: the Petersons had a swimming pool, so I ran to that – she wasn't in there, just pool noodles floating around – so I'm running around, screaming, and I go to their barn and I get round the corner and I see her.'

Selena breaks off, grabs a Kleenex and scrunches it into a tiny ball. Her head goes from side to side as if she's struggling to find the words.

Dr Shreve gives a sympathetic smile. 'That's OK, Selena, don't force it; let your mind come slowly and naturally back to what you were saying. OK? You were coming round the side of the barn: do you remember what were you feeling?'

'Yes, my God, I mean I was *terrified*.'

'But you saw McKenzie.'

'I did. She was lying, um, f-face down, and at first I thought she was dead. I screamed and ran to her and she was like – I dunno, half buried in the sand, as if she was trying to burrow into it.'

'Burrow into it?' McKenzie asks. 'What do you mean, *burrow*?'

'I don't know. I thought someone had pushed your face into the sand – it was so bizarre. So I grabbed her, and she rolled over and just stared up at me like she had never seen me before. She was … you were breathing, and you seemed alert, but you didn't look natural. You pushed me away and turned back to the sand; you put your hands in it, like it was the most enthralling, entertaining thing imaginable – almost like it was dancing for you.' She sniffs and glances up at Dr Shreve. 'You know, like it was telling her some crazy fairy tale. If I had to describe what she was doing, I'd say she was trying to … *listen*. Listen to the sand – if that doesn't sound too crazy.'

'No need to apologise, Selena, you say it as you experienced it. It's really helpful for me, and I hope it'll be helpful for McKenzie. So what happened next?'

Mom takes a long breath, lets it all out in a big sigh. 'Well, nothing really. I was like: *It's time to get up, honey. The sand is dirty.* But you kind of ignored me; you didn't blink or turn your head or anything – I might as well not have been there. Honest to God, it was like something inside the sand was talking to her, and it made me so scared, so I snapped at her – I was like: *McKenzie. Please now. Get up*. And then, kinda like a spell was broken, she rolled sideways onto her back, lifted up her little arms and looked at me so serious. She was crying. Then she said, "MA" real loud, and I suppose it made me happy that suddenly she's speaking, and how the first thing she's said is "Ma", so I grabbed her up.

And by that time the others had arrived, and I was in shock – kinda – so I went to them and I was jabbering away about how you'd said your first words, bragging to your dad that the first word you said was "Ma", et cetera.'

'Traumatic for you, Selena?'

'Terrifying. The woman – Nancy – she'd been a nurse and she thought McKenzie was having some kind of epileptic fit, so we got her checked over and then, when we got back to Virginia, she had all the scans, all the tests: they all came up negative. And what was weird was that she hadn't spoken a word until Nevada, then suddenly she's speaking alarming stuff—'

'Alarming?' Dr Shreve asks.

'I don't mean scary. I mean like she was way, way beyond her years. When she was two and a half she looked up at me, after I'd made her some cookies, and said, "*I really appreciate it, Mommy*." So you can imagine – a not-yet three-year-old.'

'It turned out she was a very bright young lady.'

'Christ, yes. And she kept talking about sand – all the time, *sand* – and asking me about deserts and why they happened, and how long could you live in the desert before you died, and is there water in the desert? And soon she got old enough to look on the Internet and the first thing she did was pull down all these images of the desert. We kind of let it ride, tried to ignore it and …' She trails off. 'Yeah – so I guess that's what I needed to tell you.'

There is a long, long silence in the room. McKenzie can feel Dr Shreve watching her, expecting some kind of reaction. McKenzie rubs her nose and glances out of the window. The sky is dark and it's going to be snowing before long, she can feel it.

'McKenzie,' Dr Shreve says at last. 'Have you got any questions for your mother?'

'Maybe.'

'Go ahead.'

'We were in Nevada, right?'

'Uh-huh.'

'Did we ever go to Phoenix?'

Mom frowns. 'Yeah; I mean I think we drove through it at some point. Not on that trip – another one.'

'Was there a weird rainstorm that you remember? Like the photo on my wall?'

Mom puffs out her cheeks, shakes her head. 'No, not at all. I have no idea why you love that photo so much. No idea at all.'

'We just drove through Phoenix – that's all?'

'Yes.'

'Dad never had a job there?'

'No. Why?'

McKenzie shrugs. She leans back in her chair and folds her arms. 'It's going to start snowing in about twenty minutes and you don't like driving in the snow, so maybe it's time for me to talk to Dr Shreve on my own.'

The house sits back from the road, with no barrier or yard in front. It is painted blue with Arabic writing above the door lintel. Around the entrance, their ears and nostrils twitching nervously, sits a gang of cats. They are looking patiently into the house, and when Spider comes down the road, with Splendour in tow, they glance up.

'In there,' Splendour whimpers, pressing herself against Spider's leg. 'Inside.'

This section of Mithi is the one he and Forlani searched. He remembers seeing this house and that they made a quick search; as with a lot of the houses on this street, one glance in the interior told them it was the wrong shape for the Sarkpont, nor was there space for a pool of any description.

He doesn't recall either of them looking at the ceiling.

'Move away,' he tells the cats. He's ready to kick them to get them to move. 'Get out of my way.'

They blink mildly at him and, moving as one, divide to allow him passage. He eyes them all carefully as he walks to the door, painted in white and hanging from the rusting hinges.

He pauses, then dips his head and takes a step through the doorway. The room is long and rectangular, with a *mardānah* at the front and a kitchen area in the back. There is a window at the far end with rusting bars on it and, standing on the sill, a fading plastic effigy of Snow White holding a small bouquet of flowers. One or two pieces of furniture are dotted around: fading sofas and armchairs with rusting springs lolling out. Last time his perusal was swift and he didn't notice what is now painfully obvious: the way the light is unnatural, disturbed by what is overhead.

Slowly he raises his eyes to the ceiling. It is high – higher than most ceilings in the city. The rafters are exposed, and hanging from them, like so many lengths of drying meat, are the remains of about fifteen human beings. They are all sucked dry, the way the Djinni leave their corpses.

‘See?’ Splendour calls from outside. ‘Can you see?’

‘I can see.’

Draped as if they are bending over the rafter, so that their legs and arms dangle downwards, they are all in different stages of mummification. He thinks of the Dulyeowos, but sees that the corpses haven’t all arrived here at one time, but have been added to, as if a creature has been slowly building its collection over the months and years. Some have skin that has dried to a crisp, leathery texture. Shiny and treacle-coloured. The skin of others has more recent signs of putrefaction, green mould growing on them. Only their faces, pointed down at the floor, are recognisable as human.

In the corner a scrawny cat, interrupted in chewing something, stares at him warily. It mews sadly and then he sees what it is eating – a piece of skin. The cats are starving and they are living on human remains. That is why they tried to bite the children yesterday.

‘Get out of it!’ he hisses. ‘Go.’

Startled, the cat scurries out of the door.

‘Spider?’

‘Yeah – I’ll be with you in a minute.’

He breathes steadily, calming his heart rate. He’s seen these warning stations before; in fact all the adults have, although they shield the little ones from this reality. In other cities the method of storage has differed: some bodies have been stacked, some buried, others preserved in an upright position, as if standing. In Abu Dhabi the skin-corpses had seemed to be waiting to break into a walk directly towards him, and this had scared him the most. What all the charnel houses have in common is the message; and, sure enough, when he turns now, he sees, daubed in something brown on the wall next to him, two phrases.

For illegal invasion.

And for incest.

He stares at the messages, his nostrils flaring: he knows the Djinni have killed these humans, but who has written the words? The Djinni can't write. This desiccated man's face with a beard, his skin dried walnut-brown – what did he do wrong? This woman with her long dangling hair turned red by decay and the dry air, her arms stretched above her head as if trying to reach the floor – was she simply found out of a Shuck on a grey night?

Splendour appears timidly in the doorway and runs to him. Spider puts a consoling arm around her shoulder and squeezes her tightly, turning her away in the direction of the door.

'It's OK, it's nothing to be afraid of. They're just . . . puppets – they can't hurt you. You know how Mardy likes to scare you?'

'Uh-huh.' She clings to his legs, tears coming as he leads her away, her head turned back to stare in horror at the bodies. 'But they look like people.'

'Well, they're not. OK?'

He takes her outside, where the cats are still arranged in their reverential circle, slightly braced on their back legs as if astounded by the humans' boldness. Spider ignores them and crouches to look Splendour directly in the eyes.

'It's like this: it's . . . you know when Madeira brings in the maize? And we husk it.'

'Yeah.'

'We get rid of the part that's not important – the outside – because the important bit is on the inside, isn't it?' He places a hand on his chest, though he feels ridiculous doing it. He hasn't thought through this clumsy analogy that he's offering her. 'What's important is on the inside; what's left on the outside it only a husk. The husks. Our bodies are like . . . like spacesuits. We don't need them when we die.'

Splendour is silent for a while. Her gaze goes to the door, then back to him. 'So where are the rest of them? The important bit on the inside?'

He sighs. She's a genius for the difficult question, this child. He takes time to find his answer. 'Like I said, they were merely puppets. And I think you know where the important bit on the inside goes.'

Eventually Splendour seems to accept the situation. Rubbing her eyes with her fist, she picks up the spade from the sand and walks away, her head low. When she's disappeared around the side of the house to find a more suitable place, he steps back into the room once last time and contemplates the ceiling garlanded in human skin. The message on the wall.

For illegal invasion.

And for incest.

Before he leaves the house, he picks up a stone and throws it at the message. It skims the wall, slicing a line in the brown lettering, and that small act of disobedience makes him feel better.

13

MOM GOES OUT into the reception area and, when the door is closed, Dr Shreve comes and sits down opposite McKenzie, her legs crossed. 'She can't hear out there – don't worry. It's your time to tell me how you're feeling.'

'Right now? Devastated. Pissed I lost my temper with Joe Marino, but mostly like I have nothing to look forward to. I wanted to go to Caltech so bad, but I can sunset that dream – it'll never happen.'

'"Never" is a difficult word. I wonder sometimes why we use it.'

McKenzie looks up. Dr Shreve is watching her steadily, the smallest glimmer of a smile on her mouth.

'Tell me if you remember what happened in Nevada.'

'No.' McKenzie shrugs. 'I mean, I dream about sand. A lot of sand.'

'How do you know it's sand?'

'It feels like it.'

'Describe the feeling.'

'It's like grit on my skin.'

'I can imagine grit, but how do you know it's sand and not grit?'

'I can see it. And smell it.'

'Smell?'

'Yes. There's this constant smell of rust and salt. Everywhere I go, I can smell it. Sometimes it feels like it's trying to suffocate me.'

'Why would it do that?'

'Because I don't belong here.'

Dr Shreve turns her head slightly. Narrows her eyes. 'Tell me about that feeling. Of not belonging.'

'My family. I think they hate me.'

'That must be very difficult for you.'

'It's my brothers, mostly. I don't think they like me or even care that I exist.'

'Did they come to the Science Fair with you?'

'They did. But only cos Mom and Dad said they had to. So they saw me hallucinating too. It was live on a Facebook feed. Everyone saw it – it's there, for good.'

'I'm interested you've used the word "hallucinating", McKenzie. Would you like to talk about what you mean by a hallucination.'

There's a long silence. Outside the window the first snowflakes begin to fall, like a dream. The box of Kleenex seems almost like an invitation – as if crying is acceptable, even desirable.

'McKenzie?'

'Yes. Yes. I mean – I'm sorry. It didn't feel like a hallucination. It felt very real to me. I know it can't be real, I do know that. I know there was no lizard. So I know it was a hallucination. And there have been other things happen too. I think maybe I'm adopted.'

Dr Shreve stares at McKenzie. 'You aren't adopted – I know that for a fact.'

'But I feel like I belong with a different family, a different place altogether.' McKenzie bites her lip and raises her eyes to the window. She likes the way the snow creeps down into the street – even between the tightest-packed buildings, the weather asserts itself. 'I love Mom and Dad. I even love my pain-in-the-butt brothers, but honestly? I don't mean to sound like I'm sorry for myself, but I'm not supposed to be here. Not in Virginia. I'm supposed to be in a place with open skies. Heat.'

The doctor is silent for a long time. She seems to be working out a complicated equation in her head. Eventually she says, 'Do you have any physical symptoms, McKenzie? Do you feel nauseated? Or headachy?'

'Not really headaches. But I'm thirsty all the time.'

Dr Shreve makes a note. Her lipstick has dried in a sharp crimson line around the edge of her mouth. 'Your father's insurance has okayed a bunch of tests. They'll be useful to rule out any other factors.'

'Like a brain tumour, you mean?'

Dr Shreve doesn't reply to that. She writes a few more notes. McKenzie tucks her hands between her knees and stares down at the doctor's ankles, thick and arthritic, wondering why they seem familiar. The rugs on the floor are decorated with stylised fish in yellow and turquoise, but it's the doctor's ankles that are riveting.

Dr Shreve finishes her notes, puts her book down and smiles at McKenzie. 'Is there anything you'd like to tell me?'

'Like what?'

'Tell me about your friends. Do you have lots of friends at school.'

'I'm a nerd, so I pretty much don't have any friends. India. She's about the sum of it.'

'Is this India Jespersen?'

'How do you know her name?'

'I think she was the one who took the WhatsApp to the principal. Boyfriends?'

'No. Evidently I'm undateable. Or at least "semi"-undateable.'

'Says who?'

'Says guys my age.'

'You believe that?'

'I've got quite a lot of empirical evidence to back it up.'

Dr Shreve scratches the side of her face thoughtfully. 'Do you enjoy drinking alcohol, McKenzie?'

'Nope. And no drugs, either. That's not what's going on, and I promise you that. I'm Gen Z – we don't get high.'

'I've heard this before.' She cocks her head on one side. 'Have you ever felt angry about not having friends?'

'Yes. But not to the point I'd do something about it. Apart from what I did to Joe Marino, I don't think about hurting anyone else, and I don't think about hurting myself.'

Dr Shreve smiles. 'You seem to know the questions I'm going to ask you.'

'I did some research.'

'It's clear you're very switched on, highly motivated, so I'm not surprised you're a few steps ahead of me.' She folds her arms and considers McKenzie carefully. 'So, McKenzie, it strikes me you've already decided what is wrong with you and you simply want me to confirm it.'

McKenzie takes a long, slow breath through her nose. 'Yes. That kinda sums it up.'

'But you know I can't do that. Not until the CAT scans and MRIs come back.'

'So it's a toss-up between early-onset schizophrenia, including visual hallucinations, and a brain tumour, right? Either of which makes my chances of getting into Caltech low to zero.'

Dr Shreve sighs and settles herself back in the chair.

'Shall we wait until the results come back and pick it up from there?'

On the way back Tita Lily sits on top of a roll of turquoise silk they discovered in Mithi. Ordinarily she'd be joking with the others about what she would do with the silk – the conversation would be about the dresses and the shirts she was planning to make.

'I was the chief fire-lighter in Bugi Street,' she'd murmur, throwing the silk one way and tossing her hair haughtily. 'The dance of the flaming assholes, and me, yours truly, dancing around lighting farts – can you believe it? The boogie gal from Boogie Street – I could have had anyone.' She'd hold out a handful of the silk to Cairo. 'You're going to have a shirt made from this, you know that? For very formal occasions.'

Today, however, she is reflective and silent in her splendid hat – gazing off at the horizon. Forlani keeps touching her foot, asking if she's OK, and Spider watches her. They can't lose another person, they just can't.

Cairo, Mahmoud and Splendour walk alongside Tita Lily, Mahmoud holding a stick, occasionally using it to push away from his face the pots of Hugo's that hang from Camel's *mahawi* saddle blankets and clank robustly with every step. Splendour is subdued, with tear stains in the dust on her face.

The wind is perfect – enough to keep the air moving, but not so fierce that it drives the sand into the family's unprotected skin. The Mithi cats gather at the low road to watch the Dormilones' departure, as if they want to be sure the family are really going.

All morning Spider can't stop thinking about the other family – moving fast because they'd discovered where the Sarkpont was. What if there is a chink in the Chicane over there that the Dormilones haven't discovered, where the city is? When the family stop for lunch, though, Spider stands for a long time studying it.

Forlani and Elk help Tita Lily off Camel and make her comfortable on the sand.

'She's not looking good,' Forlani whispers to Spider.

'We can't lose her – just can't.'

After lunch they are about to gather themselves up for the remainder of the trek when Elk suddenly freezes and sits up abruptly. 'Amasha,' he mutters, putting down his food. 'Can you ... ?'

'Yes,' she responds distantly. She turns and stares raptly into the desert. 'I can.'

All the family stop what they are doing and stare. They know what this is – it's the call that only the Futatsu can hear. Usually it happens on white nights, when Elk and Amasha rise in silence and creep away from the camp. They never say where they are going or what calls them – so when it happens in the daylight, the rest of the family is transfixed by this strange behaviour and watches in awe as the Futatsu get slowly to their feet, their faces hypnotised by something in the distance.

Amasha and Elk wander into the sands, their backs straight, going on and on towards something invisible to everyone else. Eventually they are tiny dots and then, in a blink, they are invisible even through binoculars.

Cairo sighs and pulls his helicopter from his pocket. 'So-o-o boring,' he mutters to Splendour, then yelps as Madeira gives him a swift clip to the back of his neck.

'You show a bit of respect. What they're doing is dangerous, and if they don't, we never know what the Scouts are thinking.'

'We never know anyway,' Cairo complains, nursing his neck. 'They never tell us. We gotta sit here an' wait for hours and hours.'

'It's never hours and hours – so shut your blowhole, you hear?'

Cairo crawls away moodily and sits with his back to the family, arms folded angrily. Mahmoud ignores him and wanders away into the desert alone, staring at the distant city. Splendour comes to sit next to Spider, lying down with her head on his knee and cradling the little rag doll that Tita Lily made her, moving it around as if it's a puppet playing out a scene.

'Spider, what's INKEST?'

He looks down at Splendour, who is watching him thoughtfully. 'What's *what*?'

'Ink – est. What was written on the wall.'

'Oh yeah, that.' Incest is the ghost that moves between this family, who haven't always been family. In Paris, Spider's girlfriends were ever-changing – they arrived easily and often left as fast. 'It's just a word. Don't worry about it.'

She continues dancing the doll across the air, telling it off for not walking nicely, telling it that it will have to eat its vegetables tonight.

Spider sighs and ruffles her hair. 'You keep going with that doll – she's going to listen to you before long.'

The sun crosses its zenith, and a small herd of lizards appears from the direction of Dubai, stops and eyes the family, then skitters off. Hugo and Noor sit cross-legged in the sand, discussing Dubai – the times they've been there: Hugo on banking business, and Noor with his family.

'I think you're right,' Hugo says. 'It is Dubai. And if it is, it's full of pools and fountains.'

'And water parks. If we can't find a pool inside a square in Dubai, then …'

'Where the buggeration will we find it?' Hugo finishes for him.

The two men begin making maps in the sand of what they recall from Dubai's layout. Their excitement is palpable; they pace around it, pointing things out to each other, smiling in the bright daylight. Madeira snoozes and Forlani sits with Tita Lily, holding her hand. Tita Lily lies on her back, her hat over her face. She is pale.

After what seems like an age, when the sun has moved towards the horizon, the Futatsu reappear from the distant dunes. Spider gets to his feet and watches them approach. He wishes he could tell from their faces what has happened – what they have seen or heard. Usually they are sombre, closed off, but today there is a buoyancy to their appearance that everyone notices instantly. They don't speak, but Elk is jovial as he helps Madeira repack the provisions, and Amasha has a secret glow to her. She accepts the water gourd with a small, shy smile and drinks deeply. Satisfied. In the breeze her blue-and-silver scarves flutter like birds around her face.

They rouse the children, wake Tita Lily and get her back on Camel with a lot of wincing and pain, then they head off.

Mid-afternoon, when the Shuck is becoming larger and more visible, Amasha draws level with Spider and begins casting him meaningful glances, smiling curiously at him. He speeds up a bit, then, when she keeps pace, he snatches away the keffiyeh.

She smiles benignly, but her face is secretive.

'Did it go well?'

Her smile gets more self-pleased. Still she doesn't look at him. 'What do you think?'

'I look at your face and I assume it did.' They walk on for a bit, Amasha humming lightly under her breath. 'Can you tell me?'

Amasha arches her eyebrows, suggesting she knows that he's crossed a small line. But it's an amused look she's giving him. 'It's good news. Elk saw Knut, they're in communication – Knut is responding.'

Spider comes to a slight halt. Camel almost lumbers into his shoulder, so he corrects himself and resumes moving, automatically. 'That's never happened before.'

'I know.' She glows. 'Look at Elk. Haven't you seen a spring in his step?'

'Yes, yes, I have. In fact he's got that dancing-in-Valhalla look. Any clues about where to go?'

'Not yet. But maybe it will be quick.'

They walk on for almost ten minutes in silence while he digests this information. There is sand in his left boot, rubbing the leather against his bare ankle. It doesn't bother him, though, not with this news.

'Amasha, you know why Splendour seems unsettled? She stumbled on a hiding place. Bodies – not as many as the last few times, but enough to scare her. The work of the Djinni.' He glances back at Splendour, who has her fingers in her mouth and is glancing cautiously at the long tracts of desert – as if she has never really seen them properly before. 'Anyway,' he hisses, 'I lied, said they were dummies, but she's getting closer to understanding what happens on grey nights and that's made her start asking even more questions about when we'll find the Sarkpont. And ...' He paused, making sure he wasn't meeting her eyes for a moment. 'And about what happens if we don't.'

'You answered her?'

'No. I can't, can I? I don't know.' He tightens his grip on Camel's tether. The timespan they are allowed for discovering the Sarkpont on each Regyre is unlimited – the only thing that ends the Regyre is when another family discover the Sarkpont. 'There isn't much time left. The Djinni are already circling, like they did around that other family.'

The wind gusts then, making Camel brace and blink. Tita Lily shifts in the saddle, raises the keffiyeh to her mouth and turns her back to the wind.

They arrive at the Shuck with hours to spare. The sight is so welcoming, its pastel-coloured flowers visible even from this distance. They found it late on the sixth day. Yes, the outside was damaged, a little battered; nevertheless, for a family that felt disadvantaged, down on its luck, it was astonishingly good fortune. When the family dared to enter, though the main access gate on the northern flank, they discovered the Shuck's previous occupants had left remnants of their lives, things they hadn't been able to take with them. The giant preservation lockers that hung like udders from the underside of the Shuck were half full of supplies: dates and honey in jars. There was bedding drying in the lantern room, and children's toys.

Hugo had been the most practical-minded of anyone. Under the untidy, half-dead crops he discovered the remnants of an irrigation system, which presumably had been created by a long-ago inhabitant of the tower, with a few chickens scratching around in the sand outside looking for corn; and when, within a few minutes of the family's arrival, a pack of skinny, mangy-looking kangaroos appeared at the entrance to the tower, as if they expected feeding, Madeira put her foot down right there and then. There was enough here to cultivate good crops and produce breeding animals. In short, she declared it the perfect place to survive.

The outer tower they secured from invaders and the elements by grilling and blockading all access points at ground level, save for the lockable northern access. There remains one enormous hole – they call it the 'the Eye' because it is roughly oval and is fringed with spikes of rusted iron that correspond to eyelashes. Through the Eye the sun reaches a delineated area of the ground inside the tower structure. Its existence has allowed the farm to flourish, with the seeds and cuttings that Forlani and Madeira found in the cities, and the livestock pens that Spider created, which fringe the tower's inner perimeter. The bedraggled kangaroos have fattened and are breeding, and there are ten sheep – all dragged back from the family's various sorties.

No wonder no one wants to leave, Spider thinks wearily. It's going to be like making the family cut off a limb.

14

DAD WAKES AS usual at six. He's in the shower for ages, the TV blaring loudly in the bedroom, while in the room above McKenzie lies on her back, rigid, listening carefully to the house slowly shaking off its sleep. The boys get up at 6.30 and she can hear them grumbling and bitching, heading down to breakfast. She hasn't joined them at the table since she was suspended from Harbinson – no one has said anything.

She checks her phone, wearily. She's still the subject of truckloads of sub-tweets, constant sly jokes about lizards and thermoregulating, and the penis-shaped sand dune keeps coming back to haunt her too. There's a comment on one of her Insta pictures, from @NewtinSeattle. It says – *I saw the lizard too*.

She frowns. It's the same guy who commented the day of the Science Fair. Before deleting it, she goes onto his account and his profile stops her short. The profile shows a fractal-generated desert scene, the sun setting behind a cactus in lurid pink. His bio reads: 'Desert artist trapped in the body of a Seattle software scrum-master.'

A sliver of curiosity works its way through McKenzie. It's the illustration of the desert that's working on her – as if she's being pulled by an invisible line from somewhere in the far distance. But what does it mean to @NewtinSeattle? And what does 'desert artist' mean? Is he trying to draw her in? She hesitates, then presses 'follow'. The follow-request 'sent' bar pops up and, before she can even scroll away from the page, it's accepted. She stares at the screen. He was waiting.

Quickly she scrolls through his account – no images of him – but the pics are all of desert scenes and maps. The maps are extraordinary, like nothing she's seen before, beautiful illustrations of desert lands, some annotated 'Dunes' and 'Salt Bed'. There is a recurring pattern in the maps, like a many-pronged fork lying on its side.

A comment pops up on her page.

@NewtinSeattle – *Contact me. Message me as* ***soon as poss****.*

McKenzie stares at it. Then, frowning, she switches off the phone.

The boys head off to college. McKenzie dresses methodically, trying not to think about what she's going to do. She wears jeans and a thick turtle-neck that she can fit an extra jacket over. She fills her pockets with her phone, her bank card and the wad of cash she's been saving for years. Like an outlaw.

She tiptoes downstairs. Tatum hasn't ever been suspicious enough of his sister to hide his car keys and leaves them in his room, hanging on a peg next to an ironic trucker's cap. She snatches them up, goes silently back to her room and sits on the bed, hugging herself, rocking back and forward, her heart thudding.

She can drive, though Mom and Dad hate it when she does, especially now she's a bona-fide mental case. They occasionally allow her to take Dad's Duster, which is easiest to handle out of all the family's cars; and frankly, Mom says, if you crash, at least you'll come off better in that than in one of the small cars. She's never driven Tatum's old Subaru.

At 7.15 Dad clatters down the stairs, whistling, and goes into the kitchen. McKenzie creeps to the top of the stairs and watches the empty hallway, waiting. After a while the waste disposal starts – he's dumping the coffee grounds, just as he does every morning – and moments later the door opens. Dad, in his normal work suit, his hair still damp from the shower, heads to the front door, checking his phone as he goes, his scalp shining pink through the salt-and-pepper hair.

The front door slams. McKenzie slides silently down the stairs and into the hall. The door is closed, but when she stands on tiptoe she can see out through the glazed panels. On the driveway Dad's in his car, the engine running – white smoke rising from the exhaust, startling in the blue air. He takes a few more moments to check his phone, then locks it into the glove pocket, puts the Duster into reverse and backs down the driveway.

It's now or never. McKenzie drops back onto her heels, forces herself to stand still for twenty seconds and waits until she can hear the Duster change into a forward gear and begin to move along the street.

Moving very fast, she slips out of the door and into the unlocked Subaru. It smells of chewing gum and Tatum's sweaty lacrosse bag. She starts it and backs it gingerly down the driveway, shaking with nerves. Dad's Duster has already disappeared around the corner, so she drives fast, sticking to the snowploughed lanes. There isn't much snow left at the sides of the roads, but her parents have rammed it into all the kids over the years how dangerous it is to drive on ice or snow. The Subaru terrifies her with its skinny steering wheel, the way it rattles and jolts over every uneven part of the pavement, but she keeps going, sunglasses slotted over her eyes because somehow they make her feel like she knows what she's doing.

As she comes round the bend in the street she sees Dad's car at the junction, signalling left. She slows and creeps along until he pulls onto the country route that takes him down to the boulevard. Dad must be listening to the radio, or in his own world, because he doesn't appear to check in the mirror once, and she's able to keep track of him quite easily, the dusty bronze colour of his car readily visible among all the grey and white cars, even from a distance.

There's no satnav in the Subaru, but Tatum has a phone-mount on the dashboard. Her phone app tells her the quickest way to town is I66. That makes sense; every night Dad will bore them with stories about the traffic on I66, how there's a 'slug' lane where early-morning commuters hitch rides with complete strangers, just to get themselves into the high-occupancy vehicle lanes. Sure enough, he seems to be following the route, and within twenty minutes they're on the I66 and there she is with the other adults, driving along, the low autumn sun glinting off her sunglasses.

By the time they reach the Capital Beltway, she knows India was right. Instead of carrying straight on, which will take Dad into central DC, to Foggy Bottom where the State Department is, he goes onto the ring road, heading north towards Tysons. Before long they're on George Washington Parkway, with the Potomac grey and sluggish on her right. When Dad passes the Turkey Run sign and signals right, under the sign that reads 'GEORGE H. W. BUSH CENTER FOR CENTRAL INTELLIGENCE *NEXT RIGHT*', she knows.

He makes his turn and McKenzie continues on, heart thudding low and hard. As she passes she gets a brief glimpse of a wooded drive, yellow gates standing open and Dad's car further down, passing a small security building.

She is so horrified and so excited that she almost forgets she's cruising down a main street on her own. At the next lights she does a right and meanders slowly back down Dolley Maddison Boulevard, with the sun coming over her shoulder and turning the rear-view mirror into a laser of light.

Dad's a manager – like Mr Peterson in Nevada, he was in Human Resources, which means hiring and firing people. At least that's what he's told them all this time. So what is he doing at the CIA?

At Tysons she pulls over for a drive-through Starbucks. Waiting in the queue, she opens her socials. There are the usual requests – it seems it's not only the Science Fair she's famous for, but now for what she did to Joe Marino. There are two new messages from @NewtinSeattle. The first says in caps – *DON'T BLANK ME. WE HAVE TO TALK.*

The second, in calmer lower-case letters, says: *Sorry – I don't mean to hassle you. But please, please just speak to me. I know what you've been seeing because I've been seeing it too. This thing is bigger than you can imagine. Have you heard of Limbic Resonance?*

Limbic resonance? She googles it.

'*Limbic Resonance states that everyone has a capacity for sharing emotional information based on the interactions of chemicals in the limbic system.*'

The statement is accompanied by an illustration that looks a little like a Tarot card: a woman with a serpentine stream coming from her forehead, connecting her to a man. McKenzie's scientific brain is hopeless around New Age theories; she's too rational by far. She hesitates, biting her lip, then presses 'unfollow' on his account and sends a text to Mom.

– Mom, I felt sick this morning so I stayed in bed, but I wanna get some Tylenol so can I take Tatum's car? Promise to be careful

The text comes back as McKenzie collects her coffee.

– isn't there any in the house?

– I already looked. And i want some fruit too. Can I?

– OK but don't tell him. Lucky you're insured – did you think of that? And WhatsApp me to tell me you got home safe.

There's a pause, then another message comes through.

– Please honey: remember how worried I am about you … She adds a sad emoji.

McKenzie taps out a message

– thanks Mom. But how come you never told me the truth about Dad?

Her hand hovers over 'send', but she changes her mind. Deletes the second sentence and sends it. Then sends another to India.

– need to talk – come to mine straight after school.

India arrives at 2.30, straight off the bus. She's head to toe in wool – a beanie, scarf, gloves, the whole nine yards. Mom is downstairs doing her YouTube stretches, and McKenzie pulls the door closed and takes out two Cokes from the fridge.

'Coke?' India says.

'Yeah – Mom makes a living from telling everyone how to live healthy, but as soon as she's off-duty, her truth is something different. The place is packed with e-numbers and sugar – always bad shit to fill a lunch pail with.'

'She looks like she doesn't eat more than a bit of kale every day.' India sits down, pulls off her gloves. 'Fuck, I miss you at school. No one to talk to.'

'I miss you too.'

'How was the shrink? Did she lean forward and ask you how you're feeling? Did she touch you on the knee to show you how sympathetic she was. Was there Kleenex on the table?'

'Of course. There's always Kleenex.'

'And,' India asks, popping the Coke, 'what did she say?'

McKenzie gives a deep sigh. She's thirsty again, as if all the fluid in her body is being sucked away to an invisible point. 'She doesn't have a clue. They've run a bunch of tests, I'll know this week. Might mean I've got to be in hospital. Either schizophrenia – so I'll get drugs – or a tumour maybe.' She searches her friend's face. 'I'm scared shitless, but if they can sort it, I can come back to school.'

'You want to come back to that shithole?'

McKenzie shrugs. She sips the Coke, picks a couple of grapes from the fruit bowl and gazes out of the window, to where the neighbour is vacuuming leaves from the yard. 'I followed Dad. You were right.'

India's mouth opens a little. 'Whoa! CIA?' she mouths.

'Yup. And I'm like …' McKenzie shakes her head. 'I'm so upside down, just don't know what the fuck is going on.'

'I know, I know. But listen – I've been reading about, you know, hallucinations and shit. And I saw all that stuff about tumours, and I saw all the stuff about schizophrenia.'

'You probably read the same stuff I did.'

'Prolly, yeah. But did you find that stuff about retrieved memories?'

'Retrieved *what*?'

India licks her lips and glances over her shoulder at the door to the kitchen, as if she's afraid McKenzie's mom will overhear, or that Dad's co-workers have got the place wired, then she comes in a little closer to McKenzie and mutters under her breath, 'Remember what I said about your dad? What you've got to do is establish if he did something at work that's making you have all these hallucinations. So *think*. Has he ever mentioned the desert? On his trips abroad does he ever go somewhere hot? Like Africa or anything?'

'I don't think he went to Africa – it's mostly Europe. He went to Indonesia once. Or at least that's what he said he was doing. But we spent some time in the south-west, and somehow I've got it in my head that we went to Phoenix and something happened there, something really sketchy. I've always had this image, since I was little, of a storm over Phoenix and I don't know why. Mom denies it.'

'Well,' India says, slightly triumphant. 'Maybe that's what you've got to ask the psychiatrist.'

The Dormilones have the luxury of two hours' sunlight left – the sun at an angle they rarely witness, slicing down into the tower through the Eye in the rusting tower and bathing them all in sunshine. Forlani and Amasha help Tita Lily up the ladder while the children are set to work cleaning, Hugo carries the dung pots off to the tanks of his fertiliser system, and Elk crouches in the corner, scouring and sharpening cooking utensils.

Spider unpacks the *mahawi*, the kangaroo-hide wind shelters, the camping stove, then tends to Camel, washing her and checking her feet, keeping patient because she's at an age when sometimes she has to be forced to eat and drink. When she's settled, he straightens and goes to the ladder and climbs to the Shuck.

He remembers this, the day they lost Nergüi. They had been out sharpening arrows and swords, and when Spider came back inside, Nergüi said he'd follow on later.

Noor had been the one to lock the doors. He had been the one. And later, when they were upstairs in the Shuck, it took a while for the Futatsu to notice there was no Nergüi.

'Where is he?' they said. 'Where the hell?'

The sun was sinking low, and then came the pounding. 'What the fuck?' Spider said, going to the balcony. 'What the fuck?'

Noor stood in the centre of the room, his arms held wide. 'I locked up. I thought we were all here.'

But Spider knew Noor wasn't as innocent as that. Now he could hear the screams – the screams of Nergüi locked out – and the pounding on the metal. He ran to climb down the ladder, but there were shouts from above. Night had come and he could hear the chattering of the Djinni and knew the pounding had stopped.

'Spider, no. No!' Hugo called. 'Don't risk it. It's not worth it.'

Spider hesitated. He was furious with Noor. And then, when the Djinni started to clatter against the bottom steel-lined barricades, he knew in his heart that he had to make his way back up.

He strode into the kitchen and went to the window. There was Nergüi's corpse being thrown into the air, so high he could see it. Spider saw he was dead. His heart fell into a place beyond anywhere it had gone before. His rage with Noor – his incandescent fury – lit him up, but he knew not to turn to Noor or blame him. He knew that Amasha would be onto him, insisting the family were as one.

He drank a little of Elk's alcohol and begged some ganja and went to bed. He kept imagining how he could fight Noor, maybe push him off the Shuck.

But the next morning there was Nergüi's corpse, stretched out in the sand, his skin sucked clean of anything. The family wept, they consoled each other that he would come back . . . maybe when they'd found the Sarkpont. They promised to keep him in their prayers, and no one – no one – looked at Noor. Noor remained clear-eyed. Gazing off into the distance as if he was innocent.

They didn't let the children see the corpse; they changed their route that morning to avoid them looking at him, and when they came back two days later the corpse was gone, covered maybe by sand.

'Where's Nergüi?' said Splendour. 'Where him gone?'

'He's gone for a wander. Maybe he won't come back,' said Amasha.

Spider went a little crazy after that. He knew not to attack Noor, but he watched him everywhere he went, he didn't let a moment go by when he wasn't observing him. He knew that if something had happened to Nergüi, it could happen to anyone. Nightly he dreamed he was in a fight with Noor; he would wake, sweating and angry, ready to walk down the corridor to find him and beat him to a pulp. It would be so easy – Spider knows he has twice the strength of Noor.

And yet he hasn't done anything. The family go on as they mean to go on, still searching for the Sarkpont. And yet they are afraid of the Djinni, what they can do in a blind second: hurl a corpse into the air, so high it almost reaches the top of the Shuck.

Spider is strong and tall, long-legged, it takes him almost two minutes to climb the ladder, knowing the Djinni are close behind. The others, especially Forlani with his injuries, can take up to five minutes. If anything ever entered the tower unexpectedly when the family were on the desert floor, how would they escape into the Shuck? It eats at Spider to wonder how he and the other men would carry the weaker ones. Especially now Nergüi is gone.

Inside the Shuck the children are showered and are wandering around, dripping water everywhere, and the salts that Forlani insists each family member takes are lined up in earthenware pots in the corridor. Spider swallows his, with what is left in his water gourd. Mahmoud must have brushed against a stinging plant while he was in Mithi, because he has a rash on his legs and chest and sits sullenly on a bench with his legs stretched out, while Forlani and Amasha inspect it and discuss what creams to apply.

Spider goes to the shower room, hangs up his jacket, kicks off his boots and unhooks his tool bag, then all the weapons strapped to his thighs. He pours his daily shower ration into the reservoir, drags off the dress and his shorts and stands under the shower nozzle, his hands against the wall, his head down, letting the water wash over him.

Here in the shower room a former resident must have spent time drawing maps, because the wall is covered in hieroglyphics that appear to be diagrams of cities. One of them the Dormilones have already matched with a city – the strange city of Casablanca, with its tortuous streets and souks – but there are countless others that are too decayed to understand, or that simply match plans of places they haven't been to yet.

He thinks again of the family running along the horizon. The feeling of urgency comes up like a wave. He scrubs up quickly and towels himself off roughly, throws on shorts, a dress and his boots and goes to the common room.

He steps over the place where Yma sleeps when she's here – her sextant and pillow are still there in the corner – and draws the shutter half closed behind him. He pulls out his binoculars, wipes clean the lens and holds them to his eyes. First, only half a kilometre away, the shores of the Virgule, a vast, dried-out ocean bed stretching into the distance, their closest neighbour, which has a habit of shifting consistency. On some days it is white and reflective and one can walk out onto it. On other days it dries to a crisp orange, like caramelised sugar or tiger bread, and just one step crumbles the salt underfoot. The name Virgule comes from the French word for 'slash' or comma, given for the way it hacks down the middle of the visible desert, like a sword slash. No one would dare traverse it. It's dangerous – full of holes and abandoned animal corpses.

He gives the binoculars another polish and refocuses on that far horizon. There's another city out there too; he lets the glasses skim over it and onwards. There is a small nub far to the west that they've always taken to be a Shuck. How long would it take to get there? he wonders. Less than a day?

'Spider?'

He starties. Forlani is standing behind him, one hand on the shutters.

'Jesus, don't creep up on me like that. Hey, come here.' He reaches out and gathers Forlani to him. Forlani stutters forward and leans wearily against Spider, who gives his fragile, wiry skull an affectionate rub with his knuckles. 'Little bro Forlani, don't knot yourself, OK? Hey? S'up? You OK?'

'No. Bin thinking about that diary.'

'We all have.'

Forlani nods. His hands are stitched and swollen and, glancing down at them, Spider has a moment's regret for how poorly he understands the suffering of the rest of the family.

'What you looking at?' Forlani gives him that confrontational brown-eyed stare that Spider can't wriggle from. 'You're not looking where Nergüi's corpse was. So come on. Tell me.'

'You'll think I'm *fou*. Crazy'

'I'd be sad if you weren't. I'd be disappointed.'

Spider sighs. 'This morning I saw a family out there, moving fast. Like they'd found the …' He trails off, not quite able to bring himself to say the word 'Sarkpont'. 'Like they were in a hurry. Told Noor, but he couldn't see anything.'

Forlani doesn't smirk, or react. He holds Spider's eyes for a long time. Then his thoughtful eyes swivel out of the tower, past the Virgule and upwards to where they know the Chicane is. He goes inside to the big trunk at the far end of the room where all the maps are kept, finds what he wants and limps back to the balcony, with the giant chart rolled up under his shrivelled arm.

'We need to look at these. Maybe there's a mistake.'

The map isn't new to Spider. Knut drew it months ago, after a family meeting that agreed on what they had learned of the Cirque. Now it is called 'Knut's Founding Map' and it has been the family's bible. For as long as they've been in the Cirque, it's been sacrosanct.

With Spider's help, they unravel it on the floor of the balcony. They squat and pore over it together.

'Here.' Forlani runs his crooked finger over the border to the north. 'Do you think something could be wrong here?'

Spider rolls onto his knees, places his hands on the map and studies the squiggles. In those first few days the family had spent almost a day experimenting with the border they call the Chicane: handholding themselves along it, astounded by its trickery. Some members stood back from it, others leaned into it, some even lay on the ground to look at it and discover its magic ingredient, but they never understood how they could be so close to the edge of the Cirque and yet believe utterly that the desert stretched on forever. Mahmoud, in his frustration, had thrown his newest toy plane at it. It had bounced back.

The family walked along it until they were convinced it went on forever. When, later, they began their tentative forty-eight-hour expeditions looking for the Sarkpont and collided with more sections of the eastern Chicane, they learned how the boundary curved, and from this Knut had drawn this map.

'We didn't cover this part,' says Forlani. 'It was my fault. I slowed you down.'

He is tracing his finger over a small section of the border that the family have never touched. Spider knows there is a city there. In some lights it seems pocked with green, as if grass is growing there, and there appear to be enormous gates with something like a spearhead mounted above them, though their binoculars aren't accurate enough to be sure. Even the weather formations across it change so incredibly: giant thunder-bursts and swirling clouds the shape of cathedrals or huge mushrooms.

The only way is across the Virgule, which crumbles in places. They'd never make it there and back in two days.

Both of them raise their eyes and look back over the balcony. Sunset is coming and another grey night. The horizon is darkening, and soon the Futatsu will be here to order the shutters closed. There are just minutes to witness the lights twinkle on in the huge, familiar shape of the far city, an ink-stain against the dusk.

Elk appears in the kitchen behind them, one of the pod blankets draped around his shoulders. His grey hair, which is usually fixed in a topknot on his head, flows down off his shoulders. He opens the nozzles on the methane-gas canister, fires up the gas rings, sets a pan of water to boil and measures out cornmeal from the storage bin that sits in the corner. Madeira is carrying six full, ripe pineapples they discovered in Mithi. She hands them to Elk, who pulls the segments out and arranges them on a platter, while Noor sets out the crude knives and forks in the common room.

Elk wipes his hands on his apron and comes to the balcony, cocking his head to one side, studying Spider. 'What's happening? Why the powwow?'

'I saw people this morning, next to the city near the Chicane. They looked excited – as if they knew the Sarkpont was close.'

Elk frowns. 'Spider, my son, we'll save some time if I tell you the answer to your question. It's no.'

'I haven't asked it yet.'

'You don't have to. I'm not dragging the children up north for nothing – no one has crossed the Virgule, and to get to the other side we'd have to walk around the edge, which is more than a twenty-four-hour march. We're going to Dubai – a city that is not imaginary – and we won't be scratching around the Chicane again.'

Spider sighs. Amasha he can reason with, but Elk? He's a different matter. A genial man, never angered, though no one has tested how far his patience stretches, and no one would provoke him – he is a giant and, angered, he'd be terrifying with his booming voice, his vast chest and his biceps like ham hocks.

'I did see people,' Spider mutters.

'Well, no one else did. Did you, Noor?'

Noor lowers his eyes and puts his finger to his nose, embarrassed. 'Not really.' He can't meet Spider's eyes, because Spider watches him constantly. 'I saw Dubai, though.'

'Maybe there's the makings of a new shelter for us all in Dubai?' Elk scratches the side of his face nonchalantly. 'We can't go on in this place, so tomorrow we search Dubai for the Sarkpont, but also for a place that will serve as another shuck.'

15

'RETRIEVED MEMORIES?' THE idea brings Dr Shreve up short. She takes off her spectacles and leans forward in her chair towards McKenzie. Her eyes are very grey and shiny. 'Is that what you said?'

'I wondered if the hallucinations are linked to something that happened in my childhood. That maybe I was traumatised when I was little and the memories are still painful, but they're kind of bubbling to the surface, like a—'

'I know what retrieved-memory syndrome is. It's a very 1990s concept. Rather abandoned by the mental-health community.'

Dr Shreve is wearing a deep-blue cotton dress, a brown turtle-neck, a thickly embroidered crimson scarf and little boots trimmed in red fake-fur. Clearly she's read the weather forecast. Outside the window it's snowing again, dampening all sounds of the traffic. Mom is waiting in the reception room downstairs. Her anxiety about the results of the tests are probably being added to by the fear of driving home through yet another snowstorm.

'I feel like I've been to Phoenix, Arizona, sometime in the past and something happened to me when I was there.'

'McKenzie …' Dr Shreve knots her embroidered scarf and rearranges it, brushing away a few invisible specks of fluff. 'We did discuss this with your mom, and maybe it's for you to approach her again on that subject? I'm anxious not to avoid talking about the results of the tests. So maybe we could address ourselves to that problem now. Your mother says you want to be told the results yourself, but that then you'll be happy for her and your father to know my assessment.'

'That's correct.'

Dr Shreve turns over her paper. 'I'm going to launch right in and tell you. The MRI scans, the blood tests, showed nothing.'

'Nothing?'

'Nothing physical that would explain your symptoms.'

There's a short silence while McKenzie absorbs this.

Dr Shreve leans across and places the sheaf of test papers on the table in front of McKenzie. 'You weren't lying when you said you weren't taking drugs and you don't have diabetes, which was a kind of niggle in the back of my brain. Which is a mixed blessing, as you know, because that leaves us with one other option.'

'Schizophrenia.'

'A very broad term, but we need to investigate whether your symptoms can be classed as indicating that you are on a spectrum that includes schizophrenia.'

'Except the olfactory hallucinations – I can smell things and feel them? Sometimes smells are the first warning of an epileptic fit.'

'I've got no reason to think this is epilepsy.'

'I read the DSM-5 classifications and those sorts of hallucinations are incredibly rare, almost unheard of with early-onset schizophrenia.'

The snow falls outside, calm and silent. Snow does come to deserts occasionally, because they get cold enough at night, but usually the air is too dry.

'McKenzie, I understand your anxiety.'

'Do you?'

'Let me share this with you: as a professional, I am expected to care equally for every patient. However, McKenzie, I take your case very personally, and getting answers for you is of the utmost importance to me.'

'You don't think it's worth talking about retrieved-memory syndrome?'

'I don't. I think you're clutching at straws.'

'Though it would make sense of some of the anomalies.'

'I'm sorry, McKenzie. I understand how difficult this is for you. Please don't think you're alone; the diagnosis of schizophrenia is an extremely difficult reality for any patient, and no one expects you to find it easy.' She begins shuffling with her laptop, scrolling through lists, her spectacles pushed up her nose. 'Of course if you feel that the notion of retrieved memory is one you need to explore, there are still several practitioners who will take the idea seriously. I'm sorry I'm not one of them. And I'm sorry that to give your parents the best service I can, I would not recommend you take that route, and I would not be able to continue to treat you. Which is a shame, because your school principal and I have very open lines of communication.'

'What *do* you recommend then?'

'We start you on a trial of a drug named Seroquel. It's a very well-used drug, a second-generation antipsychotic, which has undergone extensive clinical trials. There's a good generic on the market, quite affordable. Seroquel has strong anxiolytic effects – so it will help not just with the hallucinations, but also with the anxiety attached to this change in your circumstances and the consequent change in your expectations.'

McKenzie tucks her hands into her armpits and raises her eyes to the window, where the white flakes drift and dance. *A change in her expectations*. Is that how this seismic, life-shattering news is going to be referred to, from now on? A change in fucking expectations? She's read about Seroquel, or Quetiapine, and knows how it works, by interfering with the transmission of dopamine through the brain. Every review has led her to the same conclusion: the hallucinations will stop, but at the cost of brain fog, drowsiness, a lack of motivation. She'll gain weight, and her speech might become slurred. Caltech can't be a reality of course, but on a drug like Seroquel she could struggle to get into even the state universities – the ones that until recently she thought of as also-rans.

Tears come to her eyes, but she blots them away using her sleeve, not the Kleenex that sits on Dr Shreve's table. She won't let anyone see her cry. She doesn't have a tumour, she isn't going to die. She's simply facing a 'change in expectations'.

*

It's night in the desert, and Noor leaves arrows at the entrance to the Shuck and beds down under the table in the common room, using a pillow from the family sleeping pod, a thin throw over him. He's still dressed, Spider notes, still has his shoes on.

Amasha is fierce about Spider being able to access his tools when he needs them. '*Don't you see*,' he once overheard her hissing at Elk, '*that boy is as wild and dangerous as a scorpion, but treat him right and he's got the skills. One day he'll prove it – he'll make something that will save us all.*'

A scorpion, he thinks wearily as he unpacks the springs and the cogs and the O-rings he's been trying to assemble into a watch. He doesn't feel much like a scorpion, and while his screen for Camel appears to have held, his work on this timepiece has made no progress.

He isn't as tired as he should be; the thought that the Djinni are out there in the darkness keeps his nerves alive. He thinks about Nergüi, the night that they came for him and what was left, then he checks his weaponry – the arrows are in the right place and the spears too: he will be ready if something happens, but for now he needs a diversion.

He doesn't put the big methane-gas light on, though this aversion makes no sense – the Dormilones have kept lights burning on grey nights, have kept the windows open. He uses a single tallow candle to work with, cross-legged on the floor, hunched over the mechanism.

At present the family have a rudimentary timing system – they count heartbeats. Hugo's theory is that minutes and seconds come from the average human heartbeat of sixty beats per minute. From this, the family have compared pulse paces – whose goes faster and who goes slowest: Hugo and the children have fast beats, and if they are told two minutes, they count 180 of their beats, whereas Madeira and Spider count just 120 for two minutes, with the remainder of the family somewhere in between.

They need a timepiece. The primitive spring he's forged – by beating and torturing a sliver of wire – will not retain its tension, however he protects it: it's the Achilles heel of this watch. He rests it on his fingertip and contemplates it; he doesn't know how to change it. Out of the window the stars are inching their cold way across the heavens. He puts the spring back into the cloth roll, closes it and rests it in its box. Folding his arms, he drops his head forward, thinking about Tita Lily and the fact that, with Nergüi, it will make two people missing.

He sleeps, but it's not his internal clock that wakes him – it's the noise. A distant whine, a slight percussive element to it, as if something is being rhythmically beaten out beyond the dunes. He opens his eyes and stares at the ceiling for a few moments, then tips himself up and crawls carefully to the place where the weapons are. Tongue between his teeth, he lifts the bow from the pegs on the wall, automatically running a finger across the arrow-nock to check it's sound.

He carries the bow to the lantern ladder and climbs as quietly as he can, tiptoes around the room, peering out at the desert. There are no shadows or shapes on the ground and, leaning into the polymer pane, he squints at the horizon where he thinks the sound originates, then fleetingly sees a wavering in the horizon – a patch of the sky slightly darkened by what appear to be human shapes, deformed by the length of their limbs, as if they are on stilts.

There is a brief flare of fire, the line of figures rearranges itself, re-forms and billows, then disappears, leaving merely a cloud of sand on the horizon.

'Spider.' Noor has woken up under the table and is crawling out. 'See anything?'

Spider shakes his head, puts a finger to his lips and stealthily manoeuvres himself back down the ladder. He stands behind the glass at the southern balcony, his blood ticking fast in his temples. The noise is getting louder. Noor comes in silence to Spider and stands next to him, staring wordlessly into the night. Spider puts a little space between them – he knows what this man is capable of.

'You think they've gone?' Noor hisses.

The two men wait: Noor's eyes shine hard in the semi-darkness, horrified but fascinated too. He reaches for one of the spears and stands next to Spider.

There is silence in the desert. Just the flap of wings – a vulture circling overhead. Spider counts his own heartbeat: 200, 300. He's reached for the window to open it when there is a rush of noise like a tornado. The ground trembles and Spider raises his bow, slots the arrow into the riser and moves himself into position so that he can watch.

There is a billow of sand, a long line in the air marking the progress of the Djinni. They cover the ground in next to no time – they must move a hundred times as fast as a human – but the churned sand keeps them invisible. He holds his breath as the billow of sand arrives at the Shuck. He can't see how many creatures are down there, but in the next second one propels itself at the side of the Shuck and the place shudders.

'How many?' Noor whispers

'I don't know. Maybe three – four?'

The Djinni mill amongst the sand, their chattering rising up through the echoey girders, too close to the bottom of the tower to see them clearly. Then another one makes a leap, and this time it doesn't slither away but hangs for a moment. Spider gets the impression of a small, white, baby-like face on a huge head, then the creature loses its grip and slithers back down. There is a faint mewling noise, and again that staccato chattering.

Spider unlatches the window and kicks it open.

'Are you fucking insane?' Noor hisses. 'This is suicide.'

Spider adjusts himself; in the balcony where Noor can't get to him, he pulls back the bowstring, clenching the muscles between his shoulder blades, looking down the shaft of the arrow, waiting for something to become visible. The creatures keen and turn away, seem to be readying to leave. He releases the arrow as they do so and hears its whip-crack through the dark. There is a moment when he thinks he sees the arrowhead carried out towards the Virgule, on the back of one of the creatures perhaps.

Then they are gone and there is nothing except the plumes of sand and the skirmished tracks left silent and dark in the moonlight.

'Did you hit it?' Noor says, peering out into the darkness.

'I think so – in the back.'

'Didn't have any effect, though.'

'No.' Spider rehangs the bow on the pegs, shutters the windows and clicks the lock closed. He stands for a short while with his hands on the bow, listening to his heart race, thinking about what just happened. Elk and the others arrive in the corridor, shock-faced and white.

'What happened?' Elk asks.

'It wasn't our smell drew them. Was it, Noor?'

'No,' Noor concedes, his voice heavy. 'It wasn't. They were coming anyway.'

Coming home, another blizzard roars up. The highways to the cheapest pharmacies are bad, so they collect the Seroquel from the nearest mall and go straight home. India comes in after school and tries to make light of the situation, asking to see the pills, and is there a blue one or a red one; and is McKenzie going to make like Alice in Wonderland and grow out through the roof?

The boys aren't home, and Mom cooks the girls pulled pork from Trader Joe's, followed by her own lemon-and-frosted-orange cake. She reads the contraindications on the Seroquel from cover to cover in a loud voice, which gives India the giggles; she has to lower her face and stare hard at the table to avoid laughing.

After dinner they go to McKenzie's bedroom with the pills. India is on a high – Twitter is full of the fact that Harbinson students are lobbying senior management for a snow day. #closeFPS was trending not just locally but statewide on Twitter. People in Iowa and Washington State were tweeting – *Never even been to Virginia but feeling sorry for you guys anyhows #closeFPS!!!!!!*

McKenzie opens the blister-pack of pills. 'I guess I get this over and done with,' she says.

'I think you better. I promise not to let you climb out the window. I'll wait with you.'

McKenzie takes the pill, swallows it down whole and sits on the bed, trembling. She expects there to be an instantaneous reaction, but nothing happens.

'You're not getting any bigger,' India says solemnly. 'And you're still in this dimension. You think you took a dud one?'

McKenzie sighs and lies back on her bed, her hands behind her head. She watches the snow falling. The snowplough is making its screeching way down the street, its lights flashing through the flakes. She thinks she'll never, ever stop being amazed and fascinated by all this stuff coming out of the sky – the snow, the rain, the endless clouds and vegetation.

'You know, I keep asking the shrink about Phoenix – about that picture – and she keeps saying it's nothing. But with what I know about Dad now … I keep thinking: something happened when I went to Nevada; you know, when they think I had an epileptic fit.'

'Like what?'

'Well – I guess I dunno, but we were staying kind of near Phoenix, I guess.'

'Nevada? Not that close.'

'True.' McKenzie yawns. 'But I was thinking – the Petersons worked for the government too.'

'What part?'

She shrugs. 'Human Resources – FEMA I think.'

McKenzie whistles. 'FEMA? The military wing of the environment agency.'

'What? No. I said FEMA – the emergency agency. You know, it got all that shade for Hurricane Katrina?'

'Don't you read *anything*, Em? You never saw America under siege on Vimeo?' India swings her legs off the bed and goes to McKenzie's desk. 'Jesus, looks like I've got to educate you. Look at this.'

She opens the laptop and taps in the words 'FEMA CONSPIRACY THEORY'. Instantly thousands of matches come up. McKenzie gets up and goes to the desk, leaning over to peer at the entries. She sees links to sites with meta tags like: *FEMA internment camps … Military rule … Dispense with the Constitution.*

'This has been around for ages,' explains India. 'Basically the theory goes that FEMA's real, hidden job is not to manage disasters but to *create* them.'

'Create natural disasters? How does that happen? You don't create a hurricane.'

'You're the meteorologist, I'm sure you'd figure out a way – you can seed clouds, can't you? The idea is that the disasters are rehearsals for when the government finally takes over the country with the military and puts all the undesirables in concentration camps. Political realignment camps – to make them fall into line, right? The camps have already been built, they're just hidden or disguised. Like this one.' She taps on an image of a row of huts. 'On Google Earth it looks like an Amtrak depot, but actually, if you get inside, it's some sort of camp.'

'You believe all this?'

India doesn't answer. She clicks on Google Maps. 'Where in Nevada did this dude live?'

'Lake Tahoe. And before you look, yes, it is near Area Fifty-One. At least not a million miles away.'

'I can see that.' India clicks into the satellite and rests her chin on her hand, leaning thoughtfully into the computer. 'Not a million miles at all. Apparently they do weird experiments on people in the camps.'

'What the hell kind of experiments?

'I don't know; they fuck with their brains, make them undergo weird trials, maybe hallucinogenic drugs – who knows? See how they'd cope with a complete climate disaster, I bet.'

McKenzie watches the desert moving under the cursor as India drags the map between the two locations. The stark mountainsides dotted with stunted trees, the long stretches of sand, some criss-crossed with tracks. And patches of light that draw her closer to the screen, a creeping unfamiliar sense of déjà vu coming over her. 'Stop,' she says. She reaches over and taps the screen. 'What're those white things?'

India zooms in, pulling up labels on the map. 'Lakes? They don't look like lakes to me.'

'No,' McKenzie says wonderingly. 'They're silver because they're dried out. That's salt reflecting the sunshine.' She can't take her eyes off the white patches. Were they something she's dreamed of, amongst the other crazy dreams?

'What about them, McKenzie? What?'

She puts a hand on her temple. 'Jeez, I feel sleepy AF.'

India grins. 'Oh, goody, I get to watch you go wobbly.'

McKenzie goes and lies down on the bed. Blinks, but her eyelids are too heavy. 'Is this it?' she asks, and India says something like, *I guess so . . .*

But McKenzie is too far into sleep to pay any attention. When she wakes, it feels as if ten minutes have passed, but the sun is up above the trees. She blinks, rolls over and finds her phone. It's 9 a.m. She's in her pyjamas – she has a vague memory of India helping her into them – and next to the bed is a note from Mom:

> Honey, when you wake up, text me so I know you're OK. Breakfast on the table – no pressure to do anything, don't forget to take your pill.
>
> I love you, Mom.
>
> PS I did take your pulse about three times in the night ☺.

McKenzie opens her phone, texts Mom. There are texts from Dad, sending her love; and from India, crowing because there is no school today, so can she come over and hang and eat brownies? And then of course the obligatory hundreds of follow requests. Idly she unblocks @NewtinSeattle and her screen fills – all his messages. She feels mildly nauseous looking at them, so reblocks him, then tips herself out of bed and goes to the shower, where she takes her next pill, swallowing it down with lots of water.

She showers and throws on her sweats and her 'Fuggs' – the fake Uggs all the girls slouch around in – takes a blanket and goes to the verandah, where she pulls up her knees and sits sipping juice and snacking on biscuits. Winter has drawn in so fast, long before Christmas, and the neighbourhood is silent and muffled: snowdrifts, deceptively smooth stretches concealing holes and gullies that McKenzie doesn't want to think about.

She's getting dozy when India comes over and pokes her into something like life – raiding the brownie stash in the kitchen and forcing her to watch old Disney classics.

The hours melt into a whole day. Tatum and Luke are home, bitching because college isn't having a snow day, while the high schools are, and Dad is extra late because of the weather. McKenzie thinks vaguely about asking him, 'How were the spooks?' and it makes her laugh to imagine it, but she doesn't say a word, and before she knows it she's in bed, and then it's morning again, and India is back squealing about another snow day, and how today they're going to binge-watch *Gossip Girl* and cook more brownies, cos she has a banging low-fat recipe and they can eat as many as they want – no worries. And then one day McKenzie wakes up and hears her brothers downstairs and realises the weekend is here again and she has done nothing, thought nothing, slept through most of it.

Is this how it's going to be? Really?

'Give it until you see the shrink next,' India advises her. 'Then ask. Cos, not being funny, but you look a mess.'

'Do I?'

'Yeah – you haven't washed your hair. That's a piece of brownie on your T-shirt, and you're wearing the same pants: hasn't your mom said anything?'

McKenzie washes and changes in a kind of fog, and feels better when she's had some coffee. She checks her phone. Still the same trolls, though now they're dwindling to the occasional person who's seen the Science Fair on YouTube. She unblocks @NewtinSeattle and a message pops up that she can't ignore.

– A horned toad!

She stares at the words. Mr Blonde was a horned toad.

Her mouth dry, she opens the message.

– You saw a horned toad, it's also known as a Horned Lizard. It has a huge ruff – google it. Your horned toad waited a moment getting used to the light, then it pushed itself up and down: you are right, it was thermoregulating. I know because I see these damned things every day – I've got one living in my apartment, for Christ's sake, and you're the only person who will believe me.

'Kenz?'

She snaps to. India is staring at her.

'Kenz, what the fuck?'

McKenzie closes her mouth. Shakes her head.

'You OK?'

She has to put her coffee cup down and lock her hands between her knees, they're trembling so much. 'I think so.' She licks her lips. 'Any chance of another espresso – I think I liked that one.'

When India has gone, she hurriedly types out a message.

– who the hell are you?

There is a long pause; maybe he's sleeping, if he lives in Seattle, but then the icon blinks to show he's picked up the chat. He sends a message back that is so long it must have been pre-prepared. McKenzie crosses her legs on the bed and reads.

– My name is 'Newt' Herrera – that's a nickname I chose, don't know why, but then I don't understand a lot about myself. Sound familiar? I was born Gaston Herrera in Córdoba, Argentina,

where my father had an engineering business. My father once had a position as a civil engineer within the government, and I suspect later he used that experience to gain contracts. In 2007 he was working with a company on a gas pipeline into Bolivia, when suddenly overnight everything in our family changed. My parents decided to move out of Córdoba, they bought a remote house in the foothills of Mendoza near the Chilean border and suddenly there was a lot of money my father wanted to get out of the country. He did it by sending me and my brothers overseas to study – my brothers went to Europe, while a family friend sponsored me to get into the United States. I went to the University of Washington – that's when I formally changed my name to Newt; I always preferred that name to 'Gaston'. I did a computer-science degree, got a place in a start-up. In the first year, members of my mother's family, her sisters and cousins, visited me in Seattle. Each time they came they'd arrive with bundles of cash strapped to their bodies. It was mine to spend (I don't imagine they didn't take their own percentage for their services), but my father's instructions were to spend it on property or investments in US technology stocks, which I did. I'm lucky, I'm financially stable. Oh, and before you doubt me – have to let you know, I'm gay. This really isn't a come on, I promise.

McKenzie combs through the words, trying to understand what links her to this man, who comes from Latin America and lives in Seattle. Córdoba is in the north-west of Argentina. She zooms in on it, an unremarkable town surrounded by industrial parks that give way to a patchwork of green-and-brown fields. Then, dragging the map, she tracks her way across half of

Argentina, going very slowly, searching for something, any clue in the lonely Andean mountains near Mendoza where Newt's parents live. Nothing in the long tracts of mountain and greenery draw her or give any clue to hang on to.

– *The money stopped arriving in 2009. My parents kept writing, but they never attempted to visit. When I went back to visit them in Mendoza, I found they had changed totally. My mother had lost a lot of weight, but my father had become a hermit. He wouldn't sleep in the house any more, my mother said, and would only sleep in the car, wrapped in blankets, even when the temperature was below zero – as if he felt trapped when in the house. The first night I was there I walked into the living room and saw my parents asleep on the floor, wrapped in each other's arms. Weird though it was to see them on the floor, it made me happy to think that, in spite of everything, they still held each other like that. But then I heard a noise on the landing. My mother, my real mother, was standing at the head of the stairs looking down at me, wondering what had made me wake in the night. My father was still in the car. The parents on the floor were a hallucination.*

A light sweat has broken across McKenzie's face. She scrolls further down.

– *McKenzie, I'm a software engineer, except I'm not: I'm something more than that, and you are the first person I've encountered who I think might help me see whatever it is that's been evading me all these years. I'm a round peg in a square hole. Software-developing only sets me alight if I can use it for my art, and so far I haven't landed a job in one of the app developers – my work is usually in retail systems. I'm going mad.*

Look at my Insta page and you will be able to see from my work where my heart lies. And you will be able to see why your hashtag #dreamsofdesert made me follow you. Then I noticed you were on a Facebook feed and I watched it. What I saw blew my mind. I SAW YOUR LIZARD, MCKENZIE. I know you don't believe me, and I can't explain it myself, since no one else who watched that video saw it. BUT I DID. You have to believe me.

She types in the name 'Herrera' and within a few seconds comes up with Newt's father, who, as Newt says, was in the oil industry, then in the early part of the century disappeared from the scene. She taps in 'Newt Herrera' and 'Gaston Herrera' and comes up almost instantly with the software company in Seattle, and a picture of him in a surfer T, looking seriously into the camera.

She drags in a breath. She's seen him before – he has dark skin with a fine Roman nose. She *knows* him.

16

MORNING COMES, FAST and demanding, the sun white – ferocious as a quarried diamond. Within an hour it's frying the Shuck metal and popping sweat on Spider's back. After breakfast the common room empties, but Forlani sits there, disconsolate, and the Regyre fruit casts a long shadow across him. The shutters to the balconies are open – Amasha has arranged washed bed sheets to dry, draping them over the edge, secured in place by wooden pegs.

'What?'

Forlani shrugs. In front of him is a clear glass phial. 'Tita Lily. And I'm like so bugged about taking her with us today. I don't know for sure, but she could get sepsis: blood poisoning. She can't come with us – I need to get this into her somehow.'

'Can she swallow it?'

'I don't want to risk it. We need a proper syringe.'

'I've seen syringes around the place – nothing you'd want to use, though.'

'Right now I'd take anything I could get.' Forlani chews the side of his thumb. 'All I need is to make a hole into her vein. That's all I need to do.'

It's decided to leave Forlani with Tita Lily. Forlani takes her temperature three times and gives her a white satin eye-mask. She doesn't look good, she really doesn't, her breathing is shallow and her face is yellow. Spider's heart drops a little more.

The family get on the road, though Spider and Noor make excuses to stay behind – just for a short time without the kids, so they can inspect the damage made to the Shuck in the night. It's a windless day and, when Spider gets to the outside, he is gripped with the conviction that he can smell the Djinni here on the walls of the Shuck. He knows the places to grab onto, should Noor sway the ladder; knows the parts he can cling to.

'Noor,' he yells. 'Send me up some of those nails we found in Casablanca? They're in the bottom box.'

'What about the rivets you've got? They not big enough?'

'No – I need bigger: fifteen centimetres.'

Noor – on the balcony twenty metres above Spider – doesn't argue or question him. He winds up the basket and goes inside to hunt out the nails, leaving Spider in the harness that dangles from the balcony.

When Noor is gone, Spider watches the space for a moment. What is it about Noor that bothers him? The way he pointed the arrow, as if he's been imagining pointing it at Spider forever, and the way he locked Nergüi out of the tower that night. Something will come for Noor. Spider is sure of it.

He sighs and turns to look at the bright-blue stretches of sky; at the line in the sand where the Djinni were last night, and the line of footsteps left by the family heading eastwards – tiny little dots. He turns his back on the desert and runs his hand over the surface of the Shuck.

One of the Djinni hung here for more than a second, right here. The gouge in the metal ends in a hole about two centimetres wide, through which he can see the polythene coverings across Madeira's plants. The rivets and the epoxy he's mixed up will fix a big enough plate across this, and then he will do the same on the inside, but he wants to know something first.

'Here,' Noor calls, lowering the bucket hand over hand. 'Got it?'

When Noor has gone to the inside of the tower, Spider pulls out a nail from the basket. He holds it up to the groove, rejects it and chooses another one, which he tries against the groove again. He goes through eight before he finds one that is short and fat, which seems to be about the right size.

These are soft clout-head nails, maybe meant for floorboards or horses' hooves, and when he places it over the handle of a saw and uses a mallet, it bends easily with a small amount of hammering. He holds it up to the light. A short, fat claw-shape. Then he inserts it into the hole. It fits perfectly.

'Hey.' Noor appears inside the tower, his breath sharp with anxiety. It's evident he doesn't feel comfortable this high in the air. 'What am I doing?'

'Double plates – I'll push the bolts through, you tighten the thread on them. Then we'll reverse it.'

The job is a long one, as two large sheets of metal are riveted, then epoxied onto the side of the Shuck. Afterwards they wash and change, and load water onto Camel's back. Spider finishes adjusting Camel's halter and leads her to the tower door. While Noor secures the door, Spider takes a short time to look at the scuffle marks from last night. The sand today is dry and powdery; it doesn't hold impressions.

'See anything?'

'No.' Spider kicks around a little longer, wondering if he'll see a human footprint, or a print from something unrecognisable, but there is nothing, so eventually they set off across the desert – forcing themselves not to look back at the Shuck.

'Can you smell that?' Noor asks as they approach Dubai.

'Yes. Been smelling it for the last half hour.'

'Where do you think it's coming from?'

Spider shrugs. 'The city?'

'You ever smelled a city that bad before? Dubai is clean, man – cleaner than Paris, cleaner than New York.' Noor sighs. 'There used to be magnificent lakes in Dubai, fountains that could dance to music. I stood right there in the centre and watched it as the evening drew in.'

They walk on, awed by the size of the city. Glittering buildings rise high above the biggest dune they've encountered – a city-sized drift of sand reaching to the waist of the buildings, studded with coiling towers, anvil-shaped skyscrapers. The Burj

Al Arab is the first place they wander past – even abandoned, it presides over the desert like a ship in full sail, pointing proudly into the skeletal landscape. It is up to its girth in sand, but its majesty is undiminished.

Noor is disturbed – the place is parched and desiccated beyond what he recognises. Every window they pass shows glimpses into a once-lavish lifestyle, smoked mirrors, silk curtains destroyed by the sunlight, carved onyx and marble fixtures. The balconies have wind-dulled chandeliers and expensive gold-leafed furniture – an elaborate but dry fountain in one, nymphs pouring empty amphorae.

They climb up the dune, which is steep and relentless; they cover their faces with their keffiyehs against the smell, stopping from time to time to hand the gourd of drinking water back and forth between the pair of them. They come to a javelin – Hugo's – then after a few more metres another – Madeira's. Habits die hard, even in new cities. The trail leads on, always climbing, up and up towards a leviathan of a building: like nothing Spider has ever seen.

'Well,' says Noor, wiping his face with a cloth and peering up at the building, 'here we are. The tallest building in Dubai, the Burj Khalifa. Though it's not as tall as I recall it.' He stamps his foot on the sand. 'Must be eighty or ninety storeys buried under this.'

Spider feels dwarfed by the place, which blocks out the sun and gives a chill to the air. They approach the windows at the new ground level – they are smashed, and sand has drifted in here too, covering the floor and the tattered furnishings. Maybe the sunset is creeping through a far corridor from the other side of the building.

Sitting on the sand, inside the nearest window, is a small, dark figure. Cigar smoke looms above her.

'Madeira?'

She looks up, sullen. She has her hands on her ankles and her face is like thunder. She takes out the cigar and clicks her tongue dismissively. '*Ça va*, my friend? Are you here to join the party?'

'What party?'

'The celebrations at the new Shuck – our new crib.' She flicks an angry finger to the ceiling. 'Apparently. They've decided we're going to make our home right here in Dubai, though how the hell we're going to transport Tita Lily is anybody's guess.'

Spider licks his hands and uses them to half clean his face. He's desert-weary and probably disgusting. He climbs through the window and sits next to Madeira, puts an arm around her, which on this occasion she allows – just the briefest flare of her nostrils, like a thoroughbred horse, to warn him that she's not a pushover.

'We did talk about it,' he says. 'It's difficult, I know, but there's no rule that says we can't live in the cities. The Shuck in Mithi?'

'Yeah – and remember what happened to them?'

'Maybe the same as is happening to us?'

She ignores him, turns her beautiful carved face to the winds and the distant Shuck they've come from.

'I think everything that you've done could be brought out here, if here is the right place.' He rubs his face again. 'But what's the smell all about?'

'Elk and Hugo think it's the dead creatures in the aquariums. The place is littered with them. And everything is dead. Stinking.'

Noor comes in, glancing around. He looks at Spider and Madeira, then across the room. Spider follows his gaze and realises someone else has been in the room all along. Hugo, his back to them, arms crossed, is staring at a painting above a sofa of a Bedouin woman who is wrapped in a cloak that blows in the wind.

'Hey,' Noor says, but Hugo doesn't turn. In his faded blue Oxford shirt, his cream linen jacket, he's always given the impression of a man who would be at home guiding a punt along one of England's tranquil rivers, ducking to pass under willow trees; someone so ill at ease with what he's become in the Cirque, where he carries dunny-pots and sleeps rough on the sand with nine other sweaty humans.

'Hugo?'

He turns, only his head, slightly imperious. Looks the two men up and down. Defeated, but determined to keep his poise.

'You'll find a shelter on the one-hundred-and-tenth floor, which is only thirty floors above this. The sand took the other eighty floors. You'll understand if I don't come with you?'

Spider gets to his feet, flattens down his dress with his palms. He puts his hand on Madeira's head. The heat coming through her hair is enormous – she's holding so much in that pressure-cooker head of hers.

'Can I leave Camel with you?'

She rolls her head back, looks up at him and lets a breath out from her nostrils. 'Sure. I'd like to think I have some purpose in this new world we're creating.'

He massages her head, careful not to make her uncomfortable – she is his sister – then plants a kiss on it. He turns and levers himself back outside, where Camel stands. 'Come on, girl – you're looking shit, you know, like you just woke up. You gotta drink something and eat, and then I'm going to be back.'

He leads her to the window and drapes her leads down to a place where Madeira can hold them. He unhooks the water gourds and hands them through. 'Water for her – make sure, huh?'

Madeira scrambles to her feet, glad to be doing something. 'Yeah, sure. I've got it.'

McKenzie can't explain Newt Herrera to India, partly because she can't explain him to herself and partly because she knows the answer she'll get: *he's a perv, a troll and bitch, haven't you learned a single solitary thing from those online-safety talks at school? He is literally everything they're warning us about.*

And so McKenzie is left in private with her thoughts about Newt Herrera, day after day, as outside the winter gets colder and spikier. She won't close the windows, she needs the cold and the air to keep her alert. The lengths of snow between the houses seem to stretch and thicken until it's impossible to remember what the ground of the back gardens looks like. The deck has four inches of white on the side rails, and the twin potted shrubs that stand outside the neighbour's front door have been swathed in blue plastic to protect them from the frost.

Newt Herrera's story all adds up, he seems to be who he says he is and while, yes, she can grasp the concept of relating on a deep non-verbal level to people around her, she can't understand connecting to a man she's never met. Unless they have met. He is familiar. Has Newt also been exposed to it – to something in his dad's job?

The snow days at Harbinson evolve into a snow week. India is at the house every day, and Mom and Dad have again met with the school principal. One more session with Dr Shreve, a meeting with the principal, and McKenzie will be signed back on at school. 'It's a miracle,' Mom says. 'You didn't miss *anything* – it's been just snow, snow, snow. They're going to have to make up the days at the end of the semester, I guess.'

The day before the meeting with the school principal, McKenzie wakes from her sleep in the afternoon, all the hairs on the back of her neck standing up. She blinks, listens to the house, keeping her breathing very steady. The world is going on inside the house, the old boiler firing up, squirrels scampering in the branches overhead, acorns dropping off the trees and hitting the snow on the roof in distinct muffled thuds. She looks out of the window and sees a woman staring at her from the branches of a nearby tree.

McKenzie jolts backwards on the bed. The woman has dark eyes and is wearing a scarlet sari. She blinks in the snowflakes.

'*Who are you … ?*' McKenzie stammers. '*No! Please, go away.*' She blinks, rubs her eyes and opens them, but the woman is still there, smiling bemusedly, peering at McKenzie.

'It's you …' the woman says. 'It's you, and you've spoken to Newt already, haven't you?'

'*Go away. I'm calling my parents.*'

'Tell Newt about the desert, the Shuck.'

'*What? Who are you?*'

McKenzie jumps out of bed, runs to the door and throws it open. But something stops her. She stands, frozen like a scarecrow, one hand to her face, the other extended, caught between opening the door and going back to the window. Her heart is thumping, the blood thick in her head.

'Mom,' she screams. 'MOM!'

'Kenz?' comes Mom's voice from two floors below. 'You OK?'

McKenzie swallows, licks her lips. And then, hardly breathing, she tiptoes back into the bedroom, leans on the bed and looks up at the window.

The tree is empty.

'Kenz? Wassup?' Mom calls from the kitchen.

She takes six deep breaths, straight from her diaphragm.

'Kenz, what the hell?'

'Nothing, Mom. Just, uh – wondering what's for dinner.'

She hears Mom's exasperation. 'You yell at me like that cos you want to know what's for dinner?'

'I'm sorry. I'll text next time.'

A door slams – Mom furious. McKenzie sits on her bed, trembling, fishing her phone out from under the pillow. There's a note from Newt.

– It's happened again. I've seen a ghost.

She scrunches up her face. Then she pulls on a gown and slippers and crawls out onto the roof, where it's snowing. She hits FaceTime and calls him, her fingers shaking. The screen is dark for a while, her own face barely visible, the FaceTime camera icon flashing, then the screen fills blindingly with light. In Seattle it's nearly lunchtime, and her first impression is of a glorious orange sun through an open window. A white room, not much furniture, and in the centre of the screen: Newt – coffee-coloured skin and extraordinarily dark hair in tight curls.

He isn't the way she pictured him; she's imagined someone serious and intense. But his face is lively, sensitive, with kind, mocha-brown eyes.

'McKenzie? Are you there?' His voice is high-pitched, with a slight South American accent. 'Hello?'

She keeps her hand over the phone lens. 'What ghost, Newt? What did you see?'

'I saw a guy outside my window,' he says, speaking rapidly as if he knows she might hang up at any second. 'Just now. An old guy, grey hair, sitting in the branches of a tree.'

'No, no,' she pleads. 'No. How the hell do you—'

'He said he knew we were in touch – that we needed to meet. He said to tell you about the desert, the Shuck, whatever the hell that is. He said you'd know what that meant.'

'*No – you can't be telling me this …*'

'All I'm doing is telling you the truth. I'm like … McKenzie – I can't explain it to you, but I do know this thing is bigger than both of us.'

She bites her knuckles, panting.

'McKenzie? Are you going to let me see you?'

She wipes her nose, trembling, and eventually takes her hand off the lens and lifts up the camera, in spite of the fact that she's bleary and dirty and crumpled from sleep. She squashes herself back up against the chimney, as if by making herself small she'll protect herself from the thing she can't explain.

Newt peers into the camera lens. Up close, his eyes have amber striations jetting through the brown. 'Where are you? Are you on a roof?'

'Yeah. I guess.'

'It's snowing.' He smiles, and it's the easiest, most natural smile she's seen. Not a winter smile, but a summer smile, full of sun and wide places. 'Sunny here; I'm in my office.'

She nods, taking long, calming breaths. 'I know you,' she breathes when she has control of her voice. 'I've met you before.'

'Yes. I know you too.' His curious smile fades and he nods seriously, almost sadly, as if he's deeply troubled. 'The moment I saw you at the Science Fair I knew I'd met you before. Hold, will you? I'm taking you out of the office, can't do this here.'

'Sure.'

She waits while he walks fast down the sunny steps of a giant office block. She can sense the grace that he moves with – a natural sway – and now she can see he's wearing a black T-shirt with words she doesn't understand: *The Modems Number-One Hit: beee-boooop-shhhh-kaching-kaching-kaching*.

She relaxes her shoulders and sits forward, resting the phone on her knees so that she can look at him more carefully. His movements are fluid and beautiful. 'You believe me, don't you?' he asks. 'You believe we've met before?'

'I don't know what to think, what to do.'

'That's OK. Because I know what to do. I've had longer to think about it.' He pauses at a busy crossing, looking around him. 'I'm going to find somewhere quiet to do this. Bear with me.'

He walks for a few minutes without finishing the call. She can see pavements and people's feet, in Skechers and Nike shoes, some open-toed sandals. It's so warm there. All that way up in the far corner of the country she expected snow, but on an autumn day they're all in sandals. She can almost taste the sunny air, like sherbet melting on her tongue.

When Newt stops walking and rights the phone, he's in a garden full of vibrant jewel colours. Huge poker-straight tubes in the deepest blue, turquoise balls as big as giant pumpkins. It takes her a moment to realise they're glass sculptures.

'Like it?' he says, settling on a bench where a glass tree like an anemone extends orange-and-red tentacles above his head. 'It's by Chihuly – a glass sculptor. My favourite place in this town. And that blue? It's Berber blue, the purest blue you'll ever see. I'd like my hair done that colour, if my parents weren't so conservative.'

'You know about the Berbers? I thought I was the only geek who knew about the Berbers.'

'I told you – we've never met, there's nothing to connect us in our pasts, and yet …' He shrugs. Opens his hands as if to say he's out of explanations. 'I feel it every second of every day – like my body is here, in this city, but the real me is in another place entirely.'

'Like your posts on the 'gram?'

He nods. 'There's a shape I'm plagued with – I have been since I was little. It's in some of the drawings, a shape I can't explain. I drew that when I was ten. I drew it over and over until my father forbade me to draw it again. It made my parents nuts that I couldn't forget it.'

'I saw it. I have an image too – of a storm. That drives my parents crazy too. I don't know where I got it from, either.'

They regard each other in silence for a long time. The snow gets thicker, the lantern on the garage comes on, its dim spectral glow uplighting the swirling flakes.

Newt says, softly, 'All I know is that you, somehow, are the key to it.' He is silent for a while, regarding her. Then he draws the phone closer to his face and says, in a low, confidential voice, 'When you fall asleep you smell rust. You're constantly thirsty, aren't you?'

She nods mutely.

'You see sand where there should be none, you dream of living in a desert, but you don't know why.'

A tear gathers and spills out of McKenzie's right eye, runs down her face into her mouth.

'You're crying, McKenzie, because you're feeling everything I've been feeling since the moment I heard your name, since the moment I read your Insta feed. The only sense I can make of it is what I said in my messages: limbic resonance.'

She shakes her head fiercely and sucks back the tears. 'No.'

'Why not? There's no other explanation.'

'I looked it up, it's feasible for some situations, but not for what's happening here. It can't make any sense for people who've never met.' She pauses, then says tentatively, 'I'm sorry – I'm a nerd, I should have warned you. And I've got another idea.'

'What?'

'But I don't want to talk about it – not yet. I don't know if I can trust you.'

Newt is silent. A cloud crosses the sky and muddies the reflections on the glass sculptures behind him. He puts his finger to his lips, lowers his eyes as if he's looking at the floor and murmurs, 'We need to meet.. Conversations like this can be listened to.'

'I can't meet you – I …'

'Yes, you can. We've got to meet. You know it; you know it's true.' He glances up at the screen, his eyes narrow and tense. 'If you don't come and meet me, I'll come and find you.'

Startled, McKenzie hits the red button and sits back, banging her head on the chimney in her shock. She turns the phone face down on her knee and breathes for a while, trying to calm herself.

If she's scared of anything, she realises, it isn't this stranger from Argentina appearing on the doorstep. No, what she's scared of – *really* scared of – is just how much she wants to meet him.

17

SPIDER AND NOOR pick their way through the stifling-hot apartment, pushing through the vestiges of forgotten luxury. The walls are of silk, dotted with a delicate bamboo motif, and the furniture is of the finest polished teak. It's easy to imagine the champagne opened here, the cigars smoked, the women and the camel-racing parties.

They reach a wedged-open door that leads to a vast marble atrium. To their left is a bank of lift doors, beyond them two more doors to residences, to their right a stairwell, all festooned in sand and debris. Here they discover a sweets machine, lights on. Spider cracks the glass and for a while they both gorge on Reese's peanut-butter cups and Snickers bars.

After eating his fill, Spider shoves more sweets into his kit. He leans back and lets out a puff of air. Sugar must be a drug of some sort, he thinks, because his unaccustomed heart is racing a million beats a second.

Noor is licking the inside of a Butterfinger wrapper, slowly and lovingly as if it is manna from heaven and needs to be worshipped. Behind them comes the sound of voices; they turn and see Amasha and Elk emerging from the apartment where Madeira and Hugo are. Amasha has sweated so much that her sari is clinging to her body, there are unflattering marks around her crotch and under her breasts, but she's smiling broadly, beaming at everyone.

'What happened?'

'Oh, very little,' she says lightly, though the delighted, complacent spark in her eye says something different. 'We spoke.'

Both Noor and Spider turn and stare.

'Have they found anything?' Spider asks.

'I think they must have. We only need to make sense of it. And I don't want you saying a word to the children, not yet.' She sighs, looks up the stairs. 'Let's hope Tita Lily won't succumb – we have to find a syringe – we have to find the medical rooms here.'

Spider begins to follow the Futatsu up the stairs, counting the flights as they go, nosing into every apartment to find a clinician's practice. No joy. The 107th floor has a different feel to it – there are vast screens above the lifts, and a security desk with an array of screens and phones. Only one door leads off this lobby – and when Spider taps on it, it's clearly reinforced steel.

Mahmoud opens the door to them; it is heavy, thick as an encyclopaedia, and opens into a marble-floored vestibule with a private lift. The main room is enormous – sofas sweep in a curve around the dark rosewood walls, now dried and cracking in the heat – and everywhere are dotted little cup-seats, placed to enjoy the view. Food is already laid out: cheeses and smoked meat in grease-stained paper, ready to be cooked, while someone has used stripped wood from the walls to create a makeshift fire in the centre of the marble floor.

Cairo, Mahmoud and Splendour are on the floor, drinking yerba in gold-leafed mugs.

'Here, kids. Sweets.' Spider throws them a few bars of chocolate. They fall on them, grinning – glancing at Amasha, who wags her finger.

'Not too much, kids. Not too much.'

The windows are all intact, and Elk goes to the far end of the room, which stretches maybe thirty metres from the central axis to the back of the building. He stands for a bit, staring out of the window at the sunset. It's the first time Spider has seen what lies beyond Dubai and, when he realises what he's seeing, he's momentarily stunned.

'Is that what I think it is?' he says, throwing down his kit and going to Elk. 'Has that been there all this time?'

Elk nods, half amused. 'This city has some secrets it's been keeping from us.'

Spider put his palms on the window and presses his nose to it. Below them the long shadow of the Burj extends across the city, its tip reaching out to the desert itself, and beyond it an entirely new section of the desert has opened up. A vista with far-off cities, dunes and mountains. The late sun dips behind the mountains.

They all gather next to the pair. Maybe twenty clicks away, a city is splayed like an ornate cloth over a hill, its low crenellations catching the evening rays, almost as if it's trembling.

'I recognise that place,' murmurs Noor. 'It's Astana. See the golden mosque domes?' He shakes his head, awed. 'So beautiful, so affluent.'

They all squint, or raise binoculars, and see sun glinting on the low gold curves. There are large cranes too, spidering up above the horizon. 'Astana?'

'In Kazakhstan. My father worked on a trade treaty there – something about oil.'

Amasha is suddenly all business. 'Could we get from here to those cities and back in two days?'

'I'm sure,' Noor says. 'That's what? Thirty, forty clicks? We could visit more than one – easy if the weather works for us. Wind speeds, et cetera.'

Spider stays for a while, looking out of the window. He gets his portion of pineapple and yerba-maté and carries it around the apartment, through a kitchen area the size of a squash court with a curved staircase leading up to another floor. Beyond the kitchen is another room, a bedroom, which faces back the way that he and Noor have just come. He stands at the window. Below them Dubai is spread out. Long rows of glinting, twisting skyscrapers, like fingers sticking out of the sand. At the foot of the sand dune he can see the shoreline, with remnants of strange shapes, and beyond it the place Spider now calls the Chicane city.

Does this new discovery mean he gives up his dream of getting there? The cities to the east are too compelling to convince the others to go north. He gets out his binoculars and focuses them on the Chicane; it is subtly different from this angle. He can see the flank of one mountain, greener and lusher than it looks from their own Shuck. In front of it there is the lump that he's been able to see from their Shuck.

He twists the focus setting on his binoculars and sees that it's a tower, exactly like their own. Maybe the same height. Except there appears to be a ring of something around it, a series of … what? Figures? It can't be. They are standing absolutely still, as if praying.

'Look at this.' Elk wanders in and stands next to the bed, which is high on a platform. 'Have you ever seen anything like this?'

He twists and throws himself backwards onto the bed. The mattress is still firm and it bounces him a couple of times before he comes to rest. He stares up at the ceiling.

'Shit! It's the old farmer himself.'

Spider looks up and sees the ceiling is mirrored. Elk, gazing up at his own reflection, is surprised to see this stranger that he has become, over the months in the Cirque.

'He doesn't look the way I remember him, back in the day.' Elk makes faces at himself, stretching his mouth in a grin, pulling his eyebrows into a frown. Then he waves his arms up and down, like a bird on its back trying to take flight. Eventually, bored with his own reflection, he sighs and runs his hands over the satiny blue bedcover. 'They must have had fun in here, eh?'

'Yes,' Spider says vacantly. 'I imagine so.'

Elk's face is suddenly contemplative. 'You know, wallah, it gets to me sometimes. Missing my wife. We weren't soulmates, of course I know that now, but still. The touch of a woman. There's nothing can top it. I liked my women proper women – none of this skinny-as-a-strip-of-biltong stuff for me; I liked them big and properly built.' He holds out his hands to mimic breasts. 'Liked to know it was a woman on top of me, or under me, and not a thirteen-year-old boy.'

Spider's mind slides instantly to the women he's known. In Paris he had an allure that fetched him girls by the dozen, like fishing in virgin waters, putting a basket in and having the cod jump into it. It makes him sad and achy to recall it all.

He glances up at the mirror, sees his own reflection – thinner and more muscular then he recalls. And that fighter's face.

'Amasha.' Elk drops his hands over his face. He shakes his head. 'She's a beauty, my kind of beauty. Just spend one second looking at her, *one second.* That woman has it all going on – she's an eleven out of ten. But the rules here are different, we all know that. Now, you go eat.'

Spider does as he's told, putting back the binoculars and going to the main room to drink and eat. The sunset continues, fanning up above the new mountains. He wants to like this place – he really wants to. It makes all the sense in the world. But something … something's not right.

Hugo and Madeira appear eventually. Madeira sits in silence, picking at her food, but Hugo won't join them to eat. He walks back and forth, scratching his head. 'Right,' he says. 'If you're serious about this, we've got to find water.'

Everyone looks up. 'Water?'

'Yes – the most important thing.'

'Shouldn't we make sure the place has no – uh – *vulnerabilities*,' Spider says, choosing his words carefully because the children are here.

'It hasn't,' Madeira says. 'Look at the glass. Not cracked.'

Spider gets up and goes to it, touching it. He puts his head on one side and, where the sunrays are lancing up at it, he can see the thickness of it. And further over, near the edges, there is a spidering that has only affected the outside. 'It's bulletproof,' he murmurs. 'And how! There must be six or seven layers.'

'Bulletproof? This high up?'

'The sheikhs all used to go around in helicopters – even if they can't fly the damned things.' Noor gets up and comes to the window, running his fingers across it. 'You'd be surprised how common it is. My father could spot bulletproof glass two kilometres away – I guess that's what a job in the diplomatic corps does for you.'

Spider goes to the far corner, where no one will see what he's doing, and pulls from his belt the nail he fashioned earlier. Keeping his back to the family to cover what he's up to, he digs the claw shape at the glass. The tops layer nicks slightly, but even when he does it harder, the first layer of glass doesn't shatter.

'What you doing, Spider?' Splendour asks. 'Whassat?'

He puts it back in his belt, turns and smiles at her. 'It's as tough as old boots, this glass. Great.'

'Right, listen up.' Elk immediately takes control. 'We need to check the floors above and below, the lift shafts, the windows two floors above and below. The door is strong enough and the glass, but that doesn't mean anything. So, kids, you stay here and you wash up – OK? Get the beds ready; the grown-ups are going to check the place is weathertight.'

'Weathertight?' Cairo asks suspiciously. 'Why's that important?'

'We're going to make it our new home and don't want the weather getting in.'

'Is that all you're checking for?'

'Course it is. What's this – interrogation, now?'

The adults spread out around the building. Noor and Spider go together to check the lift shaft. 'The boy's a friggin' nightmare,' Noor says.

'Not just him – Splendour too. They're starting to catch on to things. They saw the hole in the tower this morning, I'm half certain they did.'

'Young minds: too damned enquiring for their own good.'

Spider rams a chisel into the lift doors and together the men prise them open. It's not the polished steel of a lift interior that they were hoping for, but the oily black cables of the lift shaft. They lean in and peer down.

The shaft is black and impenetrable, the smell overwhelming. Spider covers his face. 'It's a sewer line to hell. The others think it's dead animals in the aquariums.'

He uses the small torch that Elk has lent him, but it's no match for the big torch back at the Shuck and can't illuminate much more than the sides of the shaft. He turns it up and sees the hydraulic cylinders, and under the concrete ceiling the flat metal casing of the system and the motor. He shines the light around very carefully.

Noor takes the torch and does the same inspection. 'Yeah. But what about down? I can't see a thing.'

Spider leans in and inspects the sides of the shaft. Below the pulley wires there is a girder holding in the lift casing that runs round the shaft. He tests it – it's strong – and about four centimetres below it is another similar one. He'll have to crouch, but it'll take his weight.

'What're you doing?' Noor is alarmed when Spider swings himself out over the chasm. 'You insane?'

'No – I wanna test that pulley.'

'Jesus shit!' Noor rubs a hand over his face, screws up his eyes. 'Sure, I will.'

Spider gets to the pulley, knowing he'll have to cling tightly. He doesn't trust Noor. It is filthy in here, black with grease, and the smell is making him gag. He gives the pulley a yank – nothing happens. These things are counterweighted, he's sure, and a small pull should at least show some give.

'What's happening?'

'It's seized up, I think. Rusted probably – the axle grease dried out.' He peers down into the gloom. The lift could be at the bottom of the building, 107 floors down, buried in the sand. He makes his way back to Noor and stands, wiping the sweat from his face. 'There's gotta be a service hatch somewhere.'

'The place is built in tiers, like a wedding cake – maybe lower there are service areas for the lifts.'

They go down the stairs, past the two floors where Madeira and Amasha are inspecting the ceilings and the walls of the apartments below. Amasha calls to Noor, 'All good. The ceilings are solid concrete. Steel girders.'

Spider follows Noor down the stairs, both of them holding the handrail because the sand has blown in unpredictable patterns – on some floors there is none, on others the floor is invisible, like walking the desert itself. They get glimpses of the darkening sky through some open apartment windows, but then they go down below the place where they entered. Now there is no sky visible out of the window, as they are below the sand, moving down the hollow core.

'The smell,' Noor says. 'It's worse here.'

'Tell me about it.'

'Need to figure that out before we move here. And, hey, this isn't creepy as fuck.'

He moves more slowly, making sure he's shone the torch into every cranny, every corner, before he goes on. Eventually they arrive at a place where the hallway is different – Noor studies the wall, damp and derelict. Where there had been three doors opening away to three parts of the building, which must have a trefoil footprint, now there are four doors in two of the wings.

Noor lets the torch linger on the door, which has warning signs in English and Arabic. 'What do you think?'

Spider tries the door. It opens easily and, when he pushes it open, an automatic fluorescent light comes on overhead. The two men look up, surprised. Electric light is random in the Cirque – but it happens from time to time.

This is a maintenance area. Overhead are fat air ducts, covered in galvanised spiralled zinc, pipes meandering; and electronic circuit boards, rows of red and black levers, all the monitor lights dead. There is a door on the wall adjacent to the lift shaft. Spider goes to it and, when he puts a foot on it, it creaks open.

'OK?' Noor asks, his voice thick. 'What's in there?'

Spider takes the light and shines it inside. There is a safety cage and a bank of lift shafts 'Six – no, eight shafts.'

Noor steps inside, looks up and down the shafts. Here the lifts travel through a communal space, but on the floor above and below they are sectioned by steel separators. Spider's light picks out one or two lifts below, two above, an array of counter-weights and pistons. Five of the shafts seem empty; the cab must be so high or so low that all Spider can see is impenetrable gloom above and below – no beginning, no end.

'The smell,' Noor mutters. 'Like it's coming from down there.'

They are silent for a while, while Spider has his back to the wall. He knows Noor. Eventually Spider crawls out along the girder, making sure Noor is in a place where he can't push him.

'Jesus, I thought I told you not to do that.'

'Shhhh.' He gets to a place where he can angle the light down-wards. Again, the torch isn't strong, but he thinks he can make out a pale blob of light, an object paler than the rest of the shaft. Spider leans further into the shaft. He can hear something coming from down there, a snuffling or a snoring?

'What is it?'

'I don't know.'

Spider crawls out and stands for a while, peering back down. He doesn't like this place. He really doesn't like it. He shines the torch to the side, trying to decide which shaft leads to their apartment. He sees now that four lifts at the two far ends of the bank are slightly narrower. 'Those must be the private lifts – they're smaller. Where are we on the floorplan?'

'This is the end the apartment's on,' Noor says.

They go to the side that is near the centre of the core, which corresponds with the place where the lift enters the apartment above. When they shine the torches up, they see in both shafts the bottom of the lift cabs lodged about five storeys up. 'Dope,' Spider says. 'Good news. The cab to our apartment could've been on the ground floor – imagine trying to dislodge it from there? I mean, obviously it'd be better if it was in our apartment. But this at least may be doable.'

'You just tried.'

'Yeah – the counterweight has seized up, that's all. There's a spare rope ladder at the Shuck, and some proper axle grease: remember that tractor in Casablanca? When we come back I'll get down there, grease it up and raise the lift cab. It'll plug the shaft perfectly.'

Noor is silent for a while, maybe trying to get a perspective on how many floors are below them. In the end he gives up and spits down into an empty shaft. It feels like an act of defiance. 'This is sketchy as shit. Let's find the others.'

Elk and Hugo have been into the apartment above theirs and the glass is bulletproof there too – not compromised – while in the lower apartment one of the windows is broken, but on further inspection they realise the glass there too is bulletproof, but not as high-grade as further up the building. The men think they can use the steel mesh of the kitchen panelling to shore up the windows – it's an extra security measure, but it will make them feel safer.

Everyone looks at Spider. He puts his head back and breathes in through his nose, choosing his words carefully. 'Yes,' he says eventually. 'I suggested we move to another Shuck because I believe it's the only way to keep us safe. Do I think this is the correct place to start?' He opens his eyes and lets them rove to the stars above the mountains in the east. He thinks about the snuffling noises in the lift shaft. 'I don't know.'

Cairo lets out a barely concealed snort of derision. 'Because it's not near the Chicane. And we all know that's where you want to go next.'

Elk breaks away from the group. From somewhere he's found a telescope. He lifts it to his eye, though Spider reasons that it must be fairly useless as a viewing device and is more of a prop. Everyone watches Elk sweep it around the horizon at the cities. He says, 'We split into parties for the night. We do a sweep for the Sarkpont, and we watch for water too. Tonight we won't sleep: we will spend the night searching. If we see a syringe too …'

The family are arranged on the decaying couches of the sky lobby, all tired. Amasha is anxious about Tita Lily and Forlani, and the idea of spending more time in the skyscrapers, picking their way through the discarded corpses of the old city, is getting to her. But she says nothing and eventually they all begin to move, collecting up plates and backpacks.

Elk pairs himself with Spider and they go to the ground level. Spider attaches one or two useful oddments that he's found to Camel's *mahawi* and they fill their water gourds from the containers, then head into the dark. From one or two windows electric lights flicker – a chrome-and-glass kitchen blazes on the fifth floor of a small block nearby, and if a well-dressed woman walked in, carrying a glass of wine and a plate of canapés, it wouldn't seem out of place.

They begin to walk the streets, aimlessly, going into the buildings that are accessible and searching for swimming pools, fountains – the array of water features that, according to Noor and Hugo, made Dubai so spectacular. But the city seems dry; drier, in fact, than any place they've been before.

They go into a building that looks from a distance like a giant gold armadillo shell, but turns out instead to be a subway station, with banks of lifts, walkway tubes criss-crossing in every direction and vast glass pendant lights hanging from the ceiling like clumps of sandy stalactites. There aren't even cacti here, and the stinking air is dry in Spider's throat. But he doesn't say anything to Elk, who seems to want to keep drawing attention to the eastern mountains beyond the city – as if to make a point about the breadth of opportunities that Dubai has opened up to the Dormilones.

They pass the rusting turnstiles of a water park, derelict, no water, the glass windows now fogged and dirty – and rising above it, a stepped, geometric tower of fibreglass fashioned to resemble stone blocks like an Aztec temple. There are cracked white rapids tubes sweeping from it. Spider kicks a tube once: its Plexiglas is clouded, scratched by sandstorms, but he gets a whiff of decay and, when he trains his light on it, he sees there are marine creatures piled in the sand, decomposing: sharks and dolphins, moray eels with their saw-like double jaws, skeletonised, slimed, upside down, curled over, pressed against each other, rotting into a soup in the oven-like heat.

Spider wipes his forehead on his petticoat, straightens and stares out at the city. Really, he thinks, is this making the smell that permeates so far? 'It's not the same smell as in the lift shaft.'

'These fancy hotels, they have aquariums all over the place. The lobby, the restaurants.'

Spider is silent for a few moments, thinking about it. Then he lifts up his pack and straps it on his back.

He goes into the medical centres in all the hotels and finds nothing, except, inexplicably, a TV playing. An endless loop of a man twirling the tassel on his fez in time to music from a *hajhuj*. Spider searches around the back of the TV for a lead and pulls it out. Elk laughs and does an impression of the man, whipping his crooked head round gleefully.

'You know,' Elk ruminates later, scratching his head, 'this place is such a labyrinth, we'll never find the Sarkpont here. So I command you – as Futatsu – to go off.'

'Go off where?'

He laughed. 'Come on, my boy. The place you're so interested in.'

18

THAT NIGHT MCKENZIE doesn't take her pill – instead she crushes it up and drops it in the toilet bowl, then lies awake most of the night, looking at the pictures on Newt's Instagram account, thinking about how he said he doesn't belong in his body. That he's been plagued by an image: the strange shape like the devil's trident turned on its side. Plagued and unnerved in the way she has been by the image of the microburst above Phoenix.

The next day Mom, tight-lipped, drives her to the principal's office. The school is still closed and it's so weird to walk the echoey corridors without hundreds of other pupils there. There's a faint smell of burnt food in the air.

'I need a commitment from you,' the principal says. He has very white implanted teeth, the gums drawing back to show something dark silver at the root, and a thatch of blonde hair that doesn't look real, as if it might slip at any moment and reveal the bald person underneath it. 'A commitment that no matter how hard you are pushed, you won't take the law into your own hands.'

'I promise.'

'And how are you doing on that new medication you're taking?'

'I'm . . .' She hesitates, thinking of the grains in the toilet bowl. 'A little drowsy sometimes. But it seems to be working.'

He tilts the chair forward. 'I'm speaking to your therapist later today – she's going to give me an update on your condition, and we are confident she'll confirm that you're fit to come back to school.'

Mom smiles. 'She's a good doctor, sir, really good. A colleague of my husband's, really "up there" in the medical profession.'

'Good. That's great to hear, it all sounds solid. So – tomorrow, McKenzie?'

She doesn't answer. She is staring at Mom. What did she just say? That Dr Shreve is a colleague of Dad's? Sprung free from the Seroquel fog, her mind goes into overdrive. A colleague of Dad's means CIA, and maybe therefore part of the whole set-up.

'McKenzie?'

She snaps back into herself. 'Yes, sir,' she says, her thoughts burning. 'Yes, of course you can depend on me.'

'Very pleased to hear it, young lady. And any time you need to speak to me, feel free to come on right ahead and make an appointment.'

McKenzie leaves, feeling as if she's just carried a load up a mountain. There are still two hours before they need to leave for

DC, so she tells Mom she's going for a jog round Burke Lake, the man-made lake that is used as a running trail by all the DC professionals and the lines of Korean women in their white sun-visors.

It's midday, but the sky is overcast and in the half light the dirty snowdrifts among the trees seem to float a few feet off the ground, eerie like night-time clouds. McKenzie finds a little bench on a promontory overlooking the lake. The water is frozen in places, and below her feet icicles hang from exposed roots in a keyboard curve, like the sparkling white ribs of a dead creature.

She calls Newt, her fingers numb from the cold. He answers instantly. 'McKenzie. McKenzie.' He speaks breathlessly, as if she's rescued him from drowning – as if he'd only have lasted a few more seconds if she hadn't called. 'I thought you'd never call.'

'Newt. My God, Newt. I missed you.'

'I missed you too. Where are you?'

'I'm next to a lake. It's cold, but . . . Newt, I want to see you. I think we have to talk in person. But I don't know how. I can't let you come here. There's my parents – they'll think it's inappropriate, because you're older; and then there's school, and where would we—'

'McKenzie, calm down. It's OK. I'm not coming to Virginia.'

She pauses. 'You're not?'

'No, it's OK. I get it. I know it's threatening to you – I do understand.'

'Oh.' She should be relieved. Instead she's oddly deflated. 'OK.'

The ice on the lake is patchy. In places it has a grey rime, in other parts it is black and deadly clear, reflecting back the twilight sky. The snowstorm is coming. She doesn't think she can take another blizzard.

'Listen – I've got to tell you this and you're going to laugh, but look up CIA and FEMA.'

'I'm sorry?'

Shyly, ready to be laughed at, she tells Newt about the conspiracy theorists, the FEMA camps, about the silver salt lakes in the Nevada desert and the tests on humans they are performing. 'And though I know it's all crazies, still I wonder if I was exposed to *something* when I was a kid. See my dad is in … well, he's in government intelligence, and I feel like that's connected. Please look at the CIA FEMA stuff. Will you? I mean proper internment places. And I'm not wearing an aluminium helmet, I promise, and yes, I know it's all bullshit, I read Snopes, but regardless, whatever *is* happening, I feel like it has to be connected to that somehow.'

Newt's voice comes, calm and low, down the phone. 'I hear you. And I don't think you're insane – I think it must be one explanation.'

'I mean, your dad: he was shady, right; something weird happened to him?'

'Yeah, and how. Look, McKenzie, we need to think hard, because whatever is happening to us, we need to be efficient. I'm going to think the way I've been trained as a coder: to look at it in algorithms. And you? It's easier for you – you do what comes naturally and think like a scientist. There's a logic in all this.'

Her hands are cold and she can feel the tip of her toes getting red from the icy air, but Newt telling her she's a scientist – a real scientist – that she thinks like one naturally, has started a heat in her belly. She sits up, alert and engaged, her mind whirring.

'If we're going to meet, it has to be in a place that is relevant. Don't you think – haven't you been thinking, like me, for the last few days – that maybe we're both dreaming or hallucinating about a place that exists? The horned lizard, it only lives in the south-western states; don't you think there's a reason that's what you hallucinated, a reptile that only lives in one corner of the world?'

'I hadn't thought that. No.'

'Newt. Have you ever been to Phoenix?'

'Phoenix? Arizona? Nope – not even close.'

'Nevada?'

'No, but I've looked at it from the air – studied the lines in the sand – the driveways on the military installations, tried to make it look like the diagram I've been dreaming about.' Newt pauses, thinking. The signal fades in and out briefly, and far on the other side of the crystalline lake a bird screams. Then Newt says, 'OK, here's what we're going to do. We're going to have twenty-four hours thinking about this. Then we're going to meet – like you say, somewhere relevant.'

'How am I going to get there?'

'You can drive, can't you?'

She bites the cuticle of her thumb, thinking about how she drove Tatum's Subaru all the way to DC and survived. Is there any reason she can't drive out of state? She's got enough money for petrol – all those bank transfers from her friends for doing their homework. But it would take days: days and days.

From beyond the trees rises a thick arrow of Canada geese, their harsh cries threading out over the trees. As they fly over the lake their reflections shine back, but over the iced section they grow blurred.

Ice and salt, they are the same, she thinks. Nothing reflects clearly in them.

'OK,' she says getting up from the bench. 'OK. Twenty-four hours, then we speak.'

It is almost a full moon and the desert is lit an eerie blue. White nights are rarely as clear and beautiful as this. Other families must be out exploring too.

For Spider, the light is a mixed blessing. Though he can see where he is heading, he is also starkly visible to anyone else – heading straight out like an arrow from the sail hotel, not even backtracking to get Camel from where she is tethered at the open window of the Burj. The first half hour he steels himself not to look back, keeps his head locked on his goal, ready at any second to hear the sharp cry of his name from behind.

In the distance the city in the Chicane twinkles, the sand dunes and mountains around it look as real as any city they've ever visited before. It knocks at him that he is suddenly so fixated.

The Shuck is what he's pursuing. No one knows for sure how the Shucks arrived in the Cirque – if they were here at its inception or if they have been constructed over the years by other families. What is noteworthy are the similarities between them all: they have roughly the same formula, a living area high off the ground, walls that cannot be scaled and a single entrance point. The Shuck ahead, which now is less than two kilometres away, could be an option as good as Dubai. It's bound to have water, and it's far enough north to have the same views of the cities beyond Dubai.

It is a lonely walk without Camel or Elk. Spider's body is still fizzing with the sugar-load from the sweets machines, and he is more thirsty than usual. He's already finished Elk's water and is conserving his own ration for the walk home. A part of his right boot that he thought he'd stitched well has come unravelled, so the sole flaps with each step and sand creeps inside.

About a kilometre from the Shuck he grinds to a halt. He scoops out his eyeglasses and trains them on the Shuck.

It's a strange, unsettling sight. It is larger than their own Shuck, and something has been daubed in white on the sides of the tower; and the ring of figures that he saw earlier indeed appears to be people standing in a reverent circle around the tower, facing inwards, all completely motionless in the moonlight. For a moment he thinks of Druids and an ornate religious ritual, but on closer inspection, when he sees no movement, he realises they must be statues.

Or … He winds the binoculars into the nearest figure. It is roughly of human height, but the shape is wrong. A cactus? No. It's a pile of crystals. A Desert Rose: the thing Mardy asked him to get. Raising the binoculars, Spider studies the tower. The white splashes, he realises with a shock, are a painted skull-and-crossbones. The words *VERBOTEN* and *KEEP OUT* are splashed everywhere. Moonlight shines through in jagged shapes, and it dawns on him with a dull thump: the place is destroyed. Uninhabitable and quite useless.

If Camel were here, she'd pick up on his despair and nuzzle him. Eventually he opens his water gourd, drinks it all in one go and trudges despondently towards the Shuck, the empty gourd dangling from his fingers.

He passes the Desert Roses, like a stone circle of worshippers, and feels a shiver of unease as he steps into their ring. As if he's crossing a boundary and is being watched. More than once he glances over his shoulder at them, half expecting one to have moved when his back is turned.

The tower is huge; it blots out the night sky and is even more decayed than he'd thought from a distance. There are the tattered remains of banners and tarpaulins, as if someone has made an effort to patch it up at some point. A dead, defeated smell emanates from the interior.

He stands at one of the gaps in the hoarding and clicks on his torch, reaching inside to shine it around. There have been no attempts in here to cultivate crops, but captured animals have been raised here – their scattered remains lie around the perimeter, some of the skeletons still chained at the foot to their cages. They've died of thirst, or starvation. Most families, when they leave, are at least humane enough to cut their animals free.

There's a ladder in the centre, running to the living area high above, but it is rusting and unstable; its lower twenty rungs have disappeared entirely, as if ripped away by a giant hand. Looped in a leather belt across Spider's pack are the few things of use that he's scavenged from the hotels they've already been through. He gets everything out: there's a rope, but he discards most of the tools, then sets to work dismantling some of the banners from the exterior. They are cracked and attached to the frame by what appears to be parachute silk. This silk has survived the desert conditions and he strips it off, metres of it coming away from the tower with a crisp popping noise.

The sugar-rush is over, replaced with a dull weariness, but he finds the strength to throw the rope into the air. It takes five attempts, but eventually it hooks onto the bottom of the ladder. He tests it by putting his weight onto it. The ladder above creaks, flakes of rust cascade onto his head, but the contraption holds solid.

He begins to climb, awkwardly, clinging to the rope until he gets to the ladder, which drops rust down on his face. At last he reaches the top and hauls himself inside. The entrance is smaller than the one at his own Shuck, the ceilings lower. He shines the torch around. The walls are dirty, smeared in brown, and someone has left a pile of stained rags on the floor. It is cold in here, colder than outside.

'Hello?' he calls. 'Hello.'

Spider waits, but no sounds come back to him. Not a single creak or whisper. He's alone here. Taking it slowly, using a combination of the moonlight and his torch, he creeps along the corridors, peering into rooms, pushing open doors. This Shuck is bigger, but it isn't well organised. The rooms are fractured and jumbled as if they've been thrown together.

The bathrooms have cracked mirrors mounted above the water pipes, and there are discarded brushes and scattered bottles of pigment on a low, crude table. In the kitchen, stacks of bottles are piled on the floor. Spider sniffs one. The pungent smell of alcohol. Madeira has been able to ferment dates to create a type of gin that the family enjoy sometimes, but they have never consumed it on this scale. This family must have been drinking constantly. There is the heartbeat of unhappiness here.

He pushes the bottles aside and steps out onto a small balcony. To his right, partly obscured by the vast curve of the Shuck, he can make out the distant shape of Dubai, glittering darkly in the crystalline night. To his left, on the northern reaches, is the Chicane city, slightly different from this angle. He raises his eye-glasses and studies it.

There isn't any movement, no people scurrying across the sand, only twinkling lights in the city, but he thinks he can see adobe-red houses, boxy with angles sharp and precise, patches of grass trailing up the mountain behind it. There are wide avenues and the roads appear to be of tarmac, not dirt – a wealthy city then, one that can afford to import enough water to grow grass; one that has tarmac roads, not dirt tracks. From this side the formation on top of the gates – what he's taken to be some type of spearhead – appears now to be a sort of animal straddling the gates. It must be more than thirty metres in height.

He sighs and fits the binoculars back into his tool belt, retraces his steps to the main hallway and uses another corridor to complete his loop of the Shuck. This corridor has several doors that are ajar or open, but all bear rusting padlocks.

Spider stops at one and studies the padlock, wondering why it makes him feel sad. There are no locks in the Dormilones' Shuck. Usually the family sleep together, and they have never had to lock their doors. Their showers are unlocked – there is no sense of having to create barriers. Living without trust? Never.

He gives the door a nudge and peers inside. It's a sleeping pod, with a filthy jumble of bedding heaped in the corner. There's a whiff of something salty, like sex. And something else. More bottles in the corner.

He opens another door. In the corner is tangled bedding, glass pipes and syringes. Everything filthy and stinking. He closes the door, then remembers Forlani saying he'd take anything – literally anything – to get antibiotics into Tita Lily.

Spider shines the torch on the floor. There is worse: something that must have been human shit on the floor. Something that looks like underwear. How can people let themselves go this far? And the drugs – where do they even get these things, or is it simply clever chemistry? Maybe all it takes is one Walter Hartwell White and one Jesse Pinkman.

He pulls on gloves from his backpack and steps through the muck towards the syringes. He's gone less than a metre when the floor splinters underneath him.

It happens so fast he falls first forward towards the far wall, his right leg slithering through a hole, ripping at the flesh. He comes to a stop, sees the floor is flaking, rust everywhere, maybe from the human waste. His leg is half trapped and he feels it grate against the splintered floor as he twists backwards.

He has just enough strength to scramble across the breaking floor and get to the door. He grabs the handle and heaves himself up. But this salvage point lasts only seconds, before the door itself, exhausted and rusting, folds in on itself, dropping him through the floor so that he is hanging onto it, out in the moonlit night under the Shuck.

He dangles there, stunned. He's never before misjudged the strength of something. In Paris it was his skill – he always knew what would hold his weight. He looks down: past his feet are maybe fifty metres of drop. A girder, at an angle, about a metre away. But if he swings himself to it, he will tear most of the muscles in his arms on the shattered floor. The syringes are above him.

He closes his eyes. '*Merde*,' he whispers. 'And fucking shit.'

19

'SO, YOUNG LADY.' Dr Shreve is breezy and smiling when McKenzie goes to DC for her two-week assessment. 'You look well. I like that orange on you. It's a—'

'A brave choice?'

Maria Shreve smiles. '"Edgy" was the word I was going to use. "Brave" makes it sound like it's a mistake, don't you think?'

McKenzie looks down at her scarf. 'I really don't know.'

Dr Shreve gets herself comfortable, crossing her legs and pulling her woollen skirt down over her big calves. It has stopped snowing but it's still freezing in DC. 'So, let's talk about how we're feeling. More than two weeks on the Quetiapine, the Seroquel, and you haven't called the office with any side-effects. Does that mean you're feeling OK?'

'I'm feeling …' McKenzie folds her arms across her chest. Then unfolds them. 'I don't know how to explain it. I'm feeling calm.'

'Calm. That's good to hear. Any nausea?'

'No.'

'Any palpitations?'

'No.'

'Constipation? Vomiting?'

She shakes her head.

'Sleep?'

'Great. I sleep like the dead.'

'And the problems you were having before. The hallucinations?'

McKenzie lowers her eyes, thinks about this. She'd like to raise her chin, nail Dr Shreve's eyes and say, '*What's your game? You're CIA, so are you just posing as a doctor? Or are you the sort who tries people out for how psychologically robust they are, before they join? Is that how you know Dad? Did Dad do something in the desert he really shouldn't have, and are you and Mom helping him cover it up, in the nicest possible way?*'

In her jeans pocket her phone is buzzing discreetly.

'McKenzie?'

'Yes, yes. I'm sorry – I missed the question.'

'The hallucinations you were having?'

'Gone,' she says, smiling. 'Completely gone.'

'That's a nice result. Isn't it?'

'It's the best result.'

'And are you alert?'

'A little groggy. But I'm OK.'

'So, McKenzie. On a scale of one to ten, where would you rate the success of Seroquel?'

'A nine,' she replies, looking Dr Shreve straight in the eye. 'A nine or maybe even a ten. It's close to a miracle.'

'Then I guess I'll be calling the principal with good news.'

McKenzie smiles sweetly. She knows the ringtone that set up that particular vibration in her pocket. It's Newt calling. He's got news.

The muscles in Spider's arms where he's holding the door are screaming, lactic acid racing into them. He kicks, bounces his feet off the Shuck struts. He collides with bone-shattering speed into the floor, making wounds on his biceps. He can't let it go, just can't.

He clenches his teeth through the pain and kicks again. This time he has more of a swing – it's starting to work. Another kick, another slamming of open muscle into sharp metal, but on this time forward he is almost at the other side of the floor. One more swing, one more stab of infinite pain.

This time as he swings into the darkness he uses his stomach muscles to lift his knees, and at the highest arc of the swing throws a leg into the bottom of the remaining floor. He is rewarded with the silvery tinkle of syringes falling out of the floor into the darkness, landing in the sand below him. He slams back harder this time – so hard he thinks he's going to lose consciousness with the pain. He plays a trick he used to play in the Foreign Legion: lifts his eyes and looks up. For some reason this always stopped him fainting, be it from fear or pain, or just from the remains of what his men had done to a village.

Pray the syringes aren't broken – pray they aren't.

He turns, gets more momentum working up and, with a twist, rams his legs against the strut under the floor and slows himself. From here he can wrap the top of his foot around the strut and pull himself towards it. When he has more leverage, he wraps the other leg round it and slowly winds his way into a frog-like position under the floor.

One last push. He counts to three, then takes a huge breath and throws himself off the door handle. He means to whip-crack his upper body to meet his knees, but he misses and falls backwards, so that he is lying downwards against the strut, upside down, hanging on by his lower legs.

He lies there for a moment or two, taking in the upside-down skies, the underside of the Shuck: moonlight coming through the window and through the floor. His knees are aching, he can feel the rush of blood to his head, his whole neck filling up, so with the last of his strength he does a sit-up – the sort of sit-up they'd do in the Legion, but a hundred times more important.

He brings himself up in excruciating slowness, until he can grab the strut. Then he hangs there for a while, gasping, so dehydrated that his tongue has swollen against the top of his mouth and his lips are cracked.

At last, when there is nothing more for it, he begins the climb down. It's an easy climb – finally he drops into the sand under the Shuck and scrambles around for the syringes. One is broken, the rest aren't.

At last – *at last!* Maybe they will be able to save Tita Lily. Or maybe they won't. If she is already dead … With what Mardy said, they can't afford to lose more people.

He gathers up the parachute silk and makes a container to drag across the sand. He rips away a portion of his dress that has been snagged and tattered on the climb and, last but not least, he cracks a bit of the nearest statue – a piece of Desert Rose to take to Mardy.

And then, for good and for bad, he wants to see his family again.

It's 6.30 in the morning when McKenzie pads downstairs, and already the boys and Dad have left the house. Only Mom is in the kitchen; dressed in yoga pants and a pink training top, she has her toothbrush in her mouth while she whizzes up a smoothie for McKenzie.

'Honey, the bus is only twenty minutes away and you're not even dressed.'

'I know. But I need to talk to you.'

Selena Strathie pauses. She gives her daughter a long, concerned look. 'Talk? What kind of talk? Are you OK?'

'Sure. But I have some questions.'

'OK. But *now*?'

'I'll be quick.'

Mom takes the toothbrush out of her mouth, bends over the kitchen sink and spits out the toothpaste. She wipes her mouth on a sheet of kitchen paper, then stands, her hands on her hips, looking at her daughter. 'OK. Talk, sweetie. But let's make it quick, then get upstairs and get ready – you heard the principal, no second chances here, babe. What do you need to know?'

'I need to know about Nevada.'

'*Nevada?*' Mom frowns. She has a white rime of toothpaste on her bottom lip. 'I thought we'd left all this behind in Dr Shreve's office.'

'Not really. What were we doing in Nevada in the first place?'

'Visiting the Petersons. They're friends of Dad's. Why?'

'How do they know Dad?'

'I don't recall. I'm sorry, baby, I'm completely confused. Why are we talking about the Petersons when you haven't even eaten breakfast? You're going to be late.'

'Not if you answer my questions.'

Mom takes a sharp breath. She narrows her eyes slightly and peers at her daughter. 'Have you taken your medication today?'

'Yes. I have. I've had no hallucinations. Just tell me: how did Dad and Mr Peterson know each other?'

'Work, probably. Their jobs.'

'Because Dad's in the State Department?'

'Yes.'

'Except it's not strictly the State Department, is it?'

'*What?*'

McKenzie holds Mom's eyes. 'I said, *it's not strictly the State Department.* By which I meant: that's a euphemism for something a little more hidden.'

There's a pause. Then Mom sinks a little at the waist. A physical resignation of the fight. She puts a hand to her brow. 'This is not a conversation to be having at six-thirty on your first day back at school.'

'When then, Mom? When were you going to tell me the truth?'

'You've been told the truth, young lady, and there's no need to push it. Now,' she takes a few breaths and, as if finding the will to pull herself upright – a gesture that irritates McKenzie for the subtle message it's sending: *You, my daughter, have brought me to my knees, with all you've demanded of me over the years* – she straightens and, putting a little authority into her voice, says, 'I've got a class in half an hour at Burke, so you'll understand why I can't stand here and chat. Not to mention the bus that will be pulling up in under fifteen minutes. Excuse me.'

She pushes gently past and leaves the room, her back straight. The staccato trot of her feet in the hallway, the slam of the front door and the crunch of tyres on the gritted driveway as she reverses the Jetta out of the drive.

McKenzie listens. She knows for sure that she's heard all she needs to.

She runs upstairs and throws on some clothes, shoves a few last things into her backpack, including Cuddle Bunny, then runs back downstairs, pulling her phone out from the pocket of her hooded fleece as she walks. It's 6.30 here on the coast, and 2.30 in Seattle. She plugs in @NewtinSeattle's address and taps out a quick message, then grins at India who is waiting at the bus stop.

'First day back at school, *biatch*.'

'Homecoming queen.' McKenzie winks.

'Awww,' India drawls. 'Love you. I'm going to be your shadow, I'm going to be here all day – you hear me?'

There's been no more snow overnight and the highways are clear. The bus arrives at school a few minutes early and McKenzie uses the opportunity to stop and talk to Mrs Spiliotopolous in private. At first it's difficult to convince her that McKenzie's suggestion is feasible, let alone moral or legal, but eventually Mrs Spiliotopolous glances dubiously over her shoulder to check they're not being watched. 'I'll think about it.'

'Please?'

'I said, I'll think about it.'

At the locker bay India wants to know what's going on. 'You're as tight as a fish's butt, McKenzie Strathie. You're not the person I used to know.'

McKenzie stops rummaging in her locker and turns to her friend. She searches India's face. 'India? Will you do something for me?'

'Of course. I'm your slave right now.'

'I need someone to trust, *really* trust.'

Her frown deepens. 'What's happening, McKenzie? Are you in trouble?'

'I don't know. I will tell you, eventually, but for now I need you just to do something for me. No questions asked.'

India licks her lips and shoots a few hesitant looks around them. The bell for first period will ring in less than five minutes and no one's interested in the two of them, standing next to the locker in deep conversation. She takes a step nearer and lowers her face, speaking in a quiet voice so that only McKenzie can hear.

'Go on then. What?'

'I'm telling Mom I'm staying with you tonight. She won't ask any questions, but if she does – will you cover?'

'Where are you going?'

'I said no questions.'

'OK, OK. Yeah – I'll cover, but what if she asks my mom?'

'If she does, then I'm blown out of the water, but she won't ask. And tomorrow, at registration, tell them I'm in the washroom. Eventually they'll figure it out, but it'll buy me some time.'

'This is the best. You're having a full-on adventure. So sick!'

'I hope so. Now, at the end of Latin, take my textbook off my desk and put it in my locker – you know the code. I'll text you: tell you where I am and what's happening.'

'But if you're meeting someone, aren't you supposed to tell me? You know, in case you don't come back. Get kidnapped and, next thing we know, you're Stockholmed and radicalised and you turn up with a Kalashnikov, freedom-fighting for ISIS or the white supremacists.'

McKenzie bites her lip and is silent for a long time. Then she shakes her head. 'You don't need to know. I'm safe where I'm going.'

She hopes it's true.

20

AT HARBINSON HIGH School, Latin is the first period, and this works well for McKenzie because the teacher has long become disillusioned at trying to teach Latin to an honours class that has students ranging from seniors down to freshmen, none of whom have studied to the same level. She often simply switches on a video and leaves them to it, while she prepares another lesson or marks papers. People say she's leaving the school, doesn't give a shit any more, which is ideal for McKenzie.

She registers, sits down and opens her textbook, then lets five minutes pass, her eyes on the clock. If Mrs Spiliotopolous has thought about it and decided the answer is no, McKenzie's going to use the last of her precious 200 dollars on an Uber. That or she'll have to steal Tatum's Subaru, meaning the whistle will be blown the moment Mom or Dad or her brothers get home this evening and she'll have lost her head-start.

Mrs Spiliotopolous has to say yes. She *has* to.

Shakily McKenzie gets up and tells the teacher she needs a washroom break. Leaving her textbook open on the desk, she grabs her backpack and heads to the door. She just has time to see India look up and mouth, '*Be careful, for fuck's sake*' and then she's gone, walking fast down the corridor, her head lowered.

It's so soon after the start of first period that most of the counsellors and teachers are in their offices, and no one's organised enough yet to be patrolling the corridors for slackers. She doesn't look left or right, but heads straight to the back door, pushing it open.

Outside it's freezing, the wind has picked up and the last of the autumn leaves are being tossed around the juniors' car lot, flattening against the piles of unseasonable snow. Lined up in the bays are the forty school buses that service the school. Putting her face into the wind, McKenzie begins walking in the direction of number seventy-two, halfway down the bays. As she gets closer she sees that number seventy-two is missing. Nowhere to be seen.

Mrs Spiliotopolous has thought about it and decided not to help. McKenzie's heart sinks; she can feel the plans turning to jelly. It was the call she got from Newt during her session with Dr Shreve that made up her mind. He was breathing hard.

'McKenzie, you're righter than I ever guessed. The answer is in that place you were talking about, OK? The city is built on an ancient network of canals – the native Hohokam tribe built them, and guess what their schematic looks like?'

She knew. And when she googled it, she was sure. The ancient canals in Phoenix are exactly the pattern Newt's been obsessing about all these years.

Something is ticking away and coming together. It really is.

She gets her phone out, her hands trembling with the cold. A decision now – it has to be *now*. Uber and 200 dollars or stealing Tatum's Subaru?

'Hey, Bonnie Parker.'

McKenzie turns. Ten feet away, pulled up between the buses where she hadn't noticed it, is a 4x4, the engine running. In it, Mrs Spiliotopolous is giving her a serious look. 'The longer you stand there, the more chance you have of being seen.'

She runs to the passenger door and jumps in. Inside, the heater is on and the speakers are blaring out a piano concerto. 'Belt on, please,' says Mrs Spiliotopolous, then she puts the car into drive and they sail out of the bus bay and out around the car lot, going straight down the exit.

McKenzie can hardly believe it. No one's stopping them. She turns and looks at the gates receding behind them. No blue lights, no security, no teachers running out of the school, shock-faced.

'I know. Absolutely zero security.' Mrs Spiliotopolous gives a wry smile. 'Which makes it easier for the bad guys.'

'I'm not a bad guy,' McKenzie says breathlessly. 'I promise.'

'I know you're not. I'm just worried I'm *delivering* you to the ones who are. I feel like I'm taking you somewhere dangerous.'

'You're taking me to Baltimore Airport. Is that dangerous?'

'You know what I mean.'

'I don't want you to get into trouble, Mrs S. I really don't, but I am desperate.'

Mrs Spiliotopolous is silent for a while, thinking about this. She negotiates the traffic expertly, weaving in and out of lanes, doing much better than either of McKenzie's parents can do.

'You won't get into trouble,' McKenzie says again. She hugs her backpack closer. 'I really appreciate this, I really do. I'll pay you the gas money.'

'No, you won't.' Mrs Spiliotopolous indicates right and pulls onto the highway where the traffic is moving freely, the morning sun blazing off the windscreens. 'You won't pay me, because you're paying me already.'

'What?'

Mrs Spiliotopolous smiles. McKenzie has never noticed that she has beautiful eyes. And clear, unlined skin. 'Every day you, the cleverest kid in the school, get on my bus, and what have I seen? Sadness. All these years, a little girl lost. Until this morning. When you got on the bus and I saw your face this morning, that's payment enough. Wherever you're going today, McKenzie Strathie – weather genius – whatever you're planning on doing, it's what you're meant to be doing.'

Spider drags the parachute silk behind him, exhausted, despondent. The sun comes up when he is still more than four clicks away from Dubai. It slices up between the skyscrapers, making him pull his peaked cap lower over his eyes and bend forward as he goes.

After about three kilometres, from the corner of his eye he sees a shadow pass fleetingly over the sand to his left.

It is so quick that he almost misses it and doesn't have time to register the shape exactly. But wings? He is sure he saw wings. He whips his head back and studies the sky, his heart suddenly thumping fast, but the sunlight is so strong, and is at such a blinding angle, that he can't see anything. He drags out his binoculars and sweeps the horizon. Licking his lips, he waits for another shape to come at him, but it doesn't.

It's your imagination, he warns himself, setting off again. *You've pushed it too far, you're hallucinating – never eat chocolate again.*

As he gets nearer Dubai he can see, coming down from the long drift of sand, the whole family coming out to meet him. Camel has been prepared and is being led by Hugo, Amasha is at the spearhead of the group.

Spider grinds to a halt. He is beyond a fight. He will take whatever Amasha slings at him, and will accept all Noor's disdain, Cairo's gleeful gloating. He drops the parachute in the sand. He can't take another step.

The family get closer and closer. Camel, who is carrying the pieces of a bench they found in the hotel strapped to the *mahawi*, is loaded with blue-and-gold curtains torn from hotel rooms. Now that Spider can make out their expressions, he sees Amasha isn't frowning. She is holding a water gourd out towards him and she is horrified by his injuries.

'Ladeela, we were so worried. My boy.' She hands him the water and, before Spider can speak, embraces him. 'We missed you so much – we weren't a family without you.' Her hair is so familiar to him, with its faint cardamom smell, and the memory of the locks on the bedroom door in the tower so strong, that Spider almost breaks. He is head and shoulders taller than her, but for a moment he leans helplessly against her.

She listens to his heart for a short while. Then she drops her head back and peers up at him. 'You found something. What?'

'Syringes. They've been used, but I found lots.'

'We can sterilise them,' Amasha says. 'Let me see.'

Spider pulls them out of the pack. Everyone gathers round while Amasha inspects them, holding them up to the sun. 'Where were they?'

'In a Shuck. I don't know what they've been used for, but maybe injecting something to get high.'

Amasha grins. Her face clears, as if all the worry there has been wiped clean. 'I've got to get these back for Forlani and Tita Lily – got to get back to the Shuck. Can we take Camel?'

Spider is too tired to run with them, so when Amasha has finished checking his wounds, Spider helps her onto Camel's *mahawi* and shows Noor how to use the switch. 'Click-click in your throat,' he explains. 'Like this. She'll listen to you.'

Eventually the two head off towards the Shuck, Camel being mildly obstinate, glowering over her shoulder at Spider.

'Drink now.' Elk steps forward and helps him lift the water gourd to his mouth. Spider nods and drains it. He lets Madeira finish bandaging his arms where they are cut, and accepts the oil she gives him to put on his mouth. He chews cautiously on a handful of dates that Elk gives him. 'Did you find anything?'

'Not yet,' Hugo says. He looks tired, his shirt is dirty and sweat-stained. 'We'll go home now for the grey night and come back first thing tomorrow.'

As they set out, Splendour trots along next to Spider, holding onto his skirt and prattling on about the sweets machine.

'We're going to come back to Dubai and make a Shuck here, and then we can eat sweets whenever we want, and then we're gonna find the Sarkpont, aren't we? And get sodas off of Mardy in the apron, ain't we, Spider?'

'If you say so. Yes.'

Splendour lets out a whoop of delight and runs backwards, hugging Cairo, planting a kiss on the side of his face and pulling him off-balance.

'Hey,' Madeira scolds. 'Keep calm, children, keep calm.'

Splendour is about to listen when something stops her. Her eyes are on the distant horizon and her mouth drops open in a shocked oval shape.

Spider whips round and sees what she's looking at. The horizon to the south is dark. But the clouds are not normal clouds. They seethe like a million ants moving together as one.

His body sags. The bird he thought he saw earlier wasn't his imagination. It must have been an outlier, a predictor of what was to come.

He gets up. Walks swiftly to where Elk is and puts a confidential hand on his arm. Surprised by the touch and by Spider's expression, Elk's smile fades.

'What?'

Spider turns and nods to the south.

Elk follows his gaze and his face falls. On the other side of Camel the children have started to whimper.

'No,' Elk says softly. 'Please no.'

But there is no answer to this.

The Regyre is over. Another family have found the Sarkpont.

From the aeroplane McKenzie watches the first of the Phoenix mountains come into view. Their clear-cut silhouettes in the midday sun soothe part of her that she can't identify, as if the view is opening up pathways inside her thoughts that have never been unlocked before. When the doors open, she stands at the top of the steps leading from the 737, the sun on her face and people pushing her from behind. Phoenix is spread out in the distance; she can see mountains and a few white clouds, the sweeping glass structure of the terminal building. The textured, scratchy air comes into her and gives her the sense that home is somewhere here – out in the Arizona desert, waiting for her.

Eventually the impatient passengers behind jostle her down the stairs. McKenzie gets to the hot tarmac and walks in silence, dragging her backpack with her, gazing all around her at the high sky, the contrails in the blue above. The slight, almost imperceptible breeze, tinged with the smell of sand and drought, makes her excited and nervous all at once.

Since the moment Mrs Spiliotopolous dropped her at Baltimore, not a single person has attempted to stop McKenzie or ask her where she's going. She's seventeen, and all she needed to get on and off the plane was her driver's licence and the QR code for her plane ticket. It's incredible. Even more incredible is that now in Phoenix, six hours since she left Harbinson, the only people who've tried to contact her are Newt and India. India's message reads simply – *No questions asked yet. Keeping head low. I'm so looking forward to hearing what this is all about.*

McKenzie has typed out a nervous reply – *I'm meeting a stranger. He is Argentinian, Newt Herrera. He's from Seattle. Don't tell anyone, unless I don't come back.* She considers the message, then changes her mind, deletes it and retypes – *Arrived safe. I will tell all, be patient. Love you, M x*

Newt's message, from three hours before, reads – *I've landed, I'm waiting in Arrivals on the second floor in a coffee shop, Cactus, opposite Starbucks.*

A coffee shop? She feels a moment's anticlimax: she's imagined somewhere different, somewhere more significant. Near baggage reclaim is a bank of seats, where she stops and takes a few moments to change, peeling off the Virginia layers – jacket and sweatshirt – stripping down to her T-shirt, kicking off her boots and pulling on the summer sandals that are at the bottom of her backpack. Heart thumping, she zips her winter clothes into the pack and continues on to where the escalators lead up to the next floor.

At the top of the escalator is the Starbucks sign, lit up above the heads of the other passengers. There are ten or so sports dudes waiting for their coffees at the end of the bar and beyond them, hanging from the overhead joists, the word 'Cactus' in pale pink and olive-green painted above a shop front.

The jocks follow her with their eyes, staring at her legs, which she's not used to. McKenzie skirts Starbucks and heads for the coffee shop. It's an unusual place for an airport – with a single door to enter it, instead of the open shop front. Hanging in the display boxes are single fibreglass sculptures finished in high-gloss purples, greens and yellows, each a replica of a fruit.

Tentatively she pushes the door open. It's a brick-walled room with a reclaimed wood floor and adobe ceilings – empty save for the barista, a young woman in a pink T-shirt, who doesn't look up from the bar, where she's changing coffee grounds; and, standing next to a free-standing sculpture of a desert flower in crimson fibreglass, Newt.

He hasn't heard her come in. He's standing turned three-quarters away from her, looking at a photo on his phone. He's taller than she'd imagined, and thinner. He wears black skinny jeans and zebra-patterned Doc Martens, a velvet jacket in olive-green and, on his straw hat, a black-and-white band. The bones in the side of his face are visible, highly sculpted, like a piece of art, and there is a hint of the curly dark hair emerging from under the hat. He makes McKenzie think of the iridescent dust from butterfly wings.

She lowers her backpack to the floor, conscious that her knees are like rubber and that she doesn't know how or where to stand. Newt seems to become aware of her presence; he stops looking at his phone and his posture becomes stiff. Slowly, agonisingly slowly, as if he doesn't trust himself to make the move properly, he turns to her.

Neither speaks. They hold each other's eyes for what seems like hours. The barista continues clattering around with cups and milk cartons, the announcer reels off flight and gate numbers, but all of it is a sea of sound, none of which touches the lozenge of air between the two of them.

It's Newt who makes the move. He slots the phone into his pocket and comes to stand in front of her. He's taller than she is and bends his head slightly, peering at her carefully. If anyone else had done that, she'd have run away, but with Newt it feels completely natural. She stares at him too, unselfconsciously taking in every crevice and curve of his face – the way the flesh lies over the bones, his eyebrows, his amber-brown eyes, the faintest shadow of stubble under the skin.

He takes her hand and holds it. She squeezes his hand and he breathes out, as if she's answered a huge question, then gently encircles her in his arms.

McKenzie leans her head against his chest and listens to his heartbeat. A low, natural rhythm that sounds just like her own. She crosses her arms around his back, feels his muscle and bone so light under the velvet jacket.

They stand in silence, holding each other, not needing to speak. They're like that for such a long time, lost in their own space, that it's only the barista, clearing her throat and calling across the shop, 'Can I get you anything?', that makes them break apart.

21

THERE IS NO need to run, but no one wants to be out in the desert when the Regyre is ending. The family stumble numbly across the sand, their heads lowered. No one can speak; the children are crying silently, the women stumble and are careless about their belongings, which drag and get dropped or forgotten along the way.

Overhead the flocks of birds drown out the sunlight. Haphazard shadows skitter over the sand. The wind is blowing and the dunes begin to sing – low and bellowing. Spider has heard this sound outside the Cirque, on his trips to North Africa with the Foreign Legion; it's a universal human sound, he was told, a deep vibration, the 'Ohm' of the Thai monks, the humming of the imam.

In the Cirque the noise is terrifying; it reverberates through the desert, seems to pierce the organs: the heart, the liver, the lungs.

Spider keeps pace with the others, and all the time he thinks only of the family he saw the other day at the Chicane – is it that family who have found the Sarkpont? The memory of them is as bright as a blood-red bloom in his brain.

They clatter into the tower and climb the ladder, then head into the common room, where they collapse, weeping and shivering. Forlani and Noor, who are in the kitchen boiling water for the syringes, wander in, wide-eyed. But from the faces of the others and the sounds of the birds outside, they understand. Their expressions sag.

'Oh, shit. Shit!'

'We have failed today … again. Another Regyre; another Regyre, which is nearly our …' Amasha's voice wavers a little. She seems about to say the words no one wants to hear, but changes them at the last minute, mustering some confidence. 'Another Regyre. Ha'shem, please think of us, and please think of Tita Lily who is injured – please spare her.'

They all sit in silence for a while, gripping hands, while outside the birds rain noisily against the Shuck walls. After a while the pot in the kitchen is bouncing around so much that Forlani releases the hands on either side of him and gets up to hobble over to it. Spider follows and stands, watching the syringes bouncing amongst the bubbles.

'How do you know it's going to work?'

'It will work – it has to.'

Spider follows Forlani to the pod where Tita Lily lies. The window is open and the room, which faces south, is the coolest in the Shuck; air comes through from the distant reaches around

Mithi, but Tita Lily is covered in sweat, her cheeks bright red and swollen. She breathes fast.

'The infection – it started this morning,' Forlani mutters under his breath as he clatters the single phial of antibiotic in the bowl, knocking it against the boiled cloths and needles. 'She's got worse since you all got back. I don't know if I can save her.'

Spider sits on the end of the bed and smiles at Tita Lily. He takes her hand. 'We left you so long.'

'It's OK,' she says sweetly. 'I sang to myself. An old song called "Mindanao", which used to be sung in some of the piss-poor neighbourhoods in Manila when I was a small child. You wanna hear it?'

'Sure. When we've got this injection into you.'

Tita Lily lifts up her shift and shows them her side. All the old injuries from the cactus spines have disappeared and instead there is an ochre-red flash across her side. In the centre of it is a poisonous black hole that has pus building up around it.

Forlani squeezes his eyes closed briefly. He chooses one of the needles and punctures the phial in the rubber at the top, drawing up the clear liquid.

'OK, let's roll up this sleeve. Here. Just a tiny scratch.'

Forlani's hand is trembling; maybe only Spider sees it, but the guy is nervous. A small line of sweat develops on his upper lip, but his hands are steady as he probes around the inside of Tita Lily's arm. Eventually he takes a breath, holds it and plunges the needle in.

Tita Lily yelps, but Spider presses down on her shoulders, massaging them. She is hotter than the thirstiest desert, he thinks, as Forlani squeezes the contents of the syringe into her vein. She might well not survive, and Forlani doesn't know if it's the right medicine. Then Forlani pulls away, hot and shaking. His eyes are like moons, his breathing fast.

Spider sits and whispers to her, 'All over, all over for now.'

'I want bourbon, I want tuba. Please, Spider.' Tita Lily tries to reach up and touch his face. It's clear she's delirious. 'Please get me something to drink.'

'With antibiotics? Sure you won't puke?' Spider looks at her; her breathing is rapid. 'I'll ask Elk. Let's sit for a while.' He smiles at her, conscious of Forlani's own breathing, so fast in and out, afraid of what the medicine will do. But Tita Lily continues to breathe, continues to talk, stroking Spider's face.

'Just a little drink, my beautiful Spider.' Tita Lily has always flirted with him; she knows there's no harm in it, it's merely the way she's built. 'A little drink.'

'When we've got that spine out.' Forlani licks his lips. He pulls a bandage from the pack around his waist, comes to the bed and sits. 'We've got to get it out.'

Spider breathes through his mouth as Forlani sits and pushes both fingers into the flesh around the spine. There is a long silence, while Tita Lily clenches her eyes closed and Spider squeezes her hand. Forlani mutters under his breath and moves his fingers, reapplying the pressure. But it produces only a small amount of clear fluid. He manoeuvres his hands again and squeezes.

'Please,' Tita Lily is whimpering. And as she does so, a slim line of yellow pus jets out. Forlani narrows his eyes and keeps squeezing. More pus, thicker now; the smell is terrible, but Spider won't react – he doesn't want to offend her. And then at last a fat, black lump like a slug pushes itself out of the flesh and drops onto Tita Lily's skin.

'All the saints, bless me,' she mutters. 'Bless me for this pain – bless me, please.'

'It's over. You did great.' Forlani mops the area. Then, from his pack, he pulls a little pot with grey unguent and with a tiny wooden spatula spoons it into the wound.

Spider nods at the door. 'Go and get her something to drink.'

When Forlani has gone, Spider sits on the bed, holding her hand.

Tita Lily is groaning. 'I'm disgusting. I'm so disgusting – did you see what came out of me?'

'It's not your fault. You fell on a cactus.'

'But the smell, Spider. Look at me. My legs. My legs are disgusting, and under my arms and my chest. It's prickly. I can't be like this, Spider. I can't.'

And so Spider finds himself heating Tita Lily's water supply, putting it in a bowl with shaving cream and a razor and going back to her sleeping pod.

'Here,' he says. 'Let me lift your sheets.'

He does so, to reveal her slim, muscular legs. They are covered in a light sheen of sweat and the bristles are almost invisible to Spider, but he knows this means a lot to her, so he whips up a lather and smoothes it on her legs, carefully drawing the razor up them.

'Does that hurt?'

'No.' She leans back, her arms over her head.

Her skin is so hot, he doubts she will make it through the night. When he has finished, he shaves under her arms and then across her chest. When he's done, she grabs his hand.

'What?'

'Tell me the truth, Spider. Tell me – do you belong here?'

He stares at her. She has very narrow dark-brown eyes; a small amount of mascara has gathered in the corner of her eyes, and there is still the slight stain of lipstick on her mouth. Her breath is fetid and sour. 'I mean that I think they've made a mistake.'

'A mistake?'

'Yes – why would I be let in, with everything that I've done? Hmmm. I mean, I tried to help a few of the street girls in Manila, but, you know, I was not Mother Teresa, and then there was all the shit I did before that.' Her eyes go over Spider's face. As if she's seeing straight through him. 'And you know what? I look at you and I know you did something you're not so proud of, either.'

Spider stares at her. The shaving foam is drying on his hands, caking on the hairs of his arms. He thinks of that water tank, the puttering of the gas lamp, the way the tank rocked. He is about to speak when Elk appears at the door, holding a goblet of golden-coloured liquor.

'I heard a beautiful lady wanted a drink, so look at this.' He looks at Tita Lily and pretends not to notice she is leaking life. 'Herbal sleeping potion – the finest. Guaranteed to rev up those dreams.'

The car Newt has hired is a huge Audi Q5 in white, with leather seats and a Bose surround-sound system. He places McKenzie's backpack on the rear seat and holds the door for her, his movements fluid, the posture of a gaucho in a tango, straight-backed, his head movements very slight and controlled.

McKenzie nervously crosses and uncrosses her legs as they drive through the rush-hour Phoenix traffic, the sun blazing off buildings and car windscreens. Newt's hands on the steering wheel are dark with clean, pale nails. She's too nervous to ask where they're staying, but when they arrive she instantly feels shabby and inadequate. The hotel is in the Dove Valley neighbourhood, with views of the golf courses, bright-green lawns punched in the blonde flank of the mountains.

'It's OK,' Newt reassures her. 'I worry about many, many things, but money isn't one of them. My father was generous, so I can be too – this is on me. I'll settle up your air fare too.'

The foyer is marble, with a fountain and a café bar decorated with tubes of light. At the reception desk Newt asks for two keys, for rooms with an interconnecting balcony on the top floor. He carries her bag up.

'I'm right next door,' he says. 'Right here. Give yourself some time to get organised, I'll be back in twenty minutes.'

He's gone, and McKenzie, solitary in the room, doesn't know what to do. She's only ever stayed in Days Inns and Travelodges – nothing like this place. Everything is so big and gleaming, she's afraid to touch anything and walks around gingerly, glancing at the furniture, as if there might be a hotel employee waiting to admonish her: *Madam, please don't use the curtains in that way; they are reserved for the first-class customers only . . .*

Out of the window are golf buggies with sunshades in pistachio-and-raspberry stripes, and the huge white clubhouse is something between a ranch and a wedding cake, with its white verandah and tiers. McKenzie feels small – as if there isn't enough of her to fill the room. Her tiny backpack looks ridiculous on the luggage rack, Cuddle Bunny is dog-eared and her toothbrush seems timorous and ashamed of its ordinariness, when placed on the marble bathroom sink under the sparkling downlighters.

There is also a sensation in her stomach that she doesn't recognise. Something like excitement, or the feeling she gets when she drinks two Starbucks flat whites in a row: a vibration at a high frequency that isn't unpleasant, but not entirely comfortable, either.

She plugs in her phone. There's another message from India.

– *I've been in my room all night, hardly seen the parent. She hasn't said anything. Think you've got away with it. What do you want me to do tomorrow? And, serious, let me know you're OK?*

McKenzie taps in a message – *I'm more than OK. I'll tell you all when I call.*

The answer comes straight back – *SKRT*; India's slang for OK, cool. Then – *BTW maths double period was CRAP without you, McKenzie, serious, CRAP without ur banta. Frickin quadratic equations, kill me if I ever talk about majoring in maths, k?*

– *KK*, McKenzie answers – *Preferred method of death?*

A long pause, then – *Short and sharp, plz, and not involving Justin Bieber.*

Maybe, just maybe, when all of this is over, she and India will go back to being friends and McKenzie might end up being the cool one, who ditched school and ran away to Arizona.

After twenty minutes, when she's got Cuddle Bunny comfortable on the pillow, hung up her few clothes, showered and got redressed in her hasty grab-bag of summer gear, there's a knock at the door to the balcony. Newt. She opens it, glancing outside, suddenly self-conscious that they could be seen here. Newt doesn't wait to be asked in – he's carrying a leather portfolio under his arm and he walks straight in, taking it to the seating area next to the window.

'Look at these.' He spreads them out on the floor. They're pictures that she recognises from his Insta account, desert scenery, but today he ranges them in an order. 'This one is the first,' he explains. 'I drew this when I was thirteen.'

'It's awesome.'

'Not really. It was straight from the hallucination I'd had the night before. You recognise it?'

The picture shows row after row of Joshua trees, dunes and distant cities. A huge pylon-shaped structure – the familiar fingered shape ungainly and stark against the pure sky. McKenzie runs her fingers across it wonderingly. 'I've dreamed this shape before.'

'Me too. It's a study for a painting I made for my mother. I presented it to her in the hope she'd get my father to see reason, let me go to art school.'

He unrolls another one: a splashy painting in acrylic, shades of lime and pink.

She smiles. 'Dune formations – that's a parabolic and that's a seif dune. And, here, a star dune – you get that formation when the wind changes direction a lot.'

'I knew you'd recognise them. I wish I could say my parents were as interested as you are. Yes, my mother pretended to love this picture, but my father threatened to burn it. I didn't dare tell him I dreamed one day of mapping the deserts: in those days my dream was to be a cartographer.'

'A mapmaker?'

He smiles sadly. 'Can you imagine how that went down with my parents? The most they would let me do was a course in church architecture – that was their limit. Kept me in the faith, kept me on the straight. They were happy. I knew my naves, my piscinas, my tholoi and my basilicas. When I got the job in Seattle they were ecstatic.' He shrugs. 'Me not so delighted, though at least the company I work for now has a division that's looking at map apps – so maybe I've got something to cling to. Here, this is a map of Phoenix that I did this morning in the airport at Seattle.'

She kneels on the carpet to study the map. It's ink on a thick watercolour paper, done with pen. It occurs to her that it's rare to see hand-drawn art. The map is so beautiful and full of things she understands. She could run through those canals and arroyos and never miss a step.

'I feel strange,' she says. 'Since I arrived I've had a feeling. Here.' She places her hand on her stomach. 'It's like I'm supposed to be doing something. It's the feeling I've got when I know I've left a book at home, or left my door keys somewhere or done something stupid, but can't quite remember what. It's the way the air feels before a storm. My skin gets so prickly.'

Newt grins. 'It's because we're close to something.'

She grins back. 'But we don't have long. By tomorrow morning, at the latest, the school will call my parents to tell them I haven't registered.'

'What time?'

'Nine, eastern.'

'Which is five here. You're right – we need to work fast.' Newt tips back on his heels, gets to his feet and begins gathering up the paintings. 'Let's do this.'

After the Regyre it is the time for reassessing maps, mending, patching equipment – the family are forbidden to stray more than two kilometres from the Shuck. It is also the time when new families are introduced into the Cirque, the Scouts are recalled from their mission and the families who have failed to find the Sarkpont after twelve tries are disposed of.

Elk and Amasha don't even talk about what happens to them. They can't.

Usually the Dormilones go to bed drugged by tears, defeat, alcohol or ganja, and often sleep late into the next morning and wake gradually, long after the gentle sunrise. Maybe it's this, combined with his exhausting exploration of the skull-and-crossbones Shuck, that absurdly grants Spider the deepest sleep he's had in weeks. He lies naked, with the Shuck window wide open to the night, and drowses long into the morning.

In his dreams he's visited by a woman who exposes the remainder of her milk-white body, her breasts rose-pale and hard with lust. He thinks it's Yma.

He wakes at the centre of an orgasm. Bang, bang, bang. The blood courses around his head. Shame and lust, shame and lust. He stares at the ceiling for a while, then drops his hands over his eyes. Shame and lust: can the two ever be pulled apart? Is it Elk's conversation the previous night that's set him off – *the touch of a woman*? Or something else?

Eventually Spider gets up and goes to the shower to clean himself up. He stands for a long time, staring in silence at the strange map on the wall, the trident on its side. It's one of the cities they haven't visited – and may never. When he's dressed, he goes to Tita Lily's room.

'You good?'

She is lying on her back in a white robe. Her face is still red, still highly coloured. His heart plummets.

'Forlani gave me another jab.'

'You're going to be fine,' he lies, thinking that her face being that hot means only a matter of time. 'Just fine.'

Spider goes to the common room, worrying about Tita Lily, to find that breakfast has already been eaten. On the table are cheese and fruit for latecomers. Spider takes one of the leftover knuckles of bread, presses a cube of sheep's cheese onto it and chews thoughtfully, looking at the Regyre sculpture. Someone has closed the eleventh segment. There is only one segment left.

He goes to the balcony and looks out. Last night the sand was dotted with bird carcasses from the collisions with the Shuck during the frenzy, but this morning there is no sign of them, as is always the way at the beginning of this period. As if a giant hand has swept the area clean.

The family are dotted around the sand outside the tower – the children sitting cross-legged in the sand, helping Amasha to stitch sleeping bags. Madeira is digging under the polytunnels, while Noor is examining the sheep, maybe deciding which one to slaughter. Someone has spread out the silk curtains from Dubai on the sand, in a blaze of blue like water, while Hugo has dug up one of his pots and is examining it, presumably considering how he will transport it.

Dubai, then – that's where they are going. Spider raises his head and closes his eyes, feeling the wind on his face. He stays that way for a long time, thinking about the smell in Dubai. The faint shapes in the lift shaft. He thinks about Camel – the ship of the desert.

The ship of the desert.

Then he opens his eyes and stares at the salt lake – the Virgule.

I've got it, he thinks. *I know what to do*.

22

MCKENZIE AND NEWT get into the car and begin driving into the city. The Audi smells of oranges and suntan lotion, and has little buttons to readjust the seats and endless computerised dashboard displays showing the road ahead, the local amenities, the time of sunset, the weather, et cetera. Newt drives, because McKenzie knows she's too clumsy and will drive them into an arroyo or something. He follows the network of canals that run sometimes under the city and sometimes through it. The long concrete-banked structures are everywhere: sometimes they are derelict, with weeds growing and rubbish-strewn sand piles on either side; in other places they have been rejuvenated, with apartment buildings reflected in the silent canal, a waterfall, the water rushing on either side of a viewing platform, lit-up balconies casting their otherworldly light as the sun goes down.

Once this was a flourishing Hohokam settlement, thanks to the genius engineers' irrigation system that allowed them to grow squash, corn and cotton. Five hundred years ago they abandoned the region, and the new city that centuries later rose in the ashes was named Phoenix, after the mythological bird. A celebration of renewal.

The Phoenix that McKenzie sees out of the window is placid and non-confrontational: the adobe houses, the endless boulevards, which are so stretched out and connected to the sky, drift past leaving a haze of images on her retina. Here people walk more slowly, with none of the clip-clipping, hurry-hurry business-like walks of the DC lawyers and military bigwigs; and no one wears the buttoned-up business suits and flesh-coloured tights of the interns and lecturers. Instead the women wear cotton frocks in shades of *gelato* – peach and strawberry. Or shorts and sneakers, little yellow T-shirts with glitter motifs, even the older grey-haired women. Men wear baseball caps and bandanas, and some grow their hair long.

'People will watch us,' McKenzie tells Newt. 'We're two young people in a top-dollar hotel, with a fuck-off awesome car. We'll be very obvious to anyone who's trying to find us.'

'I don't know who'd be trying to find us.'

She chews the side of her thumbnail thoughtfully. Outside, she sees scrubby carob and mesquite trees on the pavements, and tall palm trees. She sees sleek electric trams covered in advertising, and native jewellery stores painted sandstone-red. She sees the reflection of their Audi, ghost-like, sliding along the windows of the car showrooms.

'Like you said – we're closing in on something big,' McKenzie says. 'I've been reading about FEMA and all the camps.'

'Me too. There aren't any in Phoenix itself. They're all south of here, near the Mexican border.'

'But there is a FEMA office here. Except – well, I've looked at it on Google Maps and it's straightforward, they're not hiding anything. It's based at the fire department. No blurred areas, nothing weird. You wanna see?'

She holds up her phone and Newt glances at the image. 'But you said it wasn't the FEMA base we're looking for; it was other camps they're creating.'

'Yes, I'm still working on that.' McKenzie puts the phone back onto her map. 'I really want to see the city from the distance. I want to see Phoenix the way it is in the storm-cloud picture.'

'It's getting dark now. Tomorrow?'

'Sure. And nothing you recognise at the moment?'

He screws up his face, frustrated. 'I feel like the canals are important. They've been in my head so long. Except I'm not recognising anything right now.'

McKenzie doesn't say that she agrees, and that nothing – not a thing in Phoenix – is tripping off any light bulbs in her head, in spite of the vibration she feels in her core. But the canals stream on and on, and whenever they stop to look at the water, they see nothing that seems relevant, only their own bleary faces peering uncertainly back at them, the stars vague points of white light behind them.

Driving through the Alhambra region, just north of the city centre, they cross a canal into an area that seems to comprise a huge grid of low residential houses, dotted with the occasional church or towering hotel. Newt turns a corner and begins to slow. 'Look at this.'

McKenzie, who has been monitoring their progress on her phone, raises her eyes. Something in the neighbourhood has changed. In several windows glow tiny oil lamps. On doorsteps here and there, young woman can be seen crouched in groups, working on ornate patterns on the ground. A shop with gold and silver jewellery is full of people in colourful saris. She sits forward and gazes at the lights, set in every conceivable window and porch. On some of the houses have been painted tiny footprints in vermilion powder.

'Have you seen this before?' Newt asks.

'I have. I don't know where, but I've seen this. Have you?'

'I have. And I don't know where, either. It looks Indian. Hindu.'

They take another turn and see a queue of traffic waiting to turn off a road between ornate wrought-iron gates. Beyond the gates in the centre of a huge parking lot is a tall white building with twin *sikhara*, luminous against the darkling sky. Cars are pulling into the parking lot and the building is drenched with tiny white lights.

'It's Diwali,' McKenzie says, looking at her phone. 'The first day. It says here it's called – oh, I can't pronounce it – Dhanteras? You're supposed to draw beautiful patterns for Lakshmi: she's the goddess of wealth and prosperity. That's why they're buying jewellery.'

She closes her eyes, presses her fingers on her lids.

'You OK?'

She nods, her eyes still closed. 'I can't explain it. I've seen all this before – I've seen these petals and saris and gold, and the footprints.'

They park in the car lot and follow the crowds into the building. One or two of the congregation give them strange looks – McKenzie is the only pale-skinned person there – but in general people are smiling; young girls adorned in red and gold run in small gangs, giggling and hanging flowers on cars. Inside, the floors are of polished marble, and the doors are modern, glass and aluminium, the ceiling have air vents and fire-retardant tiles, but everywhere is decorated with strings of orange, yellow and pink flowers, and with statues of the elephant god with polished gold urns and pots placed in front of them. The smell of incense and coriander makes McKenzie's head tight, and the sense in her stomach that she's being pulled along a strand of history – the excitement, the panic – builds until she struggles to keep her footsteps measured.

Newt takes her hand to hold McKenzie back. They enter the main hall and together they stand, gazing at it.

Everywhere people are sitting cross-legged on carpets, distributing flower petals or praying with eyes closed, hands clasped. People chant; some of the women are crushing spices and placing them in front of a four-headed idol, who is pictured clasping a bundle of herbs in one hand. Everywhere are dotted flames in tiny clay lamps.

Newt lowers his head to hers and whispers, 'Does it remind you of anything?'

McKenzie frowns, looking up at the soaring ceiling, the ornate tiled walls. 'Not the building itself. The decorations, though, the statues, the flowers. Yes, I've seen it. That elephant, it's called Ganesh, but I haven't got a clue how I know that.'

'Me neither,' Newt says wonderingly. 'But you're right, I'm sure it's Ganesh and that's Lakshmi. And though I don't know why I know, I'm also fairly sure that's Yama. The god of death.'

They're both silent for a while, staring at the statue of Yama, a blue-faced god. Piles of gold coins have been placed in front of him. His eyes are almost human – balanced and fixed, as if he's registering them across the heads of the congregation, noting them as intruders.

'What do we do?' Newt hisses. 'What do we do now?'

'We walk.'

They walk quickly but silently away, resisting the urge to turn and look at Yama. They skirt the great hall and exit into a hallway, then into another room where stalls are set up, piled high with sparkling metal goods, teapots and chains. They keep walking, passing devotional rooms for individual gods, promotional posters and women doling out food onto plates.

Eventually they've been around the entire temple and found nothing new. Deflated, they go back to the car and sit for a while, staring out of the windscreen at the temple, the dark sky above it.

'Have you ever studied Hindu gods?' she asks Newt.

'You're kidding! What sacrilege that would have been for my parents. You?'

'No – I mean my grandparents were Chinese; they really didn't have a religion, because of the country as it was. My dad's family were more WASPy – but, you know, they're not full-on churchgoers. Not like lots of my friends.'

'Did you do Religious Studies?'

'I swear I never even knew where Hinduism comes from.'

'It's India. There are deserts in India.'

'Sure. But how the hell do we know about Hindu gods – this is beyond freaky.' She thinks back to the woman in the tree, her swirling orange sari, the way she blinked at the snow. 'I've been somewhere else, Newt – I think we both have.'

'Of course. I've known you somewhere else.'

'My parents promise me I'm not adopted.'

'Mine too – I went on and on at them about it. I don't even look like them.'

McKenzie shakes her head, bites her lip and looks out of the window as Newt puts the car in gear.

For the rest of the night they thread their way through the interminable lattice of Phoenix streets, Newt stopping every now and then to get out and study the canal, black and punched through with the reflection of the stars. On her phone McKenzie scrolls images of deserts in the Indian subcontinent and tries to recall who told her about Ganesh. The name Anna comes to her, but she dismisses it. She can't think of anyone called Anna.

Eventually, at 1 a.m. local time, the day catches up with her. She drops the phone in her lap and lolls her head against the window.

'Come on,' Newt says, swinging the car round and pointing it in the direction of the hotel. 'You need some sleep. We'll start again in the morning.'

'First thing. I haven't got long, and I want to see the city from where that photo is taken – up in the hills.'

'First thing, I promise.'

At the hotel they grab crisps and biscuits from the hotel shop, collect a parcel that's arrived for Newt and go up to McKenzie's room. She showers, then sits in bed eating biscuits while Newt is on the sofa, unpacking the delivery.

'What the hell?'

'A Phantom drone.'

'A what?'

'It's a remote aeroplane. Cost me five grand, but it'll go into places we can't go.'

She frowns. 'Serious?'

'Serious AF. Tomorrow we've got to look at FEMA.'

'You're going to fly that over FEMA?'

'I might.' He holds it up. It looks like a miniature four-cornered helicopter – white with red flashes. 'My little quadcopter. What do you think?'

She sighs. 'I'm scared,' she admits. 'Very, very scared.'

The next morning in the common room there are two piles of belongings on two pieces of the silk from Dubai – in one pile go the necessities of life; in the other are the luxuries that can be left behind. Amasha's gems and saris go into one pile, along with the early maps that Knut made and Elk's fancy serving dishes. Cairo and Mahmoud will be permitted one tiny toy, and Splendour can take her rag doll.

The Regyre fruit sculpture has been the subject of a lot of debate. It is symbolic of all the family have struggled for and has been their constant companion, yet it is heavy and has no function for survival, as there is no need to count Regyres any more. The family all know they've reached the last one. The sculpture lands in the luxuries pile.

The good news is that Tita Lily looks a little better, though Forlani whispers, 'She's not out of the woods yet.' It plagues Spider constantly. One gone – Nergüi – and one so sick …

Tita Lily is sitting up, with Forlani and Hugo to support her – her hands resting on the sleeping-pod walls. She's horrified that the family are moving Shuck. 'How am I going to transport all the clothing? It's insanity,' she says. 'Santa Ninjo didn't reckon on me having to carry all this shit.'

'You'll ride,' they tell her, and she lies back on her pillow, her eyes roving across the ceiling.

Spider goes down the ladder and wanders around the place, checking on the livestock cages, the equipment lockers. Camel is drowsy in the midday heat, but her hump has swelled rock-hard and she's eaten all the mimosa in her net. 'You've got a lot of work to do, old girl,' he tells her, crouching and giving her topknot a rub with his knuckles. 'We're going to feed you up and you're going to be fine.'

He doesn't glance up at the hole in the side of the tower – he's going to wait until the family are inside, eating lunch, for that; instead he opens all the hatches that have been clamped shut during the last Regyre. These lockers are where he stores the oddments he's scavenged over the months that he can't fit upstairs in the common room.

When lunchtime arrives, and Elk is bellowing instructions in the kitchen, Noor and Spider take the opportunity to place a ladder up the side of the tower. Spider goes to the top of it, his tool belt filled with chisels and soldering equipment.

'What can you see?' Noor calls from halfway down the ladder. 'Has it held?'

Spider picks around a little, easing the chisels under the steel plate. The metal is so hot that just a small contact with his skin is enough to blister it. If the Djinni have worked out that two blows in the same place are enough to rupture the metal, they will come back for more.

'It's held,' he calls.

He comes back down off the ladder, wiping his hands. They move the ladder to the interior of the Shuck and check the repair – that too has held.

'Still, it feels precarious,' Spider says, squinting up at it.

'I know it. The sooner we get to Dubai, the better.'

After lunch Spider spends a long time packing up any grease he can use on the lift in Dubai, a lot of rope and a wheel that he thinks he might be able to use as a rudimentary block-and-tackle to winch the cab up. He wants to see it locked in place; he wants the shaft blocked completely.

Then he arranges the parachute material from the skull-and-crossbones Shuck in a dirty heap on the sand. Lolling on top of it is the metal skeleton of the bench that he found in the hotel. He looks at the subtle curve of it for a long time, his thoughts slowly turning.

He's interrupted by chatter and children's shouts from outside the tower. Spider straightens in time to see Elk and Amasha walking silently out of the southern haze, shoulder-to-shoulder, not speaking. The family stop what they are doing and go to the gate to watch them arrive.

Spider watches the pair climb the ladder. Then, when a few minutes have gone, he marches across the tower and climbs the ladder too. He finds them in the common room, sitting in silence at the table. They both have large bowls of water in front of them, and there is a plate of half-eaten kangaroo meat with gnawed cob ears. They both chew in silence, exhausted.

Eventually Amasha wipes her mouth and hands with a cloth. She puts it down, takes a sip of water from the bowl and pushes it aside.

'Spider, staring at us isn't going to make them arrive any quicker. To set your mind at rest, we contacted them.'

'And?'

'They know it's time to come back.' She shakes her head. 'So please stop staring.'

That night Spider can't get rid of the itch of the silent stretches of sand out there. He doesn't go to his own pod, but lies in what was Yma's usual place – the spot she watched the stars from. He pushes aside her sextant and telescope and makes up a bed from cushions. Noor follows his lead and lies down a metre or so away. They have spent a long time sharpening arrows and swords, which Noor has brought and placed under the table, just out of sight, so that the children won't see them.

The rest of the family are in the sleeping platform getting ready for sleep – Hugo reciting his centuries-old poems to himself, Cairo and Mahmoud bickering softly over their toys,

Forlani grunting as he tries to get his tortured legs into a comfortable position. Spider lies on his side, gazing thoughtfully out of the window at the darkened desert. The Virgule is blue in the moonlight, its giant scale-shapes glistening like ice.

Ice, he thinks drowsily. There is something important about ice that he should focus on. And wind. Wind too.

A noise.

Propping himself up on his elbows, he blinks around at the shelter. Noor is awake, staring at him where he lies on his side.

'Did you hear what I heard?' Noor mouths.

Spider must have been asleep, because the stars have shifted a long way and the rest of the family are snoring. He gets gingerly out of his covers and stands at the window.

'Don't open it,' Noor hisses, coming up beside him.

'I won't. Get me the bow.'

While Noor moves around stealthily, trying not to wake the others, Spider lifts Yma's telescope and peers at the desert. There is a huge cloud of sand between here and the Virgule. Inside it, white forms are coiling and uncoiling, as if in a dance. From time to time something darts from the broil and is retrieved so rapidly it leaves only a white blur. It takes Spider a while to understand it's humans who are trying to escape.

Noor returns with the bows. Spider selects an arrow and slots one end into the nock, the other into the rest.

'Don't open the fucking window,' Noor hisses again as he locates his own arrows in position.

'I heard you the first time.'

The two men stand shoulder-to-shoulder, their thick sleep-breath steaming up the window. They say nothing, just watch as the helix of sand moves around the shore of the Virgule. Spider can't get out of his head Noor's face that day in Mithi when he pointed the arrow at him. Was he joking or wasn't he? And the way he went low and uncontactable after Nergüi's death.

'I think it's a show for us,' Spider says. 'Since we'll be next.'

They stand in frozen silence, every muscle on alert. As the spiral of sand moves, a path of destruction is revealed – blood and the sucked-dry remains of people in the sand.

'Why don't they eat the skin?' Noor murmurs.

'I don't know. But we don't want the kids out there tomorrow, OK? Let's find a way to keep them from it.'

Slowly, very slowly, as if they are teasing them, the Djinni allow their circle of violence to drift along the side of the Virgule. Then, when Spider and Noor have been waiting for almost an hour, there is a pause. For a moment Spider thinks he will see a Djinni standing up erect and plain, but the sand doesn't settle long enough. All he has is the chance to see three tall spectral creatures with large heads, before they fork, lightning-fast, towards the south, churning up the sand, making the tower echo with their progress.

Spider and Noor just have time to get to the other side of the lantern before the creatures disappear, over the horizon beyond the Joshua-tree grove. They wait for a long time, but the only things moving are some thin clouds drifting across the moon. Eventually, without a word, they go back to their sleeping pods.

Spider lies awake, stretching his ears out, thinking about the show they've seen, thinking about Noor. Eventually, when he's heard nothing, he goes back to sleep.

McKenzie opens her eyes at the top of a shocked breath. It takes a moment or two to recall where she is – in bed at the Valley View hotel, in the dark; on her right, the panoramic view of the golf course, the stars clear and unblinking. She isn't alone. Someone is in bed with her. She doesn't sit up or scream, but lies as still and silent as possible, waiting for her heart to stop thundering in her chest.

The body is warm, lying on its side so that she is spooning it. At first she thinks Newt has crawled into bed with her, then she notes the softness, the warm curves, the dark, feminine hair tickling her nose.

It's Mom.

McKenzie holds her breath, the creepiness of this situation worming through her. Mom has found her, has crept into her room and is sleeping, waiting for her to wake up.

'Mom,' she hisses. 'Mom – how the hell?'

Mom stirs drowsily. She lifts an arm and drops it wearily over her forehead. 'McKenzie?'

'How did you find me?'

'It wasn't easy,' she says dreamily. 'We've been searching for ages and ages; every time we thought we'd found you, you just disappeared.'

'Mom, you're making no sense.'

'I'm sorry – I know.' She pauses, breathing in rhythmically. 'But, McKenzie, it's important now. You need to come back. I'm going to call you and you need to come.'

'*What? Mom, what do you mean? You're scaring me.*'

'Don't be scared. You're safe.' Mom smells vaguely of coconut and firewood. She rolls slightly sideways and she has the kohl-rimmed eyes of the woman in the tree. 'You're so safe, but we're getting close.'

McKenzie sits up, her heart racing. '*This is insane. Please, who are you? I'm going mad.*'

'No,' the woman replies soothingly. 'No, quite the opposite. You're saner now than you've ever been.'

She rolls away from McKenzie to the edge of the bed. And keeps rolling, off the bed. She falls, but makes no sound as she lands, and when McKenzie leans over, there is nothing on the floor.

McKenzie throws herself off the bed and runs to the bathroom. She throws the switches and light floods the room. It's empty. Trembling, she slides down the wall, hugging her bare legs, digging her upper teeth into the skin on the top of her knees. This is exhausting; exhausting and senseless. She wants her old life back – she wants the normality of her brothers farting and belching in their bedrooms, Mom doing her yoga stretches on the verandah on hot summer mornings, the huge skylights above her bed; even the drama-lama squad and their sneery faces.

She gets shakily to her feet and goes to the bedstead for her phone. It's 5 a.m. There's a message from India.

– On the bus, no alarms raised yet. Mrs S is the best – she hasn't said a word. First registration in half an hour, I'll try to cover for you but can't guarantee anything.

It's been sent an hour ago. Her parents – her *real* parents – still don't know she's missing; they think she's on the bus with India. Fingers shaking, McKenzie pulls up the phone icon, but before she can press it there's a noise on the balcony. Someone rapping hard on the window.

'McKenzie? It's me. Let me in.'

She pads barefoot to the window and lifts the curtains a bit. Newt's outside, dressed only in shorts, his black hair mussed, a haunted look in his eyes. She drags back the door and he steps straight inside, the warm night air coming with him, bringing with it a hint of the desert.

'Jesus, Jesus!' He goes to her bed, gets in it and pulls the sheets up over him, as if he's cold. 'I'm never going to sleep again.'

'You had a dream? Or saw a ghost?'

He clenches his teeth, raising his eyes seriously to her. 'Same happened to you?'

'Yes.'

'They say about it almost being over?'

'Yes.'

He gives a long shudder, closes his eyes. 'I want this out of my head. I want to drag it out.' He digs his finger hard against his temple. 'I'm so fucking tired of it. Tired. I'm a software engineer – an artist – for fuck's sake. Why are they picking on me? I haven't got anything they need.'

McKenzie crosses the room and climbs into bed next to him, slotting herself against him. Wearily Newt lifts an arm and drapes it around her shoulder. She lays her head against his chest and he gives a long sigh.

'I know, I know. You're just a high-school junior from Virginia. You didn't ask for this, either.'

She doesn't reply, simply presses her head harder against him. They sit in silence for a long, long time while the stars fade and the sun slowly climbs up over McDowell Mountain. When the first rays hit the ceiling, Newt stirs.

'OK, I'm not sitting here feeling sorry for myself. We've got to keep looking.'

23

NEWT SPENDS HALF an hour on the balcony as the sun rises, learning how to operate the drone – watching it rise like a strange, squat bird into the early-morning air. He complains that it doesn't have a gimbal, and that he's struggling to keep it steady and in range, so that the images will download.

McKenzie sits on the sun lounger in her terry-towelling robe, Newt's phone on one knee so that each time he raises the drone, she can watch the feed – the sweeps of green, the white hotel, the pair of them on the balcony, looking up at the drone, her hair like a bright-orange flame.

On her other knee she has her own phone, and in the pauses when Newt fiddles with the drone, she ponders the FEMA conspiracy theories, zooming in Google Earth onto the places listed. The rows of FEMA cargo trailers, the fields surrounded by barbed wire, the places that the theorists describe as 'killing fields' with the pits ready for the bodies of the politically opposed, the coffins ready in piles. She notices that all the identified camps in Arizona were once POW camps.

'Did you have any idea how many prisoners of war there were in Arizona?' she says to Newt as she clicks through the sites on her phone.

'Nope. I didn't grow up here, don't forget.'

'Well, I swear I don't remember doing this in eighth-grade history of the Union. They're all over the place. In fact …' She sits up, peering at the phone. 'In fact there's one here in the city.'

'What?'

'Oh, yeah, call me super-sleuth, Sherlock Holmes, Howard Stark – there's an old POW camp right here in the city.'

Newt looks up from the drone. 'Serious?'

'It's in a place called Papago Park. The POWs – they were German mostly – escaped. Dug tunnels …' She frowns. 'There was something else about tunnels under Phoenix. What was it?'

'I dunno.'

'Somewhere there are tunnels – I saw it. But I can't think where.' She shudders. 'I hate tunnels, absolutely hate them. That's my Kryptonite: enclosed spaces.'

'The tunnels in … what? Papaya?'

'Papago. Yup, they were dug through the clay when it was wet, and the Germans escaped and – oh, OK, so look at this, Newt.' She holds the phone up to him. 'It's a military installation and what's housed there is DEMA.'

'DEMA? Like FEMA with a D?'

'Department of Emergency and Military Affairs. I'm sure there's no connection to FEMA – it's just a weird acronym: only the state of Arizona uses it.'

Newt takes the phone from her and frowns. He presses a few buttons and shakes his head. 'That looks kinda sketchy. I think we'll put that on our—'

He stops. Her phone is ringing. Her turns it to her. India's name flashes on and off.

'Fuck!' she says, grabbing it. 'I guess that's the alert call.'

She's about to answer, when another call flashes up: the school. And simultaneously one from Mom. She looks up at Newt.

'Put it on silent,' he tells her.

She does, pushes it down in her pocket and pulls on her sandals.

'Are we going out?'

'Bet your ass we are.'

They buy bubble tea, a tangelo/cara-cara mixed juice, with a sweetcorn and quinoa tortilla, which is stuffed with papaya and Greek yoghurt. It drips all over the place, and McKenzie spends twenty minutes cleaning up the rental car after they've eaten. Her phone is filling up with missed calls and messages.

Newt heads the car out of the city, up towards Anthem and Cave Creek, to lush land where the air is green and cool. 'Those mountains, you reckon?'

McKenzie turns in her seat and squints back at the city, thinking of the image on the poster in her bedroom. 'I dunno. Probably.'

Suddenly in her back pocket her phone screeches. She pulls it out; she's never heard it make a sound like that before. The screen says: *iPhone Alert*. She presses OK; it goes silent and instantly an iMessage pops up – *McKenzie, what are you doing in Arizona? We can see where you are.*

Trembling, she hits 'delete'. She thinks of Dad's job, the CIA building. 'Mom knows I'm here. She sent an iPhone alert. What's an iPhone alert?'

'Jeez,' Newt says. 'You know you can switch that off, don't you? It's just a way of tracing lost phones.'

'*What?*'

'Yeah – switch it off.'

She's never heard of it. McKenzie desperately scrolls through her settings, trying to figure out how to turn it off. How could she be so stupid: stupid enough that her parents understand technology better than her. Except that maybe Dad isn't as naive about technology as he lets on.

Another message – *Honey, India says you're fine, but please come home, the police are going to be involved soon.*

'I can't see how to switch it off. Newt, they said they're getting the police. What am I going to do?'

They're driving through a place called Carefree and Newt pulls over at a mall, where one shop is open, selling coffee and fruit. 'I've got a headache; I need Tylenol,' he says. 'Give me your phone.'

He navigates his way through her iPhone settings, killing her texts from her parents, then goes inside and comes out with pills and bags of fresh pomegranates and dates, citrus fruit, pots of yoghurt and honey.

'The irony of this place's name isn't lost on me,' he says as he washes down the pills. 'Carefree.'

'Yeah.' She looks at the vast sundial in the centre of the mall. A sun-shaped metal cutout with the word 'Carefree' scrawled across it. 'If only.'

They drive on, the sun rising blindingly in the east. Newt's sunglasses aren't good enough, he says, and he keeps pulling the visor down and squinting in the sun, shaking his head as if the rays hurt him. He parks the huge white Audi at a viewpoint and they both get out, cross the two-lane street and look back down at Phoenix, splayed out in the morning sunshine.

'Is this about right?'

McKenzie nods, tilting her head on one side and back on the other side, trying to reproduce the image. 'I think so. It feels right, except it seems . . .'

'What?'

'I don't know. It's like there ought to be something in the front of it. Like a . . .' She holds up her hands in the shape of a pyramid, superimposing them over the city, turning them around until they feel right. 'Like there should be something big at the edge of the city. Here, in the front.'

'Is it in the photo?'

She is silent for a while. It's not in the photo – she's being crazy. She lowers her hands. 'Can you see FEMA from here?'

'I can see where it is.'

'Can you fly the drone from here?'

'Nope. We gotta be closer.'

'So – FEMA and, after, Papago Park?'

'Sure.' He takes off his sunglasses and winces in the sunshine. 'I've got the king of headaches coming on. Let's eat something first.'

McKenzie gets the food out of the back and spreads it on the bonnet of the car. She snacks on dates and mango and watches Newt eat. He is slow, forcing the food down. He keeps the sunglasses close on his face, but the light is bothering him.

Before they leave, she crosses the highway back to the viewing place and gazes at Phoenix again. Her phone is still in the car. Eventually she'll have to look at it, face the music. How long will she have? And what pressure will Mom and Dad be putting on India? It makes her cold to think of it – that India's going to get into trouble for all of this.

'It's time now,' says a voice from the other side of the road. 'Time to come back.'

She turns, frowning. It didn't sound like Newt, but theirs is the only car parked in the lot. He's hidden from view by the car, yet it must have been him calling.

'Now,' comes the voice again. 'Come now.'

In a trance she walks back across the road. She hears the blare of a car horn, the screech of brakes, and turns in time to see a white pickup truck coming at speed around the corner. Just in time she throws herself backwards, falling into the gravel at the roadside. The truck swerves, skids sideways slightly on the road, but recovers and, after a moment's pause, continues onwards in its headlong rush, a window opening long enough to allow a man's fat white arm to thrust itself out, one finger raised.

McKenzie lies winded, her legs scratched, her elbows scraped, and stares at it. Road sense. It's true what India says, then: she has no road sense. She didn't hear it coming. Opposite she can see Newt frozen next to the Audi, his face rigid with shock.

'What the fuck?' He races over the road to her. 'Shit, McKenzie, what happened? Are you OK?'

She nods numbly, licking her lips. 'I thought you were calling me. I thought I heard you calling.'

She leans over and spits into the dirt. Her mouth tastes like salt. She wants to go home; she wants Phoenix not to exist and none of this to have happened.

'I wish I was like the other girls in my year,' she tells Newt. 'I wish my head was a quiet place to be.'

'Well, sistah, trust me – we all wish that. Come on. Get up – we've got some visits to make.'

The next morning Spider is focused – he knows what he has to do. He has a lot more of the corrugated iron in the lockers under Camel's cage and he drags it out, lifting it into place, using a series of bolts and rivets to fasten it in place.

He sits in his secretive cage and untangles the iron braces that once held up a hotel bench. When rested on a flat surface like the floor of Camel's cage, the braces reveal themselves as very slightly curved. That curve enthrals him. He studies it and measures it, making sketches in the sand with a stick. He begins to pull out from the lockers some of the items he's collected, squatting on his haunches and sorting through the oddments of rope and screws and offcuts of timber.

He works all day, while the sun passes over the Shuck. It's only when Noor appears, his face solemn, that he packs everything away in the boxes behind Camel.

'The kids are upstairs,' says Noor. 'Time?'

Spider nods, wiping his hands on a rag. They go silently out into the desert. They carry rakes and shovels, but as they near the Virgule, they see almost no sign of the violence from last night. They stand for a long time, kicking at the sand with their feet, finding one or two hardened trails of blood, but no bodies. It's as if the wind has blown the sand over the event, denying that it happened at all.

'It happened,' Noor says.

Spider nods. 'It sure did.'

They cover the blood up, kicking it around, trying to hide it from the kids.

Much later Spider untethers Camel and, with a few clicks in his throat, coaxes her out onto the scorching sand. She walks obediently behind him. He is thinking about ice and the way the wind blows. He squints up at the sky, the relentless eye of the sun.

Eventually, after a kilometre, he reaches the Virgule. The salt lake's shores are imprecise, tattered and vague. They creep up to the walker. Sometimes the first thing you encounter is a diamond of salt crust alone in the sand; a metre or so later it will be accompanied by another crisp white scale; then after another few minutes' walking you might happen upon a cluster and eventually the beginnings of the lake, the sun glancing blindingly off its white surface. In other locations the lake shore is as abrupt as stepping off a New York pavement into a gutter – suddenly it's there: hundreds of square kilometres of salt.

A few steps later the sand crumbles audibly with each step, and Spider realises there is nowhere else to step except directly onto the fragile surface of the lake. In the blazing sun he stands with his hands thrust into the pockets of his leather jacket. The wind stirs his petticoat a fraction, but otherwise the Virgule is silent and still, all the way to the Chicane city.

'It's like ice,' Spider says. 'Today it looks just like ice.'

For as long as Spider has been watching the Virgule, it's had a habit of changing colour. This morning he noticed a section of it halfway across had darkened, as if a cluster of sand rings had opened up. That's the problem with the Virgule, its inconsistency: one section might be strong while the next could be non-traversable and dangerous. It changes hourly sometimes.

He steps gingerly onto the nearest salt-flake. It holds firm. He crouches and touches the salt wonderingly, amazed by its strength and transparency. When the water dried and dropped away, it left the crust in place, so there is half a metre or more of air between the lake's surface and its floor. Under it he can see the sand, with the remains of a dead cactus splayed out down there.

Then he realises he's looking at a human skin spread out on the sand a metre below him. It's as if a whole human has been unpeeled and painstakingly splayed out there.

Someone from last night. One of the missing victims.

24

MCKENZIE USES THE serviettes Newt picked up when he bought breakfast to stem the flow of blood from her elbows. They wind their way down Interstate 17 until they are downtown, where Newt pulls off, blending with the rush-hour traffic. They pass the Bharatiya Ekta temple, its lights still switched on but fainter against the intense sunlight, and continue on downtown.

Her phone is hot with all the contacts; there are forty-three notifications on every platform imaginable: Facebook and Snapchat, and a whole host of voice messages. The ones from India are apologetic – *I tried to keep them off your back for as long as I could. Did my best . . .*

The ones from her parents are at first angry, then cajoling, then increasingly desperate. In the latest voice message, Mom's crying: 'India says you're OK but she won't say what you're doing in Phoenix. Please, please, whatever we've done to make you do this, we are so sorry. We miss you.'

Even Tatum has left a post – *Hey, sis, let me know you're OK. Love you. T x*

She slides the phone into her shorts pocket. It's hot now, getting above thirty, according to the dashboard on the Audi. She licks her lips and looks at Newt. His voice is weak and he looks really sick now, sweat beading his forehead. A sense of vague dread and tiredness crawls into her – a gnawing futility at every Jack in the Box, Jiffy Lube and Latter-day Saints church they pass. The shopping malls and the Native American art outlets, the upmarket houses in Arcadia, the orange trees and huge palms.

As they roll into 22nd Street, where FEMA is based, McKenzie says, 'It looks like what it says it is.'

'Still we're going to look,' Newt says.

'But we don't gotta use that thing?'

'Only if we can't see anything.'

He slows and she leans forward to study the compound. It is surrounded by palisade security fencing, which she can see straight through, to where all the emergency vehicles are parked. There are one or two administration buildings, in the usual adobe format, a geometrical roof lined in red, and rising above everything a fire tower, pale with dark windows. Beyond that she can see an area with cars on their sides, a bus with windows blown out.

'Training ground.' Newt cruises slowly past, his eyes on the road ahead, ignoring the guard who stands at the entrance booth. 'Standard for a fire department. See anything else?'

She strains to see as they drift past, but there is nothing that isn't like the Google Earth image. 'No,' she says as Newt turns the car for a second loop. 'Genuinely. Nothing.'

He drives another block, then stops the car. He sits for a moment, his hands over his face. 'Shit,' he groans. 'What is wrong with me? Fucking great time to get sick, isn't it?' He raises a hand to the sky. 'Awesome timing, dude. Thanks for that.'

'Did you eat anything bad?'

'Dunno.'

She tentatively touches his neck. His skin is hot, and now she can see he has sweat stains on his T-shirt. His skin looks mottled, angry red in some places.

'You're burning up. You need to lie down.'

'Can you drive?'

She hesitates. 'I dunno – I'm not that great with roads. Kind of careless …'

'You don't say. Don't think about it; just do it.'

They change seats. She pushes the buttons until his seat goes back, and he grabs a sweatshirt from the back and pulls it over his face. 'The light is making it worse, I swear.'

'Relax, try to sleep.'

She plugs Papago Park into the satnav and puts the car into drive. Everything in the Audi seems so big, so remote, as if anything she does can't really connect to what happens out on the road, but she nudges the car into the traffic and after few blocks decides the Audi is easier to handle than Tatum's Subaru or Dad's Duster – the boulevards of Phoenix are broader than the old Fairfax country routes and the crazy highways that feed DC. The drivers are more considerate and slower, hordes of big SUVs all driven by tiny wizened men and women in golf gear. Or Latino contractors in their white Chevvy pickups. No Uber drivers terrorising the streets, weaving in and out of the lanes.

She concentrates hard, keeping her eyes off the sky and on the road. According to the GPS, they are halfway to Papago Park when she gets a sense of something behind her. She adjusts the rear-view mirror and there, in a black Mercedes, is a Latino-looking guy in sunshades following her.

The next traffic lights are red and, when she stops, the guy pulls into the right-turn lane behind four other SUVs. But she notices, when the signals change, that he doesn't make the right turn – instead he pulls back out into her lane, about four cars behind.

She clears her throat.

'What?' Newt asks. 'Wassup?'

'Not sure if we're being followed.'

'By who?'

'I dunno. A guy in a Mercedes.'

'Do a right.'

She signals and pulls into the right-hand lane. Behind her the Mercedes seems to hesitate, lets a couple of cars go by, then copies her manoeuvre. A prickle of sweat starts in her armpits.

'He followed.'

'So do another right.'

She continues on to the next traffic lights, but there is no right-hand lane, so she waits for the next one and makes the turn at the last possible second.

'What happened?'

McKenzie looks in the mirror. 'He did the same.'

'Another right – come back to where you started.'

She obeys, coming out on the wide boulevard where she picked him up. This time the Merc doesn't follow, but continues straight on over the intersection.

'What the fuck?' She takes a deep breath, realising she's trembling. 'He's gone.'

'OK – you did good. Keep going.'

'You think it's my parents?'

'Nah. I disabled your services.'

'But someone *was* following us.'

'Or maybe he just lost his way, and you put two and two together.'

McKenzie bites her lip, looking in the mirror. 'Maybe,' she murmurs. 'Maybe.'

Papago Park is a long way to the east of the city, out where the land gets free and wide and the highway slowly inches up into the red mountains. The military base is on the other side of the highway, but she gets a good look at it, the low marble monument declaring it as the Arizona National Guard, the entrance on Bushmaster Boulevard, with all the flagstaffs rising above the guards' low sentry post.

She has to head way out past it, to where the land opens up into a great gulping expanse of desert, all pocked with red rock and cacti, before she can make a turn in the road and backtrack. This way, she has time to observe how the perimeter fence curls around the red rock formations, to see the buildings and the way the roads inside the base wind around the mountains. The places that are blurred on the map are further inside the zone.

'Can you find somewhere for me to start the drone?'

'What? You're not going to do it, are you?'

Newt holds up a weary hand. 'Time is short, my sistah, time is short, and I'm struggs to funk right now.'

'What?'

'Struggling to function.'

The end of the installation is about a hundred feet ahead, so she signals right and turns down it. The perimeter fence is doubled up on this stretch of the base, with an opaque interior screen – maybe because there is residential property on the left – and beyond the fence are the vehicles, sprawling parking lots full of canvas-coloured trucks, bulldozers and jeeps, various imprecise buildings and more red rock formations, as if the base has been built around the hilly structures.

'Weird,' she says. 'So many hills in there. Makes you wonder why they chose this bit of ground.'

Newt kneels up, turning round, but the movement is too much. He leans over for a bit, holding the seat back, his head lowered, and makes desperate retching noises.

'Jesus, Newt.'

He breathes hard and sinks back down on his heels. 'It's OK,' he hiccups. 'I'm not going to puke on you – it's kind of a point of pride. I promise I won't.'

'You got to've eaten something bad.'

'Maybe.'

When he's got past the nausea, he ferrets around with the drone, pulling it out of the box. He's sweating freely now, makes no attempt to hide it.

'Pull over – like anywhere: let's just do this thing.'

She takes a right on the back road, East Oak Street, and continues on until the eastern part of the reservation, where there is a small amount of coverage from the mountains. They pull into the driveway of a low Spanish-style house, with orange roof tiles and acacia trees in the front. It looks empty, and when she looks back down the street behind and sees no cars, merely a couple of contractors wandering along talking, for a second she feels slightly sheltered, but not calm.

'You're going to do this? Seriously.'

'Yup. But we won't have much time. Where's the place that's blurred on Google?'

'Over there – in that corner, see the two low hills?'

'Yup.'

'In between that, it's all blurred.'

'OK.' Newt throws his phone at her. 'Code is two-zero-one-seven-one-eight, you know where the app is.'

She catches the phone, opens it and jumps out of the Audi, leaving the engine running. Everything is happening so fast – faster than her brain can cope with. Almost as soon as she has the app opened, Newt has made the quadcopter lift up off the roof of the Audi. It floats up almost inaudibly, only a faint buzz, like an outsized butterfly. It heads across the street and way above the perimeter fence – when she taps into the app, she sees the red cinder of the pavement, the fence, the bulldozers and the jeeps.

'Lemme see.' Newt leans over. She turns the phone to face him and, tongue between his teeth, he toggles the controls, squinting at the screen.

'More right,' she says. 'Back that way.'

The drone flies on, sending back almost unbelievable imagery of the stretches of military base, the road markings, the buildings and the vehicles. A row of helicopters – and still nothing stops them. On and on it goes, then suddenly there's a low drone, a klaxon-like alarm sounding from somewhere in the depths of the installation.

'They've seen us.' Newt stares at the screen, still toggling the controls. 'But don't sweat yet. They'll have to scramble to find us. Am I close?'

'Yes – those hills. Just there.' The phone shows a shaky image of two red hills, a snake of a road going between them. A parapet of some sort. 'Can you go low, Newt?'

'Yes, but we won't see the drone again.'

'I need to see low.'

He shrugs. 'This is it, then.'

As he moves the drone in and the picture on the phone becomes clearer, it shows a rock face, a small guarded entrance to what looks like a door into the rock, with ten or so guys with Barrett M82s standing at attention. The entrance to a tunnel, McKenzie's sure. It will lead into the desert somewhere – to the place where they do the experiments.

On the base, doors open: people stream out of the buildings, running across the reservation. Onscreen, the guards are seeing the drone, the alarms are blaring now, and in McKenzie's throat a bubble of panic lodges.

'We can't do this, we can't—' she begins, but is cut off by the image of a guard on Newt's phone, raising his weapon, taking aim at the drone. She sees the glint of his eye, quite clearly, as he fires. Then the screen explodes in a blast of white noise and Newt drops the control and bends over. At first, irrationally, McKenzie thinks he's been shot. But he hasn't. He's throwing up on the tarmac, his body trembling like a snake.

25

IT TAKES ALL of Spider's concentration to complete his task. Mid-afternoon he holds the object up to the light and inspects it: a tiny replica of a sailing vessel, with spars and a parachute-silk sail, except that in the place of a keel, two skate-shaped pieces of polished metal are attached to a wooden cross-runner. It is basic and crude, but it will test his theory.

'Hey, Sandwalker,' he murmurs. 'Welcome to the Cirque, Sandwalker. Good luck with the weight that rests on your shoulders.'

He loops the miniature yacht into a sling on the other side of Camel and turns her, so that it won't be visible to anyone watching. He tightens the straps, winds Camel's leash into his hand and gives her the tap on her hindquarters that she needs to get up. She does it slowly, clumsily and, once she's up, he leads her towards the tower entrance, conscious of any eyes on him.

He leads Camel down to the salt lake, talking to her in a quiet voice. The sun is low in the sky as he crouches next to the giant salt-flakes of the Virgule and examines his strange little balsa-wood and iron beast.

The little boat is square-rigged. Spider doesn't know how else to construct it, because he isn't sure of the physics of making a fore-and-aft-rigged yacht, so he will have to make do with this unwieldy shape. He arranges the mast and the spars, whittled from a spruce floorboard that he peeled up in an Abu Dhabi hotel, then attaches the sail to the lanyards using a sheet-bend knot around a small pebble.

Satisfied, he sets the contraption down on the white salt. It is only about thirty centimetres in height, and in most ways this prototype will tell him little about what would happen if he scaled it up, but he thinks he's got the relative weights correct. All he wants is the satisfaction of knowing that it won't tilt, or fail to move.

Slowly he shuffles back from the sailing boat and waits, squatting on his haunches, holding his ankles, staring intently at it. At present the desert is quiet and motionless, but often as the sun comes down, the breezes lift. Sure enough, he has been there for less than ten minutes when a decaying smell wafts across him, and with it the slightest hint of a breeze. The sailing boat stutters forward a few centimetres, like a living creature, almost startling Spider with its speed.

It stops. There is a breathless pause, and the stern jitters from side to side, like a racehorse kept in rein. Then, just when Spider thinks it must somersault stern-over-bow, it takes off fast, heading away from him in a smooth, continuous line.

'*Merde, merde*,' he yells delightedly, standing up to watch the boat skitter away. It is going so fast away from him that he has to find eyeglasses in his tool belt to keep track of it. It bounces gaily along, the sun catching the tiny reinforced tip of aluminium on the mast. 'See that?' he yells in delight to Camel. 'Did you see her go? My own goddamned Sandwalker!'

Eventually the tiny boat goes so far onto the Virgule it has disappeared completely. Spider lowers the binoculars and frowns. He realises his mistake. He's made no note of the weights and measurements – all of which were done on pure guesswork – and now the boat is gone. He looks at Camel, dismayed. 'Fuck, fuck-fuck-*fuck*!'

Camel lowers her neck and moves her head round and round, grunting low and soft. They stand together, perusing the silent Virgule, and beyond it lights coming on in the Chicane city. And then, far to the left, hundreds of metres away, the Sandwalker bounces suddenly out of the distance. The wind must have changed, because now she is hurtling south towards them, like a homing pigeon. Spider lifts the glasses to watch her race back.

About thirty metres away she tilts a little and veers sideways, unbalanced. There is a large bounce, which lifts her clear of the salt, then her stern flies up, to the side, she flips twice and crashes – upside down in a tangled heap.

Spider lowers the glasses, half smiling. He isn't sure whether to be dismayed by the crash or delighted she's got that far. It was more – much more – than he expected. He tucks the glasses into his belt and uses his skirt to wipe the sand from his face. What now? The craft is still out of reach, though. There's no way to examine her and understand what caused the crash.

As if reading his mind, to his left Camel calmly takes a step onto the salt lake. Spider freezes, expecting the salt to crack under her. 'Hey, girl, no – stop.'

But she doesn't stop. Camel continues walking placidly, plonking her great soft feet down evenly, unperturbed by his fear. The salt holds firm, shows no sign of cracking. She looks if she's been doing this forever. When she reaches the crashed boat, she turns and uses her nose to give it a nudge. Slowly and erratically, she propels it along the salty surface towards Spider.

'Hey, you're better than a dog.' He takes a few experimental steps out onto the salt to join her. At first he's tentative, but the surface doesn't crack under his weight, either. It feels solid. Maybe he's been overestimating the fragility of the Virgule. He meets Camel halfway and gathers up the broken Sandwalker to examine it. In the failing light it is impossible to see what has happened, but it's certainly beyond repair. He ties it into a fabric loop on Camel's *mahawi* and leads her off the Virgule. The salt doesn't crack or creak under their combined weight. That changes his thoughts on the walk back and, when he gets to the Shuck and finds Amasha standing in the opening, watching him seriously, he has made up his mind.

'Where have you been?' she asks, leaning casually on the doorway.

'Just looking at the Virgule.'

He leads Camel past her, going into the dark interior of the tower.

'When we go to Dubai,' he calls over his shoulder to Amasha as he works on settling Camel, getting her into the cage and brushing her coat, 'Camel is staying here. The kids can walk that distance on their own, so can Forlani. If we need her, it will be to carry Tita Lily.'

He waits for a reply, a sarcastic 'Of course', meaning that she understands exactly what Spider is up to and can read his every thought. When she doesn't speak, eventually he turns to look at her. Amasha is standing with her arms folded, a tiny insignificant figure in the huge tower.

She holds his gaze for a few more moments, then, without another word, unfolds her arms, shakes her head and walks slowly to the Shuck ladder.

McKenzie has never moved so fast. She throws Newt into the shotgun seat and floors the accelerator, sending the Audi into a rubber-burning screech on East Oak Street, then left into North 60th, speeding past all the low bougie houses, adorned with big gates and ornamental cacti.

Newt lies on the seat, grey and exhausted, puke all over his T-shirt.

'What now?' she yells. 'The drone controls are all over the street – what do we do?'

'Keep calm. It's not the end of the world. We are kids; we wanted to do a dare. If we're stopped. Which we won't be.'

She glances at him. He is lying on his back, his hands over his face. 'You need a doctor?'

'No. Just get me the Tylenol, will you? I must have thrown up the first lot.'

She drives on – looking constantly in the mirror for a tail. Nothing happens. She gets into a more residential area downtown, where the buildings are low, the yards piled with junked-out cars and the palm trees grow in high banners. Eventually, when her pulse has calmed, she pulls over in the parking lot of a Home Depot.

'Here.' She hands him the Tylenol with a bottle of water, and Newt manages, painfully, to sit up long enough to swallow them. Then he drops back and pulls the sweatshirt over his head, pressing it into his face. She stares at his elbows where they poke up.

'Newt. Lemme see your arms.'

'Wha?'

She puts her hands on them – the skin is hot, and it's peppered with raised splotches.

'Did you get meningitis shots when you were a kid?'

'What? I don't think so.'

She takes a deep breath, holds it, then lets it out. 'Have you got health insurance?'

'Of course. In my billfold.'

'Where? Your pocket?' She reaches around the back of him, where he is drenched in sweat, finds the wallet and opens it. There's his identity card, his driving licence, credit cards and a red-and-white health-insurance card. The name Gaston Herrera.

'I'm sorry – but you've got to see a doctor. Is your insurance good anywhere?'

'It's the best.'

'OK.' She hurriedly plugs in a search on her phone. The nearest emergency centre is the HonorHealth in Scottsdale. Only five minutes' drive away. 'If we get stopped, I'm driving you to the hospital, OK? Not because we're running away from anything – remember that.'

'Fuck,' Newt manages. 'Fuck!'

She finds the hospital easily: on a wide street, it is the tallest building around, with a curved central building and annexes on either side. The blue sky and clouds are reflected in the glass, and for a second she loses attention – just briefly, long enough to mount a kerb, with a grating sound of metal from under the huge car.

'Please don't fuck the hire car,' Newt groans.

She parks near the emergency entrance and, not bothering to pay the fee, helps Newt inside. He is shivering now and barely able to stand. The clerk at the desk frowns and pushes back her chair. If McKenzie had any doubts about how serious this is, that uncertainty vanishes, simply with the expression on the clerk's face.

'OK, a wheelchair.' She presses a button and mutters something into it, a code of some sort. 'Insurance? And sit him down – now!'

McKenzie puts down Newt's insurance card and takes him to a seat. 'It's OK,' she tells him, stroking his head. His clothes are soaked through and the rash is everywhere now, a creeping blaze of red. 'We're in the right place.'

'I let you down.'

'You didn't. You've got some amazing footage on the phone. You're going to get some antibiotics in you and everything's going to be fine.'

They wait only three minutes, but in that time Newt throws up again. This time it's pathetic brown bile, which she catches in the kidney bowl that the clerk has given her. The triage team arrives and wheels him down the passageway. The chief nurse is named Rose and has a Vietnamese accent like lots of McKenzie's friends' parents.

'*Cam o'n ban,*' McKenzie tries shyly to Rose, who is bustling away down the passageway, her hand on Newt's shoulder.

Rose turns and smiles at McKenzie. 'You speak Vietnamese?'

'No – my friends do, though.' McKenzie feels tears pricking at her eyes out of nowhere. She's so tired. 'Please take care of him, will you? He's all I've got.'

'Are you next of kin?'

She hesitates, then nods. 'Yes.'

Rose leans into Newt. 'Gaston, honey, is this your next of kin? McKenzie?'

He nods.

'You happy for me to speak to her about your treatment?'

'I am. More than happy.'

He is wheeled into a cubicle. A nurse in a well-pressed pink tabard and trousers smiles and draws the curtain.

'Do you want to wait?' Rose asks. 'There's a vending machine down the passageway. I'll come and give you news.'

But before she can go, Newt grabs McKenzie's hand and holds it hard against his hot face. 'Don't wait for me. Search – and search well. You hear me?'

McKenzie waits fifteen minutes before Rose comes back. She sits down and holds McKenzie's hands. 'We've got the best guy in the place working with Gaston. At the moment we're looking at whether it's meningitis, but we won't know for sure until we've got some more tests back, so don't go telling anyone that – OK?'

'What happens next?'

'Assessments and IV antibiotics and lots of rest.'

'What's going to happen?'

Rose gives a smile. It's edged with doubt, though – any idiot can see that. 'He's going to be just fine: a little rest, the right meds, he'll be fine. You wanna give me your number in case you want to go out and get something to eat? You look tired, you know that?'

Search – and search well . . .

Those words won't leave McKenzie that afternoon; everywhere she goes, they haunt her. She sits in the car lot and opens her phone. More messages and texts and Snapchats from Virginia. She taps into Google: 'Phoenix tunnels'.

The 4G isn't great; there's a wait, then suddenly the pages come up. The first one shows the university. McKenzie chews at the inside of her mouth as she navigates through to the page. She saw this page last night, and now it comes back to her: there are maintenance tunnels all the way under the university. Apparently they are used by the students as a music venue – there's a kind of vibe about them that's attractive.

She swigs some water and pushes her hair back, checks her reflection in the visor's vanity mirror. Rose was right: she looks appalling. Her eyes are red and there's an artefact from her earlier scrape with the truck on the mountain highway – a swipe of blood on her cheek like a tribal marking, bisected by streams of sweat.

She licks her finger and wipes it away. Then, pretending to be checking her hair, she uses the mirror to scan the parking lot.

There's nothing obvious – mostly parked cars, windscreen sunshields in some of the windows. SpongeBob SquarePants on one, and Elsa from *Frozen* in her blue dress on another, her arm around the snowman. A couple nearer the hospital entrance, older, the wife helping the man to manoeuvre his walker.

'Newt,' she whispers at the blank hospital wall, 'good luck. Good luck.'

She heads to the university, not that far from the hospital, thinking about that entrance between the rocks at Papago Park military reservation and the way it was guarded. There were more guards there than anywhere else in the entire camp. What did that mean? Could it be an underground entrance to something? All those years ago the POW prisoners burrowed their way out of the camp, but they were Germans, not prepared for the colossal skies and dry air of Arizona. When they found themselves out in the desert, they couldn't survive. Most of them crawled back through the same tunnels they'd escaped from, just to taste water and shade.

From the little information online, it's impossible to tell where the tunnels took the prisoners, but the fact that there are tunnels in the centre of the university has to mean something, McKenzie reasons, chewing her thumbnail as she heads into the campus streets. What do the tunnels lead to? Do they connect somewhere underground to Papago Park?

From time to time she imagines she's being followed, and she stares at the man in the Jeep Cherokee next to her at a red traffic light, noticing the way he pulls on his sunshades when she turns to look at him. Or those two middle-aged businesswomen in a black Prius, who look so out of place and don't overtake when she slows the car to a crawl.

She passes the Arizona Science Center with its rising adobe-coloured wall, its glass-mounted entrance lobby, its strangely diametrical walls and walkways, and the colourful montage of hands and planets, the cells mounted on its blank white edifices. When she was researching colleges she read through the options at ASU: there's a world-class hydrology and atmospheric-sciences programme here, it's still on her list of alternatives to Caltech. But that was before – back in the road behind – before she went publicly crazy, then escaped from her parents and ran away to break every law in a distant desert state.

At last she finds a place to park, though the Audi feels ostentatious and gauche in the uni parking lot. She's embarrassed, getting out of it, as she drops to the baking tarmac in her thin sandals. She shoves her phone in her back pocket and takes stock of her surroundings. A vast anvil-shaped building with white zigzags within its concave scoop dominates the skyline behind her, but her senses tell her that's north, backing the Salt River, and she wants to be deeper into the campus.

She turns and begins to walk down East University Drive, with the huge spaceship-like Desert Financial Arena on her right. She passes 'Urgent Care' medical centres and nail bars, a playhouse, then left into the main campus, along the wide avenues, past the bike racks, the yellowing grass and the huge palm trees. The students are all in shorts and vests; some wear Sun Devils hats and Ts. A few of the guys check her out as she walks, but when McKenzie meets their stares, something about her eyes makes them look away hurriedly. It's not good day to try to make small talk with her.

The buildings are mostly sand-coloured and adobe-red. She passes a huge formal square with a fountain encased in red stone pillars, and then turns into Tyler Mall, where cycles and electric maintenance carts cruise along the wide boulevard. There's a booth-like structure that has been covered in flyers, advertising lectures and local gigs and student housing, and for a moment or two she lingers, reading the events board: 'God and the Cosmos', 'A Christian and an Atheist discuss Racism', 'The Human Rights Film Festival' and 'Future Sun Devils Day'. There's an indy-looking flyer in black and white, with a mask floating above an image of Phoenix, which reads: *Clusterfest. Explore ASU's underground.* She unpins one of the flyers and examines it more carefully.

'You should go to that,' says a voice next to her. A tall African-American guy, dressed more stylishly than the other students in a tight-sleeved floral shirt and loafers, is smiling at her. 'That'll open your mind.'

She eyes him carefully. He stands loose-hipped, his hands shoved artlessly in his low-riding skinny jeans.

'Will it?'

'Sure.' He grins. 'Look at this one: dystopian punk for millennial scum. Nice!'

'Why are they flexing about *ASU's underground*?'

'Because they're subversive? I don't know.' He stamps his heel on the ground. 'They're down there, under us all. Like rats.'

'The tunnels? Where do the tunnels go?'

The guy frowns, studies her a bit closer. 'You don't know about the ASU tunnels? Where are you from?'

'Virginia.'

'*Virginia?*' He makes it sound like she's said, '*The Moon*.' He gives a long, loose laugh. 'Well, girl, what're you doing here? You just about a million miles away from home.'

'Not a million miles. Only a couple of thousand. And I'm here because I …' She hesitates.

'Because you … ?' he prompts. 'Because you what?'

She smiles and shakes her head. This guy. So well dressed, with his pearl cuff-buttons. Almost a parody of a seventies campus rat. He's out of place here; he doesn't belong.

'You were saying?' he presses. 'About what you're doing here?'

She mumbles something under her breath, twists on her heel and walks hurriedly away – heading in what she hopes is the direction of the car. She can feel him behind her, following her, so she picks up her speed until there's some ground between them. Shooting a look over her shoulder – he's following her, smiling, hands in his pockets – she puts a little more urgency into her step. At last she reaches a corner and turns out of sight. Up ahead are the cars on the perimeter road, and in her pocket her phone is vibrating.

The pedestrian signals are red and she has to wait. She snatches out the phone and looks at it, expecting Mom or India or the school. But it's an Arizona number. 'Yes?'

'McKenzie, this is Rose. From HonorHealth?'

'Yeah – hi, Rose.' She shoots a glance behind her. The guy is standing between two buildings smiling at her, as if he's not sure whether to sprint after her or not. 'Any news?'

There's a silence at the end of the phone that makes McKenzie feels momentarily sick.

'Rose?'

'Can you come back to the hospital, McKenzie? Are you in a position to do that?'

Her throat dries. 'Is he OK?'

'We'll talk when you get here.'

'Just tell me – is he OK?'

'McKenzie, I think you need to come back: will you be able to do that? Safely?'

She lowers her face. The guy is still watching her and her phone is full of messages. The pedestrian lights change to green.

'Sure,' she says and cancels the call. She stands for a moment, breathing through her nose, her mouth dry. It occurs to her that Rose is so polished. And the guy in the floral shirt, only a few hundred feet away, looking like he's ready to start sprinting towards her. Ultimately, she wonders, where does madness lead? Does it lead you through a wormhole that you never crawl back through, or is it a series of ventures into a place you don't recognise?

Eventually, as the lights are about to change back, she steps into the street, her heart thumping hard. She draws the car keys out of her pocket, feeling the drag of tiredness in her bones, imagining the sap of oxygen in her muscles, the build-up of lactic acid drawing her down, always down. What will she find if she goes to the hospital?

'McKenzie, come back now,' says a voice, very close to her.

She stops, turns and looks behind her.

'*McKenzie! McKenzie! Come back now, come back.*'

The voice is close, so close. But no one is there.

McKenzie is standing motionless in the centre of the street when a huge GMC Sierra with a chrome pushbar, going at forty miles an hour – seeing a green light and not expecting a young woman to be stationary in the street – ploughs directly into her. She's lifted easily into the air.

She flies for several feet, her thoughts suddenly slow and clear. An image of Newt in the hospital, his skin mottled. A picture of when she was in first grade and met India; how they hollowed out pumpkins and made faces in them, and laughed until she thought she was going to pee herself. The long, rolling forests of Virginia, the eagles circling above the grey roads, the malls and the Korean churches, the suburbs, and Dr Shreve in her office, peering at McKenzie, saying, 'Just speak what you're feeling.' Mom and Dad, Tatum and Luke.

Her head hits the street light first, breaking her neck and crushing her skull. The impact folds her arms backwards, up around her head, at thirty miles an hour, dislocating both shoulders and shattering further bones in her wrists. There's a flowering of pain in her belly, and an image of the posters on her wall in Virginia, and a memory of a little hamster the Strathies had, which Dad used to keep in his top pocket.

Her ribs break, perforating her spleen, liver and lungs. Her thoughts slow even more, to encompass her whole childhood, every trip to school as clear as a bell, every exam, every look from

Joe Marino, every time the drama-lamas looked at her, the great milkshakes at the Silver Diner, the models she made of the dunes.

The large arteries from her heart are sheared, her phone flies from her pocket, the messages scrolling up it – *McKenzie, please call me*, India says. *Please please please call call …*

But McKenzie is moving fast towards the place she can't come back from. She senses a moment's pain, then her body is liquid. She feels her legs hit the tarmac and her head go thudding back.

Before she can even think about her injuries, or why she's so cold, McKenzie Strathie is dead.

PART TWO

THE SANDWALKER

THE METSE'HAF

Eti Metse'haf

Kniga von patefactio, Chapter 18, Verse 2

(The Book of Ymå)

2. And so it comes to pass that her corporeal self
floateth away from Ymå with no more heed than a seed
blowing in the wind.

3. She comes to know the blaze inside her, understands
it is inextinguishable. An anima that faints not in hot sun,
dries not in the wind, drowns not in torrents and starves
not in the years of famine …

26

SPIDER SITS CROSS-LEGGED in the sand, hunched over his secret project. He is using a thick needle he's stolen from Tita Lily and some purloined kangaroo gut that Madeira has been hoarding for months, which he uses to stitch the skull-and-crossbones parachute material. He is planning to cross the Virgule, come hell or high water – to get closer to the town on the Chicane.

It's a small tube shape that he constructs, without understanding the physics or the maths and working on instinct alone, the way he has ever since he had to survive mending clocks on the streets of Paris. Every time he hears someone come near, he arranges the material into a bag shape, in case someone dares to peep over the barricade that he has made to shield him from view.

It is close to noon and Spider has just broken off from work, come out of the shelter to feed Camel, when there is a shout from the far end of the tower. Madeira is running to the entrance. He knows what this means: the Futatsu are back. Hurriedly he shovels everything back into the locker behind Camel, settles her, wipes the sand off his bare legs, off his hands, and heads fast to the entrance.

Everyone is gathering there, looking out into the desert. He stands at the back of the group, head and shoulders above the others, and stares, his heart thumping. It's not two of them today, it's Elk on his own, and this means news.

'Noor, Spider and you, Madeira.' Elk's ten metres from them when he starts to call. 'Bring water and blankets. Forlani, make sure the beds are prepared.'

The blankets have been waiting for days now, so it takes Spider and the other two less than five minutes to collect up everything they need. They each take three blankets in a stack, and on top place water gourds and food. Elk has set out a jar of preserved oranges, one of the last of a precious stock that he made with oranges picked in the place they identified as Palm Springs. This is intended for Yma, her favourite fruit; and for Knut, a plate of pineapple and dates.

Spider, Madeira and Noor jog out into the scorching sunlight to catch up with Elk, who has turned and is marching back the way he came, retracing his steps in the sand.

'He asked for three of us,' Madeira says breathlessly. She has a cigar behind her ear, and her half-shaved hair is long and bedraggled. 'That means they're both back.'

They have gone more than a kilometre to the west when they spot a huddled figure in the wavery heat. Elk is heading straight towards it and, as they draw closer, they see it is Amasha, crouched on the sand, her sari being whipped around her in the wind.

Next to her on the sand, splayed out face down, are the two Scouts, silent and still as corpses. They are both naked and have a vague, unearthly gleam to them. This stickiness is something Spider has witnessed before – he is the strongest, so he's usually the one sent into the desert to help collect the Scouts and has seen this unsettling mottling of the skin, the appearance of being half in and out of death. Which, of course, they are.

Yma lies with her head towards him, her long apricot fall of hair blazing against the white of her skin.

'Wait,' he tells Noor and Madeira. 'Wait.'

They both stop and turn to Spider, frowning.

'Here.' He hands two blankets to Madeira. 'You go ahead. We'll come when you've done it.'

She nods, takes the blankets, turns and pads towards Amasha, who takes them and carefully tucks the blankets around the two Scouts. Madeira is trying to coax Yma to drink water, though she is still barely conscious and can't yet swallow. Elk is talking in a low voice to Knut, whose bright-blue hair blazes in the sunlight.

Spider unscrews the lid of the water gourd and starts off towards them, where the sand is disturbed, with strange smears in it. Often when the Scouts return they leave similar tracks to those left by the families being dragged by the Djinni, as if their return to the afterlife has been as violent and messy as a death.

Amasha and Madeira are tipping an unconscious Yma to a sitting position to try to rouse her. Elk is in a squat next to Knut, holding his head, speaking to him gently. Noor and Spider help him arrange blankets across Knut, who has started to shiver. Spider crouches and takes Knut's hand, rubbing it between his own, bringing the warmth into it.

This part is always the hardest part for the Scouts. The shivering, the pain and the dizzying disorientation. But between them they'll get them through it and they'll come back to where they belong.

Eeeeeema Eeeeema Eeeeema.

Yma opens her eyes. Her mouth is dry, her head is dangling forward and below her face the ground is moving rapidly. She hears people's voices, familiar.

She realises she is being carried. She thinks there are two women and a man. She can feel the warmth from both of them, can sense their bodies, their muscles and their strength. Paramedics maybe. But the ground they are crossing isn't tarmac, isn't a hospital floor. It's sand. The bitter scent of rust in the air. A faint memory of something she can't quite grasp …

The man to her right is huge. Bear-like. The name 'Elk' comes to her, but she's too exhausted and bewildered to know what the name means. What happened to the cars? And her phone? Where is Newt?

Ymaymaymayma goes her heart. *You are Yma Fitzroy-Hughes.*

They keep walking. They are going fast – she can sense their urgency. She closes her eyes and, when she opens them, she sees the sand again. Then the boot of a man ahead of her swings into her vision. And out. In. And out.

A sturdy man's desert boot. A khaki-coloured sock. And above it, a hard, tanned calf muscle. Spider?

Yma Fitzroy-Hughes is your name.

Her mind squirms, worm-like. Yma Fitzroy-Hughes? Is that her name? Yes, it is … of course it is. Isn't it? She's dreaming, must still be dreaming. In a hospital? She tries to speak, to cry out, but she's too weak.

You're home now, Yma. Welcome home.

Slowly she starts to remember. She remembers the desert. She has time to recognise it, to think: *Elk and Amasha. This is it. I'm back* … before she loses consciousness again.

The family wait at the Shuck, gathered in an expectant huddle at the entrance, the children and Forlani limping out on his crutches, a tentative smile of hope on his disjointed face.

'How are they?'

Spider is at the front, helping Hugo and Amasha carry Knut, who is still unconscious. 'No better and no worse than any of us, after what they've been through,' he says.

Inside the tower, where it is more shady, he lowers Knut to the floor. Madeira and Elk do the same with Yma and the family cluster around, crouching, reaching out tentative, yearning fingers to touch them.

'How did they die?' Forlani wants to know.

'Knut, meningitis. Yma, a car crash.'

'Sudden?'

'Instant.'

'She'll take longer then.' Forlani puts a hand on her forehead and closes his eyes, taking an inventory of her health. She is breathing shallowly, but her skin has lost its mottled blue-white appearance and her eyes have begun to twitch. The blanket she is draped in covers her from her shoulders to her knees. Spider looks at her skin, so unblemished, white and clear, as if her veins and muscles are trapped in milk and solidified there.

Forlani gets up painfully and moves to Knut, who is also showing the first signs of recovery. He puts his finger on his wrists and nods to himself.

'Ages?'

'Uh.' Elk rubs his face wearily. 'She was seventeen, he was twenty-seven.'

Forlani nods. 'That's good. Not a big adjustment. All they need is rest, fluids – the usual. Take them to their rooms. We'll monitor them overnight.'

There's a sling that can be lowered from the Shuck to carry people back up – sometimes Forlani has to use it at the end of the day. It can be looped around a barrel to decrease the lifting effort and, as usual, Spider and Noor do the winching. Yma first, then Knut. Each one is delivered to Madeira and Elk to carry them back to their own pods, where Forlani and Amasha are waiting to administer to them.

When it's done, the tower falls strangely silent. Noor wanders into the desert to practise with his bow and arrow, while the children sit drowsily in the common room, playing with their toys. Elk is in the kitchen and Tita Lily in her own pod – lying still, staring at the ceiling.

Ill at ease, Spider climbs down into the tower. Hugo is outside, Camel is snoozing in the sun, and Madeira crouches next to the furrows of crops, making notes and puffing robustly on her cigar.

Spider can't keep still. He goes to the hideaway behind Camel's cage where no one can see him, pulls up his petticoat and fumbles inside his shorts. He draws out his penis, already hard, and, with one hand against the metal of the tower, quickly and efficiently brings himself to orgasm.

Afterwards he sits in the sand, knees drawn up, and wonders about many things. He wonders about incest and about love, and about the wolf inside him that sometimes opens its jaw and peeps out.

27

THE NIGHT IS long. When morning comes, it is quiet and lithe, creeping up the side of the tower, inching its fingery way inside the Shuck. In her sleeping pod, half asleep, Yma rolls her head feverishly from side to side, her nostrils twitching. The air is hot and salty, not an atom of moisture in it.

Phoenix, she thinks. It feels different because she's in Phoenix. But her head is tight as a drum, she is drenched in sweat and can't understand why the bed feels different. She opens her eyes, sees the underside of a polished walnut-coloured ceiling. And it comes back to her in a flash.

She is not McKenzie Strathie.

She is Yma. Her first word to Selena Strathie … was 'Yma'. Which was her own name, more or less. Selena had understood it as 'Ma'.

She stares at the ceiling, blinking through the steady throb of pain, at the paintings there.

This is her real ceiling. Her real sleeping pod. This is her real home. McKenzie is dead on a road in Phoenix, but her soul has come back here to be with her soul family, the Dormilones. Everything about McKenzie Strathie is over. There was no CIA plot, there are no FEMA camps, McKenzie's father was guilty of nothing. Everything she dreamed were her memories of the Cirque – this strange limbo beyond death.

She breathes through the pain, slowly, every breath sparking off new jets of agony in her head. Her shoulders and chest ache unbearably: these are the ghosts of her fatal injuries in the car accident, and they'll stay with her for a day or so while she adjusts to being home. Someone has turned her bed round so that her head is near the window – they've opened it, so she can see the sky. Her family, she thinks hazily, always know what she needs.

A small sound and, when she glances down, she sees a familiar blonde mop of hair. A skinny tanned arm curled up in front of her face.

'Splendour?' she whispers.

The little girl doesn't react, just continues breathing in and out. Splendour, lying here on top of the thick cover, all bunched up, the way she always likes to sleep. She's got a half-crafty smile on her face as if she's broken the Futatsu's rules to creep in here, simply to reassure herself that her big sister is actually back and safe. The rest of the family must be here too, probably tiptoeing around the Shuck to allow her time to recover. Amasha, Elk and Hugo. Forlani, Madeira, Tita Lily, Cairo, Mahmoud and

Spider. Those must have been Spider's feet she saw yesterday in the desert, walking in front of her. His hard, tanned calves. Noor too. He must be here somewhere.

All their lives lived, and not one of them understanding why they were brought here. Amasha in Sri Lanka, Splendour in Stockholm, Spider in Paris, and Noor in Jaisalmer – whatever their faiths, whatever they believed about their afterlives, in fact they have all ended here, with the people they know instinctively they belong to.

A wave of shivering overtakes her and she hunches under the covers. Against her skin she feels the familiar texture of the cotton shift she has been dressed in, and when she rubs her feet together she realises she's wearing thick animal-hair socks. Tita Lily and Amasha will have done that, to help with the shivering. *Amasha*, she thinks. Her Cirque mother, and so much more familiar than Selena Strathie. Amasha, the most loving of mothers – the woman in the tree.

'Yma?' She glances up. Splendour is sitting up, rubbing her grey eyes, staring at her. Her face is steady for a moment, then it breaks into an expression of wonderment. 'Yma.' Splendour launches herself at Yma, burrowing under the blankets to get her arms round her. She doesn't seem to care about the sweat and the smell – all she wants is to hug her. 'You're back. You're really back.'

Yma closes her eyes and hugs the little girl, in spite of the pain. 'Of course I'm back,' she whispers. 'Why would I ever not come back to you? What a mad idea!'

Splendour hugs her harder. Yma smells Splendour's hair. Blackness is coming back, tiredness, a need to sleep again, but now it's OK. Because, in spite of it all, she is home.

Splendour leaves mid-morning and Yma sleeps off the rest of the transition alone, restless, twisting and turning on the low bed, vacillating between extreme shivering and sweating. There's a flagon of water next to the bed, and preserved oranges in an earthenware jar, which she knows she must eat when the shivering stops. Eventually, in the mid-afternoon, she wakes to find the pain has eased and the sweating has stopped. Cautiously she drags herself up to a sitting position. Her head isn't spinning any more. The aches where the car hit her have lessened too. Maybe she'll be able to get to the shower room and check that her hiding place hasn't been discovered.

Tentatively she nibbles on some of the oranges and waits for the sugar to hit her system. The sun is getting low out of the window. The timescales are different in the Cirque: days pass here while years pass on Earth. Some Scouts find themselves reborn in the twentieth century, some in the twenty-first; no one ever knows where they will hit Earth, in what country or what year – the only constant is that they always die and come back here, to the Cirque.

Yma's pod is exactly as she left it. Sketches that Knut made of clouds, and ships under sail for her to look at. One shows the familiar mushroom cloud of a microburst.

She stares at it, her eyes dry. It was a sketch Knut made one night using pigments he'd produced by grinding shells: a depiction of one of the many microbursts she's witnessed in the Cirque – out in the north, where the Chicane is. He did it because the family wanted to coax Yma to use this pod more. If she wouldn't sleep with them, she should be sleeping in here, and not up on the balcony where it is cold and uncomfortable.

The painting is an exact replica of the photo McKenzie Strathie had on her wall. How could she not have understood why that image meant so much to her? She dreamed it so often, but didn't remember this ceiling, this familiar ceiling?

There's a gently knock on the door and Amasha's sweet brown-eyed face looks through.

'My beautiful girl.'

Yma tries to get up, but finds she can't. She sinks back, shaking her head.

Amasha comes to her, sits on the bed and takes Yma's hands with her coconut-coloured fingers. She is round and soft, like baked bread. 'My beautiful girl, my beautiful girl. You're home. How do you feel? Is it still hurting?'

'A little. It's worse than it was the previous two times.'

'Because of how quick it was. Try to stay still; better if you keep calm – you had injuries to your ribs.'

'We didn't find it then? We're in the last Regyre, aren't we?'

'Shhhh – shhhh, don't think about that now.'

'It's true, isn't it? We didn't solve the puzzle, didn't find the Sarkpont.'

'But you and Knut got further than anyone has ever got before.' Amasha holds her closer, kisses her hair. 'It's the first time any Scouts have actually met on Earth, but you and Knut did it. You gave us so much to work with. You are a shining star to all of us.'

It's true that Scouts criss-cross each other all the time on Earth, they pass each other in the street and never fully know how close they have come. But when they do meet face-to-face, it's the most powerful feeling imaginable. It's the feeling she had when she met Newt Herrara.

'But why didn't I know where I'd come from? How could I have forgotten why I was there?'

Amasha pulls back, holds Yma at arm's length. She smiles and pushes away a strand of Yma's hair. 'You were so brave. Those brothers of McKenzie's, and that psychiatric person.'

'Dr Shreve. Did you see her?'

'I saw your thoughts of her, and a little glimpse. Poof, what a manicured and dressed-up sheep *she* was.'

'And, uh …' Yma blinks, says in a small, anxious voice, 'Did you see what I did to Joe Marino?'

There is a pause. A smile flickers lightly around Amasha's mouth. 'Some people deserve what they get, Yma, and everything Elk and I heard from you made us proud. You didn't take any of their bullshit.'

Amasha reaches down and finds the jar of oranges. She encourages Yma to eat a little more, helping her to take a slice and swallow it. Slowly its sugar makes its way into her system and Yma begins to feels a little stronger. She winds her hair off her face and tries to straighten her shift a little so that she looks more presentable.

'Knut? How's Knut?'

'Better than you are. Still sleeping. Another day for you both. Everyone's desperate to see you. Mahmoud has a rash, Forlani's hands aren't ever going to get any better, and Tita Lily's really been through the mill, thanks to Cairo … but apart from that, we're fine. Especially now you're back.'

'Something happened. We found something – something big.'

Amasha nods. 'Something good?'

'Yes.'

'You can tell us all about it. When we all eat together.'

Yma closes her eyes. Concentrates very hard on keeping her head steady.

'Amasha,' she says. 'I need a shower.'

'I'll bring you a basin. Stay still.'

'No, I want to get up – go to the shower.'

'And I'm telling you no. Forlani would have a fit. You have to rest.'

'But I'm OK.' She pulls the covers off and drags her legs to the side of the bed.

Amasha lays panicked hands on Yma and tries to still her. 'Are you crazy, girl? You'll hurt yourself. Please, please – stay still.'

Yma tries to push past her but pain shoots through her side, bringing a wave of nausea. The room spins.

'Lie down, girl, lie down. I've told you I'll bring you a bowl and wash you.'

It's not a wash she wants, it's what's in the shower room. Yma lies on her side, panting shallowly.

'See? You're not fit for anything. You understand?'

'Yes,' she murmurs weakly, feeling the room heave and wallow around her. 'I understand.'

Lunch is disorganised and piecemeal – people grabbing food where they can. Amasha is buzz-cutting Madeira's hair outside the tower, great tufts scattered in the sand around her, and Forlani is busy with his apothecary jars in the centre of the farm. Tita Lily has taken up residence in the corner of the common room, still wearing a giant fluffy robe and smoking. She has pain etched on her face, but her colour is better.

Spider doesn't eat in the common room, but carries a corn-meal burrito stuffed with sheep's cheese down to his place next to Camel's cage and eats while he works. He has nestled in one pocket a T-square and two French curves, all carved several Regyres ago by Knut from kangaroo bone. The day is strangely cool, and he worries that the Scouts won't warm up quickly enough.

It's impossible, Spider thinks as he works, quite impossible for anyone to grasp this reality. He thinks of all the other people who haven't been chosen for this afterlife – all of them living lives and never suspecting how limited their view is, how boundless the true universe is, and what a tiny segment the majority of the human race can see.

Before he was chosen to come here, Spider lived near the boulevard de Beauséjour, Paris, at the turn of the twentieth century. Aged ten, because he had no other choice, he taught himself the fundamentals of engineering and mechanical repair. He lived as a tinker, fixing and improving, endlessly curious about how things worked, in spite of his lack of formal education. Those skills have come back to him now; there is little he can't troubleshoot, with the right material and tools.

As he works, Camel stands a metre or so away, her chin up, blinking away the sand in her eyelashes. Her attention seems to be on something far in the distance; she appears disinterested in Spider's preparations.

And so the day unfolds. While Yma dreams, floating in and out of her life in Virginia – while Knut lies solid and silent as stone in his pod a few doors away – high above them, in the common room, Elk cooks.

Eventually Spider goes up to the Shuck, swinging his legs up the ladder. Inside there is a kind of hush: Elk and Amasha are in the corner, discussing desperately. He knows what this is – it's the Scout choice.

Spider has washed and dressed sombrely, though the backs of his eyes are itching. He's spent the whole day in the sun and maybe that's part of why he feels so weary, so moody. His anxiety is like a boiled stone lodged in the back of his throat. The children are tired and are sitting barefoot, wrapped in their Shuck blankets, tousle-haired and yawning. Cairo cradles his toy helicopter, wedged against his chest by his crunched-up knees. Mahmoud is sullen, his legs sticking out in front of him.

Madeira catches Spider, at the edge of the kitchen. She has her shears and her twine in her dungarees. There's a cigar, as usual, behind her ear. 'It'll be me,' she says. 'Just wait. Just when they need me the most – when they need someone to set up a new farm.'

'No, it won't. It'll be me.'

'I don't think so.' She closes her eyes. 'Hug me then – before I go.'

Spider hugs her awkwardly, not sure how to hold Madeira; she is so fragile and small, he's afraid he will crush her. Her bones are as fine and light as an antelope's. He is conscious of the smell of expensive cigar tobacco.

She hisses at him. 'Promise me something, you fucker.'

'Promise you what?'

'I need you to make sure the sheep are OK – and the kangaroos. There's one: Jack. You know?'

'I know.'

'He was the worst, when they came in – he was so thin his spine was sticking up through his coat. Like some kind of dinosaur.' She thrusts out her arm, which is so slim it's like a carving. 'See the bones on me – it was worse than that. Someone had kept him tied up the whole time, and he had a sore on his hind leg that took all of Forlani's herbs to cure it.' She lets out a long sigh. 'I'm not sentimental, Spider, I'm really not. I'm a farming girl, I've seen it all in Ghana, but that poor little dude. He needs to be helped. Please promise me you'll look out for him. If it comes to it, let Jack free, but best I think you just kill him. He's old, too old, and he won't make it. Do it quick, tell him something nice while you do it – you promise?'

Spider's head throbs, his limbs are aching. Every Regyre, they go through this – the fears of the Scouts for what might change here.

'I promise. I promise, Madeira.' He kisses her hand.

28

WHEN YMA WAKES she can tell from the way the light comes through the window that almost a day has passed. At last she feels clear-headed. She eats some of the oranges and dates next to the bunk, then gingerly sits up. At first her head spins, but the pain is less, and when she breathes carefully the vertigo ceases.

She stands; her legs are trembly but surprisingly strong. The Shuck is quiet – she can hear the children outside. She feels furtive, and has to remind herself it's normal to want to shower after what she's been through. Carefully she wraps herself in her house blanket and tiptoes down the spindly spiral staircase, then pads down the corridor, with its shined walls and floor like the polished interior of a nut.

The women's bathing room is exactly as she recalls it. Positioned on the north of the Shuck, it is placed slightly off-centre to the corroded Eye in the tower. The exterior wall is glazed from floor to ceiling in the usual transparent polymer, affording the bather a panoramic view out over the desert. Here the women store all their washing products. Yma glances at the door, then quickly pushes her hand into one section and finds all her belongings safely in there – a loofah made from desert brush, a cake of the green-and-orange soap Madeira makes in the farm.

She pulls out the loofah and inspects it. It is dry and crumbly on the outside, and a small puff of matter lifts off it and floats down when she handles it. Gently she pushes her fingers into the core of it, moves them around and finds what she's looking for.

Two murky crystals, each the size of a hazelnut, grey in places, transparent in others.

She closes her eyes, breathes through her nose, not giving in to the urge she has to sit down and shake with relief. Licking her lips and thinking fast, she unpicks a tiny part of her blanket hem – Tita Lily's careful stitches, so small they could have been done by an elf – and pushes the two crystals into it. They are too big and rip more stitches, so she hurriedly folds the blanket with them carefully concealed and places it on a shelf that overlooks the desert. There she can watch it, in case someone else comes in.

Hugo has left her ration of water – double for the Scouts on their return: two buckets full, which she pours into the reservoir.

The action makes her arms ache and she has to rest for a moment before she stands under the nozzle. She washes slowly. Her body is more familiar than it has been in previous Regyres. McKenzie Strathie died at seventeen, and Yma is twenty, so the difference in their bodies is subtle. On her last Regyre she was born in a Korean village where she lived to the age of fifty, childless, husbandless and completely unaware of her destiny. When she arrived back here to her young body, full of vitality and health, the shock was overwhelming.

For a brief, aching moment she feels regret for her life as McKenzie Strathie, and for everything she left on Earth: Harbinson school, Mom, Dad, the Caltech Science Institute and even her brothers. Mostly India, though – mostly it's India she'll miss. Now they seem so remote, so small. Something to be pitied. She remembers leaving the Cirque, the final moments: Knut holding her hands and saying, 'We're going to meet. We will do it.' Then nothing, and she was McKenzie Strathie, the memory of the Cirque something vague and dream-like, until the moment she woke up to being carried across the desert floor by Madeira and Elk.

She switches off the shower. The heat of the day is still trapped in the upper storeys of the Shuck, and sitting wrapped in her towel at the opened window is enough to dry her. She rubs oil into her hair and skin, then carries her blanket back to her little pod.

The cot she sleeps on has a thin mattress. The chances are that Tita Lily or Amasha will come and try to air the mattress after this long lying-in – she needs somewhere else to hide the crystals.

The walls are crenulated, like the shell of a nut, and she stands on her cot and runs her fingers around until she finds a hole the right size. A good place to hide them, as long as she is here.

She drops them inside, presses her hand to them, whispering, 'Keep safe, keep safe.' Then she gets off the bed and goes to the hanging rail where all her clothes wait, clean and stitched. Tita Lily must have come in here and curated them while Yma was on Earth. She chooses khaki dungarees, a white undershirt and a pair of white shoes that she's never seen before. When Elk scavenges food, wherever they go, Tita Lily scavenges clothes. These shoes will be her gift to welcome Yma back.

They fit perfectly. She ties her hair back and is about to leave the room when she pauses, her hand on the door. A homecoming is always a celebration, but it's also subtly edged with regret. It acknowledges that the family have lost another Regyre. And on this occasion it's the last Regyre they will ever know.

The common room is full of light and noise, the octagonal table set with food and candles, a centrepiece of the strange flowers that Madeira grows in the farm under the Shuck. The family are buzzing around, bringing plates to the table. There is a whole kangaroo haunch, and mutton, ears of corn and melting sheep's-cheese burgers. There is a bong filled with a little ganja, and wine too, made from dates and served in a giant demijohn that Knut recovered from Ghat. The children scamper back and forth from the kitchen, giggling. Their excitement is palpable – the fizzing anticipation of seeing the newly returned Scouts, who've had contact with a world that is lost to the family.

Spider hasn't spent a morsel of his time missing his life. He clearly remembers the Parisian brothel he was born into, the secret he keeps. His mother was a prostitute in the sixteenth-arrondissement *maisons closes*, and she was allowed to keep her baby only when she declared to the madame that the child was a girl, therefore promising the brothel owner a future worker.

Believing Spider would be left alone until he was strong enough, and man enough, to go out in the world on his own, she dressed him as a girl, cosseted him and grew his hair into messy blonde ringlets. The owner called him 'Angel' and pinched his cheeks, told him to swish his skirts. Meanwhile he was learning to climb, to scale buildings and run across rooftops. When, at the age of nine, the owner decided it was time for the pretty blonde girl to go into service, Spider kissed his mother goodbye, opened the window and simply climbed straight out of the brothel onto the mansard roof, clinging on to the chimneypots and zinc gutters. A girl showing her frothy pantaloons to the world.

Knut appears, dressed in a lime-green tabard. He stands for a moment alone in the corridor. His expression is tired, a little shell-shocked. Spider brushes off his hands and comes forward.

'Dude,' he grins. 'Dude.'

'Oh, man. It is too fucking good to see you, bro.'

They embrace, laughing. Spider and Knut have been two of the closest in the Cirque – their ages and strength have demanded that they fulfil a lot of tasks together, and they have had a lot of time to talk.

'Missed the bones of you, bro. Missed ya. Let me look at you.' Spider holds Knut at arm's length and examines every centimetre of his face. Knut is a brilliant artist and draughtsman. His dyed blue Mohican is a little lopsided and sad, but whatever happened to him on Earth hasn't changed his muscularity – he's still honed and lean and handsome. 'Psyched to see you. How're you feeling?'

'Bit rough, to be fair, but not as bad as it could have been.' The life Knut first lived was in Rio de Janeiro. He still wonders out loud why he was chosen, out of all the souls that could have been selected. He has been Regyred three times, but the Scout life seems to leave more of a stain on him than it does on the others, and this time he's come back with an American lilt to his voice.

'Elk and Amasha made me sick – meningitis, if you believe that? It was hell, but I had some time to think about what was happening. You know.'

Spider does know. The shock of dying in an accident takes much longer to recover from than the lingering deaths where the psyche disintegrates and has a chance to understand its destiny.

'How long have we been gone? Was it very long?' Knut asks.

'Not even three weeks. Just a little longer than last time.'

'The timespan changed again?'

'Yes. I guess we're learning – each Regyre something new. This time only three weeks. It felt like a million years, to be honest,' Spider says. 'You going to come and sit down?'

'Sure. I mean, I …' Knut's eyes go across the family – the placings at the table. Noor and Madeira are sitting at the far end, in the two tall chairs fashioned from the seats of a broken tractor. They face the other two grand chairs, which are for him and

Yma, as homecoming Scouts. His face drops. 'Oh,' he murmurs. 'Madeira. Noor.'

They give him tight smiles, both poker-straight and dignified in their places. Their glasses are already filled with the amber wine that Elk saves for these occasions, and on Madeira's plate rests a cigar and a small ganja pipe, which she's been sucking on.

'It's OK,' she says with a defiant shrug. 'We're ready.'

'But … do you have to go? We've come back with information. I'm sure we don't need the Scouts this time.'

Spider notices Amasha clearing her throat. She glances at Elk in the kitchen. He's in his apron, stirring a bubbly pot, but as if by psychic recognition, he stops and comes to stand in the entrance, holding a ladle that drips on the floor. Maybe, Spider thinks, watching first one face, then the other, this is what they were arguing about earlier.

'What information?' Spider asks.

'So I was gay – like, you know, I guess that part doesn't change.' Knut brings with him a history of sadness: in his life, the first life he lived before he was brought here, he had a lover, a boy from Madrid, who turned out to be a vicious drug addict, who stole from Knut and slept with all his friends. 'But that was secret till I went to Seattle. I was also a secret artist – guess all that shit kind of bleeds through, you know? Had to hide it from my folk; they were big, big Catholics, wanted me to make a living, ignore my art. But,' he says, 'them being Catholic. Turns out to be a great thing.'

'How come?'

'Because I learned so much. I learned what a "piscina" is.'

His comment brings the room to a standstill. Everyone looks at him, amazed.

'We all think a pool, right? But Tita Lily, you remember: the word "piscina"? How it bothered you? It's because it can also mean a font in a Catholic church – a place where holy water can be disposed of, like a sink or sluice; a place where you can wash the Communion vessels. I did a course on church architecture – and that was something that kept coming back to Newt. The term "piscina". He – *I* – couldn't work out why it stuck; but it means we should be looking for a Catholic church, a place with a rectangle.'

'Hindu temples have *padas*, *mandalas*. Not rectangles,' Amasha says.

'I mean, don't get me wrong: I was limited by my parents – Roman Catholics from the toes up – and if a mosque or a Hindu temple had been the most beautiful building on the planet, I'd never have been allowed to know about it.'

'And I think,' Spider says quietly, 'that somehow the way faiths intermingle is the key to all of this.' Everyone turns and stares at him. But no one questions him, or argues. He shrugs. 'Just a thought.'

Knut shakes his head. 'But I'm sure it has to be Catholic. I'm ready to swear on it. And that's a clue, right?'

Yma comes down the corridor towards the common room, checking her hair is neat, rubbing her eyes in a hope they will open, look bright and alive. She hesitates in the doorway because there seems to be an argument going on.

Spider and Knut are together – Spider looks exactly as she recalls him; most of his limbs and a lot of his chest are visible, by virtue of his wardrobe, and he's wearing his leather jacket and a tattered lace skirt and bears the marks of a day in the desert: sand and grease in his hair. He carries a sort of sexiness with him, but it's a danger too, and that's scary.

He glances up at her with his flinty blue eyes, holds hers, then looks away quickly, as if he's seen something that troubles him. He's always like this – a kind of disregard for her that seems like hatred. Nergüi is missing; it's something she still doesn't understand.

Everyone stops talking, and they turn to her.

'Hey,' says Spider. 'Welcome back.' He shakes her hand and turns away – heading off to the other side of the table, leaving Knut standing there staring at her, a crooked smile on his face. He's wearing a green tunic and his hair is dyed a shocking blue. He looks so much younger than he was on Earth.

'Oh, Knut. How didn't I know?'

He smiles and opens his arms to her. 'Come here.'

Yma goes to him – Knut wraps his arms around her and she leans into his chest, hearing his heart thud. 'You've got back the hair you wanted. Blue as those glass sculptures.'

'Are you OK?' he asks, muffled against her hair.

'I don't understand how I didn't recognise you.'

'But you did. We both did awesome.'

She closes her eyes, tries to smile.

Just then Elk, who is carrying a huge plate of steaming cornbread to the table, notices her there. He pauses, a wave of delighted tenderness crossing his face. He puts down the plate and opens his arms to her. 'My girl.' Yma comes shyly into the room and lets him hug her, bear-like: the smell of him, smoke and woody herbs. He is a giant – at least twenty-five centimetres taller than her and twice as wide.

Behind him Hugo is waiting. He smiles, gives Yma a hug. 'Well done. Finding Knut was astonishing – truly astonishing.'

'He found me!'

'Yeah, but you know. You both did brilliantly.'

Forlani stands patiently next to them, smiling awkwardly until she breaks away from Hugo and puts her arm round him – kissing his head. He laughs, wraps his skinny, buckled arms around her waist. 'Missed you so much, you won't even know.'

'Yma, Yma, Yma . . .!' The three children are jumping up and down next to her.

Cairo hugs her around the knees, pressing his face against her legs. 'I missed you, Yma, I missed you.'

She smiles and puts a hand over her heart. It is so good to be back. But when she looks at the table, piled with plates and wine and food, she sees – beyond everything else – three people who don't stand up to meet her.

Tita Lily, who looks pale. Yma crosses the room and stands behind Tita Lily, her hands on her shoulders. Tita Lily covers her hand with hers, and Yma plants a kiss on her head.

'I've been sick, my honey.'

'You better now?'

'Getting there. Cactus spines in my stomach. I had blood poisoning.'

'But you're OK?'

'I am.'

And Noor and Madeira, sitting at the tall chairs denoting the next Scouts. Noor smiles calmly at Yma. His hair shines, his skin seems to have a radiance. There is something in the glint of his eyes that tells her he would break the rules, just something ... He doesn't stand to greet Yma, merely nods his head. She smiles, noting the way her lip catches on her teeth as she does, hating herself.

Madeira scrapes back her chair and smiles grimly. Her dark hair is shorn back on one side almost to the roots. She's wearing the plaid shirt that she farms in, a leather gilet with pouches for tools, and her gardening gloves are tucked into the front pocket of her cargos, even though it's a formal dinner. She hugs Yma tight. She smells of sheep's milk and the sage she cultivates.

'How's the farm?'

'Oh, I'm still the Frankenstein of agriculture. Still trying to speed up the way the kangaroos mate. You know me, I'll never change.'

Eventually, when Yma has hugged everyone, Noor stands, gives her a formal peck on the cheek, then takes her to her seat. 'Good to see you back.'

He sits back down just as quickly, leaving only the tingling impression of his skin against hers: salt and vaguely grazed roughness. He's wearing cargo trousers and a T-shirt that is blinding white against his dark skin. Avoiding his eyes, Yma quickly slides into the chair next to Knut, where her place has been set.

'Roast pumpkin and cheese-steak for dinner,' says Elk, clapping his hands. 'Everyone sit down.'

Everyone settles in their place and Amasha holds up her hands, opening them to where Knut and Yma sit, the homecoming king and queen.

'Thank you, Ha'shem, for bringing them back to us. Thank you for your munificence.'

The family mumble 'Amen', give a round of applause – as if Yma and Knut are in the Carnegie Hall and have delivered an award-winning concert. They smile back, thank everyone. Then the meal begins. They eat slowly, giving their bodies time to get used to the new air and food. The first few bites are salty and sour, to Yma's tastebuds, still with their ghost memory of an Earth diet, but gradually the food becomes familiar and comforting, like every good family meal she can remember. From time to time Yma can feel Spider's eyes on her, but she ignores it. She doesn't want to be scared.

Halfway through the meal, when the children are getting sleepy, Yma places her hand over Amasha's. 'Listen,' she whispers, 'I don't think the Scouts need to go.'

Amasha stares at her white nails over her dark-brown skin. 'It's not me you need to convince. It's Elk.'

Next to Yma, Knut nods. 'We were talking about it.'

'Did you mention Phoenix?' Yma asks.

Elk looks up. 'Phoenix? Like the bird – the legend?'

'There's a city called Phoenix,' says Knut.

'There is. In the United States. In Arizona.'

'When I was on Earth,' Knut says slowly, 'I remembered a diagram. I couldn't work out where I got it from. But it's drawn here in the Shuck on the shower wall in the men's. Left over by a previous family. It's the Hohokam canals in Phoenix.'

Everyone stares at him.

'This is our discovery,' Yma says. 'We find Phoenix and maybe – *maybe* we find the Sarkpont.'

There is a long silence, then Amasha clears her throat. She sets down her own spoon and carefully wipes her mouth. She looks at Elk.

Elk shrugs. 'You know, you have a way, Amasha. It's just a look from you, and you know I'm putty in your hands.'

Noor gives a small smile, though he tries to conceal the way he's feeling. Madeira draws more deeply on the pipe – she doesn't want to waste a chance to get high.

'What about Dubai?' Elk says.

Amasha nods. 'OK, so we're leaving here. We need to move on. We've searched all we can in this area, we need to relocate.'

'*Leaving?*' Yma shoots a look at Knut. 'Where are we going?'

Amasha explains it then – all about Dubai and the apartment. On the other side of Knut, Spider is staring hard at the plate in front of him. He presses his thumb and forefinger into his closed eyes, still shaking his head.

'What?' Yma murmurs, and Spider shrugs.

'We have to leave, but I don't think Dubai is the right place.'

'Stop whispering,' Elk says. 'Maybe one of the cities past it is Phoenix.'

The sun sets outside the rusting tower and Forlani distributes bread, knifing out little globs of ghee with it; and Hugo tells a joke about a banker he once knew, who fell three storeys from a building in Kuala Lumpur, through a plate-glass roof, and landed face up on someone's dining table mid-dinner, so drunk and limp that he survived with only a few scratches. How he became lifelong friends with the family, after destroying their dinner plates and candlesticks.

'Did you remember any of this?' Yma asks Knut quietly. 'Is there anything at all you recalled when we were alive?'

He lowers his head to answer. 'Snippets mostly. Amasha and Elk I recognised from dreaming them on the floor of my bedroom. How about you?'

She shrugs. 'The microbursts.' She closes her eyes, struggling to find the right words. 'I saw them here. It's like … it's incredible. But I only remembered some little things.'

'Me too. I can't explain it, but I had this feeling on Earth that I was growing away from the person I really was. Apparently, when I was four or five, when my baby sister was born, my mother found me in her room, staring at her in her crib. I frightened the fucking life out of my mum, because when she asked me what the hell I was doing, I looked her in the eye and said, "*I'm asking the baby to remind me what God looks like. Because I'm starting to forget.*"

*

Yma goes to her bunk – this might be the last night she can sleep here without claustrophobia setting in – and lies wakeful in the dark, her chin dropped up and to one side, so she can stare out at the night. She remembers those long days at school, the teasing, the girl gangs hurling insults, the bullying from her brothers, how she didn't recall the skies here, the endless aching sweeps. The storms that gather in the distance, the lightning that ignites distant dunes and ragged trees.

As she falls asleep she watches the stars nudge slowly across the heavens above the Chicane city – the manipulated lights there blink off slowly as the city descends into darkness. She dreams of microbursts and canals lying in complex diagrams on the desert floor. She knows they have to get to Phoenix.

When Yma wakes, the sun is high and beyond the dried-up Virgule the Chicane city is hazy on the horizon. She blinks a few times. The Shuck is silent, she must have outslept everyone. When she listens she can just hear voices outside and the sounds of people working.

Raising herself up on her hands, she tilts her body sideways so that she can look out of the window to where the distant sky-scrapers of Dubai are glinting in the sun. Then she stands on her bunk and feels for the crystals. They are there, comforting little shapes that she loves and hates in equal measure.

'Yma. Yma?'

From below comes the sound of Splendour's voice calling. Excited and scared. 'Yma, come quickly. Come down.'

Hastily she pulls on khaki shorts, a shirt and rubber shoes. Splendour's voice is coming from the pod lock.

'Yma! Come on.'

At the pod lock she shuffles out into the space above the ladder and sees Splendour halfway up the ladder, waving up to her.

'Splendour! You can't be on the ladder on your own. Where's Amasha?'

'Come,' the little girl calls and begins to scamper down the ladder. 'Come quickly.'

Yma lowers her head and sees the rest of the family gathered near the tower walls at the western end, their backs to her, staring out into the desert. She swings out onto the ladder, pausing for a moment when vertigo hits her. It's a long time since she's climbed down this ladder – the roof in the Strathies' house was a dwarf compared to this height – and it takes her a few seconds to recover, swaying perilously above the yawning space.

She continues more slowly, concentrating on each rung. Below she can see familiar things: the livestock pens, Camel's cage and Madeira's farm, where parts of the polythene have been peeled back to better access the crops for transportation. There is a lot of dug-over earth, but two rows of fat shiny pumpkins remain, the suckers and tendrils curling like antennae around them. They must be the mutant giants that sometimes spring up in the farm, with no taste or nutritional value.

There is a new repair to the tower too – a giant square of metal riveted to it – and the sight of it makes her cold. She looks at it warily. The endgame?

At the edge of the tower Splendour has joined the group – they are all intent on whatever is out there. Yma reaches the sand at last and breaks into a run. The group is arranged with their backs to her, all gathered behind Spider, who stands at an unlocked shutter. He has rolled up the sleeves of his jacket and is holding the wall so tightly that the muscles in his wrists are standing up. His binoculars hang around his neck. Noor stands to the other side, silent. Concentrating.

'What is it?' Yma murmurs. 'What?'

Forlani has clambered monkey-like halfway up the side of the opened shutter and clings there, his head bent down so that he can crane his face out and watch. He turns to Yma and, with his free hand, grabs her shoulder and pulls her forward. 'See?'

Crunched between Elk and Madeira, Yma stands on tiptoe and is able to see what has fascinated them so much.

'Who's that?'

It's a family, moving brazenly across the desert floor about two clicks away. They are in a long stream, obviously carrying belongings and maybe livestock too – it's difficult to tell without glasses. There seems to be something large being dragged along behind them, a round object that might, judging from the proportions, be almost as big as a small house. All in all, they give the impression of a string of ants carrying home an enormous husk or grain.

Knut asks Amasha, 'How can they be walking out there? It's against the rules.'

'They're new,' she murmurs thoughtfully. 'They've just arrived, still finding their way.'

'How can they be new? I mean – how can they have the cojones?'

'They're strong. They're confident. It's not such an impossibility. Looks like they've found their feet very quickly.'

The Dormilones are silent for a while, dwelling on this. A family so confident that they're marching across the Cirque as if they own it. Yma's spirits sink. The Dormilones crept in, terrified and humble. If this is their competition on the last Regyre, what hope do they have?

The sound of laughter comes across the desert. And the low notes of an instrument. The name 'harmonica' pops into her mind, though she has no idea why. A family playing a musical instrument? And wearing clothes that makes the sun glint off them.

Wearily Spider turns and hands Forlani the binoculars. Forlani swings further out of the tower on one hand and focuses the binoculars. Instantly he becomes tense, his face clenching.

'They're turning towards us.'

Spider snatches the binoculars back and focuses them.

'Spider?'

'Keep still.' He focuses furiously, but it's plain even to the naked eye that Forlani is right. The shape of the procession has changed and is narrowing to a point, as if it's an arrow that has been turned to face the tower. The large shape at the back, which this close up appears not to be a cart but maybe a creature of some description, shuffles around to the tail of the train until its silhouette overcomes those of the people, and all that is visible is its girth against the morning sky.

There is silence as the silhouette gets larger and larger. Yma feels everyone in the family shrink slightly away from the advancing shape.

'What do they want?' Cairo hisses, clinging on to Elk's leg. 'Are they coming here? Are they looking for a Shuck?'

'Don't be a baby,' Mahmoud tells Cairo. 'Baby from Tripoli.'

'Shut up. I'm not a baby.'

Splendour begins to cry. 'They can't have our Shuck. It's *our* Shuck.'

'Shhhh, I promise they won't. We don't know that's what they want.' Amasha pulls the children to her and glances for guidance up at Elk. He doesn't notice – he is too busy staring out at the desert. It's Spider who eventually takes action. Suddenly he elbows the others away from him, clearing a space. He braces his hand on the ledge, opens his feet wide and, with one push, springs up onto the sill in a crouch. He is balanced there for one second, then pushes himself out onto the sand.

'What're you doing?' Noor says.

Spider straightens from the leap and begins to walk in the direction of the family. He does it nonchalantly, his long legs swinging calmly, as if he's on his way to meet a friend for a drink. Yma closes her fingers around Forlani's arm. He covers her hand with his and squeezes it reassuringly.

The family are nearer now, and they show no sign of stopping. Spider too shows no sign. He must be 1,000 metres away, halfway to the limit of what they are allowed during the fallow period. How much further will he go? He stops then, and although he is a tiny figure now on the sand, Yma can see his strong legs planted wide, the slight drift of his skirt flapping against his thighs. Slowly, very slowly, he opens his arms and raises them so that he is standing in a cross shape, arms spread.

It seems to Yma such a hopeless, senseless gesture, it makes no sense. Except that it works. The oncoming shape stops getting larger. No one in the tower breathes. Then slowly the shape wavers and changes. The train has turned to its side and is now marching due north, coming at a diagonal, which will bring them near the Shuck, but not directly to it.

Spider lowers his arms, turns on his heel and begins to wander back to the tower.

The Dormilones release their breath as one. Forlani lets go of his hold on Yma's hand and she gives him a small grateful smile. Spider's shadow is long as he walks, the sun still low in the sky. He gets to the tower and Knut leans over, offering his hand to help hoist Spider back through the window. He lands with a shudder, turns instantly to look back out of the window. The family gather back round to watch. Yma can smell Spider's fresh sweat from the walk.

The family out in the desert are going to pass the tower close enough to be visible. They stretch out into a straggly line and slowly, slowly the shape at the back emerges into its reality. Everyone catches their breath.

It's an elephant, being led along at the rear of the pack. Covered in a gaudy red-and-gold cloth, someone seated atop it.

'Well, aren't they just the shit?' Spider mutters. 'No question about it. Just the shit.'

'How come they've got an elephant?' Cairo wants to know. 'We ain't got no elephants. How come?'

Yma feels momentarily defensive. She knows how long Spider, Madeira and Noor spent hunting for livestock; she knows that having even one camel was a feat of effort and skill. Yet Cairo is voicing what all the family are thinking: how can they compete with a family so bold and skilled that already they've entrapped an elephant in their first week here?

Cairo pulls away from the group. 'If we ain't got an elephant,' he says, turning and walking away angrily, 'then how are we going to find the Sarkpont?'

29

WHEN SPIDER COMES back to the Shuck he feels achy and sweaty, as if his muscles have been loosened, and when the others break off to continue their preparations for the next morning, he goes back to the compartment and works silently, squirrelling away the things he needs, surreptitiously checking on the contraption that is folded into the locker behind Camel's cage, all the while not sure he's actually going to do it.

He isn't stupid. He saw the way Yma looked at Noor, and the way Noor almost ignored her. And the way that Nergüi died … This is the core iniquity, he thinks, the real reason he hates Noor: for his carelessness about Nergüi's death, and the fact that Yma loves him. It's an elephant in the room – no one speaks about Nergüi … no one dares say what they think about Noor. Spider hates the man's privilege and his gravity, his authority and the way he 'jokingly' aimed that arrow.

At nightfall Spider carefully secures what he's working on in the locker behind Camel's cage. He has no idea if it will work; all he has to go on is the miniature version that crashed. It's a complete punt.

In the middle of the night he dreams that Madeira comes into his sleeping pod and sits cross-legged at the foot of his mattress. She looks at him intently and says, 'You are the best thing this family has going for it. Ignore the others. Do what you need to do.'

When he wakes in the dark she's not there, and although it takes him a while, eventually he realises it is a dream. He sits back, his hands on his knees, getting a grasp on what he's going to do today.

It's still dark when he gets up and there are no sounds from the rest of the Shuck. It's the first day of their last Regyre. He tips out of bed and begins to assemble the few items he's hidden up here. He's wearing the tattiest dress he owns. Over it is a faded leather jacket with a hood and his cargo belt, which is stuffed full of tools. With the bundles of food that he's concealed in his pod, he creeps silently past the sleeping platform. He unlocks the pod lock with intricate care, each twist of the great cog seeming to him to echo through the Shuck. But no one calls, no one stirs above.

There is nothing in the rules about the last night before the new Regyre. None of them know if the desert is dangerous, but instinct tells Spider to be on his guard. He swings the huge battery-powered lantern out into the drop. Far below him on the desert floor the animals that haven't yet been slaughtered for the move are sleeping. Camel is awake, sucking at her salt-lick block. She looks alert and healthy after her two weeks' rest.

It's a risk, being out before sunrise, but he feels relatively safe in the confines of the tower. He works silently. He must be ready to leave before sunrise, before anyone realises he's gone. He loads Camel with water canteens and saddlepacks of food. The Sandwalker and camping equipment for one person collapse to a thin tube of neoprene – it weighs less than thirty kilos; the only bulk is in the D-ring that secures it to Camel's saddle. He's got his eyeglasses around his neck and a pencil and paper, because he wants a record of everything he sees, so that he can come back and convince the rest of the family what he's doing is important.

He finishes packing, checks all the buckles are tight on the equipment and links Camel's plaited halter through his grubby fingers. No time like the present. 'Come on,' he tells her. 'Let's give this thing a go.'

The first ten minutes are crucial. He wants to get far enough away from the tower that the family can't follow him, but not so far that he can't race back to it, if anything comes at him from the sand. Though the sun hasn't risen yet, the desert is light – he can see for several hundred metres around. He walks tentatively, Camel plodding obediently behind him.

Nothing tries to stop them, and he is almost a kilometre from the hangar when the first sunrays pierce the sky. He stops and turns, regards the stretch of sand he's crossed. At the end of it stands the Dormilones' tower – it is huge, even from this distance, but it doesn't appear spectacular. Now he regrets that he and Knut didn't spent more time maintaining it. Had it appeared unoccupied to the Elephant Family? Is that why they approached? Or was there another reason they were brazen enough to get so near?

So full of ostentation and bravado – the man who led the family was a short, fat guy dressed in red shorts and plaid socks, as if he was on a golf course in Florida. He seemed to be dancing across the desert, as if it was all a huge joke, cavorting across the sand almost joyously. Every now and then he thrust forward a staff of some description and, if Spider wasn't mistaken, he chucked a flexing twirl into the ballet. Back in the Parisian brothel, the madame had hung a painting on the wall of a jazz funeral in New Orleans, and if yesterday's Elephant Family had reminded Spider of anything, it was that.

He turns back to face the city beyond the Virgule, where the Chicane city lights are blinking out, one by one. He is going to have a lot to explain and a lot to live down, if this doesn't work. He clicks in the back of his throat and encourages Camel to pick up the pace. Soon they find themselves closing in on the shore of the Virgule. This time, when he checks behind him, the family have appeared out of the tower. They are small dots on the sand, but they've come far enough out that, with the aid of glasses, they will be able to see him clearly. Someone waves to attract his attention, and maybe they are shouting, but it's too far to hear.

'Pick up the pace,' he tells Camel. 'We're killing it.'

They get to the first dried scale of the lake. The salt looks more friable than it did the other day, although it holds his weight. He and Camel cross a small section where there is still some briny water mixed with the sand. A smell like fish drying on a Mediterranean quay hangs around these places.

And then he finds a spot where the salt holds Camel's weight, but makes a long cracking sound when he applies his own foot to it. It's time. He unloads the long canvas bag from Camel's back and drops it onto the salt. He taps her rump and points to the Chicane. 'Keep going. I'll catch you.'

She regards him lugubriously, as if he is of some curiosity, but not so much that she'll argue with him. She swings her long neck in the direction of the city, lowers her head and begins to amble away.

Spider gets to work fitting together the stays, made from a hardwood he found in Abu Dhabi – Hugo thinks it's *lignum vitae*. He uses his teeth to snap the kangaroo-gut twine, and wraps it time and time again around the cross-beams. He hasn't had the chance to test it for real; he knows only that the prototype works, and that this larger version will carry his weight. He attaches the canvas bag across the undercarriage, then leans onto it, pushing it out onto the paler salt that would crack if he stood on it.

He assembles the parachute-silk sail, knotting it into the mast and adjusting it so that the top and the bottom line up perfectly. The early sun is already reflecting back from the salt, and sweat runs down his back as he works. When he's finished, Camel is already a speck in the distance. What will she do if he doesn't catch up with her – if he is unable? Will she keep walking into infinity, slowly getting smaller and smaller on the horizon, swallowed up in perspective?

There is a loud whoomph overhead, and when he looks up he sees the wind has caught the sail. The Sandwalker makes a loud creaking noise under him; for a second he thinks he's got the balance wrong and the sail is going to tilt forward, spilling him out onto the salt, but the frame under him jolts once, twice, shudders for a moment and then, in one breathtaking moment, the whole Sandwalker takes off across the salt.

Now that Yma is recovered, she has started sleeping in her usual place, on the floor next to the window, a light blanket over her, her arms wrapped around her sextant. The clear view of the skies from this vantage point keeps her head clear, stops her sweating nightmares, and she always wakes, alert, when Elk fires up the methane-gas rings in the kitchen.

On the first day of the new Regyre she is wakened by the smells of fried orange and pumpkin coming from the kitchen. She joins Elk, ready to help, but he is silent and moody.

The family eat in silence, their backs to the lightening dawn outside the window. There is an empty place: Spider is missing, though no one mentions it; they are used to his erratic ways, and next to his seat Noor sits in a reverie, eating methodically, as if food is a science that he can measure and quantify. Yma watches him when she can, marvelling at his self-control, his calm. She's sure Amasha hasn't told anyone about McKenzie's temper, it is her great secret; but some days she imagines lying close to Noor and soaking up some of his self-control.

After breakfast Yma goes back to her pod to dress, in her usual shorts and boots. She smears high-factor sunscreen on all her bare skin. Tita Lily only smiles wanly. Usually she'd check each person, but she's tired. Yma is the fourth-palest of the family (after Splendour, Elk and Hugo), thanks to her father, who had red hair and pale Hibernian skin, and she's learned how to avoid agonising nights after a day in the sun. She drinks plenty of water, brushes her teeth with the sand-and-menthol mix Madeira has created, then assembles all her belongings, pushing the crystals into her bra. It's so strange not to have a phone to shove in her pocket – she misses it. How else is she going to know the time? By the heavens, and good guesswork.

Usually she's the first to climb down the ladder, always raring to get out of the Shuck into the open, but today someone else is ahead of her. Amasha. In that short window of time Amasha has washed and dressed, and now stands at the north entrance to the tower, gazing out at the desert. She is quite still, her hands clasped in front of her. Her shawl is pulled up over her head, and the wind buffets her salwar kameez against her sturdy ankles. She has the air of a small choirboy, very reflective, very contained. She doesn't react when Yma comes to stand next to her. Yma is a head taller – she has to bend her knees a little, to work out what Amasha is watching.

The sun has just risen, sending shards of light like fans around the edges of the landmarks. Ahead is the long white expanse of the Virgule and further, maybe forty kilometres away, the distant blot of the city. But that's not what is holding Amasha's interest right now. It's something much nearer that she's contemplating. Wordlessly she hands Yma her glasses. When Yma focuses them, she sees Spider. He's about a kilometre away – Yma is good at judging distances – at the perimeter of the salt lake. He is alone (no Camel to be seen) and has stripped off his jacket. His bare arms are visible, and he is tinkering with a strange collection of wood and canvas.

'What's he doing?'

'His secret,' Amasha answers drily. 'Or what he thinks is his secret. I've known about it for days.'

Yma continues to watch him. Spider seems to be folding out sails on some sort of contraption. Holding each one out – as if he wants to introduce them to the wind, give the breeze time to understand them; and they, the breeze. Encourage it.

As a child in her life, the time before she jumped from Earth into the Cirque as Yma Fitzroy-Hughes, her parents took her dinghy-sailing on the Thames estuary. She was the descendant of a great seafarer, so she should at least learn a little of his craft. Now she has fierce memories, grimy on her tongue: sea-spume in her mouth, her feet cold in their canvas shoes, her brother in a ridiculously oversized oilskin, his skinny legs bare on the flat mudbanks. Carrying home elvers in a pillowcase, bloodstained; their mother scrambling them with eggs and bacon.

Yma tries to access some of what her father taught her about the wind, but finds it's all vague. Still, she is sure the breeze on the Virgule isn't doing what she'd expect. It feels misleading and she isn't sure why. She wonders: does it always come from the south? She thinks not. Just then the wind seems to catch the sail and instantly fills it – a distinctive popping sounds travels across the desert. In the next second Spider scrambles onto the contraption and, before she can fully understand what is happening, he is bouncing away across the dried salt.

She lowers her glasses.

'He's going to the city he saw at the edge of the Chicane,' Amasha says.

'Why?'

'He thinks it's not a mirage, he thinks it's real. He says he's seen people out there – it's obvious to us all it was people who were lost, but not to Spider. Stubborn and headstrong, that boy; he doesn't change.'

'You're not going to stop him?'

'Would you? Would you force him to come with us to Dubai, in the mood he's in? I'm sure one of those cities on the other side of Dubai is Phoenix; it'll simply take time to find it. He'll catch up with us when he knows he's on a fool's errand.'

Yma is silent. It may be that the Dormilones have arguments and differences, but at the root of it lies the understanding they all have – something that goes beyond words. It looks as if Spider intends to sail across the Virgule on the contraption and, in doing so, leave them completely. If he hated her any less, she might try to do something about it, but Amasha is right: Spider is headstrong, and usually angry.

'You're sure he'll be back?' Yma feels strangely desolate at the thought of him all that way out there.

'Of course, my child, of course. Now look at you – let me rebutton your blouse, you're all over the place.'

Yma stands still and lets her Cirque-mother fuss. She watches the sky and the distant shape of the city on the border, where she once saw a microburst. Amasha refastens Yma's shoe buckles and wipes a smear of suntan lotion from her nose.

'Good. My little girl hasn't changed much. You've still got your head in the clouds.'

Yma rests her chin on Amasha's head, her arms around her shoulders – a gesture that she adopted in the very beginning of their time here in the Cirque, a gentle teasing of Amasha's tiny stature, a way to demonstrate affection. Amasha grunts softly, acknowledging her, and squeezes Yma's hand.

Then together they watch Spider disappearing until he's just a tiny dot on the horizon.

30

SPIDER CLINGS ONTO the mast with one hand and with the other desperately holds the canvas bag out of the way of the riggers. The craft seems to go faster and faster, as if it is as determined to reach the Chicane city as he is. Eventually he manages to collect up the canvas and is able to lean back onto the frame and maintain his weight in the right direction to keep the Sandwalker on course. It leaps over the brown salt as easily as the white salt, skimming across great swathes where his unaided weight would have shattered the surface. The sun pierces in blinding white dots through the tiny stitch-holes in the canvas, salt flies up behind him and Spider feels his heart elevate, lift in his chest through the sheer exhilaration of movement: the engorged sail, the wind in his face.

'Yes,' he yells into the wind. '*YES!*'

As he nears the city its shape resolves itself from the horizon. It appears to be a long, flat rectangle at the base – he assumes that's the city – and the megalith above it is looking more and more like a creature on two legs.

Be real, he thinks, *don't be a mirage – please be real*.

Two hundred metres ahead of him Camel comes into view, her giant ponderous rump moving away from him. As he nears, the noise makes her pause and turn. She watches him shoot past her, tracking him leisurely with her head, unfazed, as if he isn't that remarkable. And when he looks back, she has returned her head to its stooped position and is continuing on at her own stoic pace.

'Hey,' he shouts back at her. 'A bit of enthusiasm maybe.'

The Sandwalker tilts to one side. He whips himself round in time to transfer his weight and angles it back to the true. It continues on for a few hundred metres, but the wind must have changed because every time he tries to keep it on course for the Chicane, it keeps leaning to the west. It turns, twists and soon he is heading back in the direction he came from, going faster and faster, no matter how much he tussles with it.

'Fuck, fuck, fuck! Keep straight, *putain*.'

The words are whipped out of his mouth by the wind. The Sandwalker veers sharply to the left, her stern twisting out to starboard. He hangs onto the lower stay, though he has no idea what he is doing as he tugs blindly at it. Now he can see the Shuck getting larger and larger. He has to wrest control, but the craft twists and leaps in his hands, as if it is a living thing, sinuous and strong.

There is a breathless pause when he thinks for a moment he's conquered it, then the whole craft comes to an abrupt halt and the back flips up, throwing him off. Spider curls himself into a ball and skids along the salt surface, coming to a stop about twenty metres away.

He is unhurt, but when he pushes himself up on his hands, he sees that the Sandwalker is in worse condition. It lies hull upwards, and its sail has been ripped off and is flapping a few metres away like a dying bird. The two yardarms are cracked, and one of the outriggers has dug itself into the cracked salt.

Spider wipes the sweat off his brow and drops his face, shaking his head. *Well then*, he tells himself. *Doesn't that teach you a lesson?*

The Sandwalker is wedged in the cracked salt at an impossible angle, beyond repair, beyond recovery. It is splintered in so many pieces it resembles the dried, forgotten skeleton of a seagull frozen in a crash landing. The salt here is brown and so fragile that whenever Spider manages to get close, it cracks loudly, threatening to drop him almost a metre to the sandy floor below.

'Shit!'

Spider backs off. He uses the hem of his dress to wipe the sweat from his eyes. Then he stands there hopelessly, staring at the Sandwalker. It was going so well. Now he is stuck – frozen out here, halfway back to where he started. He's gained nothing, fucked it up and now he'll have to limp back to the Shuck, his failure like a wet rag dragging behind him. He thinks of the Elephant Family. The confidence they showed strikes fear into his heart. If it took them so little time to capture an elephant, and to find all the cloth and gold trappings, how long will it be before they find the Sarkpont? The guy at the front – maybe African, though probably American, judging by his clothing – seemed so confident. And how long will the Dormilones' Shuck lie empty before the Elephant Family decide it is fair game.

Camel approaches him. Since he stopped, she's been circling him impatiently. Now she comes forward and nudges his shoulder with her head.

'No, get off. Food later.'

But she persists, nudging him from behind. Off-balance, he takes a jerky step forward and Camel comes behind him, pushing him again so that he stumbles forward again.

'Jesus, cut that out.'

She ignores him and continues prodding him forward, keeping him perpetually off-balance. 'Stop that, stop it.' But after a few minutes of this shoving and badgering from Camel, Spider realises something. The salt hasn't broken where he's staggered on it. Wherever he's stepped, his feet have landed on the harder white salt. It's not an accident; it's Camel – she's showing him the way across the dried lake. When he raises his chin and surveys the Virgule, he can see, snaking out in front of him, a meandering milky path through the cracked brown salt-flakes.

'OK.' He holds up his hands in surrender. 'A path. You win. We walk.'

'Where's Spider? Has he done sumting wrong?'

'What? No. Don't be stupid.'

'Where is he then? He's not with us, and I don't like walking.'

'You'll have to get used to it.'

'You're just saying that cos you love him.'

Yma frowns down at Mahmoud, who lies on his stomach on the blue-and-gold rug that has been spread out across the sand. 'Of course I love him. We all love Spider – we all love each other.'

'Yeah, but …' Mahmoud shrugs and picks idly at the gold-thread logo on the rug, which reads *Grosvenor House, Dubai.* 'I don't love him right now. He's difficult to like, isn't he? Why's he got to be so different all the time?'

Mahmoud's right, Yma thinks. Spider's gone a little mad while she's been on Earth. What has made him want to drive a wedge into the family like this? Their ability to search for the Sarkpont has proved poor, and the only thing they've been able to congratulate themselves on is the way they've always pulled together. Spider wants to jeopardise all that. Maybe that accounts for Noor's silence today: the way he seems to focus his attention a few centimetres from his own face, not letting his eyes stray further.

Yma chews on the handful of nuts she's holding and shifts a little to get comfortable – the two crystals are lodged one under each breast, because she learned early that sweat doesn't activate them. The family are about one-third of the way to Dubai and have stopped to rest here in the long eastern tract. Tita Lily is exhausted, and Madeira keeps bringing her dates and water to keep her energy up.

There is no Camel to hide behind, so Elk has hung four sheets between two spiny cacti to shield the family from the sun, and has unravelled long cloths studded with candied dates and macadamia nuts.

Noor sits in silence, eating dates, staring at Dubai. Yma doesn't watch him and turns slightly away, so he's not in her eyesight. It's taking a while for McKenzie's ghost to peel away from her – her ribs still have the shadow of an ache to them, and her stomach is still uneasy. Also, all the new skills McKenzie acquired on Earth are trailing her; Yma sees the Cirque through new eyes. She can see the way the winds here work, just from the shape of the sand dunes, and although she hasn't had time to really study the direction of the winds over the salt lake, its topography niggles at her.

'Because of him, we ain't got Camel and we ain't got an elephant, either.' Cairo spits out a date stone and rolls onto his back. He holds his toy helicopter above his head, flicking the rotors so that they go round and round, slicing the sunlight over his sulky face. On-off, on-off.

'You don't simply find elephants in this place, you know that? There isn't a giant elephant tree you pick them off. Or maybe you want an elephant ranch, where you simply walk in and choose what you want.'

'No … I mean, I … I never meant that. I just …' Cairo opens and closes his mouth hopelessly. 'That family had camels too.'

'Then they are dank, aren't they?'

'Dank?'

'Yeah – sick AF.'

'Sick?'

She considers him a while, then sighs. Of course this language doesn't translate here. It's still McKenzie Strathie's or, more accurately, it's India's, because when did McKenzie Strathie ever care about using the latest slang?

'Go and help Elk. He's waiting for you.'

Cairo sighs and gets to his feet. He trails across the sand, his head sagging, to where Elk and Knut are busy packing things into the handcart they've brought along in place of Camel. It is loaded with huge sheets of aluminium to shore up the windows of the apartment that the family found on their last visit.

Yma gets up and folds the cloths into a bundle. She goes to the others and helps load up the handcart. It's like the one she used to take the sand-dune experiment into the Science Fair. This life echoes their lives on Earth, and vice versa; it's a strange and terrifying weave of dreams and consciousness.

'Look at this,' calls Hugo. He is walking fast out of the distance, holding something in his hand. 'It's a big 'un. This is dinner.'

The men all stop and look. In his raised hand Hugo holds a lizard by its tail. It snaps and writhes, trying to reach up high enough to bite him, but each time he slaps it away. Yma sees instantly that it's the same type of lizard as Mr Blonde.

'Dinner,' Hugo repeats.

Elk comes forward and crouches to look at the lizard. He squeezes its belly and pulls back the skin on its groin. Just as Yma is about to stand and argue for a pardon for the creature, Elk shakes his head.

'No. It's a female. Leave it.'

'What? There's meat on it.'

'You heard. We've got plenty of meat in that muslin bag. And if not, there's plenty more in the fancy fridges in Dubai. Let it go.'

Hugo blinks at Elk, not comprehending.

Eventually Elk leans forward and bellows at him, 'You heard me the first time. I said, let it go.'

Hugo drops the lizard reflexively. It darts away across the sand, and everyone in the family subsides a little, shocked by Elk's aggression. He doesn't look at anyone, but continues packing, unhooking the sunshade sheet, muttering under his breath.

Not much has changed then, Yma thinks. Hugo is still the outsider, privileged and entitled. He speaks only about the arts, literature and operatic music. And the family's patience is stretched taut as a singing wire, everyone so afraid of what happens if they don't find the Sarkpont soon.

Spider and Camel have been walking for almost two hours and there is no sign of anything new on the horizon, just the eye-watering expanse of salt, harlequined white and brown like a colossal dead reptile dying in the sun. Eventually Spider brings the progress to a halt. He drinks half a litre of water from his canteen, then wipes his brow, and eyes Camel suspiciously.

'You're taking me on a wild-goose chase, aren't you? Where are we going?'

Camel lowers her head and begins to nudge him, but he gives her a quick flick on the nose to stop her. 'Where then? Where?'

He opens his hands to indicate the barren stretches. He can't see much from here, as the white of the salt lake is blinding. Camel sighs, lifts her tail and spurts out a long stream of shit pellets, as if commenting on her impatience with him.

'Thanks for that. Always a pleasure.'

Slowly Spider unpacks the equipment from Camel's back. He distributes it at equal distances to spread the weight, then removes her saddle and the *mahawi*, the pad of blankets and grass mats that fits between her humps. When her back is bare, he beckons her to kneel, clicking his fingers to indicate where. He straddles between her two humps and, when he's steady, clicks in his throat for her to stand. Camel hesitates, as if she fears his extra weight will make her fall through the surface.

'It's OK.' He presses his hand on her front hump to reassure her. 'This part is solid.'

Eventually, trusting him, she does her ungainly little scramble to her feet, back end first, then her gangly front legs, spread wide in her anxiety not to fall through. Miraculously the surface doesn't buckle under their combined weight, but it's a risk and Spider isn't complacent. From his vantage point atop her back, he scans the view as quickly as possible, aware that at any moment the surface could crack.

The tiny difference in height lends him a better view. He can just make out the tiny black smudge where the Dormilones' tower is, and to his left the distant city of Dubai where the others are, with the skull-and-crossbones Shuck perceptible as a tiny blip of black. He makes a clicking noise in the back of his throat and taps Camel's right wither, getting her to turn to the north. His binoculars skim across the horizon, bouncing along new features he's never observed before: dunes and distant mountains he'd never see from the Shuck. And then they find the city on the edge of the Virgule.

The shock of how big it is almost makes Spider lose his balance. It leaps up, enormous and immediate in the glasses. The solid oblong at the bottom consists of the city's outer walls, a dull adobe-red, one or two gateways and windows in it, the sun twinkling off panes. But it is what is mounted above it that takes his breath away. A vast sculpture, taller than any tower in the desert – it must rise at least 300 metres into the air. And what it depicts makes him grin, long and hard.

It's a huge bird, wings spread, with a plumed head and a tyrannical beak turned to one side. Flames of iron lick up the sides of its legs.

'Phoenix,' he murmurs under his breath, instantly back in the common room last night, with Yma and Knut talking about their time on Earth. 'We've found it, Yma – the city you've been thinking about. Phoenix.'

Yma and Knut have lost some of their Cirque sense and they're not used to the dry air – they go more slowly than the others, and by the time they reach Dubai, Yma is exhausted, her skin crackling with dried sweat, her tongue sticky and sore around the edges. The stench that rises from the city is making her nauseous.

'Give them time to rest,' Noor says. He stops halfway up the huge dune that slopes up from the desert floor, engulfing the city. 'Take them and Tita Lily to the apartment.'

Neither Yma nor Knut argues. While the rest of the family breaks into groups and fans off through the city, hunting as always for the Sarkpont, Elk and Amasha lead the way up the scorching sand into the tallest of the buildings, which rises up and up into the cloudless sky, black and grey, its windows shattered, sand blowing through the rooms. Noor unloads the aluminium screens and follows them up.

'What's the smell?'

'Dead sea creatures,' Elk says.

'Dead *what*?'

'Don't worry about it – you'll get used to it.' Elk lets his eye travel up the building. 'You'll be able to see what we think is Phoenix from the hundred and seventh floor. That's the hundred and seventh before the sand came in; now it's just thirty floors up.'

They have drunk plenty of water from the pig-bladder pouches they use as water reservoirs, but only ten floors up, Yma is already feeling faint. She gets into the apartment and sits on the fading royal-blue sofas with the dulled gold tassels, her head hanging, trying to recover. Knut also has to take time. It will be days before either of them is fully fit again.

'The smell doesn't help,' he complains. 'I've never known anything like it.'

Elk gives them a handful of crystallised pineapple and a small cube of salt that Forlani has provided. They chew on them carefully, glancing around, taking stock of their surroundings.

A huge place, with thick, unbroken glass.

Elk and Noor help Yma to the window with Knut. They stand there, staring out towards the east. It's the highest Yma's ever been since she's been in the Cirque, and she has to focus hard on not looking down or the dizziness will return.

'Any of those look familiar?' Elk hands her his glasses. 'Anything you recognise?'

She and Knut lean against the glass and study the distant shapes. It is late afternoon and the sky beyond the cities is a pale blue, almost white. Never before has she had such a breathtaking view of the Cirque. She can see for hundreds, maybe thousands of kilometres, and every direction she looks, the sky is teeming with different cloud formations, different weather phenomena. She can see collapsed cumulonimbus to the south, which means someone has had rain; she can see cirrus and low-lying stratus. Also the mackerel clouds that, as a child, she fantasised were the ripped wedding veils of sky goddesses, scattered in a temper. She sees no microbursts, but on the extreme furthest reach of the horizon there is something that she believes might be a *haboob*. Or a sandstorm whirling away across the far lands – she isn't sure from this angle.

'There were mountains in Phoenix,' Knut says, squinting through the binoculars Amasha has handed him. 'And lots of it is green; lots of parks and water. The buildings are mostly low-level, especially amid the city spread.'

Yma scans the horizon with her telescope – she's missed it so much – studying every detail. At least six cities are out there. Three seem to be separated by, she guesses, ten kilometres or so and run along the base of a range of mountains. There are definitely, as Hugo said, green areas on the sides of the mountain, but that doesn't automatically mean one of them is Phoenix, because the same rules don't apply here as they do on Earth.

'Yma?' She turns. Elk is looking at her, his head on one side. 'Is there anything you recognise?'

'I can't say for sure. The only thing I know is that Phoenix sometimes had microbursts above it.'

'Microbursts?'

'They're a . . . how can I put it? It's what happens when a storm turns itself inside out.'

Elk's bloodshot eyes drift to the horizon. 'Can you see any above those cities?'

'Not now. But I have seen them before – out beyond Dubai, and in other places too.'

'Nothing out there, then? Nothing that tips off any memories?'

'Not right now.'

The room is a circle and has balconies facing every direction, so Yma and Knut wander around from window to window, staring at the vista, trying to latch their thoughts onto anything that feels familiar. Phoenix had been at once memorable, yet unremarkable, and from a distance she can't think of anything about it that would be recognisable, save the mountains.

She goes to the northernmost balcony and sees the giant Virgule, flat and white. On the wall of their Shuck is graffiti stating that the Virgule was named by a man who was, on one occasion, Regyred to France in the nineteenth century and became famous as a playwright by the name of Balzac. McKenzie Strathie had learned about Balzac in literature classes. On Earth in France he'd been driven mad – possibly by all his vague memories and connections with the Cirque, Yma thinks now. There is nothing else on the walls to indicate if his family survived, but from the way he used languages on Earth, she would bet his family had strong and healthy communications between Earth and the Cirque.

She can't see Spider out there, though the area of the Virgule is too great to search in detail, so she turns the glass on the city he's so entranced by. She's been so used to seeing it from due south in the Shuck and is surprised to see its difference, but the Cirque is so artful, it manages to blend and convince from whatever direction you view things. Except that it's not all perfect, she thinks now, because there's an element that feels wrong. She focuses the eyeglasses on the sand stretching towards Spider's city. There's something about the formation of the dunes all the way out there that is ringing bells. A glow of fascination crawls over her.

She reaches into her trouser pocket for her phone to google it, then realises her mistake. She's not McKenzie Strathie; she can't reach effortlessly for knowledge. It never occurred to her to be grateful for that luxury, and now she wonders if her brain wasn't the worse for it. Had she been lazy? Always able to answer questions, prompt her memory with the phone screen?

'Yma?' Amasha has come up softly behind her and is now staring in the same direction. 'What is it? Can you see Spider?'

'No. I can see sand dunes.'

'Sand dunes. That's a novelty. It being a desert.'

Yma doesn't acknowledge the attempt at humour. She moves past Amasha and goes back through the huge, destroyed room. She crosses to one of the windows that faces east. Knut and Elk, surprised by her sense of purpose, stop what they are doing and come with Amasha to stand behind her. Yma zooms in the eyeglasses on the distant cities.

'What is it?' Knut murmurs. 'What can you see?'

'Nothing. I see nothing. And that's what's wrong.'

'Come again?'

'Out there.' She lowers the glasses and looks at the other family members. 'Can you see the mountains between the two cities?'

All three of the family lean against the window, straining their eyes at the distant shapes.

'What about them?'

'Wind should be coming through them.'

'How do you know it's not?'

'Because there would be sand dunes. And there aren't.'

Phoenix is not a mirage. The reality comes like a shout to Spider as he stands at the ruined highway entrance. The city sprawls out in front of him, houses and office blocks all built in dull reddish adobe, real and tangible; the cruel bird guarding its entrance, blotting out the sunshine. It has taken Spider and Camel three hours to get over the last part of the Virgule, and his throat is scorched, and his conviction has been pressed as thin as rice paper. Yet in spite of it all, he was right. In the same way that his fingers, hands and balls exist – the city of Phoenix exists. The same place Yma and Knut were in, on Earth. Where they should be now.

He wants to run through it, wants to put a fist through every wall and trot down every sand-filled highway, but he has to be careful. If the Sarkpont is hidden somewhere, there could be other families in the city, drawn here by their Scouts.

He puts his hand over Camel's muzzle and whispers to her, 'Stay with me.' She doesn't understand the words, but she's intuitive, she knows the emotion, and as he begins to walk along the highway she stays close to him.

They go slowly up the boulevard, eyes flicking from side to side, checking the palms and the buildings, the great drifts of sand. They go through the gates, between pillars topped with adobe lions, and on into a warren of city streets, all silted up with sand. Palm trees, which from the Virgule appeared like spindly pins sticking up above the buildings, are crowded along the remains of the streets. Their tops are green, the undersides brown and withered. Ancient acacias sprout from cracked pavements and the sprawling hackberry trees sport tiny orange berries. Nothing here to eat them. Vultures don't eat fruit. Nor do the Djinni.

He moves on through the wider boulevards. There is so much here: where does he begin to search for the Sarkpont? He comes to a vast square surrounded by buildings, no pool in the corner. Most of the windows are smashed, but some are intact and there is a neon sign blinking on and off, advertising the 'Silver Diner'. That it's definitely an American city confirms his conviction further. It's Phoenix. It has to be.

Thinking of what Knut said about the piscina, he tests the door to a church. The sign outside is in Korean and English: 'Presbyterian church of Salt River Canyon'. The door opens and he peers inside. Row after row of dusty pews. Along the walls the tall stained-glass windows have been smashed by the weight of sand that has piled up outside, burst into the church and lies in long trails in the nave. The church is silent, there is no pool or font in the corners, so he closes the door and continues on his way.

Knut says that the diagram scrawled on the shower wall is a map of the ancient Native Americans' canal system, so did the previous inhabitant of the Shuck draw it from his memory of the

Earth, or of what he saw here? It's impossible to get an understanding of how the canals would look from above – they're too spread out and long for him to walk. He tries to remember anything else Yma and Knut said about Phoenix in the United States. They mentioned mountains, golf courses. A temple.

What else?

Spider can't remember, so he keeps walking, sketching and making notes. The city seems huge, never-ending. There are golf courses, the brown grass planted in geometric shapes, and a complex of buildings grouped together like so many shapes from a child's educational toy, in concrete and adobe, threaded through with stairwells and bisected by a single towering white wall. A glass hall, and a display of four coloured panels depicting the human hand and a variety of cogs and planets. He sees a sign lying in the centre of the road that says *FroYo*.

At the top of a broad avenue with trees on either side he stops, leaning his shoulder into Camel's chest to bring her to a halt. They are motionless for a while, surveying the street. There are no cars, only traffic lights at each intersection showing red, the electric glow weak against the sunlight. Electricity. It hasn't made it into the shops, which are unlit and set back from the street, and all seem to be empty ice-cream parlours, with cracked and faded signs. At the far end is a large curved roof – a stadium, he supposes – with the word DIAMONDBACKS! displayed in red and black.

But it's the trees that catch his attention. They are citrus trees and appear still to be producing fruit.

'Come on.' He leads Camel to the first – a lemon tree. She nibbles tentatively at the leaves. Spider watches her. Madeira and

Forlani are firm about treating all Cirque vegetation with caution, but Camel can usually eat almost anything put in front of her and rarely baulks, even at the thorny trees they sometimes encounter. Satisfied that the trees are not poisonous, he pulls an orange off a nearby one and examines it. It is firm and plump. He licks it experimentally, feeling his tongue tingle at the slight acid, then bites a chunk of the skin and spits it out on the pavement.

Jackpot! The juice inside is sweet and delicious. A real orange. He sucks it dry, then gnaws on the pulp, eyeing the street as he eats. It's not unusual to find edible plants growing, but something this fat and loaded with moisture is a rarity and speaks of a ready water source. Somewhere under all this, parts of an irrigation system must still be operational.

Spider throws down his kitbag and searches for the trowel – it's sturdy and has a strong joint between the scoop and the handle; it can do anything. Crouching, he levers up some of the earth in the borders next to the street. The tinny sound of the tool echoes around the silent buildings, while Camel's stomach gurgles as she chews and watches him.

It takes half an hour maybe, but eventually he hits something. Not an underground canal, but a plastic pipe about as thick as his torso. It is studded with tiny holes that are leaking water into the sandy soil.

'What the fuck?' he asks Camel. 'A pipe?' He studies it, pressing his fingertips to it to stem the trickle, then releasing it. He wipes his hands and sits back, looking up at her. 'What were they called? The Hohokos? What did Knut say? He had a word – I just can't quite . . .'

Camel ignores him disdainfully and continues chewing, staring up at the clouds, the buildings, uninterested in his discovery. A reminder that Spider's the uneducated dick amongst them all – the one who never read a book and can't remember the names of things.

He gets up, sighing. 'Come on,' he tells Camel. 'Enough snacking now. Work to do.'

He leads her down the avenue, stopping every now and then to listen either for the telltale tinkle of glass that tells him someone else is here, watching him, or maybe for the exciting drip and rush of water.

At the end of the avenue, in front of the stadium, rises a tall building panelled in turquoise and golden-brown, with multiple balconies. He frowns up at it. The windows on all the lower storeys are shattered; that is standard in the Cirque, and he can't recall ever seeing a window that hasn't been broken by the air drying out the sealants and allowing the units in modern windows to drop right from their anchors. But further up towards the top of the building – maybe sixteen storeys high – he can see sun glinting on uniform rectangles.

There's a noise reverberating in the building: a mechanical vibration that only creeps up on him as he ties Camel to a heavy aluminium seat on the plaza outside the building. Above it a sign reads: 'Summit at Copper Square'.

Cautiously Spider heads inside. In the lobby he sees the usual detritus he's come to expect from modern buildings in the Cirque: drifts of sand, cacti and *Hilaria* grasses. The occasional glimpse of masonry or marble, dulled by exposure. Two lifts – one with the doors standing useless and open, the lift in situ, and the other also open, but with the naked inside of the lift shaft visible.

The sound is louder here: rhythmic and deep-throated as if it's in the very heart of the building. He stands there for a while, trying to see up to where the cab is jammed, wondering how the others are managing with the lift in the Burj Khalifa. When he can't see it, he wanders around the ground floor until he finds a maintenance room. Mostly it's empty – the only things of use are three galvanised buckets with mops in them and a huge industrial sink in the corner, with a large tap. He turns it experimentally and nearly leaps back in surprise when the tap jerks, gurgles and emits a long, clean stream of water.

'What the fuck?' he whispers. 'Running water?'

He blinks at it, as if it's a mirage, and then, tentatively, puts his fingers into it and holds them to his nose. No smell and the water's cold – so he touches a bit to the inside of his wrist. It dribbles off, without stinging, so, knowing that Forlani would have a fit if he saw this, Spider presses a tiny bit to the inside of his lip. It doesn't itch, it doesn't burn, so he fills a bucket and carries it round to where Camel is and sets it in front of her.

She drinks sloppily, sucking up almost the whole bucket in one go – no hesitation. He stares, mesmerised, then, laughing like an idiot, goes back and cups his hands under the tap and drinks long and deep. Then he pushes his head and neck under and stands there like a dog, shivering with the delight of the water dripping from him.

When at last the novelty wears off, he brings Camel three full buckets and then, dripping everywhere, feeling as if he's been given a brand-new skin, turns to the staircase. It is panelled in a wood that has not fared well in the desert air – it has decayed back, to reveal the skeleton of the building, but underfoot the stairs are firm and solid. He climbs slowly, thinking that the air is danker in here than he expected.

The building is twenty or so storeys high, and when he reaches the top Spider finds that the doors are of steel, as if built for an oligarch afraid of bullets. There is a crude arm that can be padlocked in place, but the padlock sits open, as if expecting a visitor.

Spider stands for a moment, running his hands over the padlock and the door. He turns the handle, it opens effortlessly and he finds himself in a large hallway, windows intact and a single doorway at the end. The door clangs shut behind him and when he turns, startled by the noise, he sees that the door is equipped on the inside with a security bar, hanging from a yoke bolted to the wall. It dangles open at the moment, but when he lifts the bar to its closed position, he sees it is of the most ferocious strength. It strikes him as odd – overkill for a building like this. On examination, he finds the mount is clumsily welded in place, as if done by an amateur using the most rudimentary of tools, and when he closes the door and inspects the outer padlock system, he sees it's the same workmanship.

Which means, Spider reasons, that they've been done by another family. He's not the first person to have climbed these stairs.

He turns and looks at the door at the far end of the hallway. It is half open, with sunlight from the apartment beyond spilling onto the rug. He moves stealthily across the hall and stands at the door, his pulse thudding, low and hard.

Tentatively he pushes the door open. The penthouse is breathtaking in its size and view, open-plan and rimmed on every side by windows. He can see the whole Cirque spread out – the city, the desert, the sky. What is remarkable is that none of the windows are shattered. He goes softly to a window, touches the glass. In the late sun he can see the layers, just like in Dubai.

He presses his nose against the glass and peers out. There is the fearsome phoenix straddling the city gate, and beyond it the desert, the skull-and-crossbone Shuck, then the small but clearly jagged silhouette of Dubai, the sun reflecting back from its skyscrapers. When he puts his hand above his eyes and looks down, Spider can't see Camel, but he can see the avenue they walked along to get here, and the line of living trees.

Following the treeline from a point below the building, he sees that it adjoins another, at a forty-five-degree angle, and moves on to make other hazy green lines into the distance. He assumes these green lines are the plastic pipes, joining to other lines and reaching out across the city. What's most important about them is that they fit, he thinks, his heart thudding now, with the diagram on the wall of the shower. This is the place – it *is* the place.

He turns and surveys the huge kitchen, which looks as if it should be home to boutique gin-tasting parties, tapas and tequila, cocaine on black mirrors. There are signs of a camp fire: the carpet has been scorched and there is congealed fat on the floor where meat has been cooked. There is a door leading to a second internal hallway, and here Spider finds other doorways that lead to the vestibule, all locked from the inside, all as invulnerable as the first.

There is a plastic doll discarded on the floor, its nylon hair scattered with sand. Spider stares at it, then puts his hands on his chest and breathes slowly through his nose, surprised at the rush of emotion. Others have been here. And when they left, they did so in a hurry. Does that mean they'd found the Sarkpont? There's hope here: a sense of beginnings and a future.

For the first time he realises the vibrating sound is louder, as if this is the floor where the mechanics originate. He walks from room to room, shooing away lizards and roaches. All the time he expects to find a gaping hole in the glass, curtains fluttering and ragged, drifts of sand across the beds and chairs, but every room is perfect. Yes, the furnishings have faded in the relentless sunshine, but otherwise it's as if this top-drawer apartment has been maintained – there are even cans of Sprite Zero in the fridge.

He finds the lift entrance. As in Dubai, it's a private lift and the doors stand open a fraction, just enough for him to look through and see that the cab is wedged with its roof at floor level – blocking the lift shaft. He studies the position and decides it's the perfect place, because the roof of the cab is sturdier than the floor and will take more to claw through. Also, the rust and the drifts of sand suggest it's going nowhere, has been nowhere and hasn't budged in a long time. He sniffs, because he's often wondered if it's possible to scent the Djinni, to tell if they are near, but there is no smell, like in Dubai – in fact all that comes back to him is the salty stench of dry air and the rancid fat on the kitchen floor.

Tentatively, afraid of destroying this fragile balance, Spider slips back into the apartment and goes to the main room. Here the glass doors give out onto the large balcony. He slides them carefully, finds that the pane holds firm and he can step out into the sunshine.

The balcony must be more than 300 square metres, with an empty plunge-pool and assorted rattan furniture, splintering in a pile at one end. He walks to the end and sees the balcony wraps itself around the building. On the western flank a larger swimming pool, similarly empty, its ceramic blue floor tiles cracked and decayed. A stunted palm tree grows from the place where the drain must once have been.

He sees mountains startlingly nearby. It takes him a moment or so to realise what they are: the same mountains he is accustomed to seeing each morning from the Shuck. From here, they appear a different shape and hue. Greener and somehow flatter. He turns his head from one side to the other, trying to understand, and thinks what if he's now seeing *behind* the Chicane – through a new bottleneck that opens into an entirely hidden part of the Cirque?

He leans over the balcony to peer down at the building. It's hard to be sure, but the four floors below him appear to be glassed-in too. The Djinni, according to everything he's seen, aren't capable of climbing glass or steel, so this place is secure. In the plunge-pool next to the master bedroom there is a solitary access ladder, which has been wrenched off the wall and lies rusting on the cracked blue floor.

He drags it out and props it against the wall. He climbs it carefully, half expecting his weight to shake it from its rusty moorings, but it is solid and opens onto a baking-hot roof crowded with rusted air-conditioning units and antennae. Ignoring the warning signs and the cartoon-like outlines of men falling through open air, Spider goes to the edge and paces around the perimeter, looking down.

The light sets the desert on rosy fire. The white path on the Virgule that he and Camel used to come here has changed – in just a few hours it has virtually disappeared. He slowly rotates his body until he's facing south-east, and Dubai rises from the desert floor in sharp points, like a black dragon, scales glinting. The sun's angle makes it difficult to discern whether the stretch from here to Dubai is any different from the passage back to the Shuck, but he's fairly certain that if they continue across the Virgule, he can rely on Camel to guide him to Dubai.

It's a seven-hour trek, he estimates, and will mostly be done in the dark – he'll arrive before dawn. The others may have found water and a place to stay. It doesn't matter; he has to convince them to leave Dubai and come with him to Phoenix.

Everything is falling into place.

31

'WHAT ARE YOU thinking?' Knut says, looking sideways at Yma.

They stand together at the base of the Burj, on the eastern side of Dubai where the sand dune slopes back down towards the desert. There are a dozen or so more shattered buildings on this side of the Burj, moving away from them in a line along what must once have been a highway. Then a dozen or so rusting shipping containers. Half a kilometre past those, the sand dune peters away back to the flat desert floor, and the highway, tarmacked and new-looking, appears from under the sand, snaking into the distance.

In the Burj Khalifa the mood has not been good. Elk and Noor have successfully shored up the windows on the lower floor, but between them they can't budge the lift from its place four floors below them, even with Knut and Hugo helping. They will have to find a better way of securing the apartment, and the conversation all evening has revolved around that and the search for water.

It was Yma who suggested that she and Knut went into the desert to look at the sand dunes in the east – she was itching to see more of what seems an anomaly in the desert. Before they left the Burj, Amasha made her drink yerba-maté and eat more pineapple. The effect has been instantaneous: she has found her energy, she feels good, alive and alert, her senses hyper-tuned. She thinks she could hear a lizard move a kilometre away, could sense the cacti flowers opening on the highway in the distance. So why can't she feel wind on her face from those mountains?

Yma rubs her face distractedly. 'Come on,' she tells Knut. 'Let's go.'

The sun is low behind them and their shadows are eerily attenuated, like monstrous stickmen, with elongated legs, heads stretched to pinheads. They move between the blocky shadows of the buildings, in and out, in and out of the late heat, as if the sun is flashing on and off. As they reach the tarmac, which is hot underfoot, the sun finally sinks behind them and a chill enters the air.

Knut rubs his arms. 'Never did get used to being out here at night. It never feels right.'

They walk on in silence, glancing at the purpling desert around them. The only sounds are the flat drop of their feet on the tarmac, the faint whoosh of wings as a vulture swoops over them. Their sun shadows have been replaced by moon shadows that shiver blue around their feet.

'Did you ever dream about them?' Knut asks. His voice is quiet and he doesn't look at Yma as he speaks. 'Did you think about them?'

'The Djinni?'

Some of the family believe that even saying the name is an invitation to trouble, and Knut is one of them. He winces at the mention.

'You don't think it's weird?' He gestures around the darkening desert. 'To talk about them? You don't think it's like asking for trouble?'

'I think that if not saying their name was a sure-fire way of avoiding trouble, then it hasn't worked. Look at us now. One more Regyre. And another family with an elephant and three camels pounding the sand.'

'Jeez – don't sugar-coat it, sistah. Just, you know, say it as it is.'

She tries to smile, but can't. They walk on for fifteen or twenty minutes. There is a part of the tarmac that has inexplicably been eaten away by the elements, leaving bare tracts of sand, and Knut is unnerved by this. He slows and kicks around in the sand, as if searching for some clue to the disappearance of the road, though it plainly picks up a few metres away. He licks his lips and glances back longingly at Dubai.

This time Yma doesn't taunt him. She thinks back to their Shuck, and the few lines carved shakily by hand in the shower wall. Another epistle from an earlier dweller: *God ye shall know, yet falleth the Angels so fast 'tis not for man nor beast to 'compass their true nature.*

None of the family have entirely understood this line. Tita Lily says it means the Djinni are fallen angels, and that fact alone makes them more dangerous. Amasha says it means they might look the gods in the face, but they'll never look the Djinni in the face.

'Come on,' Yma tells Knut. 'We haven't got time.'

She turns to go, gets a few metres down the road and instantly hits something soft and pillowy. It is so unexpected that she falls back, sitting down on her bottom and rolling backwards a little.

'Yma?'

She lies on her back, blinking.

'What is it?'

She shakes her head. Rolls back to an upright position and lifts herself up on her hands. She kicks out at the barrier. Her feet bounce back. 'Chicane. It's the Chicane.'

'Chicane? Here?'

Knut comes to her and tentatively reaches out, flinching slightly when his fingers meet the barrier. '*Banging*,' he murmurs, awed. He presses his hands against it and fingers his way slowly across it. 'You're right. It's a boundary.'

She glances back at Dubai. The buildings are dark against the evening sky, just one light glowing in an upper storey of the Burj. She and Knut have got only two or three kilometres out of the city, nowhere near the cities they were aiming for.

She tips forward onto all fours and gets to her feet, brushing the sand off her hands and joining him to feel the miraculous illusion that is the Chicane. The barrier is warm against her palms.

The smell from cacti on the road ahead – the ones that don't exist – is another powerful illusion. But it's not perfect, because out where the distant cities stand proud against the dark-blue sky there is a gap in the mountains, and in front of it there should be a very distinct series of sand dunes. They should be somewhere in front of the gap, and they should be crescent-like in shape. Yma turns, looks around. They are missing.

It's almost dawn when Yma and Knut get back to Dubai, to find the family haven't climbed to the stifling hot apartment but have made an impromptu camp at the current ground level, in front of the broken windows of a restaurant. They are gathered around a small bonfire, lit on the drifted sand. The children are half awake, half asleep, curled on a sofa that someone has dragged into the open air.

Yma throws down her pack and sits on the sand, dragging her hands down her face.

'I'm sorry. There's a Chicane out there. We can't get to the cities. We can see the mountains and we've worked our way two kilometres in each direction. It's literally so clear – those cities are an illusion, a mirage.'

There's a long silence when Yma feels everyone's brains clicking forward, trying to accept this new leap. Amasha and Elk's faces are serious, and Yma struggles to decipher what they are thinking.

'I wish I could change it,' she murmurs. 'But it's true.'

Amasha looks at Elk. By the firelight his face is saggy, despondent. He glances at the children, then across at the adults, as if the weight of caring for them is immense.

It's Cairo who surprises them all by speaking. 'There's no water here, either.'

They all turn to look at him. 'What was that?'

'They have to make fresh water out of sea water. Hugo said it. And he said the place they gotta make it ain't there.'

'That's not entirely true,' Hugo says gruffly. He's wearing a white shirt that has become the colour of sand with sweat and hard work. There are white patches on his face where he has done a poor job of wiping away the dirt. 'And we haven't finished looking yet.'

Yma looks at Hugo, perplexed. She knew all along that the real Dubai relied on vast desalination plants. 'No desalination plants?' she asks, raising her eyebrows. 'No water?'

'Maybe not,' he admits.

'What then?'

Elk clears his throat, scratches his chin. 'I'm sorry. We can't secure the apartment, either – not the way we want it. We have to go back to the Shuck.'

Splendour's face crumples. Tears spill out of her eyes. 'But, Yma, what about the Elephant Family? They might be in our Shuck.'

'Hey, hey,' Yma crawls forward on her knees to where the little girl is sitting and takes her in her arms. 'No, no, no. That's not going to happen. Is it?' Over Splendour's head she appeals to Elk and Amasha with her eyes. 'Is it?' she repeats meaningfully.

'Of course not.' Elk gets to his feet. He comes and holds out his great beefy hand to Splendour's. 'Hey, shortpiece,' he says, 'wanna test Tree-Arm?'

Splendour stops crying briefly and eyes his hand. 'Tree-Arm' has been Elk's party trick since they first arrived. He proves he's as strong as a tree by letting Splendour swing on his forearm. His promise is that she cannot swing hard enough, or long enough, to make his arm tire.

'Go on,' Yma whispers, pushing her forward. 'That arm can't hold you – it's gonna get tired, I'm betting on it.'

Sniffing shyly, Splendour wipes her face and gets to her feet. She clambers up and wraps her arms around Elk's solid forearm, dangling like a monkey. Arm extended, he carries her across the dining area, making her giggle and swing, her little legs sticking out in mid-air. Not wanting to be left out, Cairo and Mahmoud get up and join them.

Yma turns back to the adults, who are all studying her seriously, as if waiting for her to give them the right answer. 'Well? Tomorrow's a grey night. Just twenty or so hours more: we should be moving.'

'Wait,' Knut says, low and serious. 'What if Spider doesn't go back to the Shuck? What if he comes here to meet us?'

'If he comes here and we're gone, he'll know we've gone back to the Shuck,' answers Amasha.

'He won't make it back in time for the grey night. We should separate into teams – some of us go back to the Shuck with the children, the others go on to the Virgule to find him?'

She shakes her head. 'Too dangerous. The Virgule is impassable. The surface changes by the hour.'

'Then how the hell did he get across it?' Knut asks.

Amasha shifts position, pushing her dark, soft legs out in front and switching them so that they are under the other side of her body. 'Spider is good at keeping secrets. Slippery, some might say. He built a sand-yacht,' she explains. 'It can travel across the salt lake. But we can't, so I forbid anyone from crossing it. Do you hear?'

Knut holds her eyes for a few seconds. There's a tiny beat in his irises, a slight engorging then shrinking, as if in time to a heartbeat. Yma wonders if this is going to be the moment when someone in the family defies the Futatsu. But eventually Knut lets out a long sigh. He lowers his face and presses his fingers into his eyes, as if trying to quell a pain in there.

'OK.' He gets to his feet. 'But we're going to leave supplies, for if he does come here. And, Noor and Hugo, we're going to make a sign that Spider can see.'

'What're you going to do that with?'

'Anything white, anything luminous. There are mirrored tiles somewhere – I saw them.'

'Well, buggeration,' Hugo says wearily. 'They'll be under all the dead sharks.'

Yma watches the three men walk down towards the derelict water parks.

'Right.' Amasha claps her hands. 'Kids, time to get going. Let's do it, let's do it.'

'I wanna go back to sleep.'

'No. It's a long way back, so get a wriggle on.'

Yma gets up to help Elk and Amasha organise the belongings, and between them they have most of the cart loaded when Forlani appears beyond the broken glass in the restaurant.

He is silent, standing quite still, holding the giant lamp that Spider uses to check the tower floor in the mornings.

Yma glances at the children, who are squabbling over who will ride in the cart, then carefully goes towards him. Inside the restaurant it is dark – once there was an aquarium set into the walls, for the diners to appreciate tropical marine life; now all that is left of it consists of sanded-up tanks, peeling walls, silent pumps and fibreglass caves, where moray eels may once have coiled.

'*What?* You look awful.'

Forlani glances at the rest of the family. Then steps a fraction closer to Yma. 'Spider told me to look in the lift shafts.'

'And?'

'You'd better come and see.'

32

FORTY KILOMETRES AWAY, in a city that miraculously has electricity to light his way, Spider at last finds the source of the rhythmic noise. It's inside what he thought was a broom cupboard, but turns out to be an engine room lodged inside the apartment at Copper Square.

He stands and stares at it for a long time – the moving pieces, the long pipes that disappear to nothing beneath him. There aren't any gaps between them and the concrete of the building. Nothing a Djinni could creep its way into.

Spider closes the door and sits against the wall, his hands resting on his knees. He thinks for a while about what he's seen: nothing of any other families. No tracks, no fresh scattered rubbish. Also no tingling sensation that he's close to the Sarkpont. No rectangles with pools in the north-west corner. This building, with its labyrinth of staircases and ladders to the upper floors, isn't a rectangle, it's a square with a notch cut into it – and anyway the pools are in the wrong place. It's not the Sarkpont.

It doesn't matter. There is a water supply right here in the apartment, running taps both here and downstairs, a mystical electricity supply and its elevation. They could live here.

He goes back down to the plaza, and together he and Camel eat a small supper – dates and cornmeal flatbreads. He fills the water vessels, checks the equipment is still tied securely to the *mahawi* and touches Camel on the muzzle.

'How you feeling? You ready to go?'

He finishes tying the kit to her saddles, then hikes his backpack onto his shoulders. Two clicks in his throat and Camel begins to move.

They walk back through the boulevards. Everything is quiet and for a long time there's no fear. Just the softness of their footsteps and the crunchy trail they leave behind. They pass the giant square with the Korean church, the Silver Diner sign still flickering, go past the bird gate and out onto the Virgule, towards Dubai and the family.

The going is easy and Camel lumbers peacefully ahead, her head down as if she knows exactly where they are going and doesn't need to be fully awake. Spider follows, trusting her confidence. But two kilometres out from Phoenix, a crack ricochets beneath him. He looks down in time to see fissures racing out from under his feet, multiplying in fractals, like lightning. Camel startles at the noise and backs away. Her feet are large and padded to spread her weight, there is no chance of her cracking the salt; but with his solid mass, aligned vertically and ending in two points where the pressure concentrates, Spider doesn't stand a chance.

A second crack, the salt explodes into a million crystals and he drops.

The movement panics Camel and sends her into a jittery sideways jig. Spider drops the rope and lets her dance around, while he gets his balance. He's only fallen fifty centimetres or so, but it takes a while to right himself.

The hole he has made is more than a metre square, and the crust must be thinner than the scales at the edge of the lake. He drags his feet out from the sand and, in an ungainly wading motion, arms in the air, makes his way to the edge of the crust. On examination, it's only a couple of centimetres thick; surprising it held him as long as it did. He puts his hands flat on it and tests it, slowly transferring his weight down. It breaks almost instantly, and a scale the size of a tyre breaks off and shatters against his bare legs.

'*Merde. Merde.*' He wipes his forehead with the back of his hand and squints at the lake spreading out around him in the dying light. Surely the crust can't be this thin all across the lake – his luck might be bad, but not *that* bad. He has to get back on the surface. He can't plough thigh-high in salt all the way to Dubai.

'Camel!'

She stops skittering instantly. She hesitates and then, head lowered, she makes her way across the salt. Her instinct won't let her come too close – generations of ancestors have written in her genes not to approach holes in the salt. But she gets as near as she dares, and Spider is able to catch the rope. He winds it around his wrist, then ferrets in his tool bag until he finds an awl. He chooses a piece of salt thirty centimetres away, raises the tool high about his head and plunges it into the salt. The crust shatters instantly.

'Shit!'

He repeats the process on another scale, but that cracks too. Soon he has cleared a semicircle about three metres wide.

He is ready to give up and try a different tack, when unexpectedly the awl hits a solid sheet of salt that doesn't crack. Experimentally Spider leans onto it. It holds his weight on his two hands and he cautiously lowers his upper-body weight onto it. He lies flat on the scale, and although a small amount of salt crumbles at the very edge, the majority holds firm.

Moving very slowly, he spreads his arms as far onto the crust as he can, his head turned to one side. He makes a soft clicking noise in his throat and Camel begins to walk away. The moment the rope is taut, he kicks off. It's like being on a sledge; he slithers free instantly, bumping along the salt for some distance.

'Halt!'

Camel stops and Spider curls his legs up and gets to his feet. He brushes off his legs and his dress. The hole is about three metres behind him, and now that he looks, he can see the difference in the quality of the salt crust. Even in the twilight it is clearly brown, not white. He must have been on the brown salt for minutes, because the patch where he fell through spreads back to the south for a hundred metres or more.

When he turns and looks in the direction of Dubai, he sees no white path at all. Nothing. The lake spreads out in front of him, hectare after hectare of dangerous brittle salt.

Many times Yma has wondered how the Djinni come into the Cirque. Mardy said they were uncontrollable. But now, braced in the lift shaft, looking down while Forlani shines the massive spotlight down, she sees things she can't explain.

Under the Burj, maybe a hundred floors down, the light glints off something liquid, something foul-smelling. She can't tell exactly what it is, but she can see white shapes smeared along the sides of the shaft.

'Yma?' Forlani puts out a hand. 'Don't faint.'

'No . . . I—' She swallows. She hands him the torch and swings herself back to the side of the shaft, where she crouches for a while, her back to the drop.

Forlani puts a hand on her shoulder. 'Let's tell the Futatsu.'

They head for the door, out to where the others are. Cairo and Mahmoud run past them in another of their crazy games. Seems they've already forgotten what it cost Tita Lily.

'What?' Amasha says, looking at Yma and Forlani's faces.

'This is not the place for a new shelter.'

'Says who?'

'Please trust us. We can't stay here.'

Elk frowns. He folds his arms, his big head on one side, and is about to say something when there is a loud scream from the direction of the lift room. Everyone heads back and finds Cairo, tears running down his face.

'What the hell?'

'It's Mahmoud. He fell.'

'He what?'

'Fell …'

'You pushed him?'

'No – no, we was just messing around.'

'Fuck, *fuck*!' Forlani goes to the lift shaft and leans over as far as he dares. '*Mahmoud, what the fuck?*'

Yma leans over. The little boy is about five metres down, clinging like a marmoset to the side of the lift shaft, his face turned up to them, his eyes wide. Next to him is the bloodied scalp of a man. White and slightly balding. They can't lose him – not after Nergüi,

'Don't move,' Amasha hisses. 'Stay right there.'

Through his shock, Mahmoud seems to realise his mistake. His mouth opens in an upside-down smile, and a low moan comes out. 'What's under me?' he wails. 'What is this?'

Beneath him the liquid seems to move, as if something can hear him.

'Don't speak, don't move. Stay there, we're going to get help.'

Already Forlani is clambering out into the shaft. Yma puts a hand on his shoulder and shakes her head. 'No – wait. We've got to think this through. Elk, bring any rope you can find.'

Elk and Amasha disappear, and Yma shines the light very carefully along the sides of the shaft. Now she sees that the white shapes are the vague remains of human beings. For sure, Mahmoud has realised. She positions the lamp so that it is illuminating the entire shaft and begins, cautiously, to make her way down the girders and cables.

Beneath her, Mahmoud is realising the danger and panic hits him.

'Yma, YMA! What is this? What is this place?'

'*Don't move, don't move. And keep quiet. Hush.*'

But Mahmoud is too young, too panicked to follow instructions. He kicks at a piece of skin, as if to keep it away from him, and as he does so, he loses his grip. There is a horrible moment when Yma is close enough to see his fingers giving up the fight – the way they scrabble, sliding off the slime – and then he is falling, his body flipped like a doll's from one side of the shaft to the other, hitting his head as he does.

Yma freezes, her mouth open in a half shout, half cry. It seems to take forever for the sound to stop. A faint splash fingers its way up the shaft.

'No, no, no!' She begins to move down faster, into the places the light can't reach. 'NO! Mahmoud? Answer me.'

From above, another light powers up. 'Yma?' Elk's voice from above. 'Yma, what's happening?'

'He's fallen – he's in the bottom,' she yells back. 'He's unconscious. *We can't lose him.*'

'Wait. Don't move. I'm going to lower a rope.'

She stops climbing and faces the wall, her eyes clenched tight, biting her lip. Above she can hear the sounds of whispering and the manoeuvring of the rope being prepared; below she can hear nothing. No cries. She thinks Mahmoud has already sunk into the soupy mess down there.

A touch on the back of her neck: the rope Elk is lowering. 'I've made a loop, it's firm. Slide into it, arms first.'

She does as she is told, wishing suddenly for Spider and his calm, his natural confidence around ropes and heights. She can hear her breathing coming off the walls, can smell its sourness. And the scent of her own fear, adrenaline mixing with the stench from below. A wallowing sound below her. She pauses.

'*Mahmoud? Can you hear me?*'

Silence. Just a repeat of the wallowing.

She looks up. 'How long is this rope?'

'Not long enough,' comes the reply. 'We're knotting another one onto it.'

'Yma – don't do anything stupid,' Forlani hisses above her.

'Please, Yma, please. *Pætiyo*, my precious girl, please …'

She tests the rope, resting her weight into it. Again she thinks about what Spider would say – how he would do this. She takes a breath and pushes herself off the side of the shaft. There is a slight tautening of the rope under her arms, a constriction and a creak of the rope as it adjusts to her weight.

'We've got you. We're lowering you now.'

Yma fills her mind with an image of Noor and Spider sharpening their arrows, ready to take on whatever the night sends to them – she grinds her teeth, thinking of Joe Marino, and summons up all her anger, metabolising her fear into fury.

Lower and lower she gets, past all the dead skins, the people who have once walked the Cirque. Children, old women, someone's eye sockets gruesomely hooked over two bolts in the gridding. Below her she can hear nothing, merely the faintest glooping sounds.

They tie another rope and she feels the knot go over the side. She must have gone down eighty storeys when she reaches the slop. It is like a charnel house down here. The rope has lasted, but now, clinging to the edge of the shaft, she knows Mahmoud is lost forever. There is nothing that could survive that fall. Mahmoud hit his head, he is under all this.

She breaks off a long mangled piece of metal from the shaft and pokes it experimentally into the sludge. Something under it stirs and for a moment she thinks it's Mahmoud.

'Grab it.' She moves the metal around. 'Take it, Mahmoud.'

Instead a long white finger emerges, tentatively curling around the metal.

She drops the metal, kicks herself up a few rungs. '*Bring me up*,' she screams. '*Bring me up!*'

The rope creaks and begins to pull her away. Yma convulses, frantically lifting her limbs as high as she can, scrabbling at the lift wall. The languorous finger slowly drops away below her, pulling the metal strut below the mulch.

She is crying when she gets to the top. '*They're down there. The Djinni – I saw one*.'

Elk and Forlani drag her away from the shaft.

'*No! Mahmoud's still down there!*'

'He's gone, Yma, he's gone. He can't be alive.'

They collapse in the apartment at the new ground level, panting hard, their eyes wide.

'He must have drowned,' Forlani says, his voice hoarse. 'He can't be alive. He banged his head as he went down – he would have been unconscious.'

'We can't stay here,' Elk reiterates.

'But *Mahmoud*,' Yma cries. 'We can't lose another one.'

Amasha grabs her hand, shakes it, forcing Yma to look into her face. 'There is a reason for everything – there is a reason for this. It's to tell us not to stay here.'

Yma curls herself into a ball, sobbing so hard she can barely breathe. Her head hurts, her throat aches, she keeps recalling Mahmoud running past her so fast. One minute he was there, and the next not. She should have done something, should have stopped him.

And then she feels Forlani touching her shoulder. 'We've got to go. Yma, it's not safe here in Dubai.'

Three hours after sunset Spider wonders if he's going to die. Every centimetre of the way has been a struggle. Camel is patient, picking her way ahead of him, finding by instinct the best places. She hasn't broken the surface once, but Spider has; with every step, it seems, he's crashed through to the lake bed. Both legs are covered in welts and sores that are open and red, as fat and shiny as newly slaughtered rabbit meat.

This time, when the salt shatters, he doesn't scramble out again. He's come to the end of his fight and his willpower. Dubai, with its glittering buildings, has been visible with the naked eye for more than an hour. It looks so close, but it is too far. He'll never make it. He sits down in the sand, his hands resting at shoulder height on the crust, lowers his head and does nothing. Absolutely nothing. The water canteens strapped to his biceps are almost empty. Camel has got used to the routine of these plunges to the lake bed and is waiting patiently ahead, her hindquarters towards him.

'Hey, girl.'

She lowers her head and twists her neck to look back at him.

'Go,' he says. 'Go.'

She peers at him, as if he's an object of curiosity, but nothing more.

'Go on. Get the hell out of here!' He makes clicks in the back of his dry throat. Hisses at her.

But Camel merely raises her eyebrows arrogantly and turns her head back to look at Dubai, as if he is beneath contempt.

He breaks off handfuls of salt and begins hurling them at her. 'Go on, fuck off.' She flinches as they hit her flanks and takes a couple of jittery steps forward. 'That's it.' He chucks more salt. 'Go to Dubai. Go and find the others.'

She dances out of his reach and stops. Shuffles back to face him and takes a hesitant step towards the hole. Spider grunts. He sits back on his heels, shaking his head, hands limp on his thighs. His left wrist is encircled with beads and twisted leather thongs. Each one was made by one of the family. He stares at the bracelets. Thinks about Phoenix. He knows they have to go to Phoenix to stand any chance of finding the Sarkpont.

A cracking noise rouses him. Moodily, reluctantly, he lifts his eyes. Camel's great moony face blocks out the moon, peering at him like a thoughtful old woman. She has risked coming close enough to the edge of the hole that the salt is cracking. She backs up a fraction at the sound, but doesn't stop staring.

He sighs. Massages his temples. The camping equipment in its protective neoprene dangles from Camel's *mahawi* a few centimetres from him. Spider takes the last few gulps of water, chews on a handful of grapes from his tool belt and eyes the kit thoughtfully.

'Come here.' He spits out grape pips, gets up and beckons Camel. She is nervous, he can tell from the wet bubbles in her nostrils, but she risks coming close enough for him to reach up and detach the sleeve. Instantly he has it, he pushes her back. She retreats gratefully a short distance and continues to watch him.

For a while Spider can't work out what on earth he is meant to do with the equipment. He unfolds it on the salt crust and studies it: the lightweight pickaxe, the nylon tent. It smells of suntan lotion and, inexplicably, the sea. Once he saw Yma's silhouette inside a tent like this – she was undressing on one of the white nights in the desert.

An idea. He stands, suddenly energised, and begins ripping the tent with his teeth. In his belt is a robust sail needle and a length of nylon, intended for repairs on the Sandwalker's sails. Watched by Camel, he begins to make the additions he needs. When it's nearly finished, he whistles to her and, catching her lead rope, firmly stitches its frayed end into the apex of the bag he's made.

It looks like something a butterfly has carelessly discarded, limp and roughly stitched. It's laughable, but it's all he has. Holding on to the bag and the rope, Spider leans his body flat on the Virgule surface. Two clicks in his throat, and Camel pulls him swiftly out. Another click and she slows. She turns to him expectantly, but instead of standing, he remains on the crust. Clumsily, aware that there's no dignity in this, he manoeuvres himself feet first into the cocoon he's fashioned. His legs are long and muscular, but he is able to fold them into his chest just enough to close the bag over the top of his head. Now he is curled up like a foetus, arms crossed around his shins, hands over the top of his head, which faces Camel's backside and the direction of travel.

He takes a breath. This is going to hurt.

'OK, girl. Take us to Dubai.'

Camel sets off. She's going at a steady pace, as if she can sense the right speed. At first the bumping is bearable: Spider keeps his face tucked in, ignoring the pain as his knuckles and shoulders bounce on the salt. But the longer it goes on, the harder it is to bear the motion. His teeth are gritted and he counts loudly – one two three, three two one – anything to distract himself. Each bump is like being cracked against a wall, and his head feels as if it will split open the next time he hits the surface.

After too much friction, the bag begins to disintegrate in places of stress: his knuckles are now colliding directing with the salt. Another rip appears on his calf. Instantly Spider feels the skin stripped away, he puts back his head and yells the words, 'One two three, three two one, fuck-fuck-fuck!'

He's at the end of his pain, he needs a break.

'Stop,' he yells. 'Sto—'

The word is cut in half. Camel has dragged him over a tiny bump in the salt, but as Spider careens over, his head meets the surface with a blackout crack. He doesn't even have time to understand what has happened before he is unconscious.

33

THEY GRAB EVERYTHING, shovelling things into packs, trying to work fast, and walk out of Dubai jerkily, wearing expressions of stone. Yma is sweating slightly, goosebumps on her back, thinking about Mahmoud, maybe swimming in the silent black under the desert, lost among blind cave-fish. When he tries to surface, his head will brush the underside of Dubai, the underside of the sand.

No, she tells herself, *don't think about it. He's dead.* They walk down the sand dune and find Hugo, Noor and Knut near the bottom, exhausted and dirty. Before she gets to them, Noor holds up a hand to stall her.

'Don't get near us. We're not pretty.'

She doesn't reply.

'Seriously. We had to move some of those dead carcasses to get to the tiles.'

They are smeared with something foul-smelling. She covers her mouth and comes down the dune, her feet sinking with each step, passing them, holding their eyes.

They stop laughing and follow her.

'*What?* What is it, Yma?'

She shakes her head and walks on, her chin up, facing the desert. Behind her, Amasha is weeping, holding Noor, explaining as fast as she can what has happened. Yma stops and turns. Knut is trying to get back to the Burj, but Elk stands in his way, dodging, fast as a quarterback, stopping him at every step.

'Knut, he's gone. He really is gone. There is nothing we can do. We have to get back to the Shuck.'

Beyond them, studded into the side of the sand dune, at the point where it rises most precipitously from ground level and can therefore be seen from possibly twenty clicks away, the message: S*H*U*C*K. Standing twelve metres high, the letters are glaringly obvious, to make absolutely sure they are clear for Spider. They have been embellished with every free-standing object available in the ruins of Dubai – the men have torn hanks of cladding from buildings, and sheets taken from beds, and mirrored tiles from the bottom of the water park. If Spider doesn't see it, he'll smell it, she thinks.

Slowly Knut is subdued. He stands in the sand, his hands to his face, shaking his head. The other two men are motionless, staring at the Burj.

'It was your fault,' Cairo says to Hugo. 'You told us there was a plant under the city – something to make water. Except there wasn't a plant.'

'What the fuck?' Hugo says.

'You're a fat slob and you're a liar,' the little boy says. 'I hate you. *I hate you.*'

Hugo is silent for a moment. He puts his hands on his sides and stares out at the desert. 'How comes I always get the blame? Is it because of my life before I came here?'

No one answers. They all look at their feet. Yma has never considered this before, but she realises he's right. He was privileged. But then, she ruminates, she was too. And Noor, and Amasha. So why do they all take it out on Hugo?

'Cairo,' she says. 'You have the responsibility of an adult. You could have stopped that happening.'

'*No, no!*' he yells. 'You're all wrong.' He runs off ahead of them in the sand, his face lowered. He's crying, no one has any doubt.

Amasha frowns. 'Let him go. He knows he's done wrong. He just needs time to digest it.'

The family turn for the Shuck. They are slower than usual, they have no energy, no high spirits. They know they can't lose anyone else. Splendour is in shock, her face a little mask of horror, while Cairo walks sulkily along ahead of the train, his face lowered.

When Yma is roughly two kilometres from Dubai she feels less sick, though she keeps casting glances over her shoulder. Forlani is hobbling much faster than usual, and she knows he is throwing her glances from time to time; and Tita Lily seems to have regained some strength and can walk now. Eventually Yma chews a piece of kangaroo jerky as she walks, the woody saltiness feeling good in her mouth. The Virgule to her right is brown and treacherous-looking.

'He'll need to have the right sails,' Hugo says next to her. 'Or he'll never make it.'

'I beg your pardon?

He squints up at the sky, as if he's considering the question. 'I used to sail myself. And there is no way he'll cross that on a fixed sail.'

She continues walking a while, absorbing this. He means that Spider needs a boom to swing the sail into the wind when it changes – which it will do, on the Virgule. Yma Fitzroy-Hughes on the mudflats at Mersea comes back to her, the dried sea water caking and blistering her soft palms as she tied clove hitch after clove hitch, trimming the sails onto the rudimentary capstans. She thinks she could recall some of the basics, but it has been lifetimes since she thought about sailing.

They don't stop for lunch; no one is in the mood to eat. About an hour after midday the Shuck comes into view. The Futatsu stop to study it – all morning the notion of the Elephant Family has been a niggling worry – but it is too far to tell if the walls have been breached.

Then Amasha turns, a strange look on her face, and stares to the rear of the family train. When Yma turns, she sees what has caught Amasha's attention. Both the children, who must have been lingering at the back, have stopped dead in their tracks and are staring out into the Virgule. Cairo is holding his helicopter, forgotten in mid-flight, his attention diverted entirely, and Splendour has her knuckles pushed nervously into her mouth, her eyes wide.

'Kids?'

Neither responds. The direction they are looking in is empty – there is nothing out there, nothing at all that Yma can see.

She and Amasha exchange glances, then backtrack to the kids.

'What is it?'

Splendour's eyes dart to Yma's, then go directly back out to the dried salt in the distance. 'Me don't like that noise.'

'Me neither,' agrees Cairo. He edges himself into Yma's shadow, peeking out cautiously at the horizon.

Yma can't hear anything. She frowns up at Amasha, who shakes her head. Yma knows that children can hear at different frequencies from adults. The men have stopped now and have come back to join the group, Splendour instantly monkeying her way up Elk's sturdy leg and curling into a ball in his arms.

'What can you hear?' he asks.

'I dunno.' Splendour buries her face in his chest, turning away from the sound, wanting to disappear into him. 'Make it stop.'

The adults stand in an uncertain cluster, their eyes darting from one face to another. It's very clear there is no cover out here, and Noor lifts his bow.

Yma tips her head back and watches a lone vulture wing its way through the blue. The second she's seen in twenty-four hours. Then a movement in the corner of her eyes: something emerging from the heat-shimmer of the Virgule.

Elk hands Splendour to Amasha, who carries her to the back of the men, using her other hand to drag Cairo with her. Elk, Hugo and Knut step forward, squaring their shoulders. Elk is huge, his shadow long and wide, but the other two are unimposing.

They don't have whatever it is that Spider had, when he stood in front of the Shuck two days ago to warn off the Elephant Family. Forlani limps to stand with them, shaking; but it's not from fear, Amasha thinks, it's from a readiness to fight whatever is coming at them.

Now they can all hear the sound – it's inhuman, as if a creature is in pain. And then the haze clears and the creature resolves itself.

Everyone in the family lets out their breath.

It's Camel, limping towards them. She is dragging a battered object in her wake. The noise is her panicked braying through her nostrils.

As Camel draws closer, it becomes clear that the object she drags is a tarpaulin or canvas bag containing something large. She stops wailing and pauses for a moment, her legs slightly splayed as if she's weary. She sniffs the air, then turns her head to eye the family standing there. Blinks. Once. Twice.

'Camel,' Yma calls tentatively. '*Camel?*'

She puts her head down and snorts loudly. She lets out a long, long breath, like a sigh, and begins to walk slowly towards the family, her eyes down as if she has a terrible confession to make. As she walks, the object she pulls leaves a dark smear of blood on the sand. Yma covers her mouth, unable to fathom what she is seeing. No one speaks for a few frozen seconds. Then, silently and reverently, Forlani limps forward. He has one hand out for Camel to sniff, to scent something familiar. She stops to smell him and doesn't flinch. She stands patiently, allowing him to go behind her rear legs and kneel painfully next to the bag.

'No,' Splendour says, getting restless in Amasha's arms. 'No.'

'Ssshhh.'

'What is it?' Cairo tugs at Amasha's sari.

Slowly, slowly, Forlani pulls at the battered canvas. The shape is motionless. It's a corpse, of course, Yma thinks; a corpse sent to them by someone.

The canvas peels away and she sees a knee. Sticking upright, pointing to the stars. A naked human knee, which she recognises as Spider's. She starts across the sand towards Forlani, a monstrous choke coming from inside.

'Don't,' Forlani warns. 'Don't.'

But she is there, breathing fast and looking down at the body, in spite of Forlani's pitiful attempts to cover the mess in there. Spider lies on his back, blood moulding to his right side. The hair is ripped away from his scalp and his dress is completely detached from him, torn away to reveal hard muscles and blood caked into the hairs on his stomach.

34

THE SANDWALKER.

Spider dreams of it skating across the Virgule's surface, powered only by the insane wind, its framework a neatly geometric skeleton of bamboo lashed with kangaroo sinew. It doesn't crack the salt, there is never a moment where it rests there long enough, always bouncing along, driven by the wind in its flapping sails. It tilts, flips over, the sun flashing on and off. Before it can hit the ground, he wakes at the top of a gasp, gulping in air.

His eyes are shut, but slowly his consciousness opens – he can feel and hear. He is sweating, his heart is racing. His head hurts, and the pain in his side is worse. He is being carried: up and up, the late desert wind on his face. Someone – Hugo – is yelling something. About water?

Spider closes his eyes and dreams of water. He drifts from the place that his mother washed when he was a young boy – two porcelain bowls, lathering herself with 'Le Sapin' olive-oil soap brought by a customer all the way from Marseilles – to the double-spouted canteens they'd drink from in the Foreign Legion: water, or *pinard* if they were lucky; a water-tank in an attic and the shower room here in the Shuck with the diagram on the wall.

The canals in Phoenix – the gauzy green lines of vegetation he'd seen from the apartment window …

'The canalsh,' he mutters through blood-thickened lips. 'Peeenix.'

'What's that?' It's Forlani's voice, anxious. 'Did he say something? Did you hear that? He said something.'

There is a murmur of voices, and Spider feels his body being stabilised – he has no idea where. Then Forlani, his hand on Spider's shoulder, speaking.

'Spider? Spider?'

Beyond Forlani, Hugo is still bellowing – again about water.

'Spider, dude? You with us?'

But the noise and the light and the pain are too much for his inflamed brain. He drifts back from it into a half world, a place of images that flitter across his eyelids.

His mother, stroking his face. 'So handsome – such a handsome boy: you are going to break so many hearts, my son.' And a girlfriend from a Scout mission when he was Regyred to Australia, telling him that he had to find water for the car because it was overheating. Walking to a petrol station and carrying back a five-litre plastic bottle along the baking tarmac, stopping every kilometre to sip at it, the smell of engine oil thick on his hands.

He's thirsty – so thirsty – he can taste the blood and the sand in his mouth like a crisp rind. And Hugo still shouting about water, people around him yelling anxiously; someone pulling at him, pain shooting from his calves, too much, too much … And he's back in the apartment in Phoenix, the engine room, with the pipes and the smell of petrol, empty cans strewn everywhere, those fat pipes like living arteries, gurgling and sighing.

It's a pump, he thinks; it's a pump, and it pumps water to the entire city – to the entire Cirque maybe. They could swim in all the water in Phoenix, they could. He has to tell them.

And here is his mother again, pressing a wet cloth to his head. Or Forlani – it's hard to tell. A little water dribbled into his mouth, something soft against his back, the pain in his legs so bad that he tries to scream but can't open his mouth.

Yma stands in the sand outside the Dormilones' tower and stares at the Virgule. Behind her the place is in commotion – Hugo is bellowing at the top of his voice, someone else is shouting back at him; meanwhile Spider is being taken up the ladder by Noor and Elk, Forlani crawling up behind to offer assistance. But Yma is silent, watching the evening draw across the salt lake.

'Yma?'

She snaps out of it. Knut is standing next to her, half angry, half confused. She blinks. They have walked almost a kilometre to the edge of the Virgule and she hasn't noticed any of it.

'It's nearly dark – time to head back.'

'Yes. But wait a second.'

'What're you doing?'

'Stay there.' She unhooks binoculars from her backpack, raises them and begins to peruse the Virgule. The salt crystals shatter the last of the day's light and throw it back at her. It's the dunes at the far end, in front of the Chicane city, that draw her. She focuses and refocuses, trying to make sense of it.

'Yma.' Knut rubs his arms nervously. 'We've gotta go. It's a grey night and the sun's hit the horizon – we got to run. Today has been bad enough, with everything that's happened.'

'Yes, just wait while I—'

'I'm going back, you're coming with me: stop being so obsessive.'

'*For fuck's sake, Knut – go. I'll follow.*'

He takes a sharp breath, seems about to speak, but eventually draws away and begins to lope back to the tower, glancing back at her sullenly. She refocuses the binoculars and peers at the sand dunes. The hairs on her body stand up at once, as if they've been polarised by a magnet and have all chosen to rise and point in the direction of the Virgule.

It's what she thought. Exactly what she thought.

'Yma!'

She turns. Knut is all the way back at the tower, waving at her.

'*Move it*,' he yells. '*Get a fucking move on*.'

The sun is on the horizon, a fizzing yellow half moon. That's less than ten minutes she's got. She sees her mistake, begins to run. Knut is at the gate, waiting for her, screaming. He grabs her hand and drags her inside.

'Do this to me *one more time … and I won't wait*,' he spits.

'I'll do the gate. You go.'

Furious, Knut turns and heads to the rope ladder. The giant red shape on the tower wall coming through the Eye is gone now: the sun has set, and Yma's hands begin to tremble as she locks the gate. It's odd – the locks don't seem like they usually do; maybe they were changed while she was Scouting, but she gets them closed, rattles the door and races to the stepladder. Knut is already above her in the opening to the Shuck, leaning down, his hand outstretched. From somewhere beyond the walls come the familiar sounds, the chattering in the distance, the thundering of the ground as the Djinni emerge.

Her hands are slick on the rungs, her legs like rubber, and suddenly she has no power in her body. The sound is getting louder, as if they can smell her, sniff her out. The patch on the side of the tower: what if it doesn't hold? They could use it to crawl up to the Eye, and drop through that way – she won't stand a chance.

'*Yma, concentrate*.'

'*I am*.'

She stares up at Knut's outstretched hand, desperately focusing on it. A sudden noise reverberates against the tower walls and, with the last of her strength, she throws herself at Knut. He grabs her, drags her inside, bruising her hips, grazing her legs. Quickly he hauls up the ladder and throws down the giant lock – in his haste, slamming it on the last two fingers of her left hand. Yma screams, drags the hand out in time and rolls onto her side, panting and trembling, her hand pushed into her armpit.

'Fuck, fuck!' she pants. '*Fuck*.'

'Oh, good God, Yma, I'm sorry – I'm sorry. Is it OK?'

She grits her teeth, nods, although her eyes are watering.

'Yes. Help me up – we've got to speak to the others.'

Knut lifts her carefully, supporting her round the waist. She doesn't move her hand from her armpit, knowing it's bleeding, from the warmth that spreads out across her tunic. It isn't as painful as it should be, Yma thinks vaguely.

In the common room everyone is sitting at the table, as if convened for an important meeting. There is no food, and everyone turns towards them, their faces etched with shock. Maybe this is a kind of memorial for Mahmoud.

'Did you hear the noise?' Elk asks.

'It's stopped now,' Knut says, helping Yma into the room. 'It won't come again.'

'Yes.' Elk taps his fingers on the table, his eyes crawling all over their faces. 'I guess.'

'What's happening?'

Elk purses his lips – looks at Hugo, who shakes his head. 'Today is not our day. Someone's been in the Shuck: they've siphoned off everything in the water tanks. All that's left is what's in the pipes.'

'You're kidding,' Yma says, sitting down, suddenly a little faint. 'Someone's been in here? While we were . . .' She wants to say *losing Mahmoud*, but she can't.

'They only took water – nothing else.'

'The locks on the gate?'

'We had to refigure them; they'd been smashed,' Hugo says, 'There's no water to wash with tonight. Enough to drink for today and tomorrow, and maybe the next day, but no washing, no cooking.'

'And no water for the crops,' says Madeira.

'I need to wash Spider.' Forlani is at the far end of the table, blinking owlishly behind his array of bottles. He holds a pestle and mortar in his crooked hands, a smear of something green in there. 'To stop him getting infected. And he needs more water than us – he's dehydrated.'

'You can have an extra two litres for him. Use it carefully.' Hugo shakes his head, runs his hands down his face. He sighs. 'I don't know what to do – just don't know where to go from here. I don't know how to get the water back. I took such good care of it.'

'I know what we've got to do,' Yma mutters. She stares at the table, breathing hard, trying to stop the pain from making her unsteady. 'I've got a plan – I know it can work.'

There's a short silence, then Amasha gasps and pushes her chair back. 'Yma, child, you're bleeding.'

'It's nothing.'

'I shut her fingers in the pod door,' Knut says, his voice tense.

'You what?'

'We were in a hurry.'

Forlani gets up and hobbles over to Yma, holds out his hands. 'Show me.'

'It's nothing. More important that I tell you what we can do. Elk, can you get me some cornmeal?'

Elk scrapes his chair back and goes to the kitchen to fetch the jar, but Amasha and Forlani won't be put off.

'Show me your hand.'

'I don't want to.'

'You're bleeding everywhere.'

'I told you,' Yma says, her voice rising. 'It's *nothing*.'

'For heaven's sake,' Noor says, suddenly fierce at the end of the table. 'Behave like an adult and show him your goddamned hand.'

Yma opens her mouth, shocked. He's never spoken to her like this. He's staring at her steadily and the intensity of it sobers her instantly, makes her look away, ashamed. Mahmoud's loss is getting to all of them. She'd love to reach for one of the crystals, but she can't admit that weakness, so instead she bites her lip and eventually, gingerly, holds out the throbbing hand.

There is a lot more blood then she'd imagined. Amasha covers her mouth, shakes her head and goes quickly to the laundry stand to collect napkins to staunch the flow. Cairo makes a gagging noise in his mouth. Only Forlani stays calm.

'OK, OK,' he mutters, touching the hand gently. 'Let me look, let me see – I know it hurts.'

Amasha puts the napkins down and Forlani sits, using a napkin to tie a tourniquet on her arm and compress the wound site with more napkins. Yma's face is hot now – stung by Noor's reprimand, shocked too by the blood that emerges in slow-moving humps from her fingertip, gloving her hand in red.

'What sort of a hurry were you in, that this happened?' Amasha tuts. 'As if Spider isn't enough.'

'Is he OK?'

'He will be,' says Forlani, tentatively lifting the napkin to check the blood has stopped. 'If he keeps quiet and still, and does what I say.'

Elk comes back with a bowl of cornmeal and a flagon of the sour mesquite that he brews from cacti. He fills a sturdy cup with the stuff and orders Yma to drink it. She does, wincing at the taste, and slams the cup down, screwing up her face and shaking her head. Then, when the taste is gone, she says, 'I've got to show you something. Got to show you.'

'Wait till I've dressed this.'

'Please – Elk, tip out the cornmeal. Here on the table.'

He hesitates and glances at Amasha, who shrugs and shakes her head, because he upends the bowl in front of her. While Forlani works on her hand, stemming the flow and making a poultice of crushed witch-hazel leaves, which he fastens around the fingers, Yma uses her other hand to move the sand around.

'Watch this.'

She scoops a few handfuls of cornflour into a pile in front of her. Then, using the edge of her hand, she separates it into two sections, with one pile making a long, wriggling shape, with the other a low, flat crescent shape.

'This is a linear formation,' she explains, pointing to the left-hand pile. 'It happens when the wind is coming from two directions: you can see how the force is equal. Whereas this, on the right, is a crescentic formation, made when the wind is coming from one direction – typically from between a gap in some topographical feature, be it natural or man-made. I didn't see this in the place I'd expect it from the eastern cities, but I have seen it over to the north-west of us, here.' She digs a finger into the cornmeal, making a small hole, recognising that the model is identical to the one McKenzie Strathie was trying to create at the Science Fair. 'They mean, to me, that there's a system in the north that is allowing wind to come through. Ow! Jeez, Forlani.'

She tries to pull her hand away but he holds it tight, giving her a sheepish smile. He finishes binding it and Yma watches, grimacing. Slowly the mesquite takes hold, and within seconds she begins to feel slightly high. 'Anyway,' she flings out carelessly, 'that, for my money, means that Spider was right. We should look at the city at the edge of the Chicane.'

There is a long silence. Elk scratches the underside of his neck doubtfully, and Splendour pushes out her lips in an anxious pout, gazing up tentatively at Amasha, who sits in silence, staring at the cornflour mounds.

'How do we get across the Virgule?' Elk asks at last.

'We build a sand-yacht like the one Spider made,' Forlani says.

'Yes, but we've got to alter it – haven't we, Hugo?'

'Yes. Spider used a fixed sail: one that can't turn from side to side. We need to change that.'

'Make a boom, so we can swing it.' Yma sighs and closes her eyes. The throbbing in her fingers is getting worse, in spite of the alcohol. She'll use the crystals the moment she has some privacy. 'We have to adapt to the wind; it's the only way.'

Forlani leans over and puts a cool hand on her forehead.

'It's going to get worse for a bit – but I'm going to give you something to sleep. We'll talk about this in the morning.'

They eat a dry dinner, feeling morose and exhausted. No one speaks about Mahmoud; he is the unacknowledged presence in the room. At some point Amasha has already cleared away his drawings and his toys.

35

THERE'S A SMELL – a comforting mixture of liniment and meat cooking. Something is tapping against the sole of his right foot, and nearby he can hear people talking.

Spider opens his eyes and finds he is lying on the couch in the window of the common room, covered with a Shuck blanket. Outside it is light, but inside the candles are lit and the meal seems to be in full swing. He blinks to clear his eyes and sees Yma, sitting a metre away, her back to him, her hair in a long orange plait down her back. She is eating with one hand – the left is bandaged – and speaking to the family in a voice that is weary, yet alert.

Blinking, he opens his mouth to speak, but can't. His mouth won't form the words, and the dream takes him down before he can attract anyone's attention. For a while once again he is on the Virgule, careening like a mad clown into the wind.

The Sarkpont won't show you God, says a voice. *It won't show you God, it will only show the way . . .* The sun bounces across the horizon and Camel's face appears close to him, inspecting him, smelling his features, testing for life.

Another sharp tap on his foot and Spider jerks upright, fearsomely awake, making a juddery *mmmphmmph* noise in the back of his throat. At the base of the couch, a sad and steady expression on his face, is Cairo, rhythmically twanging an elastic band against Spider's left sole.

'Yow, motherfuddder, what the fudddd?' Spider tries to twitch his foot out of the way. The words that stumble out of his mouth are nonsense. 'Wha the fuuuuu?'

Cairo stops the assault. He lowers the band and watches Spider try to speak. Spider realises his mouth won't move the way it wants to, and when he gingerly touches his finger to his face, he feels why. The right side of his face is a pumpkin – hot and swollen to a crust. Then he sees the rest of the family frozen in shock, turned back in their seats, mid-forkful, to stare at him.

'*Pœtiyo?*' Amasha gets up and comes to him. Draped in orange silk and black jewels, she's wearing a black bindi bead on her forehead.

He clamps a hand to his forehead, releases his head back down onto the couch and lies there for a moment or two, getting everything realigned. His body is intact, though there is pain. His right calf is on fire, but he can feel dressings on it; Forlani must have done that. Something stiff and crackly: the *Aloe vera* leaves that Madeira grows in the polytunnels, or the witch hazel he found in Mithi. Spider's left hand, which he lifts above his face to inspect, has been wrapped in a glove of the same material. He lowers it and frowns at Amasha.

'Camel?' he croaks. 'What . . .'

'She's fine. Perfectly happy and a little proud.'

Amasha snatches the rubber band from Cairo, who was preparing a further assault on Spider's sole. She takes Spider's wrist in her soft palm and lifts him. 'Come along, *Pœtiyo*, you need to refill your strength.' She lifts his head and gives him a drink of sweetened sheep's milk. It makes him retch, mixed with the blood he's swallowed, but he manages to keep it down. His mouth is so sore, it's like a million needles in his brain.

'You lost a tooth,' Cairo says, holding it up to the light. 'It was bouncing around in the bag what Camel was dragging.'

'Cairo, go and sit down.' Amasha is suddenly sharp. 'Go now, before you catch the back of my hand. And give me that tooth.'

Sullenly Cairo hands the tooth to Amasha and turns, walking casually back to his seat as if nothing has happened. Elk draws a chair nearer to Spider, and presently he has four anxious faces peering at him. He groans and puts a hand to his head, closing his eyes. He is dizzy and nauseous, and if he becomes unconscious again he'll probably puke up the milk. He has to fight.

'Dode look ad me,' he murmurs. 'Dode.'

'We'll take you to your room. But tell us, what did you find?'

He breathes through his nose, slowly.

'Spider?'

'Yeah – I foud Phoedix.'

He senses Yma take a breath. 'You sure?'

'Shure I'm shure.' He tries to make the shape of the statue over the gates with his hand. Tries to form the words 'Giant bird', although it sounds more like 'Gyreburg'.

'A giant bird?'

'Phoedix. Shhtatue. And warder and shafe place for Shuck.'

There's a murmuring. He hears people swapping places and whispering excitedly, but he can't open his eyes. The vertigo will take him under.

'Water?' Hugo says.

Spider rolls his eyes up and sees his linen trousers, his shirt marked with sweat stains.

'You're sure there was water?'

'I shaw it. Drank it.'

'Lots of water? Everything is green?'

'Shafe place to hide too.'

'What did the city look like? Anything else, so we can be certain? We're talking about going there tomorrow.'

There is a pause while Spider searches for relevant details. It takes a bit of digging, but he finds it. 'Canalsh.'

'What? Canals?'

'Yeah.'

Knut whistles. 'The Hohokam canals.'

'Treesh, churches. Tall buildings – not many.' Spider digs back in his pounding head for anything else. He pictures the panels on the front of a building, with a human hand and a plant seed. 'Hand. Picture. Buildings, buildings, streetshh . . .' He starts to waver, feels his brain is swimming in an oily blackness that is about to crest. 'Streetsh,' he says feebly; in spite of his sloshing head, he knows he has to convince them. It is so important. With the last of his energy he burrows deep for a detail that will set the Phoenix he has seen apart from any other. As he's about to go under, he finds it. '*Diamondbacksh*,' he says with an effort. '*Diamondbacksh*.'

The noise in the room wavers, in and out, like the sound of distant wind. For a second he's back on the Virgule, surrounded by an unlikely cast. A girl from the Parisian brothel, solemnly holding out to him a glass of absinthe; a dark creature clinging to the legs of the Shuck; and Camel, lying panting on the sand. Then, just as quickly, he's back.

'Whad happened to the warder here?'

'The water? We don't know. Someone broke in.'

'Fucksssh shake. Fucking Elephant Family?'

'Maybe.'

'That sand-yacht,' says a voice behind Spider's head.

It's Noor, he realises, He tries to lift his chin and focus on him but the pain is too great, the light too strong. 'The Shandwalker, you mean?'

'The Sandwalker? What happened to it?'

'Near.'

'Near what? Phoenix?'

'No. Shuck.'

'Near the Shuck?'

Spider grunts in reply. He's exhausted. He wants to sleep – anything to avoid this pain for a short time. He closes his eyes, drifts back to Paris for a little while. Then there are hands under him lifting the blanket that he lies on.

He closes his eyes. Cool hands on his forehead, Knut speaking quietly. 'It's me,' he says from a place close to Spider's head. 'I'll take you to your own pod in a bit – I brought you out here for the air.'

'We'll take you to your room,' says Elk.

Spider gets a brief swirling image of the common room, the pale faces of the children, of Forlani and Yma watching, their faces anguished as he is carried out.

'I look a messhhh?' he asks Knut, who walks next to him, supporting the side of the blanket.

'Sorry, Spider. You get back seat in the eye-candy role.'

Spider tries to smile, but it's too painful. He subsides and watches the ceiling of the corridor as they walk. They reach the door to his sleeping pod. The low-down bed is made, the window is open, allowing a deliciously cool breeze to come through. The men – Hugo, Knut and Elk – get him settled, putting out water, a plate of food for when he feels well enough, a bowl, should he vomit. They are silent and focused.

When he is settled, Knut sits on the end of the bed. In spite of his half-conscious state, Spider knows there's something bad about the way Knut looks at him.

'Whad? Why the look?'

Knut clears his throat. 'Something happened. In Dubai. You were right – the Djinni are there.'

'Smellsh of shit.'

'Yeah.' Forlani smiles sadly. 'It smelsh of shit. You're right.'

'But it's Mahmoud,' Knut says.

'Mahmoud?'

'He's gone. In Dubai, we lost him.'

Spider tries to sit up. '*Whad?*'

'We had to leave him. He fell into the lift shaft.'

'Shit, shit, shit!' Spider lies back down, his head spinning. He can't believe it. If he'd been there, he would have saved him. Little Mahmoud – the impishness, and the stupid toys he made with Cairo. What is this place doing to them? Just what is it doing?

For a moment he wants to cry, he can feel the pressure at the back of his throat, but what would be the point? He lies, his eyes closed, breathing in slowly through his nose. Slowly, as the others think he has settled, they get up to leave. Hugo is the last one to depart, after double-checking that everything is within Spider's reach.

'Hey.' Spider flops out a hand, connecting with Hugo's foot. 'Wait.'

'Yeah? What is it?'

Spider paws weakly at Hugo's leg, getting him to crouch down closer.

'You get Shandwalker: fix her.'

'That's what I plan to do.'

'Camel – tired, hear? Tired. Take care of her.'

'Say it again, mate?'

'Look after Camel.' He holds up a finger, stiff in the air, to make his point. He bares his teeth, in an effort to get his point across.

And then he releases his grip and allows himself to fall onto the pillow, closing his eyes and travelling back, back into his head, deep down, into a place where there is no pain and no light.

*

Yma doesn't want to sleep in her pod, she wants to be up under the stars. She eats everything Elk forces on her, drinks her water ration for the night and then, with Forlani's help, she beds down, lying on her back, her throbbing hand on her chest, head turned slightly so that she can see, out of the window, the silent skies moving slowly above her.

'What about you?' she asks Forlani.

'I'll stay with you for a bit, then go and see Spider.'

'You're the shit, you know that? You really are.'

He grins. 'Actually I disagree. I think you're the shit.'

'Even though I was irresponsible?'

'Impetuous and bang-obsessive – about the winds and the skies. But I guess that's why we love you. Now go to sleep.'

Yma yawns – the herbs he gave her are working. The familiar faint chattering of the Djinni comes from Dubai, and while the stars fill out their familiar patterns, she thinks about Mahmoud, the last expression on his face. She imagines him sliding along under the desert floor.

What if she's wrong? What if the dunes she's seen in the north aren't made by the wind at all? What if they are mirages?

The last thing she thinks is that she's glad she's hurt her left hand, and not her right. She wants to get working on the sand-yacht first thing.

The herbs Forlani gave Yma are like a swipe to the head: in spite of the pain from her fingers, in spite of the memories of Mahmoud, floating through the underworld, she sleeps so well she's not the first person up the next day – to be breakfasted and waiting next to the pod lock to get down, out into the open before the others. Instead she drags herself up just in time to get a little food and yerba-maté before it's cleared away.

'Slow,' Knut murmurs with a sly glance as she manages painfully to get to the bottom of the ladder. His blue mullet stands up as straight as a coxcomb and his eyes are as bright as the sun. 'Expected a full-on sister this morning. How you feeling, after I attacked you?'

Her hand is still swaddled and she hasn't dared pull back the bandages to inspect it. Her wrist is bright red, but she thinks that must be normal. 'Forlani's gonna give it a day, then check.'

'I'm truly sorry.'

'Don't be – I was the one acting lame. You sleep OK?'

'I didn't think I would after . . . you know. But I did – like a rag doll. Which is a thing I always wanted to be. Kind of careless and loving, and always passed around and hugged.'

'What a ho! Nothing changes, does it?'

The area around Hugo's water pumps is churned up. Yma didn't see it last night because she was in such a hurry, but now it's so clear. Chunks of metal from the door latches are scattered on the sand, and Madeira's polytunnels have been torn apart.

'This is what they did?' Yma asks Knut. 'Did they have to?'

'We all have to find the Sarkpont. Maybe respect isn't their game.'

She rolls her eyes up to him. 'The Elephant Family?'

'That's the betting. They used tools to get in – see the way the metal's been hacked. That's something the Djinni can't do.'

She picks up a couple of pieces of metal – sees the ragged saw-work, as if a hacksaw has been used.

'And how long will it take for the reservoir to refill?'

Knut screws up his face. 'Hugo says weeks before we're in the clear. We're going to stink like month-old cheese before long. There's enough to drink, though, but only for a few days. Like three. Max.'

Shit, she thinks. 'So … I guess it's Phoenix then?'

'Uh-huh.' They both stand and stare at the distant city. 'If we can find the yacht.'

Noor and Hugo join them, Noor wearing a blinding white shirt that the wind flattens against his chest. The four of them set out towards the Virgule, expecting the day to drag on, half expecting failure, but to their surprise they find the craft after less than an hour.

'Fucking hell,' Knut mutters, lowering the glasses and pointing to the wreck. 'It's only there. See it?'

The three men let out a joyful whoop. They'd expected an arduous search out here – it's beyond lucky to have found it so easily. Difficult to believe that Spider made it such a long way into the distance: she and Amasha clearly saw him four or more kilometres out; he'd disappeared into the white of the lake, only to come all the way back and crash here. The injustice of it seems brutal, but now Yma realises she's not all that surprised. If Spider had asked her, she would have come down here and thought for a long time about the winds and the right sails.

'How do we get to it?' Noor is taking tentative steps out towards the misshapen wreck that sticks its lonely fingers up against the sky – like a broken tree or the sun-dried skeleton of a huge beast. 'We can drag it in, if we can get to it. Is it safe on this salt?'

He takes a few more cautious steps out onto it, while Knut, Yma and Hugo shuffle closer to the edge of the lake, ready to creep out and drag him back from the splintered salt. But he doesn't fall; he stands, firm and sure. Knut ventures after him onto one of the solid white scales.

'Whoa!' He executes a couple of jumps to demonstrate. 'Completely solid. Just stick to the white parts – see, there's a path.'

Hugo and Yma aren't so confident; they hold each other's hands as they go. It's weird to feel his slightly damp hand in hers. She's never thought of him as a man before, and the softness of his hand is vaguely repellent. Noor's hands are hard and wide, the other men's too: Spider's are like vices – he could clamber up the side of the tower in ten minutes, should he want to, she's sure of it – and Elk's hands seem the size of dinner plates.

The Sandwalker is much bigger, close up. The four stand and stare at it, marvelling at its sails flapping in the breeze, its carved runners, its lanyards and capstans. It is splintered in places, but seems to be entirely free of salt. The Virgule has nasty habits; one day it will swallow something whole – an animal, a family, a yacht – and the next it will rebuild itself in layers from below and push any foreign object up to the surface, like skin ridding itself of a splinter.

'How did Spider keep this from us?' Knut wants to know.

'He hid it behind Camel's cage,' Hugo explains. 'Everyone else was too preoccupied with waiting for you to come home – planning how to make the move to Dubai. We didn't see it happening.'

'He's got slippery ninja creds, that guy.' Knut shakes his head admiringly. 'I know who to go to with a secret.'

Hugo is suddenly sharp. 'Yeah, well, you haven't got many secrets you haven't chosen to share with the entire family. Thank you for the graphic detail about you and that varsity quarterback – I am sure Tita Lily is forever grateful.'

Knut gives Hugo a nasty smile. 'Better than storing all my sins and giving the world the fake version.'

Before the bitching session can take hold, Noor interrupts by pushing between the two of them and crouching to test the wood of the Sandwalker. When he touches the structure, it moves freely on the salt. He pushes it with his foot and it glides on its two curved skis.

'We can move it, no worries.' Hugo walks around it thoughtfully, pausing to test the strength of the sail fixings, experimentally pushing the two sides of a ruptured mast together. 'It's light. The sailcloth isn't ripped.'

Yma takes a long breath. She straightens, puts her hands in the small of her back and lets her eyes wander across the horizon. The breeze, the way it is pulling her hair in wings around her face – it's calm and purposeful, and it's not coming from the direction of the Shuck. All the things that have been bothering her about the Virgule, and Spider's attempts to cross it, are now clustering in.

'What're you thinking?' Hugo asks.

'I can see you were right. The yacht needs a boom. The prevailing winds are over there, to the right of Phoenix, maybe funnelling through a gap in the Chicane. When the Sandwalker moved all that way on a fixed sail, it was because Spider got lucky. He must have caught a rogue wind that came from the south, but when it changed …' She gestures sadly at the wreck. 'Boom! This.'

'Do you think we can fix it by the morning?' Knut asks. 'It's not that bad, is it?'

Hugo wrinkles his face doubtfully. 'It needs a moving boom – we've got to be able to manoeuvre it from side to side. If the winds come from that direction …'

'The sail will have to be at this angle,' Yma completes for him. She holds her arms out at forty-five degrees, demonstrating how the sail should sit. 'It has to be set like this, but it has to turn; when you've got to the end of the tack, you have to be able to swing the sail quickly or you'll be way off-course and you'll never recover it. If you do that …' She bites her lip, gazing out over the seemingly endless stretch of salt. 'If you do that, and you do it right, then there's no reason you shouldn't get to Phoenix.'

Knut smiles. 'Because the boat is going to have to take more than one person. And supplies. And out of the three of us, you're the only one light enough to do it.'

'But my hand.' She instantly takes it from her back and holds it out in front of her, as if it has suddenly caused her pain. 'I can't sail that thing.'

'You climbed down the ladder OK,' Knut says, smiling.

'Yma – you're the one.' Noor lowers his chin and pins her gaze with his brown eyes. There is no going against Noor. And so, it seems, in that fleeting court, assembled ad hoc out on the salt, Yma is designated with the greatest role of her time in the Cirque.

Back at the Shuck, in one of the pods, Amasha is weeping, talking under her breath. A prayer for Mahmoud, Yma thinks, and then wishes she knew how to give voice to her grief. The common room has been emptied. Elk has spent the afternoon sawing the table into usable chunks of wood – after all, if Spider is correct about there being a secure place in Phoenix, there will be no more use for the vast table, and the next family will have to construct their own. He has stacked all the usable pieces of wood in the kitchen door, so that the floor is clear for everyone to work.

Hugo takes control of constructing the beams for the mast, discussing everything with Yma, testing each possible boom for grip and weight. Elk is tireless; he whittles and chops and is ready for every demand. Forlani and Amasha, helped by the children, get all their belongings into bundles. They test the weight of the bundles by straddling a beam of the old table across a chair, then placing the various loads at either end of the beam to see which will see-saw the wood to the ground. When they've done with the belongings, they start weighing people. Elk, to his slight pride, is by far the heaviest, followed by Hugo. Yma is the third-lightest after the two children, so Noor was right – maybe it's her duty to be the ferryman, in spite of her injury.

After dinner she stays up practising swinging the boom on the sand-yacht, favouring her right hand, but just able to use her left. Every time she fudges a swing, the men come forward and check the boom, the sails. Was it her fault, was it the workmanship or was it her hand?

Outside the moon comes up. She notices it but ignores it for a while, concentrating on her lesson. But then she can't deny it any longer. She stops the practice and goes to the window, watching the desert.

'What?' Elk asks.

'They live under Dubai,' she whispers softly. 'And they have us in their sights.'

Forlani nods. 'They do.'

'What else can we do?' She looks round at the men. 'Getting to Phoenix is our only chance.'

They go to their beds then. Yma lies in the dark, her eyes wide open in spite of the fact it's a white night, thinking about Mahmoud floating somewhere, her ears tuned for the smallest movement in the sand. It doesn't come. Another night they are spared.

The following day the work continues: packing and practising with the sail, carrying the yacht to the Virgule and testing out its weight – assessing the salt crust for weaknesses.

Late afternoon, Elk, Hugo and Madeira go in silence to the animal pens and free those animals that are healthy, leaving the gates open so that they can roam the tower – tomorrow they'll open the main gate and the animals will be free to come and go. Maybe a new family will stay here and tend to them.

The ones that are old, they slaughter in grim silence, with their backs to the Shuck. Yma sits in the Shuck opening and watches, her throat tight. Everyone has tried not to get attached to the animals, but it's difficult. The big kangaroo that Madeira called

Jack, which she loved and protected and talked to, is the last to go. Madeira talks to him gently, caressing him, and the creature's eyes widen only when Elk comes from behind and quickly breaks his neck with one slick movement.

Afterwards the three stand over the bodies with their hands together, heads bowed. They are covered in blood, but Yma thinks they are praying for the souls of the animals. Elk seems to admire animals more than he does human beings – he says they don't have the cruelty of a human, that they only injure if they are scared or killing for food.

Yma wipes her eyes and goes back into the Shuck, to the common room where Forlani is waiting for her.

'Final inspection, Skipper,' he tells her solemnly.

She sighs and holds out her hand. He unwinds the bandage, ignoring her winces, and inspects it, asking her to turn it over and touching the fingers carefully.

'Hurt?'

'Not like it did. How's it doing?'

'Better – much better. I didn't want you to sail, but the others do, and I think you'll be OK. Try your hardest not to bang it, open the wounds.'

'Does that mean I'm out of excuses?'

'I'm afraid so.'

'And so I am measured by an accidental day – a lucky chance. Let's hope I don't fail, eh?'

'You won't,' Noor tells her, looking up from where he's polishing one of his machetes at the other side of the room. 'I'm sure of it.'

Yma looks at him, at his beautifully shaped head, his neck and shoulder muscles. His gravity. If he knew half the things about her that Knut and Amasha know, he wouldn't have the same faith. She gives a nervous smile and rewraps the bandage.

36

IT'S THE WORST of nights. Sleep is a hard board at the back of Spider's head, always out of reach, always pulling him back down. Tiny toxic flowers of pain blossom along his side and his spine. Vaguely he knows that family members are coming in and making him more comfortable, moving him and washing down his wounds.

He's surprised that Mahmoud's loss has somehow galvanised the family, and he doesn't know what to say to anyone about it, so he keeps his eyes shut and feigns sleep; attempting to communicate would be impossible, with his head so painful. There are small mercies, though: the sheep's milk Elk's been feeding him for two days stays down and begins to nourish him. When he wakes in the silent dark of the early morning, he is grateful to recognise he is hungry. He rolls over, groping for the bowl of bread and sugared pineapple, feverishly pressing chunks into his mouth with his fingertips, washing it down with water.

Are the Djinni hunting tonight? His window is open and, in the layers between dreams, he thinks he hears breathing. The shush-shush rasping noise of sand underfoot. A shadow crosses his sleeping pod, a deformed human shape, its head hideously swollen.

It's real, or it's not. A delirium.

He wakes eventually, still in pain but with a clear mind. It's dark, and from the constellations outside the window he guesses there's another hour before the family will begin to wake. Carefully he crawls off the low pallet and begins to assemble the beginnings of a kit. The small actions tire him and he has to rest after each one. It takes almost ten minutes to get himself showered and dressed. His swollen right foot won't go into his hard leather boots, so he forces it, feeling like one of Cinderella's ugly sisters.

In the brothel his mother used to tell him the story of Cinderella and always showed him how the sisters had to force their feet into the pretty shoes. His mother had tried everything to keep him safe. Several lifetimes ago he decided never to be ashamed of what she did to put bread in his mouth.

There is a crude mirror that Tita Lily brought back from Abu Dhabi hanging in the corridor. He stands in front of it for a while, swaying slightly, astonished by the stranger, ugly as the Île de la Cité hunchback. Like a devil. His hair has been scraped away from his scalp and both his eyes are swollen to slits. His right ear is crusted and black. The clothes are clean and new – a fresh jacket and an unsoiled dress, but he knows that what's underneath will weep into the clean fabric and stain it.

He limps downstairs, using his left foot as the lead one. No one is awake, but they have been working all night – the common room has been stripped clean of tables and chairs, and in their place stands something gleaming and unrecognisable.

The Sandwalker. His own craft, polished and oiled, rebuilt with a strange new beam that is lashed to the mast with kangaroo gut. The frame has been whitewashed and the parachute-silk sail is coiled in an orderly bundle on the floor. It all looks much sharper and more professional than his attempts. Spider takes in a few breaths. He doesn't want to sit down yet. He needs to eat, get his strength. He turns his back on the craft and limps away, his head rippling.

There isn't much to eat in the kitchen – all of Elk's hand-tied bundles and curing meat have disappeared, and the gourds of sugar water and milk have gone too. All that is left are spices and slabs of cooking lard in the cool spot under the water butt, which is almost empty.

Water, he thinks – water, the most precious thing they have had in this Shuck. And in the distance Phoenix, with all the water anyone could wish for.

He finds the packed-up food lashed to the Sandwalker. It's been preserved in sealed jars; there are cheeses wrapped in cloth and no end of folded paper packets, sticking with the dried fruit they contain. Weary now, his head turning, he lies down against the wall and nibbles at a handful of dates. He closes his eyes and sleeps.

When he next wakes, he's being jostled. There's a smell of grease and sweat, echoey shouts around him. He opens his eyes and sees the interior of the tower swaying dizzyingly in and out of reach. 'What the …'

'Shhhh.'

He looks up and sees Forlani, straining down at him, one brown eye roving over Spider's face. 'Shit, you look a mess.'

'Thangsss …'

His voice is still a nasal hollow. Spider crunches his chin in, to look down, and sees Elk's head. He feels the rough fabric of the Scout stretchers and realises what's happening. Elk and Forlani are transporting him down the ladder in a cocoon. He struggles weakly in the strapped-up stretcher. A fly in a web.

'Keep still,' Elk says sharply. 'Stop it! We'll fall.'

'Where we goid? Phoedix?'

'Yes. Now stop arguing.'

The pain makes him faint and suddenly his world is a vortex of colour again, of half-remembered dreams, then he clicks awake once more, full and bright in the dazzling sunshine, his body being jolted up and down, the wind deafening. He steadies himself, uses his hand to stop his head banging and feels that he's been given a pillow of scratchy hemp to rest on. He's stretched out on the spindly plank connecting the cross-members of the Sandwalker. Above him the sky is blue and the sail is stiff with wind. He coughs and tries to sit up. Wedged next to him, her face locked in fear, is Amasha, clutching Spider's foot in one hand, hanging onto the rough gunwales of the Sandwalker with the other.

'It's OK,' she yells, without taking her eyes off the horizon. 'Go back to sleep.'

By slightly inclining his head he can take stock of his surroundings. Everywhere there is white and blazing sun. They're on the Virgule. The Sandwalker is going dizzyingly fast, but somehow Camel has kept pace with it and lopes along about fifty metres away, her head down, her *mahawi* piled with belongings. Spider licks his lips and scrunches his chin down to assess who else is on the Sandwalker. Incredibly, it seems to be happily carrying five people: Amasha, Tita Lily and Knut, who is wearing a long-sleeved black shirt, sitting as counterbalance to Spider on the other side of the vessel, his Mohican battered by the wind. And at the tiller, her arms bare, her overalls rolled up to show her slim brown ankles, is Yma.

It takes him a while to process that she could be driving his craft like this. But she is, her chin raised, a giant bandage around one hand, which is on the tiller, the other on the boom, eyes narrowed to scrutinise the horizon. She doesn't feel him watching her and Spider has time, from his sickbed, to watch the way the wind takes her sheet of apricot hair and sends it straight behind her, like the tail of a comet.

Where's Noor? he wonders. Can he see her?

A squeeze to his foot. Amasha isn't watching him, she still has her face turned to the wind, but something about the squeeze warns him to keep still. He turns his face away and closes his eyes. The pillow is sturdy enough to stop his head from being banged, but his body jolts painfully with each lurch of the Sandwalker. He wants to sleep. Again. He is the sponge that could soak up all the sleep in the universe and still need more.

It's healing, a voice from his past tells him. *Healing*.

Then his mother's voice: '*Mon enfant*, you could sleep for France ...' As if sleep was some internationally recognised sport that he excelled in. All the girls in the whorehouse were enthralled by Spider's blonde hair. They'd ruffle it and laugh: 'That Swedish captain of industry, Gustav Mortensen, who always tips so big: you think you're related to him somehow? He loved your mama so damned MUCH!'

The next thing he knows is a series of jolts. He can hear everyone talking excitedly. Knut standing in the Sandwalker and letting out a long, triumphant laugh. 'Phoenix?' Spider tries to say, but the words are whipped away by the wind and the noise of laughter.

The movement of the Sandwalker subsides and he's aware of being carried from the craft and set down on the baking tarmac of a road, a blanket and a pillow under him. He opens his eyes and sees Camel peering down at him, a long string of saliva coming out of her mouth. He hears the soft grunt and rumble of her huge belly.

Around him everyone is talking rapidly, then he sees Amasha's face, smiling. 'Hello, hero child. You were right.'

'I know.' He manages a cracked grin.

'OK, stop gloating. Drink this now.'

He drinks the water, warm and yeasty from the pig-bladder. Then she feeds him, capable fingers pushing dates between his teeth.

'You've got to concentrate, Spider. Tell me where the new place is.'

'The new …'

'The place you found where we can camp.'

He wipes his tongue around the inside of his dry mouth, trying to summon some moisture, and sits up painfully, everything around him swimming.

'Can you see the stadium? Red?'

More talking. Then Amasha squeezing his shoulder. 'We see it.'

'Brown-and-green building in front?'

'We see it.'

'Top floor.'

'OK. Let's do it.'

Knut, Yma and Amasha carry him in the blanket, see-sawing it between them. Every step, their excitement bubbles up.

'*Fuck's sake,*' Knut says. '*It's the ice-cream mall!*'

'*Remember that avenue? It's exactly the same.*'

'*I can't believe it.*'

'*Water. It's got water – he was right.*'

The blue sky rocks above Spider; street lights and the tops of buildings swim in and out of view. By the time they stop at the building, he's had enough of being the invalid. 'Let me down. Let me walk.'

Amasha is reluctant, but eventually he is lowered to the ground. He is unsteady on his feet, but he feels a hundred times better than he did this morning. He waits for Knut to get Camel fastened in the lobby, gives vague instructions about how to feed and water her and then, after a few more minutes' break, he shows the family the staircase.

They all walk, but he can just manage a crawl, clinging onto the handrail, and takes forever. He knows how Forlani feels, always at the back, always watching the able-bodied ones jaunt ahead. Eventually Knut has had enough and hoists Spider onto his back, in spite of his complaining, and carries him like a child having a piggyback for the last few floors.

At the penthouse with the pools and the heavy lock on the door Spider is so exhausted he doesn't argue with Yma, who leads him into the main bedroom and makes him lie on the huge bed. The sheets are missing and the smell of the rancid meat is strong in here, but the softness of the mattress is like a long drink of water. He sinks into it and lies there motionless, while all around him he can hear the rest of the family moving through the apartment, testing doors, opening windows, talking among themselves. He can't hear the words, but he can tell the growing awe and agreement that the place is secure. That the taps work.

Someone walks past on the balcony; someone else comes in and opens a window. He murmurs a thank-you, but doesn't raise his head. He's sure the scabs on his head are sticking to the damned mattress. There's a soft squeak, then the mattress depresses slightly. When he opens his eyes, Yma is sitting there smiling at him.

He smiles back, feeling the skin on his head pull at the scabs. 'You did great.'

'Yeah, well, I had help. There was Camel, and there was you. You built the Sandwalker. I'm completely stoked, you know; we can travel anywhere. You really know what you're doing with your hands.'

Unexpectedly Spider's embarrassed. He looks at his hands, the dirt under the fingernails. He wonders if she sees what he sees – fingers aged beyond their years by the time in the sun, the nights in the Paris underground.

'I've got to go,' Yma says. 'The others are waiting.'

'Yeah, give me a few minutes, I'll be right there.'

'What?'

'Let me get my breath back, then I'll be with you.'

She hitches in a breath. Then she shakes her head.

'What?'

'Spider, please, be sane for a change. You're not coming back with me.'

He frowns up at her. 'I am. You can't sail the Sandwalker on your own.'

'Can't I?'

He blinks. Under her expression, below her tone, is a note of derision. He's trying to put his finger on it, wheedle it out, when her face changes.

'You know what: you're right. I need you.' She gets to her feet. 'I'm going to get you a drink, then we'll go. I'll be right back.'

She leaves the room. He closes his eyes again, rolls his head back on the mattress and waits.

It is quicksilver and adrenaline mixed together in the tallest, coldest drink on a summer's day. It lights up Yma's nerve endings, makes her eyes wider and clearer, taking her close to the sky and the elements. She never thought she'd be able to do it, but she can. She can sail the Sandwalker. Spider will bitch about it, but she doesn't care. Just the fact that trimming a sail makes the boat lean in the direction she intended makes her want to yell into the wind. She has no right to feel this free, but she does. The remains of McKenzie Strathie are ripped away from her by the speed, and the soul of Yma emerges, stretching out and breathing deep.

At the other end of the Virgule, Noor and Elk are waiting for her return, standing at the lake edge surrounded by water gourds and parcels of food. Next to them is Forlani, holding the hands of the two children, who are nervous. While Elk and Noor help lash the provisions to the Sandwalker, Forlani helps the children and Madeira take their seats. They do it eagerly, gripping the rudimentary gunwales and staring into the distance.

'How fast will it go, Yma? How fast?'

As Yma makes the final preparations, checks the weight is distributed – only three people now to think about – Noor puts his hand on her arm and says quietly, 'I watched you. You're a fine sailor. Even with your injury.'

'Thank you. What I learned as a kid is coming back.'

'The place is good? The new quarters?'

'I think so. There's running water.'

'We're going to bring it all?' He nods further up the sand to where there is a pile of family belongings waiting in the midday heat. Bags and blankets and tools. Four preserved kangaroo carcasses wrapped in muslin. Jack, they aren't going to eat – Madeira buried him this morning before they set out. Even so, there is a lot.

Yma wipes her head, feeling the crust of sweat drying there. 'I don't know. We've only got time for three trips today. Forlani and the kids this time, then you and Elk last – I'm not sure about the weight.'

'Bring back Camel for the last trip.'

She shrugs. 'I don't know; she's looking ropey to me.'

'She's solid. You saw what she did for Spider.'

Yma sighs. 'OK, but bring Camel's water trough down to the lake edge for the last leg. Don't let's make her go further than she has to. And some of those nuts that Spider gives her.'

The men help her lash provisions to the Sandwalker, checking the balance. It's afternoon now and the sun is at its hottest, but the second crossing is like falling off a log. She is more confident, and Forlani is even more exhilarated by the speed than the children and keeps throwing back his head, smiling his white-toothed lopsided smile. She lets him steer for some of the trip, and when they stop for a break, she reseats him in a place where he can help switch the boom without standing and upsetting the weight of the yacht.

In Phoenix, Amasha and Knut greet them at the entrance gates, and between them they carry the provisions and water gourds down the street. In spite of the fact they've lost one of their number, the kids forget Mahmoud long enough to be delighted by Phoenix, awed by the giant bird, the avenues of orange and lemon trees; the closed ice-cream parlours with their colourful signs in the windows.

'Don't wake Spider,' Yma hisses to them as they reach the apartment building. 'He's going to bitch and bitch and bitch, when he finds out I sailed his boat all this way.'

'Bitch-bitch-bitch,' mocks Splendour as she is led away. 'Bitch-bitch-bitch.'

Camel is sleeping, her legs tucked up underneath her. Yma has to coax her awake with a bushel of mimosa. She feels bad, forcing the creature from her sleep, but Spider has always told her that Camel is as obstinate as a mule and has to be pushed sometimes.

'Come on.' She drags Camel up by the bridle. 'We need you.'

Eventually Camel gets to her feet. She's forlorn, blinking, not wanting to be moved. Yma encourages her by making a clicking sound in her throat, the way she's heard Spider do it. Eventually, with a loud resigned sigh, Camel begins to walk, dropping her feet down on the tarmac as if they are heavier than she can bear.

The journey back isn't pleasant. Yma can sense the glittering towers of Dubai to her left, and she wants as much as she can to drive the image away, but can't. Also, she has no idea how to coax Camel – it's impossible to know if she's genuinely tired or being obstinate. Eventually she adopts the attitude that it's safer to avoid looking at her, so she trims the sail to make the Sandwalker's speed slower and lets the rope trail behind her, trusting that if there isn't a sudden yank on the rope, Camel is still there, ambling along.

Sure enough, she's still there at the other end of the Virgule, although so exhausted that Elk insists that she eats, drinks and rests before they make the return journey with the provisions.

Camel seems a little livelier on the way back and walks with her head up, as if she's looking forward to seeing Spider again.

The sun goes down, blistering at the horizon, and the shadow of the Sandwalker is momentarily vast, like a creature prowling the salt lake next to them. Yma's energy is low, and as they close in on Phoenix her hand has started to throb. Tonight she is going to shower in one of those fabulous bathrooms and sleep on the balcony overlooking the desert.

There are clouds low over Phoenix. She doesn't think it will rain, but it will cool the place down. And even as she thinks of it, as if in punishment for her loss of concentration, the Sandwalker bucks ferociously, going abruptly nose down into the salt. There is a loud crunch, Elk shouts, 'Shit!' and the back of the craft shoots into the air, jettisoning everyone out onto the salt.

Yma throws out both hands, landing squarely on the injured left one, fingers first, then tumbling forward head-over-heels, crunching through the salt. She drops maybe sixty centimetres through the gap onto the sand below and lies there, stunned, the pain in her hand white-hot, blocking out everything around her.

Somewhere she can hear the Sandwalker bouncing noisily away from them, still impelled by its speed.

'What the fuck?' someone is yelling. 'Yma? Noor?'

Eventually she stands, her hand shoved between her legs. She sees Elk a few metres away, up to his waist in the salt; and further away, just dragging himself upright, Noor, salt in his black hair, a gash on his face. Further away, maybe forty metres, the front of the Sandwalker stands up vertically from the sand – Camel next to it, peering at it as if it is a great oddity.

'What happened?'

'I don't know.' She winces. 'The salt – is it a different colour?'

They look at the salt where all their belongings are scattered, everything spilling open, all the grain and the clothing heaped in a line.

'Brown,' Noor says. 'It's brown.'

Yma breathes out, drops her head, shaking it. He's right. Brown. As far as the eye can see – the Virgule has changed consistency. If she had been paying attention and not dreaming, she'd have seen the brown sections in advance and averted the crash and the pain in her hand. The wound is leaking. She can see blood running down her arm.

She half turns away from the men and uses her good hand to check that the crystals are still in her bra. They're not damaged and for a moment she is tempted, but Elk and Noor are watching her; Noor always so sensible – he must never know about the crystals. Never.

'Yma?'

She licks her lips, turns back. 'Yeah. I fucked up.'

'It's OK, OK.' Elk begins to wade towards her, his hands in the air free of the salt that crumbles with every step, releasing a fine mist into the air. 'Stay there – you're bleeding.'

He comes to her and gently takes her hand from where it is lodged and holds it up in the air. Noor meanwhile has pulled off his shirt and is wading towards them, tearing it with both hands.

'Shhhh,' he tells her. 'Sit down. Sit down.'

She does abruptly, light-headed, her eyes watering. She's an idiot to have lost control, and their pity makes it worse. Noor is gentle as he uses half the shirt to make a tourniquet around her arm, the other half to wrap her hand. And she half loves him, half hates him for it – hates her vulnerability and the way the shirt smells of him so much.

'I'm OK,' she nods. 'I am OK. But the Sandwalker isn't, and neither is the Virgule. We can't pass over it like this.'

'Like what?'

'The brown. It's too fragile. Even for Camel – look at her.'

Everyone turns to the creature, who stands anxiously, almost afraid to move her feet, her head turning first to the city, then back to the people in the lake behind her.

'The sun's going down,' Noor says. 'It'll be more difficult in the dark. Phoenix is only a click away. We can walk it and come back tomorrow for the kit.'

'Walk through this?'

'Yes – it'll break. I'll go first, clear the trail.'

And so they set off, parched and in pain, without supplies, without the Sandwalker, the salt splitting Noor's naked stomach until he has to give in and ask Elk to go first. Yma's fingers throb with each step. She can't see them inside the wrapped shirt, but they feel like a red pulp.

By the time they arrive back at Phoenix, after sunset, Yma is exhausted, Noor's belly is bleeding and Camel can barely raise her head.

'I'm sorry, girl.' While the others go upstairs, Yma stays with Camel, washing her as best she can with one hand, feeding and watering her. Camel's in such a sorry state that she has to lean her weight against the marble lobby wall while she is being washed, and the moment she can, she lies down.

Yma sits on the cool floor with her hand on Camel's withers. This place is so harsh for the humans, but even worse for the creatures. So fucking harsh.

'One day I'll find a way to make it better. I promise,' Yma whispers.

37

SPIDER DREAMS OF salt spray from a distant ocean. He dreams of sails being buffeted, of halyards clinking, of hulls groaning. He wakes as if salt water has hit him in the face and finds Amasha sitting next to him on the naked mattress, her hand on his forehead.

'What? What?'

'You're doing well. You feel good?'

He struggles up onto his elbows. The room is dark, there is moonlight on the carpet, lighting the white porcelain of the shower suite.

'Where's Yma? She was getting me a drink.'

Amasha smiles. 'She's been and come back, been and come back. You can't outfox her. You've been asleep a long, long time.

Everyone is here now. Everything is here – we're all safe. Elk and Noor arrived last night.'

'What the fuck?'

'Hey,' she says calmingly. 'You're safe, you're fine. Your scars are healing. It's all going well.'

'Apart from Mahmoud.'

'Apart from him. Yes.'

Spider subsides on the bed, breathing hard. The headache has left him and the pain in his side has gone. He runs his hand across the back of his neck, feels the scab there. Hard and cool now, not hot and weeping. Tonight is a grey night and he'll have to spend a long time checking and rechecking the apartment and the lift shaft.

Amasha sighs. 'Madeira, Knut and I have already searched half this city.'

'Anything?'

'No Sarkpont yet, but Knut is on fire. Says he can feel it, says we're hours away from finding it.' She squeezes his hand. 'You did the right thing bringing us here. Now, listen – I've left food in the kitchen. The water here is running, the drains are working. It's like being in a four-star hotel: I can wash the dishes without the smell of Hugo's pots. The only bad news is that the last crossing went wrong. The Virgule – it changed, like that.' She snaps her fingers. 'The Sandwalker crashed and they drove Camel too hard. I don't know what to say: I'm sorry.'

'Camel?'

'She's resting. Yma found her a room on the ground floor – somewhere dark. She's been fed, drank about half a lake when she got back.'

Amasha leaves, closing the door with a lively air as if she's been replenished by being here. Spider stares at the closed door, surprised by her, then tips his legs off the bed and finds that the floor doesn't see-saw in front of him. The scabs on his legs are recognisable as scabs now and not a bewildering mess of pulpy flesh; he bends them, feeling the slight stiffness around the knee where the wounds are puckering. The foot that he worried might become infected is still swollen, but there are no telltale tracks of black, nothing green or discoloured. He's got away with it, he thinks in surprise.

He goes to the window and looks out at the Virgule. Sure enough, it has turned a dull brown overnight – the worst colour for stability; there would be no getting back across it now, not with Camel, not with the Sandwalker, so the apartment had better be safe for a grey night. He ignores Dubai glistening menacingly across the sand.

His petticoat is stained, so he limps into the shower room, puts a plug in the sink and fills it. It is fascinating to him to see the water in the porcelain, something he hasn't seen for so long. He rubs his chin and peers at the cloudy mirror above the sink. He needs a shave, but that will come later.

Slowly he washes through his petticoat, scrubbing at the stains. Then he unplugs the sink and marvels at the way the water coils into a helix, disappearing down the drain. These tiny things are such luxuries. Listening to it; to the way the machine in the maintenance room whirrs when he runs the water.

From the bedroom window comes the noise of people talking far below. Men's voices. Wearing just his boxers, he stands in the kitchen and eats the yams and flatbreads left on the side. Noor's weapon bag is in the corner of the room, unzipped, and one or two of the longer blades appear, at a glance, to be missing.

Spider pulls on his jacket and his still-damp petticoat. He limps to the wardrobe, opens the door and stares at the vast array of pipes, all sweating and groaning, an electric panel studded with blinking lights and a gantry. He walks out onto the mesh-floored platform – it leads to the pipes, all intersected by valves, each of which is mounted with a control wheel painted yellow. The pipes are huge, as vast as the pipes under the city.

In the lobby he finds the family engaged in various tasks. Everyone is here now, and the search is about to start.

'Not you,' Forlani tells him, strapping on his backpack. 'You spend the day resting up.'

Spider doesn't argue. He can use the time to secure the apartment and maintain the weapons. He finds the room where Camel is – the door is open and Yma is there, sitting on the floor, her bandaged hand resting on Camel, who is lying on her side and breathing hard. Yma scrambles to her feet defensively when she sees him. She looks as if she's been wearing the same clothes for days; there is blood down her front, a look of abject apology on her face.

Camel's lips are black and dry, her hump is slumped. She's been washed and the water has left long lines of black in her coat.

'What's wrong with her?'

'I don't know. I stayed with her all night – she seems a bit brighter today. Did you hear what happened?'

'The Sandwalker? Yeah, sure.' Ignoring the pain in his scabbed leg, Spider sits next to Camel, resting his hand on her flank. Her breathing is harsh, her skin dry. In some of his Scout times on Earth he's been inexplicably fascinated by camels, to the bewilderment of his various Earth families, and has brought back to the Cirque a working knowledge of the beasts.

'It's the fault of your genes, old girl. You've been blessed with too many stomachs.' She opens her eyes to acknowledge him wearily and he scratches the top of her head. 'That's what I said: too many stomachs. You've got bloat. You snuck in some alfalfa or something, didn't you? Yesterday, while you were out?'

Camel gives a soft whimpering sigh and closes her eyes again. He hopes he's right and that her swollen belly is due to something she's eaten and not because she's dehydrated, or plain exhausted from being pushed beyond her limit. Bloat, he thinks, he can cure.

When the others have gone, he miraculously finds, abandoned in the kitchen of the apartment, a large tin of olive oil and, of all ridiculous objects, a turkey-baster lying in a cobwebby utensils tray. Spider gathers everything he needs, then limps back down the eleven flights of stairs to the lobby where Camel lies, her chin on the marble floor, her eyes closed.

'Hey, girl, come on, let's get you fixed up, eh?'

He fills the baster with oil and tests it, squeezing a tiny amount of oil onto his hand, and then, satisfied it's working, lifts the corner of her rubbery lip to expose her giant teeth. Her mouth is so tough and resilient – he's seen Camel eat dried-out wicker chairs just because she's bored, or cacti, and never flinch – and it's only when he tries to get her to open her jaw to accept the tip of the baster that she stirs.

'Steady, steady …'

She twists and grumbles, but he holds her head firmly and forces the baster past her teeth, squirting the contents directly into her throat. Camel tosses her head and tries to stand up – he thinks she might spit it back at him, but he wraps his arm around her neck and holds her in place until the baster is empty. She's too tired to fight any more and eventually swallows all the oil. There's going to be a lot of camel dung in this room by morning, and it won't be the dry stuff the family sometimes use as camp-fire fuel. But there's a tap in the room and he'll be able to clean her up.

He administers the fourth dose, squeezing the last of the oil into Camel's throat, then holding her mouth closed, massaging her neck to encourage her to swallow. She licks her lips and gives her head a fretful shake.

'That's it, that's it,' he murmurs. 'That's the way.'

Gradually she settles back into a half sleep, her head resting on Spider's bare legs, gentle rumbles coming from her belly, like echoes of distant thunder. He leans his head back against the cool of the marble wall and closes his eyes. Is it his imagination or can he smell fish? And brine and seaweed. Dreamily he realises it's not the first time he's smelled the sea since he's been in Phoenix; the idea of ocean water has been tinkering around the edges of his imagination. The sense of surf and wide vistas. Salt spray in his face.

Crazy, for a desert. He opens his eyes and looks at the door. Before the day is over, he is going to barricade this door. Camel is going to have the same protection that the rest of the family have.

38

'ELK,' YMA SAYS later that afternoon. 'Do you think the apartment is going to be safe tonight?'

Elk doesn't answer immediately. He walks on, chewing thoughtfully. They've been given the north-westerly quarter to search, a scrubby area with few buildings and weed-covered parking lots. He's carrying a tied-up cloth around his back full of food, and from time to time he pulls out a hunk of flatbread, tears it in half for the two of them.

Yma starts to think he hasn't heard the question. 'Elk?'

'I'm thinking.'

'You've been thinking for a long time. Are you afraid of the answer?'

'No,' he says flatly. 'I don't know the answer. I guess we don't have any choice but to wait and see. Anyway, I trust Spider. The boy's a skirmisher – he's not stupid. Not stupid at all.'

He hands her a chunk of bread and they continue walking. This is a street with shops on it, the first they've seen. They stop at a petrol station that has a Humvee mounted on the roof, and next to it a red Pegasus – Yma thinks it's the logo for a petrol brand that she can't quite recall. She thinks she might have driven past this with Knut, but she's not sure when or where they were going. Elk tries the door. It opens first time and, from the marks in the dust on the floor, she guesses they're not the first people here. The refrigerators are empty, no lights are on, and where the sweets should be lined up there are only empty boxes.

'It's a rectangle,' Elk muses, opening the door behind the counter and poking his head through. 'It's a rectangle and this is the north-west corner, but no pond, no pool.'

'There's a sink,' Yma says. 'Knut says a piscina doesn't have to be a pool. It's the Christian term for any sink or source of water or drain that's used for the Holy Sacrament.'

Elk smoothes back his grey hair and smiles, glancing around him. 'You're not telling me this is a Christian place of worship.'

For a while, as the day becomes thin and worn, they walk on and talk about religion. For Yma Fitzroy-Hughes, the Church of England was all she knew. As McKenzie Strathie, her Korean friends were more devout Christians than her own family, who would try to attend church two or three times a month, but in truth rarely managed it. She was confirmed and took Holy Communion, but she'd never given it much thought. It seemed to be something that ran alongside her scientific studies without ever crossing it or meshing with it. Whenever she'd tried to reconcile the two parts of her life, she'd failed.

'I was one of those awful socialists who fought everything establishment, so I became Asatru,' Elk told her.

'Asatru? I've never heard of it.'

'Why would you? It's a reversion to paganism. Very popular, when I was on Earth. In the way that Iron Maiden was very popular. And leather gilets.'

She squints at his cynicism. 'You don't believe it now?'

He comes to an abrupt stop in the centre of the street. He opens his hands to indicate the street, the city, the entire desert. 'Do you *think* I still believe in it?'

'But we think we're going to find an answer here. Don't we? We're going to know why the Djinni are like they are, and why we were chosen. Aren't we?'

Elk is silent for a while. Then he shakes his head, tears in his eyes. 'My darling child. Everything we believed on Earth, every one of our faiths – it was all leading here. All leading to this. Everyone was aiming for the same goal. I guess we just chose different routes.'

Yma tucks her hands under her arms, hugging herself. Different paths to the same thing.

Maybe. Maybe Elk is exactly right.

The bandage that Forlani set her up with last night is heavier. He told her the blood took longer to stop and she'd opened up the wound more. He tried to rinse it through, and the pain was unbearable, so she slept with Camel. She didn't want to be in the apartment and keep people awake.

'I guess. But it's incredible how we all believe it, and will kill people who don't follow our chosen route. If we really are all trying to get to the same thing.'

'Oh, we are. Believe me, child, we are.'

She and Elk walk for another hour, passing flaking mansions, tower blocks, furniture shops. They check each one with the crude compass. On they go under lonely traffic lights, swinging lazily overhead, creak-creak. They get to the university campus and Yma lingers, wanting to see the place where McKenzie Strathie died. But it's the trick of the Cirque to deny her this – so although the university is as she remembers it, with its endless adobe buildings and boulevards, the street where it happened is missing.

When the sun tells them the day is nearly over, and they are both so exhausted with the search, with its teasing, they drag themselves back to the apartment. The others have already arrived – there is laughter coming from the balcony where, overlooking the city and full of crystal water, a swimming pool blinks blue in the late-afternoon sun.

Yma can't believe it: cool, clear water at the end of the most exhausting day, the family standing in the open window in awe, and Spider on the balcony, smirking because of what he's achieved.

'I wanna swim,' Cairo says, stripping off his sand-bleached T-shirt. 'I'm in.'

'And Splendour.'

'Well, *shit*,' Knut squeals, running his hands through his Mohican. 'Make way for me, cos I'm going to drench y'all.'

The sun is low on the horizon, but everyone piles into the tiny plunge-pool, drops of water spraying high in the last light, everyone squealing and laughing. There's a palm tree in the centre that the children cling onto. Yma struggles out of the overalls she's been in for two days, peeling them carefully away from her bandages and, in her shorts and T-shirt, drops. Madeira plops in and so does Tita Lily, while Forlani removes his jeans and moves his crooked, vulnerable legs into the water, unashamed.

Amasha's sari clings to her. Elk tries hard not to look, and even Noor, who is wearing one of Forlani's poultices on his belly across the salt cuts from yesterday, dares to take off his desert shorts and get in up to the waist, wearing only his boxers.

'This,' he says, wiping the hair back from his face, giving his blinding white smile at Spider – drops of water glistening on his face – 'is the best.'

Hugo doesn't get in, but stays in the kitchen with Elk, while Spider lies on a recliner, smiling, watching them. There's a small absence moving among them like a ghost – Mahmoud. However much they pretend delight, they can't rub out his trace.

After a few minutes Spider loses interest. He stands and looks down the side of the building, sauntering casually along the railings, stopping every now and then to look down.

Yma watches him from the pool, and after a while scrambles out, grabs a towel and goes to him. 'What you thinking?'

'Nothing.'

She tries to squint down at the side of the building, see what he's looking at. Like Dubai, the apartments on the three floors below are glazed in the same glass. 'I can't see any way they'll get up here.'

He frowns – squints at the horizon. As if he's seen something there that angers him.

'Spider?'

'If we're wrong, then tonight is the night. Have you thought about that?'

'It's all I've thought about.'

And so, after a dinner of cheese-steak and flatbread, when the children are in the interior rooms, well away from the outside, the adults lock the windows and stay in the living room, with the lights out, each with a weapon next to them. They can't keep their eyes off the view out of the window – the rippling night, the star-curtain draping itself high above them, reflecting in the plunge-pool. If there are any noises out there, it's impossible to hear as the glass is so thick.

'How can we be sure they can't climb it?' Noor asks, rubbing a stone rhythmically back and forth over the blade of his sword. 'You guarantee us that, Spider?'

Spider shrugs. 'I spent the day checking. They can't get up here – even if they get onto the balcony, they can't get through the glass: it's the same stuff that was in Dubai. And people have been here before – it's been lived in.'

'Not for long.'

'Maybe because the Sarkpont is here and the families passed through quickly.'

There's a long silence. They have all searched large portions of the city and so far there has been nothing.

'And, uh …' Hugo, who has been quiet this evening, sits forward. 'Something to tell you. May I, Knut?' He gestures to the map Knut has brought with him. It is on the table, unrolled. 'Can I make a mark on it?'

'Sure.' Knut pulls from his pack a few stubs of charcoal and hands them to Hugo, who drags the map over to the place where Phoenix is marked and draws a long line down the east section of the city.

'What's that?' Noor asks, frowning.

'That's the Chicane.'

Everyone stares at him.

Noor stands, leans over the map. 'Chicane? But that means . . .' He draws his hands back and forward around the city, marking where they know the other Chicane lies.

'Everything from that office block there . . .' Hugo jabs his hand towards a grey-and-black four-storey building out of the window, 'to a petrol station way, way in the west is Chicane.'

On the map is marked a large diamond-shaped building at the furthest reaches of the city limits. Yma squints at the map, finding it difficult in the half light to understand what her eyes are telling her. 'You seem to be saying this is a tiny narrow gap in the Chicane?'

'That's exactly what I mean – no more than a kilometre wide.'

Amasha says, 'We went due west and hit the same Chicane that we found in the first two weeks, so there's another border. Then we went onto the Virgule to recover some of the stuff from the crash.'

'Did anyone hit anything north-west?'

'That was our tour,' Yma says. 'And no – nothing. No Chicanes, just regular city stuff.'

'Did you get to the end of the town?'

'Not quite.'

There is a long silence while everyone stares at the map. Spider and Noor stand and go to the window, scanning the office building and the street that runs below it. When Yma gets up to look at it, she cannot believe it's not real – it is so perfectly depicted, each storey so well rendered: the effects of time on it, the way the glass has shattered and, beyond it, the mountains. 'They're not real?' she asks in a whisper.

Hugo shakes his head. 'Sorry.'

'Then,' Noor says, 'the city is a gateway. There must be a whole new section of the Cirque to the north-west. Tomorrow we will—'

Before he can finish his sentence, Spider grabs him, leads him fast away from the window, pushes him into the sofa. 'Everyone – get down, get down. Elk, switch off that light in the hallway.'

He grabs the sword and squats, holding it between his legs, facing the window.

Everyone else grabs their weapons and copies him, in a huddle so that their backs are towards each other and they are facing every angle of the windows.

'You saw them?' Yma hisses. For the first time today she cannot feel the pain in her left hand. 'Where?'

'Coming out of Dubai.'

They all breathe shallowly, nerves on alert, using their ears to pinpoint the tiniest sound. Yma's pulse is thudding in her ears and she has to will it to slow, so that she can listen to the silence.

A lengthy time elapses. There are distant screeches, the familiar chattering sound. A long way away. Then an extended silence in which the family hold each other's gazes, but say nothing.

A tinkle of glass. Below them – maybe on the ground floor – the noise coming up the lift shaft.

'You fucking touch Camel,' Spider hisses, 'and I will eat your face off.'

'Shhhh …' Noor murmurs. 'Listen. Is that in the lift?'

They all turn and look at the lift doors, which are half closed. The cab is locked on the floor below, but it's not stopping the noise. The scratching and chattering of the Djinni, the sniffing, the searching. They sound as if they are directly under the lift cab, poking at it. Yma's blood runs cold, sweat breaks out across her skin. She's never allowed herself to consider how the end might be, but now she can't help it: the images overtake her, close up her throat until she can hardly breathe.

'Hold hands,' Amasha says. 'Hold hands now. Pray.'

She shuffles them into a smaller circle and each person grips their neighbour with one hand, the other hand still clutching their weapon of choice. 'Ha'shem,' Amasha intones, 'please remember us. Mardy, gods of the east and the west, and of all faiths, hear us. Please remember us, remember Mahmoud, bless him …'

They all mutter as much of the prayer as they dare, their eyes watering, their voices tight. And then, just like that, there's a skittering sound as if something has been dropped down the shaft, a muffled wailing, then silence. Only the tinny rattle of a street sign further down the road.

No one speaks for nearly five minutes. Then Spider stands and prowls silently to the window, holding the sword half aloft, pressing his shoulders against the glass and turning to look out.

'Anything?' Noor hisses.

There's a pause, then he shakes his head.

Slowly, one by one, the others get to their feet and sit, panting, shaking their heads.

'Did the children hear anything?' Spider asks.

Amasha shakes her head, her eyes owl-wide. 'You think if they did, we wouldn't know about it?'

Yma breathes out and stares down at her feet – still naked after the swim. Suddenly, overwhelmingly, she wants that shower she promised herself. She thinks longingly of her Earth life, of India; what she wouldn't do to see India right now. She wants to be McKenzie Strathie again, dealing only with her crazy brothers.

'How are we going to do tonight?' Elk says.

'Watches,' Noor answers. 'Two at a time. There's a clock on the cooker – did anyone see?'

'Two hours each team?' Spider says. 'And I can do more. I've been asleep for most of the last three days. I could do with a bit of stimulation.'

At last, when everyone is divided out and the watches are scheduled, Yma pulls a plastic bag over her bandage and takes herself to the shower room. The water is warm, she can hear it chugging up from the feet of the building, and it's fresh, not salt. There are soap bottles in the unit too, and washing her hair, washing her feet, her arms, her face in the non-stop water is the best thing she can remember.

Afterwards she puts on her trackies and sports bra, lodging the two crystals inside it, then lies on her bed and tries to sleep. Her watch is in four hours' time and she needs this sleep – last night was awful. But the sound in the lift shaft keeps her eyes wide.

As the only Scouts who have been to Phoenix, she and Knut have extra responsibility on their shoulders – there must be a detail in this city that is the key. Something … something she's missing that will explain the narrowing of the Chicane.

She lies, unblinking in the dark, and reels her mind back through the time they were there – starting with the accident and working backwards. The wide boulevard where the HonorHealth place was, the university and the—

Her thoughts jar to a halt.

The guy in the seventies floral shirt: so good-looking and anachronistic. What did he say to her?

'*You don't know about the ASU tunnels?*'

Tunnels, she thinks. Tunnels? The words '*ASU's underground*' and '*Clusterfest*' scatter around her head. She hates tunnels, hates losing her vital connection to the sky; she'd lose her bearings and lose her way. And then she thinks, shifting onto her right side and gently laying her injured hand on the mattress, about the Hindu temple. The conversation she had with Elk about religion, about everyone trying to find the same thing but using different routes. Every place of faith is there for a reason. A Hindu temple in a Christian city.

Bharatiya Ekta, she thinks as sleep comes at last. In the morning that's where we'll go.

39

THE MORNING COMES with a burst of light – as if it's the first morning the family have been alive. How, Spider wonders, can they have lasted a night here? And yet they have. He waits until the sun's rays have hit the ceiling, then he goes to the door with the locks inside and out and opens it.

The stairwell is clear: no debris, nothing that wasn't here last night, so he goes down a floor. He peers up the lift shaft at the cab – wedged in the space. There are scratches on the underside; he knows if he used that clawed nail, it would fit. He goes downstairs to check on Camel, aware of the scabs on his legs feeling better than they did two days ago. The barricade is intact and when he unlocks it and peers inside, there she is in the corner of the room. Her hump is pathetically slumped, frothy streams of dung surrounding her, and her belly still roils and gurgles.

'It worked?'

She looks at him, her eyes brighter as she grunts and chomps her way into alertness.

'Fuck, you worried me last night. I mean, seriously?'

Soon the family assemble on the steps outside. Some of them have blankets around their shoulders, some are holding steaming cups of yerba-maté. Yma's legs are bare, as if she's just woken up and hasn't dressed yet, and Noor is carrying the holdall full of weapons.

Elk silently hands Spider a hot sandwich with something pungent and sweet smeared between the bread. He eats hungrily, glancing back to where Camel is, checking she's eating. She is. When the food and the yerba hit his system he is instantly alive, impatient and ready to move.

'Where's the Chicane?'

Hugo points down the road. 'See the way the side of that sign looks blurred? That's the beginning of it.'

'OK – so what now?'

'The only way we can go is north-west,' Noor says. 'We're going to try to find the Hindu temple that Knut and Yma saw in Phoenix. Bharatiya Ekta.'

'Because?'

Yma shrugs. 'It meant something to us when we were there – maybe it's important.'

Spider finishes his mouthful. With a dubious glance at Knut, he carries the sandwich across the concourse. He asks for the map Knut always carries with him, then stands with his head on one side, studying it.

Maybe it's not that the horizon slides off slowly to the north, but that it actually dog-legs on itself, as if the Cirque has a peninsula beginning at Phoenix, which, possibly, travels several hundred clicks from here, all hidden by the Chicane. Maybe this is a different section of the Cirque altogether. He doesn't know, but the yerba-maté is in his system and the only way to decide is to go there.

'Where's the temple?'

'North-west,' Knut says. 'Straight that-a-way.'

Eventually, fed and ready, the weapons distributed among them, the family head out into the abandoned city. The sun sends its needles between the buildings behind them, while ahead of them the streets gradually uncloak themselves from the night. The family move through the fresh morning to a part of Phoenix that Spider recognises as the place he came to the other day. The strange artwork with the hand and the seed painted so carefully.

It's a long morning. They stop at a Christian church. Elk sighs and lowers the cart. 'Break, everyone. We need food.'

They stand at the doors of a huge ruined chapel, the stained glass broken, the walls slimed. Elk leans on the door and pokes his nose inside.

'This will do.'

They file in – to a place with an impossibly high ceiling. There are wooden pews, some of the wood rotting. A crucifix above the altar, but Jesus's head is missing. While Elk serves a midday meal, Cairo finds the plaster head behind a pew, cracked and mildewed. He starts a game of football with it, kicking it into the aisle.

Amasha is incensed. 'How many times have I taught you respect?' She cuffs his ears, drags him away by the scruff of his coat. 'Would you do that with Mohammed's head? Don't you dare let me see disrespect from you.'

Cairo glowers at Amasha. He casts the others a sullen look, hoping for some defence, but they all shake their heads solemnly.

Behind Spider, Camel lets out a long groan. He turns; she's trying to lie down. 'Hey, hey, girl. Not now. Come on.'

But she is determined and sags to her knees.

'What's happening?' Yma says.

'I don't know.' He staggers to keep Camel up, hold her halter. 'Maybe she's dehydrated. Are you thirsty, girl? You crapped for an Olympic medal last night – is that the problem? Come on, let's find you some water.'

The family empty their own gourds. Camel guzzles the water in no time, but it's not enough. About fifty metres behind them is a long line of citrus trees, clearly marking one of the pipes. 'Noor, see that? Under it there's a pipe. Dig down – there's water in there.'

Noor takes the trowel that Spider hands him from his backpack and goes to the base of the trees to begin digging. Elk helps too, but when Spider is able to get Camel up from the ground and over to the pipe, he sees the ground is dry.

'Crack the pipe. Use your boot! Here.' He hands Camel's reins to Noor and jams his boot into the plastic pipe. It shatters and a small, discoloured dribble of water comes out. Spider frowns at it, then looks back up at the verdant trees with their waxy leaves and green flush. 'Weird.'

He takes the halter back.

'Give me your gourds, and a couple of backpacks. I'm going to head back to the apartment, fill up and meet you back here in thirty. Get this grumpy old girl sorted, won't we, eh?' He strokes Camel's muzzle. 'Come on – let's get you into a good place.'

Noor gives him the apartment key and the others load Spider up with backpacks and water gourds, then begin dividing themselves into search parties. Spider walks with balanced, even paces, not rushing Camel, worried about her. His worry intensifies as the further they go, the more she tries to lie down, and by the time they get to the avenue where the apartment is he knows something is really wrong with her.

'Girl.' On the plaza outside the apartment he stops and runs his hands over her. 'Come on, girl, we're so nearly there.'

He leads Camel into the room, slides her drinking trug under the tap and opens it. It judders, spits out a few drops of water, then becomes motionless.

Spider frowns, crouches and checks a washer isn't broken or cracked. The tap is undamaged; it's simply that there is no water being supplied to it. He stands, confused. The whir of the giant water pump on the top floor still reverberates gently through the building, so maybe one of the valves is blocked or the control panel has broken. It would explain why the pipe in the street was empty.

He sighs. 'Stay here, girl. You can lie down if you want, but you gonna have to get up again, so you make up your mind.'

She blinks at him, lowers her head. He kisses her on the topknot, between her moth-eaten ears, pats her neck and makes for the stairs, swinging his way up two at a time. He gets to the floor below the penthouse and instinct makes him slow.

He stands at the top of the stairwell, looking suspiciously across the landing, his skin crawling with fear.

What is different? The lift doors are open.

He swallows quietly and shrinks back against the wall. The doors were closed when they left – it was one of the things they made sure of. And now, above the pounding of his heart, he can hear a noise coming from the lift cab. A low, scratching noise that makes his blood run cold.

40

YMA IS STILL thinking about tunnels, about their significance. As they wait for Spider to go and get water, she touches just under her breasts where the crystals are, twin nodes, reassuring her. She found the crystals in the second town they came to after Mardy's canteen. It was only two days into their search for the Shuck, and Forlani was still finding his feet as the family's apothecary. The way they fell into their roles, so easy and natural, made them laugh over and over again, back in the days when they were all so heady about the way death had turned out for them. When they were still touching each other's faces, staring into each other's eyes, amazed and gratified to see a mirror of themselves looking back.

Mardy told them they were lucky to have been chosen. She crossed her arms over her abundant bosom and frowned at them.

'With the way your species is reproducing, we can't let everyone through. Now we have to be selective. We had to start that a century ago – it was meant as a precautionary measure; we assumed that two world wars, a couple of genocidal maniacs, and you'd settle to a reasonable level, understand what you were doing to the planet you were given, and choose not to use it and put yourselves first.'

'Except . . .' Yma said, shaking her head sadly.

Mardy laughed, a coarse, throaty smoker's laugh. 'Except that human nature came in the way – the greediest produced more ways of getting around the world, by car and plane. And the selfish and greedy side of you all: you wanted children, you wanted to make more copies of yourselves, no matter how immaterial you were, how selfish and lazy, you came to see it as your right. To duplicate. And now there are far too many of you for you all to have a chance in the Cirque. Until there is room, until enough families have moved through, we can't even begin to process the souls that are dying. There they sit,' she rotated her hand, like a whirlpool, 'waiting for their chance, in a vast rotating pod, like one of your tumble dryers that you use to pollute the air and the water and burn more energy, in spite of the sun you were given and don't use. Every day thousands more get added.'

All of that stuck with Yma on the walk through the desert. She thought about human beings, about the fact they'd eat animals, yet if an animal threatened them – be it a shark, a mosquito or a tiger – that animal would swiftly be put to death. Where was the justice in that? And why did so many Abrahamic religions teach that it was OK to plunder the Earth like that?

By the time they reached Ghat on the fifth day they had a routine. Elk searched for food, Yma checked the stars for their bearing and Knut sketched out everything they'd seen. Tita Lily checked on clothes and shoes, while Noor and Spider sat in a huddle, making weapons from everything they found. Forlani had got into the habit of checking the family for dehydration.

'I need you to lick some salt,' he'd say each night, presenting them with a crystal of salt. He picked them up everywhere they went, along with the herbs he collected. Later that would evolve into the bottles of ointment and iodine – all the armoury of a physician. 'Just a little; you will have sweated out a lot of salt, you need to replace it.'

So they would lick the salt, which felt so dry after the day in the sun, always washing it down with water afterwards, some of them spitting in disgust.

Then came the day in Ghat when Yma found her own salt. Two crystals on a window ledge in a ruined shop that must once have sold dates and figs for the sweet, yeasty smell, and the pips on the mud floor. It had become her habit to lick any salt she saw, so that at the end of the day she could rightly be spared sleeping with the taste of salt on her tongue. This time she licked the salt, tasted nothing and so, confused, licked it again.

It wasn't salt.

She's kept the crystals, her only secret from them all. So far the Futatsu know nothing about it, and neither does Noor. Above all, he'd be the most disappointed.

A noise behind them, and when they turn Spider is making his way silently down the street. He's on his own.

'Great,' Knut says, wiping his hands. 'Water at last. I'm parched.'

But Spider isn't carrying the water gourds and his face is wrong.

'What, dude?'

He stops a pace from them, breathing hard.

'What the fuck?'

'There's a situation with our lift.'

'What about it?' Noor asks.

'There's something in it.'

They all stare at him.

Noor turns slightly, lowering his face, and nods at the children, who are coming with Amasha from the direction of the church, smiling because they can see Spider and think he's brought water. He says in a steady voice, 'First we are very, *very* careful what we say. Geddit?'

Everyone glances at the children. Yma can feel her eyes watering with fear, can feel the crystals hard inside her bra.

'And then we go and look.'

Knut grabs up the pack where he keeps his knives. Noor reaches for his sword.

Sensing the panic, Amasha turns to the kids, ushering them back the way they came. 'I forgot! What a silly woman I am. I wanted to ask you something else about that street.' She guides them back to the church, silencing their questions with, 'Nothing to worry about. Noor is going to go and get us some water. Just tell me this …'

Spider turns and heads silently back down the avenue, beckoning the others, ducking in and out of side turnings.

'What if it is one of the Djinni?' Yma asks Knut.

'Fucked if I know. Say our prayers, then try to capture it alive.'

They slow as they see the apartment building. The blinds are drawn on the top floor.

'Who was the last to leave?' Elk hisses.

Noor holds up his hand. 'And I didn't leave the blinds like that. I can guarantee you.'

Spider goes first – he gets to the plaza and stands with his back to the wall, giving them the signal to join him.

'One floor at a time, OK?'

They all nod and move in single file up the stairs, going up sideways, backs to the wall, as if, Yma thinks despairingly, it will help them, should a Djinni come tearing down the stairs. What do the Djinni look like? Spider has glimpsed one – that's what Noor told Knut – but he won't talk about it. He said something about the face being small, but fat and pink, like a white human baby.

By the time they reach the penultimate floor her heart is thundering. Spider and Noor are at the head of the team, weapons raised as they quietly twist out onto the landing. There is a long pause while there is no sound, nothing at all, then – just as Yma swings into the passageway, holding in her good hand the bow that is trembling so hard she hasn't a hope of firing it with her injury – a long human laugh comes from above.

Everyone freezes. Their eyes turn to the ceiling.

'What the fuck?' Knut mouths. 'Whatever the fuck was that?'

No one answers. There's another laugh, then footsteps and a child crying.

They all shoot glances between them, then look back at the next floor. Someone is up there – another family, from the sound of it.

'You locked it, right, Noor?'

'Locked it, double-bolted it.'

'Shit,' Spider hisses. 'They got in through the lift shaft. That's what I heard.'

'Dude, you said nothing could get through.'

'Not the Djinni, they can't use tools – but humans with tools? That must be what I heard.'

Out of nowhere, Yma finds herself walking up the stairs. Her fear has shifted rapidly into anger. No one can take their shelter. No one.

'Yma?' Noor hisses.

She keeps going, the anger fizzing white around her head. On the penthouse floor she goes to the door. The padlock has been removed, but when she rattles the door, it is locked from the other side.

'Hey.' She bangs her good fist on the door. 'Open the fucking door! Open the door this second!'

'*Yma. Jesus!*' Knut appears at the top of the stairs, eyes wide with disbelief. 'Yma, what the—'

'You heard me, didn't you?' she continues. 'Because you've gone silent in there. You think I can't hear. Open the fucking door! *And do it right now, before I batter it down. This is our shelter – we were here first . . .*'

'Yma!' The voice is sharp. It's Noor standing at the top of the stairs, gazing at her in amazement. 'What the hell?'

She stares at him, frozen where she is, and sees what he sees: a woman losing control. There is a long pause while she gathers every strand of self-control. She lets go of the handle, puts her hands up as if he's aiming a gun at her. 'They took our place,' she says in a low voice. 'That's our shelter – we found it.'

'There are better ways,' Noor hisses. 'Better ways.'

The other men gather behind him. He goes to the door and knocks, puts his face up close to it. 'Hello? Hello – we know you're in there.'

There is a hushed sound of someone whispering, someone scampering through the apartment.

'We can share, if you have to. There's enough for all of us.'

Silence from inside.

'We can share and help each other. There are things we can trade.'

More silence. Long minutes tick by and then, impatient, Spider throws down his sword and crosses to the door, hammering on it.

'You turned off the water. We need water. At least turn it back on.' He stands listening to the door, a closed expression on his face. '*Come on. At least turn the water back on.*'

Again no reaction.

'I asked you,' he says, very controlled, a tiny twitch in the corner of his mouth, 'to turn the water on. You know what I'm saying. Just do it.'

He waits, breathing slowly. And then, when almost a minute has passed and nothing has happened, he picks up the sword and swings it at the door.

'Open the fucking door, or I'll get in there and I will be the one to kill you all. This is *our* shelter. It's ours.' He prowls down the passageway, rattling all the doors, slamming the sword into them until at last the weapon shatters, leaving him holding only a stub. 'Fuck.' He throws it down, licks his lips and kicks the door as hard as he can. 'Get out of our fucking shelter.' He goes to the next one and aims another kick. 'Get out – get the fuck out!'

'Spider, come on – we got to think about this.' Knut puts a hand on his arm, and for a moment Spider looks as if he might thump him, but eventually he lets out a long sigh.

'What're we going to do?'

'Let's look at the lift first.'

Eventually Spider is calm enough to go back down to the next floor. With Noor, he puts his head through the doors, looking up at the bottom of the lift cab. Yma stands close by, her hand on the wall, watching intently, but when Noor comes back out he shakes his head. 'That's not good. They've reinforced it where they broke through.'

Spider turns away from the door and paces, cracking his knuckles. 'The same ones who took our water, right? Since when do we have to show respect for another family?'

'That's what we've based all our beliefs on since we've been here.'

'Well, *they* don't have the same belief system, do they? So what are we going to do about it?'

'Easy, Spider. Easy. We've got to think.'

They go back downstairs to the ground floor. There is no water from any of the taps, and when Spider digs down into the irrigation system in the street he gets the same result. No water and no sign that the family are going to turn it back on.

Yma stares up at the apartment, her heart bursting. One of the doors to the balcony is slightly open. She imagines the family up there, surreptitiously dipping in the swimming pool. Eating their food, drinking their water. It must go against all the rules in the Cirque – to prevent another family access. *But is it the Elephant Family …? They've got eleven more Regyres to get it right. Eleven chances.*

The anger comes back at her, but Noor is still watching her steadily. She turns away and breathes slowly, thinking about the crystals. But she can't – not yet, not now. She jams her hands into her sides and walks down the steps, moving, wanting to be in private so that she can punch something. Everywhere there are squashed lemons and oranges. Limes, leaking out their innards, as if something has shaken all the fruit from the trees, crushing them underfoot. As she turns the corner behind the apartments, she realises she's not alone. About twenty metres away, tethered to a traffic light, its head at an awkward angle, is an elephant.

She stops, catching her breath. The animal watches her warily, its eyes rolled back, its ears flapping. It is in pain, she can see that, and when she gets closer it shies away from her, moving its huge back legs away as if afraid she'll beat it.

Yma stands, solemnly, staring up at it. There are marks on its flanks where it has been whipped, dried blood running down its legs. She puts down her pack and, in spite of the pain in her hand, shimmies up the traffic light until she gets to the gantry where the rope is, and unhooks it. The elephant drops its head and swings its neck, relieved to be out of discomfort. But it doesn't try to run.

The men appear at the corner of the building, looking for Yma. They stop when they see the enormous beast waving its head to and fro.

'Get the fuck out,' she hisses at it, kicking it in the back of the neck. 'Get a fucking move on.'

The elephant begins to amble away. It stops halfway down the street and turns to look at her. 'Keep going,' she yells. 'Get the hell out of here.'

Eventually, when it's moved back along the street, she crawls down the sign, wincing at the pain in her hand. Mankind, she thinks sourly, has little more than intelligence. No compassion or insight that she can see. And the family in the apartment are the ones who were *selected*? Seriously?

She has tears in her eyes, but she wipes them away and goes to the men.

'They did the same to the camels,' Spider says, his eyes narrowed in hatred. 'Exactly the same.'

'All I ask is that when we meet this family you let me speak to them first. Get it? I want to be first.'

Knut takes her hand softly, puts an arm round her shoulders. 'Let's find Amasha. Elk needs to talk to her.'

They make their way back to the church. Amasha's eyes are wide and concerned, and the children are miserable.

'Camel drank our water,' Cairo says, kicking a stone. 'I'm thirsty.'

'Splendour too. You wanna see my tongue – it's all furry.' She sticks out her tongue for everyone to inspect.

'Disgusting,' they all agree. 'Like a furry rat.'

They find the temple in the early evening. It's the three moderate white domes picking up the pink blush of the evening sun that alert them, above a petrol station and a McDonald's, cracked golden arches flickering on and off.

'Is this it?' Noor asks.

Yma and Knut nod in unison, their faces rapt. Maybe, Spider thinks, maybe they are on to something after all, because although at first there's nothing special about the temple, when the family walk through the vast gate they see it *is* unusual, very unusual.

It is remarkably clean and untarnished. Although weeds grow through the pavement and sand has drifted all the way across it, the marble steps leading to the entrance are clean, the railings gleaming gold, as if they've been polished in welcome. It looks so different from any of the places they've been before in the Cirque. So *prepared*.

'Is this it?' Splendour asks, tugging at Spider's hand. 'Are we here? Does Splendour gonna get her ice-cream soda?'

'We don't know yet.'

'Splendour is so-o-o-o thirsty, though.'

'Like I said – we don't know.'

The glass doors open into the lobby, and the glass on the shrines of Ganesh and Lakshmi is intact and gleaming. Spider ties Camel in the lobby and the family drift through, poking their heads into the doors to the smaller prayer rooms, stopping to peer at the shrines, looking everywhere for water. It takes an hour to agree there is nothing that could possibly be interpreted as the Sarkpont.

Eventually Spider finds a maintenance ladder and the family climb up to the roof and wander between the white domes, the air-conditioning units, the aerials that must serve no purpose except to create the illusion of the temple on Earth.

There is a panoramic view from here. The sun is now on the horizon: a fizzing, melting white sphere beyond the city, and the floor of the desert to the north and east is at that point where every object casts an enormous shadow. The smallest stone or ripple on the ground is magnified, the cacti are giant men – lying arms outstretched, reaching across the naked sand.

On the west side of the building they find the end of the city. From here the tarmac peters out, into sand – just like in Dubai – but further out, snaking around the edge of the city like a hem, is a dark band, a long, almost perfectly straight line that runs in a north-westerly direction. It effectively closes off the west of the desert, where now Spider sees a range of mountains they've never known about, which rises, bruised and huge, in the distance.

All of this is behind the Chicane, he thinks, incredulous. All those days they woke in the Shuck and looked at the limitless desert to the north, not knowing they were looking at a curtain, beyond which were these expanses: the mountains … and something else.

It is lodged in the gap between that new mountain range. He cleans his binoculars on his petticoat and lifts them, focusing on it. White and blue – something about it pulls at his heart the way nothing in the Cirque has pulled at him.

He trains his binoculars on it. Everything comes back to him in a flash.

The scent of fish, sea spray bursting across his skin. The distant echo of the imam, singing out the call to prayer. A clang of the goat bell. It's a place he knows from his life as the Parisian street urchin, who once, because of what happened in that Parisian atelier, was forced to flee to the only refuge for a teen of his low birth and bearing. The Foreign Legion. The Legion went far and wide. Part mercenary, part reputable army cohort, they went where the fighting took them. And one place was North Africa. Deep, deep into Morocco, where there was dysentery and yellow fever, rabid dogs and snakes that would kill you soon as look at you. Insects too.

'Essaouira,' he murmurs. 'Essaouira, my heart.'

He'll never forget the place, as long as he has consciousness. Noor may have watched his father broker oil in Astana, but Spider lost his innocence and found his adulthood in that city. Essaouira.

'Spider?'

'I knew I could smell the ocean,' he says, not taking his eyes off the place. 'That's it. That's where we need to be.'

Everyone gathers round, peering into the distance. Knut raises his glasses, focuses. 'Shit – the sea! The freakin' sea, guys.'

'The sea!' Cairo yells, grabbing Splendour's hands and dancing around. 'We're going to the seaside!'

'Yes. It's Essaouira. A place I dream of.'

'A place you dream of?' Amasha asks.

'I went there. I was twenty – just six months before I died. I got sick there. Really sick …' He lapses for a moment, recalling the tiny open windows in the riad, the fever, the crazy imagery of his illness. The pictures of death and of deserts, and of a family who loved him and would protect him, regardless. He remembers how the wind coming through the medina whistled down the alleys and was strong enough to fork through the window and rustle the heavy silk bed linen. He recalls how, on the first day of wellness, he climbed to the roof and, although he was hundreds of metres inland, still the sea spray reached him, smattering his face with diamonds of salt. He remembers things he hasn't recalled for lifetimes.

'I survived. And I don't know how or why – but afterwards I was different, and it happened for a reason. There's a Christian church there. I remember it.'

'A Christian church in a Moroccan town?' Elk says gravely.

'The French were there, the Portuguese … I prayed in there one day.' He looks from face to face. 'Everything we see has its orbit and its own meaning; the way faiths cross – it's all part of their sneaky puzzle.'

Knut scratches his chin, surveying the road that leads out of the city to the north. 'We can cut through that corner – keep us on tarmac as long as possible. It's getting dark, but within ten minutes we can be on that road. And it's a good road. It looks like we'll have almost a kilometre of tarmac before the sand takes over, and the city is what? Twenty clicks away? We can do it easy before morning and be back by midday.'

They break apart, with a renewed sense of vigour. Bundles are shouldered, the insides of shoes checked for lodged stones, belts and buckles tightened. A beautiful city to the west, they think. Paddling in the sea at midnight.

They clamber quickly down the access ladders, renewed, excited. Slowly the buildings get smaller, spaced further apart, the shops are small, everything a little rundown. And then, just as in Dubai, the tarmac runs out slowly; first pocked with weeds, then covered in sand.

About twenty metres away from the end of the road Noor takes a step and freezes.

'Stop,' he says, holding up a hand. 'Stay there.'

Everyone stumbles into one another, grabbing to get their balance and stay back.

Noor is quite still, keeping his precarious balance, one foot out in front of him.

'Noor?'

He holds his hand up again in warning, then, rocking his weight back onto his rear foot, he wraps his hands around the thigh of the front leg and lifts his foot. He contorts himself, and Spider hears a familiar sucking sound, then Noor falls back, landing on his butt, his boot half pulled from his foot.

'Quicksand,' he yells, and everyone takes another step back. 'Stay there.'

They've encountered quicksand before in the Cirque. Noor knocks the wet sand from his foot, fastens his boot, tips onto all fours, then stands and walks to his right a little, looking down. Spider joins him, keeping a respectful distance from the quicksand.

'We saw this from the temple,' he says. 'That mark in the sand. I should have guessed.'

The ribbon bounds Phoenix, stopping all access to the western desert. There are ways to cross quicksand, but this one is maybe thirty metres across, and they've never dealt with it on this scale.

'Shit!' Spider stands with his hands at the back of his neck, staring up at the darkening sky. Essaouira, the windy, fish-smelling, stinking and beautiful fishing village. If it had sent out a harpoon affixed to a line and pulled him towards it, he couldn't have felt more drawn.

Yma and Knut crouch together at the quicksand band, in the moonlight. The stars are up. Yma has her hand resting just above the surface, as if she can divine something from it. The strip is warm and eerie.

'There's no crossing it,' Knut says. 'Nothing we can do. There's enough material in the city to make a pontoon – but it'll take hours, days. We'll have to have another grey night here.'

Yma glances up at Knut, who is staring at the mountains, a tense expression on his face. 'Knut,' she says. 'There are tunnels under Phoenix. Not the Papago Park ones, but ones that start under the university. Maybe – just *maybe* – they go under the quicksand.'

'You never told me.'

'You were dead before I could.' She bites her lip. 'We'd have to find them.'

And I'll have to – you know – fight my Kryptonite ... she fills in silently.

Knut is thoughtful for a while, looking at the mountains, where lights are on in the city of Essaouira. It's not only Spider who is drawn to it, the whole family are. The others come nearer.

'Three options,' Noor says as he comes to them. 'We're running out of water ...'

'We can last – a day or two, even in this heat, if we're sensible,' says Forlani. 'The human body can survive. We could try to get back to our Shuck, or we storm the shelter or ...'

'Or what?'

'We try to get to Essaouira before morning. If that fails, we're screwed anyway, so we can storm the shelter when we get back.'

'Wait.' Yma stands up. 'Let me help you here. The first option is out. The Sandwalker is screwed – I mean big-time screwed, already half buried in the salt, half covered. It would take a day to recover the wreck and ... yada yada: you fill in the rest, with the grey night coming in – what? – less than twenty-four hours?'

'How about we negotiate?' Amasha says. 'Offer to help them.'

'We tried already.' Yma looks at her hands. 'What comes to my mind,' she says, 'is that Essaouira seems like the key. Does anyone else think that?'

They all raise their eyes and look at one another. She gives them a small smile. 'Yeah, you all think it. So the question is: how do we get there?'

'I've thought about this.' Spider kneels up, begins to draw in the sand. 'I can build a bridge. There's a place that's got sidings on it – aluminium. I reckon if we work together, we could do it and—'

'Except,' Yma says abruptly, 'there are tunnels under the city.'

'*Tunnels?*'

Everyone turns to look at her. She opens her hands. 'Everything we learn, we learn for a reason, right? And when I was in Phoenix someone told me there were tunnels, starting under the university. There has to be a reason that he told me.'

No one speaks. Then, with a long sigh, Noor gets to his feet. 'Right, let's find them.'

41

THE SUN HAS come up, the morning has passed. The family have spent the day looking for the tunnels and it's late afternoon when Spider goes to collect Camel. She is a mess, breathing heavily, her eyes crusted and in no mood to walk. Spider has a moment of anxiety – maybe she can't make it from here to Essaouira.

'We'll see how you do, eh?' he tells her, rubbing her head. He has to drag her to her feet. 'You look like I feel.' He wipes down her face. 'Come on – not much further, then you can run on a beach.'

He leads Camel out, pausing to spit on the place where the Elephant Family will come down the stairs. He decides that whatever happens, they are going to be the ones to find the Sarkpont, not the Elephant Family. It's going to be the Dormilones.

Camel plods along obediently behind Spider, plonking her wide feet down on the unfamiliar tarmac. In the street the fruit is all squashed and trodden by the elephant, but Spider pauses at an orange tree with one or two fruit still on it and pulls them all off the branches, putting them in his backpack, although they are hard and small. Thirsty though he is, others in the family will need the moisture before he does. Already his legs are screaming with pain; he should have rested today, and his head is on fire where the hairs are trying to grow back, but his anger forces him on.

He leads Camel back to the yellow-stoned university building with the walkway snaking down to it. There is nothing remarkable about it; it looks like the side of a building in an inner-city street, rubbish-strewn and graffitied, but he enters confidently, leads her to the stairs and gently coaxes her down. She's not using her full concentration, she is so weak, and Spider worries that she's going to slip, but they get to the bottom in one piece.

The Dormilones have been down three different staircases in various university buildings, each darker and less promising than the previous one. Eventually, about an hour ago, they found one that led them into a maintenance room, where dim, glowing lamps were mounted – just as if an invisible generator was supplying electricity. The tunnel leads in the direction of Essaouira; they have been along it for more than half a kilometre. It has to be the right one.

The light is vague, slightly greenish as if harvested from fireflies, but it marks the beginning of the tunnel and this is where the family are assembled, huddled in a smelly lobby waiting for him. Beyond them the green lights march off in parallel lines into the gloom of a tunnel.

Amasha opens the door of the lobby and pulls Spider in by the wrist. He drags Camel after him and Amasha closes the door behind him.

'Now.' She claps her hands. 'Everyone – here, in a circle.'

She takes the hands of both of the children and closes her eyes. The family all shuffle forward and create the circle, half closing their own eyes. Spider joins the family, holding hands with Forlani and Splendour, and lowers his face.

'Ha'shem,' Amasha intones. 'Gods of the north, east, west and south, gods of the small things and the great things, gods of thunder and of scorpions, please bless us tonight and tomorrow in our quest.'

'*Namaste*. Amen, thank you …' comes the mumbled chorus.

'Are you ready?' she asks.

There's a long pause. Splendour, who is holding Amasha's hand, swings her arms sullenly. 'Are there monsters in the tunnels?' she asks.

Spider frowns. 'Are you kidding? Of course there aren't. There are amazing things – crystals and shit, and maybe oranges.'

'Oranges?'

'Yup. But the best thing …'

'Yes?'

'The best thing is it's so cool down there. So cool – it's like being in a breeze. No hot sun, no lizards or scorpions, and at the end of it … ta-da.' He opens his hands like a Las Vegas magician. 'The seaside! You'll love it.'

'Will there be somefink to drink? Water?'

'Of course!'

A shy smile comes to Splendour's face. 'You promise.'

'Do I lie to you?'

She looks up at Amasha as if to check she's heard right. Amasha is tight-lipped, she doesn't believe in giving the children false hope. 'I told you not to drink that pop. What did I say?'

'Pop?' Spider frowns.

Forlani rolls his eyes. 'They found half a bottle of orange soda: warm, old and full of sugar. I told them not to drink it, told them it would make them worse.'

Spider scratches his neck. 'Yeah, well, we all make mistakes. The important thing is that we learn from them. Right?'

Cairo shrugs sullenly and sets off along the tunnel after Elk, who has already broken ranks and is walking fast. Everyone follows, Splendour pulling back on Amasha's hand, reluctant to move forward, her own hand still wedged firmly in her mouth. Camel is equally reluctant to move, always trying to lie down.

The air is curiously soft and muffled. There are no echoes. Their footsteps sound as if they are on sand rather than the concrete floor. There is a huge metal door about twenty metres into the tunnel, which stands partly opened. This side of it has no markings, no handle, no lock, but the reverse side, further into the tunnel, has a massive lock of steel mounted and a huge handle.

Protection from the Djinni. It must be. In the greenish light, Spider notes lines on the concrete where the door has been repeatedly opened and closed. He feels a slight tingle of hope. People have been here before.

The family all come through it and Spider slams it closed, engaging the lock. The great door wedges into place, solid and unmovable. He puts his hands on it, then his forehead, silently telling the door he trusts it.

When he gathers up Camel's reins, he sees that the family have disappeared ahead of him, dwindling in the distant green light. He hurries off again down the tunnel, dragging the reluctant Camel behind him. By the time he gets near the rest of the family, his heart feels tight and black in his chest.

Forlani is limping along painfully at the back and is the first to hear Spider. He turns.

'You OK?'

'Sure,' Spider says, catching up. 'You?'

'Dunno.'

'What?'

Forlani shrugs. He nods at the others, who are tense, walking with their backs straight as if there's going to be an argument any second. The tunnel is larger here – it's got more of a feeling of a mausoleum than a shaft – and the family can walk ten abreast. There must have been a slight decline in the path, because the ceiling is several metres above them and when they speak, their voices echo as if they're in a cathedral.

'They're dehydrated. Big-time. Especially the kids.'

And sure enough, the kids are wailing at the Futatsu, 'I'm thirsty. I'm *so* thirsty.'

Eventually, irritated, Elk stops and turns, spreading his arms to stop the others. There are no provisions to divide up, as there usually are, so instead Elk tells them all to rest, to take five minutes to think about nothing.

Spider leans his shoulder into Camel's chest to stop her lying down and takes from his pack the four oranges. All the adults fixate on the fruit, but Spider hands them to the children. They take them ravenously and suck on them, getting nothing from their flesh but an acrid sting, making their faces pinch up.

'Give me the rinds,' he says, holding out his hands.

They do so and he passes them from adult to adult. They all take a fruit and suck, but the moisture is too tart to be a relief and they throw them down, their faces solemn. Spider understands. Already, after only a few hours, water has become a dream that they believe they can taste if they just close their eyes.

'How far, Knut?' Noor asks. 'Have you kept track?'

'I think we've done nine kilometres.' He takes a breath and stares down at his feet, licking his dry lips. It's Knut's job to record the distance, but how, Spider wonders, can anyone be monitoring that at a time like this? 'Give or take. But the direction – I have no idea.'

'What if the tunnel doesn't lead to Essaouira?' Noor says bitterly. 'What if it simply leads downhill forever? It would be good to have a direction.'

Everyone turns to look at Yma, who is slightly separate from the group, standing with her legs strangely balanced, as if she's concentrating on staying upright. 'What?' she says brightly. 'I'm sorry?'

'Are we going in the right direction?'

'Yeah.' She smiles hopefully, resting her hands against the wall behind her. 'Probably.'

'Is "probably" good enough?'

'Of course it's good enough.' Yma shakes her head, gives him a brave look. 'Of course. We're on-track. Don't worry.'

Noor sighs and shoulders his backpack. 'Only one way to know for sure.'

He has given the children a pebble each to suck. It's an old desert trick they used in the Thar; it's supposed to lessen the thirst, but still they complain. Amasha gives them a sharp talking-to and eventually they get up, brush themselves off and begin to walk, wearily, wavering slightly.

Spider has to wait to get Camel restarted, and that means he's at the back. He notes that Yma is trailing behind the others. She's not right, he sees this clearly. Not enough water probably.

She keeps falling behind, just like Camel does, and he has a wave of sympathy for them both. She drove the Sandwalker across the Virgule three times; she's injured and tired. He wants to catch her under her arms and help her, but she's too proud for that – too full of hostility – so he plods behind her, finding the right pace, the front runners getting further and further into the distance.

They've been going for what seems like hours, neither of them talking, when suddenly Camel's reins jerk. Spider turns in time to see her sinking at the knees.

'Hey,' he begins, but before he can admonish her, he sees it's not Camel being lazy or obstinate. It's because she can't. She simply can't.

Her head goes down on the sandy floor and she closes her eyes. Her breathing is shallow, her coat matted and thin. He gets on his knees and puts his hand on her neck, a bubble of panic starting in his chest.

'Girl, come on. We're nearly there. The beach – you want to see the beach: there are waves that'll go over your knees and winds like you've never felt. Come on. Just try a little further; a little further and we'll be there.'

But Camel doesn't respond. She is breathing, but her eyelids don't even flutter at his voice. He rests his head against hers, smells that chalky, sandy scent that he's come to know so well. He should stay here, lie down next to her and die here with her. It would be OK, wouldn't it? It would all be OK. Sometimes he wonders if there is a magic in the Cirque that can bring the ones you love back …

'Spider?'

He looks up. Yma is standing there, her eyes glassy. She's holding out her hand. 'Get up.'

'Why?'

'Because I can do it for you.'

'Do what?'

'You know what. She can't go on. There's every chance the Elephant Family are behind us – they could be following us – and you know what will happen to her if they find her.'

He stares at her, his pulse hard behind his eyes.

'Spider, you know it's true. And I can do it. Trust me, right now. I can do this.'

He shakes his head and takes two steps away. He can't believe this is happening.

'Do you have something?'

'What?'

'*Something*. Don't make me ask again, please.'

He understands. He swallows and pulls the pack off his back. There's a knife in there, which he hands her.

Yma touches it, has to wait a moment for him to release it, then she crouches next to Camel.

'Do you want to watch?'

Spider tips his head forward, puts his finger in the centre of his forehead. He thinks about his mother, about the day he escaped from the brothel, the way he ran like an imp. He thinks that maybe his mother cried, that maybe she screamed. He is sure she never, ever forgot him, and never let a day go by without looking for him.

'Yes,' he says in a croak. 'I want to watch.'

He sinks next to her. Takes Camel's head in his hands, holds its weight so that she doesn't have to make the effort. He strokes her eyes and scratches her topknot. 'Hey, girl, you know, I was just thinking about those waves.'

Yma takes a breath, lowers her head and draws the blade across Camel's neck. There is blood, but not as much as he'd expected, and it slows to a crawl, the way Camel's life is slowing and drifting. Her eyes open once – a moment's confusion, like a bird flying into a glass window – then she grunts and slumps, the full weight of her wet, warm head in Spider's hands.

He doesn't cry. He lowers his face, so that Yma can't see his expression, and breathes deeply through his nose.

42

YMA CAN'T BELIEVE she has done it. Camel, lying there, almost peaceful. She wants to sink to her haunches, cradle the animal, but she knows the smallest hesitation and her claustrophobia will engulf her, make her a burden and not an asset to the family. She has lasted this far without the crystals; she intends to keep going.

She rubs her face, swallows hard. None of the family have had water all day and her head is pounding from dehydration. She turns her back on Camel.

'Let's go,' she says, not meeting Spider's eyes. 'One foot in front of the other.'

She puts her head down and begins to walk towards the rest of the family, Spider trailing her in silence. She wants to cry, and she's sure he must too, but they are silent. She is thirstier than she has ever been before and now she's covered in Camel's blood, her feet hurting, her hand hurting even more.

The walls become rough-hewn stone, glittering black like coal. The tunnel is wider, with lots of little side pockets, and there's a metallic clink to the air, like in a blacksmith's foundry. They've gone almost a thousand paces when there is a screech from behind them. Something like metal being drawn across metal.

'*What the fuck …?*' Yma turns, but Spider is holding up a hand to silence her. The noises continue, screeching along the tunnel.

'It's a tool,' he murmurs. 'Another family at the door.'

The Elephant Family. Part of knowing it makes her glad: she is ready. She reaches for the knife in her belt, tasting blood in her mouth. Though her left hand still aches, she clenches her teeth and jams the knife into the soft lead of an overhead pipe, until eventually it gives way and a large chunk comes away in her hand.

No water comes out – but the weapon is sturdy and will fend off the other family. She turns it over and over in her hands, wondering what damage she could inflict with it.

'Hit them on the temple or the throat,' Spider says quietly. He is drawing the bow off his shoulder, his eyes narrow. 'Don't have any fear.'

'I won't.'

'Hey,' Spider calls ahead. 'Elk? Noor?'

There is a long silence, punctuated only by the screeching of the saw behind them, moving through metal. Then slowly, out of the green gloom ahead, come four ghostly faces of the Dormilones men.

'What happened?' Noor asks, looking at the blood. 'Where's Camel?'

Spider shakes his head.

There's a short silence, then Forlani cries, 'Oh no, oh no.' He limps over to Spider and wraps his arms around him. 'No, I'm so sorry, so sorry.'

Spider simply stands, rigid, not meeting anyone's eyes. Yma also keeps her gaze down, wretched and ashamed.

Another noise from far down the tunnel.

'What the hell?' Elk says.

'It's the Elephant Family,' Spider says. 'Tita Lily, Amasha and Forlani, take the kids, keep going. The rest of us are rearguard. Get it?'

Up ahead they hear Amasha and Forlani gather the children, convincing them to run, in spite of how thirsty they are. The pitter-patter of their feet echoes down the tunnel.

The remaining seven ready their weapons, Noor selecting an arrow from the quiver he carries. Madeira is snarling, her mouth wide open, and even Hugo looks ready to fight, holding a sword from Noor's collection. They walk backwards after the other five, stopping every now and then to listen to the noises behind.

'It's whatever they used to break into the tower, and to hack the locks in the apartment,' Spider whispers. 'They've just opened this place up wide to the Djinni.'

'You think they know we're here?'

'Probably.'

Yma is ready, in every cell, to fight. She didn't know she had this courage, but her anger and fury, her fear of the tunnel and her thirst all fire that energy.

They have gone about another 400 metres when the noise from behind stops. Everyone comes to a pause, listening hard. Either the Elephant Family have given up or, more likely, they've broken through the door.

'Scatter,' Yma says. 'Keep moving, but use the sides of the tunnel.'

The men obey her without arguing and they all creep along, skulking in the lee of the pipes, dipping into the little antechambers to glance behind. They can see nothing, but presently they hear things: a grunting, someone whispering. The Elephant Family have got through, Yma thinks, a line of adrenaline going down her neck. She and Spider paused for a long time to kill Camel, and it's taken the Elephants nothing to open up the tunnel to the Djinni and come after them.

Amasha comes running back from ahead. 'Elk, Elk! Another door. Hurry!'

'Shhhh!'

She sees their posture and reverses, diving back into the semi-darkness. 'It's less than twenty metres away,' she hisses, then turns and runs back the way she's come. Noor makes to run after her, but the others are frozen, staring back down the tunnel. Suddenly, shining out of the gloom, comes an arrow. It whup-whups through the air, like an invading angel, and lands midway between them.

After it comes a huge rock, hurled so hard it bounces and cracks against the wall.

'Run!'

They break into a canter, seeing the huge door glimmering ahead. But Hugo is instantly cut down by another rock, square between his shoulders. He groans, manages another couple of steps and collapses face down. Seeing this, Spider turns, squares himself up and fires an arrow backwards. Madeira is on Hugo, helping him, and Noor stops and readies an arrow. Another rock catapults into the tunnel, hitting no one this time.

Yma and Madeira try to lift Hugo. 'Get up, get up – not far now!'

Hugo rouses himself, blinking, and rolls onto his side. Another arrow whistles past Yma and now she can see the family coming out of the gloom. So many of them – a human wall – headed by the little African-American guy in his weird suit, tails, a moustache. Behind him is a man almost two metres tall, wide and fat as a sumo wrestler, dressed equally formally in a suit, like a bouncer. There is a large white woman with bleached hair and a mouth outlined in red, a small Italian-looking man and three taller people – all three holding bows and arrows. Beyond them children too, other people she can't see, but no elephant, she thinks in relief.

In her bad hand she readies the pipe, waiting for them to get nearer.

'Fire,' shouts the little man. He speaks in an accent that is deep south. The sumo wrestler pulls a rock from a belt around his waist and hurls it. The others release arrows. The rock misses, though it's going so fast it hits the door behind them. The arrows miss, but passing them are some of the Dormilones' arrows. Most of them miss too, except for one, which hits a white guy at the back. He is carrying the chainsaw that must have cut down the previous door, and he sits down suddenly amongst them.

The party ripples in shock around him, but their leader doesn't react. 'Fire again,' he yells and one or two arrows appear in the air.

'Their aim sucks,' Spider mutters. 'Make a run for it.'

Everyone skeeters forward, falling over themselves. Yma and Noor half drag Hugo along the floor, feeling the arrows flicker past them, one nicking Yma's shoulder. Spider stays at the back, walking backwards, firing arrows down the tunnel.

At the door Forlani and Amasha are waiting, reaching out to grab Hugo and drag him past the door. Yma is the last through, except for Spider, who is advancing towards her backwards. The man he hit earlier is still on the floor, moaning, but the light in the leader's eyes is ferocious and focused.

She reaches forward and grabs Spider. He tumbles backwards, bleeding on his leg.

'What happened?'

'I'm hit, but it's OK.' He throws down the bow, leaps up and begins to close the door.

'What's happening?' Amasha wants to know, as he screws the door closed.

'They broke down the door – they opened the tunnel to the Djinni. They fired at us.'

He rams the door shut and everyone takes a few steps backwards from it, staring at it.

'What do they want?' Splendour whispers.

'They want what we want,' Yma mutters, her tendons like wires, her heart thundering. 'They want what we want, even though they've got other chances.'

'It's not fair.'

'It's not.'

Everyone is silent. Yma glances behind her. They are in a wide, almost church-like grotto. But the tunnel seems to have ended.

'Where's the exit?' she mutters. 'Where's the way out of here?'

One by one, they peel away from the door and begin to feel their way around the cavern. No one can see the remainder of the tunnel.

'What does it mean?' Yma hisses.

'That we fucking die down here,' Knut says. 'There's no way out.'

The family gather in the centre of the space, staring at each other.

'It can't be long before sunset,' Yma says. 'And if it is, what's going to keep them on the other side of that door. They broke down one, why not this one too?'

'And expose us all to the Djinni?' Elk mutters.

'Haven't you figured out they don't have any moral compass?'

There is a sudden scraping noise on the other side of the door. Everyone turns to look at it. It's the Elephant Family, knocking, slamming their fists into the door to get attention.

No one speaks; they all stare in horror at the door.

Then Yma finds her voice. 'Let them in,' she says.

'What?'

'Let them in. We finish it with them here.'

'No! Why should we?'

'She's right,' Spider says. 'We've got more chance of finishing it in here.'

'For fuck's sake,' mutters Noor darkly. 'You serious?'

Yma nods. 'Think about it. They are out there, and it must be nearly sunset, which means they will hack the whole thing down anyway. And it seems to me they know where they're going – like they know which way this leads.'

'They followed us.'

'No. They *know*. They're through this place like locusts – no hanging around.'

Yma meets Noor's eyes, holds them. He is proud, but eventually he lowers his eyes and nods.

'Elk? Amasha?' she asks.

'You're right. We let them in.'

There's a further pounding on the door. It sounds panicked. Maybe the Djinni are already on their way.

'Open it,' she hisses, raising her pipe. 'Just open it.'

And so Spider and Noor stand, arrows raised; Elk and Hugo with their swords drawn, Madeira – cigar between her teeth – a machete held aloft. Forlani hobbles forward to unwind the giant lock on the back of the door.

'Hand me the chainsaw,' Spider hisses through the gap. 'Do it now.'

The door opens just enough and the chainsaw is passed through, handle first. Spider takes a moment to disengage it. He takes it to the back of the cave and hides it there. The door gets wider and the moment it pops, the Elephant Family burst through – first the dapper little man with his oiled moustache, then the others, all falling on top of each other. They jump up quickly, holding knives out to the Dormilones, who have assembled in a circle around them.

From the corridor beyond comes the chattering of the Djinni.

'*Close the door – close it!*' Spider yells.

Noor and Knut lean into the door; even some of the Elephant Family, pushing with all their might. As it is nearly closed, a white finger appears in the gap.

'*PUSH!*'

A hand now.

Spider launches himself at the door. It slams shut and, as it does so, the white hand spasms – the fingers shooting out. Blood spurts from the wrists and, as Spider closes the mechanism, the hand flops. It's huge, Yma thinks, panic-stricken; the size of Elk's forearms, the fingers as long as rulers.

Everyone backs away from the door, from the hand, the Dormilones holding their circle around the Elephant Family, their weapons raised. The hand is limp now, and slowly it slides down the side of the door, falling onto the floor – severed.

Amasha turns the children away, ushers them into the corner so they can't see. Chattering and scratching noises echo through the cavern. Yma stares at the hand, then the door, hardly believing what she's seeing. A line of blood trickles from her hand, but she's fixated on those noises.

No one speaks, no one takes their eyes off the door, everyone's eyes following the sounds of the Djinni as they work their way around the seal. It takes almost ten minutes to be sure that the door is holding the Djinni off.

Yma has more time to take in the other family: the brassy woman with her tanned breasts spilling over her neckline; the little man in a white shirt and black trousers, like a waiter. There's a dark-eyed woman – her body encased in black, a headscarf hastily wrapped over her thick black hair – who holds an axe; a tall black guy who holds a baseball bat; and another guy, white, wiry, a grey beard straggling down over his leather jacket, who holds another baseball bat. He's no taller than Forlani, but covered in tattoos, a look of malevolence on his face. Also at the back, looking shy, is a tiny red-haired woman and three female children.

When the noise of the Djinni stops, the leader turns and draws his hand over his moustache. 'I'm down on numbers.' His voice is New Orleans maybe. 'You hear me – it's your fault. My best man is out there. And my elephant has gone walkabout in Phoenix.'

Yma realises the guy who took the arrow isn't with them. '*Don't move*,' she hisses. 'Don't move or I'll have to kill you.'

'Yeah?'

'Yes. Don't think I won't.'

'But the rules,' he says, running a tongue over his mouth. 'Don't you remember the rules?'

'You haven't obeyed them.'

He shrugs, grins, showing a single gold tooth. 'Why would I bother? I know where we're going.'

From the other side of the door comes a wail as if an animal is being disembowelled. The woman in the headscarf falls to her knees and begins to cry silently. 'Truro, Truro!'

Another sound, something wet being slapped against the door. Only the headscarfed woman continues to cry; everyone else is too appalled by the killing taking place less than a metre away to speak. It seems to take forever – from time to time there is a lull, when the family think it's over, but then there's a small cry, or a chattering, and again the slam of the man's body against the door.

A smell comes into the cavern, difficult to define. It reminds Yma of drains and of the stink of adrenaline.

Eventually, when it's fallen silent, the Elephant Family leader turns away and drags the headscarfed woman to her feet. 'Get up. Hold your knife.'

She takes it shakily, holding it out to the Dormilones as if its presence alone will defend her. In response, Elk raises his sword.

The Elephant Family, awed by Elk's size, the light in his eyes, shrink back a little.

'No,' Elk says, lowering his chin. 'Are we going to kill each other in here? Do the Djinni's work for them?'

There is a pause – no one seems to know how to respond. Eventually the little dude in coat and tie tilts his head and smiles. 'Well, well, well. My thoughts exactly.'

'Because you haven't got the cojones,' Knut yells. 'You know we'll kill you.'

The leader of the Elephant Family looks at his fingernails as if they please him enormously. 'Oh, I doubt that.'

'We would. You suck!'

'Please. Manners.'

'What we need is a truce,' says Elk.

'A truce,' nods the Elephant Family leader. 'My thinking exactly.'

'On one condition.'

'What's that?'

'When the morning comes, you leave by that door. You hear?'

The man shrugs. Quirks an eyebrow. 'What: *that* door?'

'You heard me. Or we fight now.'

Yma flickers her attention around. The Dormilones aren't at their best. Spider is bleeding profusely and Hugo still looks grey from the stone between his shoulder blades. Her own hand is leaking from the bandages, her shoulder bleeding.

'*Answer him*,' she yells, raising the lead pipe higher. 'You leave by that door in the morning or you fight on. Answer him *now*.'

The little man shrugs and runs his fingers over his moustache. 'Oh, I see no reason to fight. Let's all spend the night together.'

Yma licks her lips. 'First you give us your water.'

He peers at her then, leaning forward and narrowing his eyes as if she's a strange and unexpected specimen, something grown up here in the darkness of this cave.

'You heard me. *Give us your water*. You stole ours, so now it's time to give it back.' She senses Amasha trying to hush her, but she is on fire. '*Give us your fucking water now, or fight*.'

He clicks his tongue against his teeth, still smiling. 'We don't have any *water*,' he says, pulling out the vowel sound to mock her British accent. 'I think you'll find it's all gone.'

'Liar.'

He lowers his chin, as if she is being immeasurably rude. Then he looks over his shoulder at the rest of the family. One by one they all pull out water gourds, upend them. One or two drips come out.

'You left the apartment without water?' Hugo says.

'No,' Yma says slowly. 'They drank it – just now on the other side of the door. Am I right?'

No one meets her eyes, except for the little guy, who lifts up his lip to reveal the front of his gold tooth.

'You fucking freak,' she murmurs. 'You did, didn't you? You drank it now because you know we haven't had any water for twenty-four hours.'

'Gosh,' he says in that infuriating British accent. 'What an accusation.'

Yma takes two breaths. And then she launches herself at him. She is no taller than him, but he is thin in limb and thick round the middle – he goes down in one.

'*Yma, stop!*'

She straddles him, her hands on his throat. Someone is yelling in her ear, someone pulling her arms, but she struggles with them, staring into the man's brown eyes. He shows no fear, only arrogance and contempt.

'Take that fucking look off your face,' she spits. 'Say sorry.'

'I sowwy,' he says, mock-apologetic.

She shakes him more. '*Say it like you fucking mean it or I'll—*'

And then she is being lifted off him. Yma kicks at him, struggles, but it's Knut and Noor and Spider and Elk together, and she's no match for them. '*Get off me, get off—*'

But they drag her to the far side of the cave and, no matter how she struggles, they hold her tight. Noor is staring at her in disbelief; then there is Forlani, squatting next to her.

'You've opened up your hand again.'

'I don't fucking care.'

'Well, you should. This isn't over yet.'

He begins to unwind the bandages, his face prepared for what she has done to her hand. Yma feels the blood leaking from her, knowing she can't afford to lose blood when she is dehydrated. She stares across the cave to where the Elephant Family are picking up their leader, brushing him off, standing him up. He reminds her of one of those balancing dolls that rock on their giant bellies and never topple. She wants to kill him, in spite of where they are and all the morality that has surrounded them for so long, she wants to kill the guy.

A clock lies on the floor in the centre of the cave. It's a possession of the Elephant Family and placed there to mark off the minutes until they can be released. The family are propped against the far wall, in various states of sleepiness, or alertness. The little guy in the circus-master tails sits in front of them all, a cane planted on the floor, his chin resting on it, so he can better contemplate Spider.

'Did you expect it to look like that?'

Spider changes position, doesn't answer. The guy is talking about the white hand, which lies in the back of the cave, out of view of the kids. Spider placed it there, he doesn't know why. The touch of it was repellent, soft and luke-warm, something greasy about the palm. But the fingers have no talons, like the ones on the outside of the tower.

'No claws,' says the guy, murmuring in a soft sibilance. 'Is that what you expected: no talons?'

Spider stares at him, knowing his eyes are watering. Funny how the body doesn't know how to hold on to water; funny that his eyes would do that, in spite of how much he's bled.

'Because a claw is what you expected, isn't it? I saw it on the outside of your tower. They'd come after you good.'

Spider shifts his bow to a more comfortable position. It is nearly the end of his watch, but he hasn't once lapsed concentration, hasn't once taken his eye off the Elephant Family. His leg has stopped bleeding, but the blood loss has made him light-headed. He wants more than anything to be back in the tower, asleep in his pod.

'Your women are awesome, by the way.'

Spider narrows his eyes.

'You heard me. That one in the back with the giant teats. I'd like a ride of her, if you'll pardon the expression.'

'I won't pardon it.'

'And the one with the hair. The red hair. Nice. Very nice. You see, my family will fuck anything they want. They just do it, and you know what? No one tells them they're wrong.'

'*Don't talk to me. Don't look at me or I'll kill you*,' Yma hisses from her corner.

He laughs. 'Of course not. Of course I won't.'

Spider rearranges the bow so that it's pointing directly at the guy's eyes. The man smiles. Then he shrugs again and starts to whistle a little song. Spider says nothing, and the man winks at him as if he knows a great big joke about him. Spider glares back, trying to get the measure of him.

He seems not to have a partner, seems to be carrying the role of Futatsu himself. The other family members are quiet, mostly sleeping. The woman in her headscarf is still crying, curled in a ball facing the wall. Next to her, his hand on her shoulder, is the giant. His chin is lifted, his eyes closed, as if he is trying to listen to the cave, to define its dimensions and dangers. It has taken Spider a while to notice the milkiness in his eyes and understand why his aim, though strong, was so wide. He is blind.

In the shadows are the rest of the family, who sleep not like the Dormilones, in a pleasant, hot heap, but separately, even the children. There is a small woman in one of the alcoves, with hair dyed the colour of a flame and her eyes a flat, unblinking gold. She looks as if she's come from New York, she is so colourful and unabashed. She sits drowsing in the corner, her back to Spider, her slim arms wrapped around her knees. She wears rolled-up jeans and is barefoot.

'Spider?'

He blinks, coming out of his reverie. Noor is sitting there, wiping his eyes.

'Is it time for my watch?'

'Yes. I mean – yes, it's twenty minutes in.'

'Why didn't you say?'

Spider eyes the little man opposite, thinks briefly that it's because he is wired enough to put an arrow into the guy's forehead, but shrugs and turns away to let Noor take control.

He goes to the corner, where the children are whimpering, their mouths so dry, already their skin like sandpaper to the touch. He can see Cairo's cheekbones, and wonders fleetingly about Mahmoud, about what happened to his bones.

He lies down, tries to get comfortable on the floor, still facing the Elephant Family, still holding his bow. Their lead man hasn't moved a centimetre, but just stares at Spider, a sly smile of intrigue.

Spider closes his eyes, pretends to be unperturbed by this, but his eyes flicker for a while in the subterfuge. He thinks about a tank, full of water, in a Parisian apartment, and imagines the Elephant guy in it. Then he forces himself to think about the hand, only a few metres from him. The way it is clenched.

Unexpectedly he sleeps, his mind meandering across the Cirque, seeing Djinni tearing up the sand. He dreams about Yma, with the comet of red hair flying behind her on the Sandwalker, and a pair of golden eyes watching him from a small alcove. His mouth is tacky, tongue glued to the roof of his mouth.

A touch at the back of his leg. He opens his eyes, looking down. It's Yma, stretched out on the ground near his feet, her finger to her mouth. With the smallest of gestures she points across the cavern.

He looks. The Elephant Family have moved. All of them. They are about three metres to the right of where they were before.

He doesn't move, just keeps his eyes half closed and creeps his attention around the room. Noor, holding his bow, has fallen asleep, his chin on his chest. The rest of the Dormilones, exhausted by dehydration and little to eat, are all asleep. The Elephant Family have arranged themselves in a semicircle, facing outwards, while the little man is standing, his back to the cave, silently moving a large boulder from a place in the rock.

Spider closes his eyes. His bow is still in his hand, the arrow still there, his fingers can brush it with the smallest movement. If he gets the angle right, he can take out the sumo wrestler, or the tattooed guy.

He counts to three and then, with a yell, lets loose the arrow. It hits the wrestler in the foot, pinning him to the ground for a short moment. Around him the Dormilones wake instantly, Noor firing a shaky arrow at the tattooed guy, who sinks to his haunches and snarls at the Dormilones like a wolf – a knife extended.

The dark-eyed woman fires an arrow, which hits Spider in the leg. She's a mean shot – the same place that bled before, and it lodges. He has a microsecond to decide what to do; he knows he should leave the head in, but he can't, so he rips a piece from his skirt, wrenches out the arrowhead, ties the fabric around the blood and stands.

Meanwhile Yma has thrown herself across the gap, launched herself at the blonde woman, who reaches out a hard, clawed hand and holds her at a distance, nails sinking into her neck. Yma raises the piece of pipe and launches it at the back of the woman's legs, toppling her, while Knut has also raced forward, his sword out, and has brought it down hard on the shoulder of the crouched biker, who now rolls backwards, as if expecting the blow, and manages to slice the back of Knut's ankle. Knut yowls in pain, but doesn't give up and raises the sword again, clapping the victim on the back of his head.

Madeira leaps up with the machete, and Spider sees his chance. He creeps up to the sumo wrestler and, with one elbow in the windpipe, fells him like a giant oak. The woman in the headscarf is slotting another arrow into her bow, but he doesn't give her a chance – he reaches forward and snaps the bow, grabs the arrow from her. She screams something at him, maybe in Farsi, spittle coming out of her mouth, but he pushes her face and she falls backwards, yelling.

The sumo wrestler is up from his place on the floor – he wraps his arms around Spider's legs and brings him down, and the next thing Spider knows he's in a brawl, a full-on insane scrap, rolling across the guy, smelling his sweat, smelling the oil in his hair, getting his face pummelled, all the scabs breaking apart. He tears at the guy's clothes, tries to throttle him with his shirt, but the wrestler gets a blow into the side of Spider's head.

For a moment he sees the walls waver and dim, then he's on his front, coughing. He looks up. The wrestler is smiling, but it's vague; he doesn't know exactly where Spider is. Spider catches sight of Knut at the end of the tattooed guy's knife, screaming in pain; Hugo faced down by the bow of the headscarfed woman; and the little guy, who, like a child, is kicking at the wall, trying to insert himself into the hole he's created.

Spider grabs his sword and goes for the wrestler's legs, hitting them in the back of the calves where the muscle is solid. A spurt of blood and a roar of pain, but the action has located Spider for the wrestler and he drops himself down, all his weight landing on his opponent.

All the breath goes out of him in one push. He has time to register Yma screaming somewhere, then Spider feels his ribs being squashed down – nothing to help him draw another breath – and knows he is going to suffocate here.

43

WHEN SHE WAS a child in England, Yma Fitzroy-Hughes didn't have much time for the sort of hobbies most young women had, like reading, sewing and playing the piano. Instead she sailed and fished and cruised the mudflats for elvers, and watched the skies. Her conversation was always about octas and areas of high pressure, and was it true that a certain type of storm could lift fish from oceans and drop them on a town? She had a newspaper photograph on her wall of the largest hailstone and she measured rainfall every day.

She died young, aged twenty-four, from an injury she got on the mudflats, which was all about her not being observant. She still remembers the things her parents never knew and the look in her mother's eye, at the end, her hand on Yma's forehead.

'It's over, my darling, but you mustn't be afraid. This life is over, but the Lord will take you to higher things.'

The knowledge of overness. The knowledge that life won't reset itself, give you more weapons, reboot you, start the level again. And in the cave, straddling the fat tanned woman, Yma has that sense of overness.

Hugo has been backed into a corner by the headscarfed woman, Knut is lying in a pool of blood under the wiry biker guy, who is sawing off his left ear. It streams with blood and Knut is screaming, trying to throw him off.

They can't lose any more people.

The biker dismounts and smiles, snuggle-toothed, at his trophy.

Madeira and Spider are unconscious. Noor is scrapping hopelessly with the little Mediterranean-looking guy, while the sumo wrestler has his arms around Elk's neck.

'*It's my family*,' Yma yells, punching the woman in the face. 'My family!'

The woman underneath her hitches in a breath and rolls – her girth enough to throw Yma to one side. She loses her grip on the piping and while she is fumbling for it, the woman charges her. What she lacks in fitness she makes up for in weight – it's like being hit by a bull, and Yma skids backwards on the ground, her shoulder and hand lighting up in pain.

'*You fucking bitch*,' Yma growls at the woman who straddles her now, all her weight pushing into Yma's ribs. 'You won't get the better of me, I promise you that.'

'I will.' She smells of alcohol and tobacco, and her eyes are bloodshot, as if she rarely sleeps. She snatches the pipe from Yma and holds it at her throat, leaning in. '*I am going to kill you*.'

The pipe is tight on her larynx, and because Yma has died many times, this constriction is familiar to her. She closes her eyes, searches inside herself for a germ of strength, just the tiniest piece of anger that she can grow.

There is nothing. Only her mother's hand, her dark-brown eyes, her mouth saying, 'Let the Lord take you.'

Another death. But this one deeper. More profound. Yma tries one last time to expand her ribs, but the woman is so heavy, everything between her legs is grinding down on Yma. She says to herself, *Help me, someone, help me*.

And then she begins to let go.

A crack, and the weight lifts. Yma opens her eyes, rolls onto her hands and knees, coughing. Cairo, Forlani and Tita Lily stand there, each holding a pipe similar to hers, while the woman writhes and screams insanely, a long unbroken string of words, 'Fucking bitch fucking bitch fucking bitch.'

Yma coughs a little more, then finds that atom of anger: she scrambles onto the woman, straddling her. With her bare hands she bounces on the woman's ribcage, once, twice, until there is a soft and satisfying crack somewhere inside the flesh.

The woman screams louder. 'Get out of my fucking face.' She throws her hands around crazily. 'Get out of my face!'

Yma kicks her in the stomach and the woman curls over in a pathetic, sobbing heap. Forlani instantly turns to the sumo wrestler, using his pipe to hit him around the back of the head. Yma picks up her own pipe and does the same. The guy moans, but doesn't let go of Elk, who is going blue around the mouth.

Cairo sees wounds in the back of the wrestler's legs and homes in on them, delivering several short, sharp blows. Yma joins him, raining blows down. Eventually the sumo wrestler bellows and rolls backwards, grabbing for them, but Elk is up in a second, punching him in the face, again and again, until there is blood coming from his nose and mouth. The man's milky eyes roll in his head.

'Spider,' Elk yells. 'Wake the fuck up!'

Forlani goes to Spider and Madeira, crouches next to them, shaking them, while Elk easily cracks the back of the biker's right leg. He screams and goes down, releasing Knut, who drags himself upright, his face wild. His neck and face are covered in blood – but he's ready to fight. Together they are able to tie the Italian-looking guy with Spider's ropes; he says nothing, lets them do it, as if it's the tiniest thing. Noor spits in his face while it's being done, and again the man doesn't react.

Last is the Persian woman with Hugo. In the end, all it takes is for them to stand in a circle around her and eventually she lowers her bow. She is spirited enough to head-butt Noor, who instantly wraps her hands behind her back and frogmarches her to the Italian guy, tying her up too.

Meanwhile Elk is busily disengaging the little dude from the hole that he's trying to scramble into – for a moment it looks as if he's going to lose him, be left with just one of his black-and-white daps in his hand – but with a last yell, Elk reaches in and pulls the little guy onto the floor.

He stands astride him.

'You broke the pact. Why did you do that?'

'Gotta be fast – gotta keep hitting it,' says the guy, wiping his forehead. 'Gotta be in it to win it.'

'Give me your hands.'

The guy does it, very, very slowly, a coy look on his face as if he's expected this all along and half hopes for a kiss along with it. Elk wraps the rope around his hands, then around his body until he looks like a little Santa Claus parcel, grinning and well oiled. 'Congratulations. You've made me into a beauty.'

Madeira is sitting up and Forlani is turning Spider over, examining his face. He leans on his chest, listens.

'Is he breathing?'

'He is. Help me get him up.'

While Elk, Noor and Hugo shepherd the Elephant Family into the corner nearest the door, Forlani and Amasha lift Spider, sit him up. He is muttering, slapping his face as if to try to wake himself up, and Forlani has to catch his hands and hold them. Meanwhile Knut lies on the floor, trying to wrap his shirt around his severed ear.

'Fucking asshole. Fucking low-class biker shit – look at the guy, he's gotta be about a hundred years old.'

The Elephant Family stand with their backs to the cave. Yma glowers at the big suntanned woman – clearly she is in pain, as she is doubled over. Only the leader faces the Dormilones. Parcelled up, he is still smiling and winking.

'So,' says Elk slowly. 'The hole. That's the way through, I assume. You were going to try to get there before we had the chance? Yeah?'

The little guy simply closes his eyes, very slowly, then opens them. He doesn't stop smiling.

'One of us is gonna try.'

'Yup – me,' says Cairo. 'I can do it.'

'No, wait,' Amasha says, but Cairo is pulling away from her.

'It's easy. Watch me.'

Before she can reason with him, Cairo has crawled up the wall and is disappearing into the hole. For a moment he pauses, and all Yma can see are the soles of his feet – caramel and so small – then he's gone.

'No,' Amasha cries, going to the hole and calling after him. 'Please, Cairo. *Please*.'

But, just like that, Cairo is separated from them. It's so soon after Mahmoud that Amasha starts to cry. Elk goes to her and holds her.

'I can't bear it. Not after Mahmoud.'

'He's going to be OK. He really is.'

Knut is running with sweat, rocking to and fro, holding the side of his head. 'Just a fucking drink of water,' he mutters to the parcelled-up Elephant guy. 'That would have made everything better.'

Splendour picks up on the mood and begins to cry too. No tears, her body is too dehydrated. She looks like a tiny prisoner of war, shaking, trying to get into Amasha's arms.

One by one the family settle back to nurse their injuries, straighten their clothing. Spider eventually stands, a little shaky. His leg is still bleeding ferociously.

'Why are you still here?' he asks the Elephant Family. 'We've seen enough of you.'

'Wait,' Elk says, but Spider points to the clock.

'It's morning. Sunrise. They can go now. Assuming the clock is correct.' He goes to the family, looks into their eyes. 'Is it correct? Because it says morning now.'

'It's correct,' says the leader. 'It is. You can let us go.'

Spider sighs. 'Yma,' he says. 'Will you open the door? Everyone else, we gotta stop these fuckheads trying one last thing on us, eh?'

The Dormilones men usher the family away from the door and Yma turns the lock slowly. It feels like longer than twelve hours since they came in here; it feels like she's never drunk water – not pure, cold, still water. When she slept briefly she dreamed she was drinking from the pool on the Copper Square balcony, sucking up the water. She can't remember, in any of her lives, what is was like to simply turn on a tap and have water run out. The thought makes her light-headed.

But she turns the cog. With Noor's help, she pulls the giant door back and stands, her head bowed. The men push the family out, not looking at them or listening to them. None of the Dormilones want to see what happened to the tenth member of their clan. They've all seen enough remnants of the Djinni's work.

There is silence from the other side – no Djinni. Maybe the clock really was telling the truth.

Yma slams the door closed and turns the cog. Her hand is screaming with pain, and again it starts to bleed. Forlani is tutting about it, pulling her to the side to re-dress it, pulling embrocations and pots from his waist-pack when, from the hole in the wall, Cairo's small face appears.

'Hey.' He looks at them all, a little owl face, eyes preternaturally wide in his greying face.

'Cairo. What did you find?'

He blinks for a moment. Then he says, 'I think this is it.'

Yma puts her hand over her mouth. She wants to weep. She wants to cheer. They are all so close to dying, she is sure of that. The lack of water – it's coming up for thirty-six hours and she's certain they won't last much longer, especially the kids.

Amasha flaps her hands in delight. 'Come here, little boy, I need to hug you.'

Cairo leaps down from the hole – suddenly transformed by his actions into a miniature Spider. They sit him in the centre of the cave. He's holding a twig with strange leaves on it, which he hands to Splendour. 'For your hair.'

'What did you see?'

He is puffed up, more important than he's ever been before. A trace of the future man he will be, in spite of his drawn face, his greying skin. 'The tunnel is long, and it's narrow … But it goes to the sea. A strange city. There's a bit where the tunnel kind of curls back on itself.'

'What?'

'It goes sort of down, then back – like a hairpin.' His gaze goes to Elk. 'I think you'll get through.'

'With my dancer's body.' Elk leans back, grinning, and pats his belly. 'Of course I will. Racing snake, me. Racing snake.'

Yma says nothing. She thinks about a long tunnel. Narrow. With a kink in it.

'I'll go last,' she says. 'Bring up the rear.'

'Don't be ridiculous.'

'Well, who else? We need men at the front – Knut and Spider are going to require help getting through. And someone needs to help Elk.'

'Hey, I told you. Racing snake.'

Forlani shakes his head. 'At least let me re-bandage your hand. And what happened to your shoulder?'

There is a short period of preparation. They whittle down their packs, so that Elk is nearly empty-handed, and remove his belt and anything else that might get caught. Noor and Hugo roll a rock to the foot of the wall, so they can get up it. 'Kick it away when you're done,' Noor tells Yma as he climbs up. 'Don't want anyone getting any extra help.'

He salutes them all, half wicked, then pushes himself, face first, into the hole.

'It's only narrow at the beginning,' Cairo says. 'Then you can walk. Well, until you get to the kink.'

Yma doesn't know where she got her fear of enclosed spaces from. Maybe the long days in the nursery with the nanny; maybe the disused ice hole in the grounds of her parents' house, which had been grated off, but was still dangerous.

'And there are mines around here, too, Yma,' her mother told her. 'When you go wandering off staring at the sky, you make sure you watch where your feet go. Or you'll be down a hole in no time.'

And that, of course, was roughly what happened. And there was another element too, the detail she never told her parents.

But that was then, and this is now, and the claustrophobia hasn't left her. She doesn't want Noor to see that she's afraid.

Knut goes in front of Amasha. Forlani has strapped his ear as best as he can, but Knut's still in pain. His face is screwed up and it takes all of them to lift him into the hole. He stops, on his hands and knees, and pants for a short time.

'You can do it,' Forlani says. 'You can.'

Yma watches Amasha climb in, followed by Tita Lily, Madeira and the children. Then minutes later Elk – he wriggles to get through the first narrowing of the tunnel, but is soon gone. Forlani and Spider are next. They stand together, waiting, staring at each other, listening to the noises from the hole. Spider looks thin and exhausted, he has lost a lot of blood. When a long time has elapsed and they've heard nothing, Forlani says, 'Is it safe to go through yet?'

Spider shrugs. 'Only one way to find out.'

He climbs up, his usual strength gone. It takes him a long time and he has to catch his breath at the top. Forlani follows. 'Give us ten minutes,' he tells Yma, and then he's gone and she is on her own in the cave. Only the black walls pressing down.

The ice hole. The shadow in the ice hole. The mudflats, birds rising from them, the smell of brine and fish and engine oil.

She takes three breaths. She can't do this alone. Just can't.

She jams the pipe into her belt and snakes her right hand up into the lower band of her bra, scratching the surface of the crystal. A flake comes off in her fingernail, and she pulls it out and studies it. Too much and she will lose all sense of where she is, will forget what she's doing – maybe she'll open the door, laughing, to the Elephant Family. She chips a tiny nip off the flake, rests it on her tongue, closing her eyes.

It takes maybe four or five minutes for the first, blissful lowering of her heart rate, a cleanness spreading over everything she sees. She smiles stupidly, as if glass has coated the cave, making it glint prettily.

Remember, she tells herself. *The tunnel.*

She climbs up, stopping every now and then to laugh at an imagined scene in her head. Her hand hurts, but she can see the pain in her body, a tropical red flower, there for a reason. Even the thirst she welcomes: it's part of the universe inside her, reminding her what to do.

Then the opening of the tunnel – narrow, with a tiny piece of Elk's shirt torn on the overhead rock. Even this makes her laugh. Yma pushes through the narrow passage and then the tunnel is bigger. The floor is slimy, as if a giant snail has been through here, and it smells of earth and fish.

'Fish,' she giggles, as if it's the funniest joke ever. 'Fish.'

She wobbles along, bouncing off the sides of the tunnel, wondering what the seaside will look like. No Mr Whippy and smelly donkeys and fortune-telling automatons. It will be like heaven, she thinks. She will drink all the sea in one gulp, the sailing boats and all.

'No, silly, the sea is salt. Salt!'

She pushes herself away from the wall, keeps walking. The ceiling is getting lower and she has a moment's panic, a moment where her rational self peeps through, but then she smiles, tells herself to get on with it, like anyone else would.

The ceiling gets lower and lower until she has to lie like a caterpillar and crawl along. How Elk got through this she doesn't know, or maybe he's ahead, wedged in the tunnel like a cork. And the others behind him.

Another flare of panic, but she quells it, keeps going. The tunnel is heading down now, there is no light at all, none of the faint greenish lights from earlier; it is pure blackness, the stone rough under her belly. Suddenly her hand hits an obstacle ahead. It takes her a moment or two to understand that the tunnel curls downwards and back on itself. Just like Cairo said. A kink.

She can smell adrenaline, and sweat, as if there has been a struggle here. That will be Elk – so big, a huge man to contort through this space. But she runs her hands down, lowers her chin and winds her body into it, head down, her chin moving back in the direction of her lower half.

And then, out of nowhere, she is stuck. She can't move.

At first she laughs, sings to herself a song her father used to sing on Mersea. 'Stuck, stuck like a barnacle. Like a blistering blue barnacle …'

She tries to drag herself forward with her hands, pushing her toes, but she's lodged.

'Think,' she mutters, licking her dry lips. 'Think!'

But her headache is back, pounding harder now that all the blood is running to her head. Why is she stuck? Why?

And then she remembers – the pipe in her belt. She scrambles for it, but can't get her hands back through the tunnel to loosen it. She pushes herself backwards, but the pipe has wedged her here: she is jammed solid.

'Like a turd in the U-bend,' she smiles. 'Like a rock in the … whatever …'

She grins in the darkness, trying not to think about her pounding head, trying to catch the tail of the drug, the exhilaration, where pain is just part of it all. From a long way back down the tunnel, beyond her wedged-in bottom half, comes a sound.

She recognises it, though she can't quite say why.

'*Because you're high, because you're high!*'

And then it hits her. It's the sound of the Elephant Family using their tools on the closed door.

Her heart begins to pound now. A clarity. The pipe in her belt is what's holding her here. Choices? Unbuckle it: impossible – she can't move her hands. So: break the belt? How? It's leather.

Once again she giggles stupidly, thinking about a turd stuck in a toilet, and then she realises the pipe is lead – it must be – and lead bends. She gathers her feet up behind her knees so that her backside is grazing the top of the tunnel. The blood is so tight in her head now, she thinks it will explode. She has no strength, too much blood loss, too little water, too long awake and no motivation.

Then the sound again: a rhythmic thumping. A screech.

She pushes again, part of her knowing she hasn't got the strength. She thinks about Noor: how long before he notices she's not with them – will someone come from the front? Pull her. But that would be impossible; it's such a small hole there's no room to manoeuvre. The drug is leaving her system, bringing with it a sense of unreality, slight pain and a shortness of breath.

Another noise, and the memory of the blonde woman comes back to her. Lipstick on her teeth, the dog-shit smell of tobacco and alcohol on her breath, and suddenly the belt in her trousers snaps, releases momentarily, catches, then releases again.

She's free. Yma doesn't stop to breathe, but pushes off her feet so that her head goes further into the blackness, her body coming out of her trousers – leaving them behind. Her legs snake round the hairpin and she lies on her back, panting hard. Her trousers have gone, so there is no Camel blood on her.

Yma can see the passage opening ahead, the familiar green lights. Her escape. But first she crawls a metre or so back up into the hairpin bend. She tests the pipe again – it is wedged solid, it will take the power of a few men to dislodge it, so she wraps the jeans around the pipe to give it more bulk.

Just enough to hold up the Elephant Family, she thinks, and another ridiculous smile comes to her. Then she turns and scrambles on after the Dormilones, until she can raise herself to all fours, then to a crouch.

They are getting close. They really are getting close.

Then she's up and running, the wind coming through her hair.

44

THE LIGHT IS changing. It's no longer the chemical green of the tunnel, it is moving through turquoise towards blue. Spider can hardly walk; he has to take a few steps, then stop and rest, holding onto a rock to steady himself. The air in his lungs is different, fishy and full of ozone. There's a distant sound of seagulls.

Forlani is with him and ahead Spider catches occasional glances of the others, about fifty metres away as the ground gets higher and higher, until it levels out. Knut has his hands to his head, being held up by Elk, who has blood running down his naked back. There are flashes of green and brown ahead of them, sunshine, a cloud. And suddenly Spider's at the mouth of the tunnel, which opens abruptly out onto the flank of a mountain. He stops, breathing hard.

'Essaouira,' he tells Forlani. 'It's Essaouira.'

The fishing port is spread out beneath them like an ornate carpet. Blue-painted boats are bobbing merrily on the choppy sea. A wind whips up wet sand and sea spray. Below him a jigsaw of painted houses, tiny streets, roof terraces with lattices entwined with flowers.

The family are about 500 metres ahead, winding silently down the path. Spider takes a deep breath and runs his tongue around the inside of his mouth, trying to release the stickiness in there; he looks at the clear sky, his pulse thrumming in his temples. He can feel life returning to his limbs, can sense the oxygen meeting his cells, clearing his thoughts, dilating his lungs.

As if in a trance, Yma appears next to him. Her face is grey, her eyes glassy. She's half naked, wearing just a vest and underwear. She stops to stare at the city.

'Hey,' Forlani says, peering into her face. 'Are you OK? You look weird – and, like, half dressed. Here, take my shirt.'

She wobbles slightly, starts to smile, then wipes the look from her face and takes the shirt, pulls it on. 'Yeah, I'm … I dunno – dehydrated maybe. Have you seen any water yet?'

'Nothing yet.'

'The Elephants – you know, that family – they're behind us. Really close.'

'Fuckers!' Spider hisses. 'Of course they are.'

They hurry down the narrow mountain track that winds through olive trees, down, down into the city. Essaouira is different from the other places in the Cirque – it has an eerie tranquillity, as if the place has been waiting for them. The path is fringed with rough gorse and fig trees and, higher up the slopes, argan trees lean in like bent old men. Perched in the branches are goats of many colours. They chew on the argan nuts and monitor Spider disinterestedly, their beady eyes flitting across his head.

Forlani says, 'Where do we go?'

With Noor's help, Spider limps to the front of the group. He feels a little strength coming back, though he knows he has to get water soon. He can't imagine what is happening inside him; he imagines his organs shrivelling up into tiny balled fists.

'We've got to go fast – the others are behind.'

'I'll fucking kill them,' Knut says through his pain. 'I will.'

'Follow me.' Everyone falls into line behind Spider, who goes more slowly than he'd like, each step an enormous effort. Splendour is emitting a low moan, pushing her head into Amasha's side and scraping her feet along, begging for water.

Soon they reach the outer walls of the city, sandy-coloured with Moroccan arches over the streets. The medina is so familiar to him, the walls on either side of the narrow streets so close and tall they block out the sunlight – it's like being at the bottom of a canyon – and everywhere there is the smell of lamb frying, burnt odours of cinnamon and aniseed. The family pass an entire wall draped in carpets that hang from windows, and Spider remembers that from a century ago.

There are signs of life everywhere; nothing about Essaouira is neglected or decayed, and yet there is not a soul to be seen.

Spider takes a serpentine route, a series of sharp turns, then heads down a wider street, past little shop fronts, with huge trays of coloured almond-paste balls displayed in the windows. He disappears again, this time into an alley that is no more than an appendix. A dead end. He's confused. He comes back out and takes them down another alley, which opens out onto a central square that is dotted with poured-concrete counters painted white, upon which are hundreds and hundreds of fish – freshly caught, laid out as if for a market.

Cairo covers his mouth. 'Smelly.'

Spider stands in the centre, surrounded by the bulging eyes of sharks and squid. This wasn't here when he visited, and he imagines what it might be like now. Cooks and servants with their baskets, striking bargains, vendors pulling back the gills of the fish to prove how red and fresh they are.

In the corner is an old-fashioned water pump. He goes to it, pulls through the first few barrels, because that is where the bacteria live, then stands back and lets everyone else drink. At last it is his turn. The water is so sweet, so cool, it's a balm – he lets it dribble down his front, down his legs.

Yma is busy drinking the water. A shadow catches her eye, just the corner of it. She looks up. 'Oh,' she mutters. 'Oh.'

Spider turns. She is pointing upwards. A shape catches everyone's eye. A bird, watching them from the roof above the square. And then, when she turns, she sees another. There are five or six birds. Another one arrives, flapping and squawking.

'No, no,' Splendour screams. 'No – they're starting.'

Cairo begins to cry, quiet and pathetic. He sits down in the middle of the fishy floor, his shoulders shaking. Amasha looks as if she might cry too, then Spider says, 'Wait.' He stands quite still, looking up at the birds, his blonde hair gleaming in the sunlight.

'There aren't that many. They're watching us. How do we know it isn't because *we're* about to find the Sarkpont?'

Cairo hitches in a breath and raises his face to Noor, curious. Hugo too is staring at him, his mouth open. 'You think?'

'I don't know. Where's the church?'

'Somewhere here. I'm confused, it's different – a labyrinth. We'll try this way.'

Spider heads into a softly lit arched street that seems to lead to nothing. He turns, shakes his head.

'Can you hear that?' Amasha asks Elk as they creep down the streets. He stops and listens. It's a strange humming coming from deep in the medina. 'Is that it?' she asks, rubbing her arms as if she has goosebumps.

'Maybe, maybe …'

They walk on in silence, hardly daring to breathe, until at last they come to another dead end. Ahead of them is a nondescript door. Tall, with a pointed arch. High above it in the white wall is a second arched window, blocked with chicken wire and fibreboard stamped with 'Fresh Fish'. This time Spider doesn't turn and walk back. He walks in silence to the door and puts his head against it, breathing slowly. In and out, in and out. His eyes are closed.

'What?' Yma asks. 'What?'

'This is where they got the water that healed me. From a Christian church, in a Muslim town.'

'It's where the humming is coming from,' she says. 'Isn't it?'

The sky becomes dark and, when Yma looks up, she sees a flock of birds circling down onto the rafters, their eyes locked on the family. Slowly Spider opens the door, pushing it wide.

Inside, the church is derelict. Old roof beams are on the floor and a golden statue of the Virgin Mary lies on her side, staring blankly at the floor and the broken pews. There are pigeon droppings everywhere, and sunlight pierces the gloom in fine, sharp beams. The humming is deafening and above the dust is the smell of harissa, mint and something else.

'Iron,' Spider says, standing there in a trance, his dress still smeared with Camel's blood. 'It smells of iron.'

And then they see Mardy.

She sits in the shadows at a low trestle table, on which are plates of teacakes, all piled in pyramids, each one with a price on it. There are tall glasses of soda with chocolate ice cream floating in them, others of lemonade.

'How lovely to see you all here – what an unexpected bonus to my day. The *Mimosa pudica* family. The shyest little flower, the Dormilones. Here to see me.'

She presses a hand to her chest. Today she is dressed like a woman at a county fair or a bakery competition, a bobbly pink cardigan with cats embroidered onto it, a pie-crust collar and a thick skirt. Her legs are encased in orthopaedic stockings, as if she's trying to control varicose veins.

'Sometimes, Dormilones, when I was watching you in the desert, I rather rooted for you. Not that I have my favourites, you understand, but I'm glad this time you've made it. Well, stand up. You all look such a fright. Come and claim your free sodas.'

The children go, wide-eyed, to the table. Cairo is the bravest; he snatches a glass and downs it in one, the ice cream all over his face. 'Can I have another?'

'Goodness, yes, I should think so, after what you've been through. Help yourselves – drink as much as you want. Though,' she holds up a stern finger, 'you need to pee, and I'll know. So please restrain yourself, my little *Knuddelmaus*. And, Knut, I know you have found it amusing in some of your lives – but it's not amusing here.'

One by one the family go to the table and the adults drink the lemonade, which isn't sweet and cloying, but cold and with the slightest lemon fragrance. Hugo groans as he drinks it, shakes his head, while Cairo gets through the second glass and begins to cry.

'Hey, hey,' Amasha says, hugging him. 'It's OK.'

'I never knew it could taste so good.'

'I know, sweet boy, I know.'

Yma doesn't drink, she's too exhausted and disturbed. She feels something isn't right. Elk gravitates to the stone piscina in the corner. He is silent, then leans over. The shock of what he sees makes him jerk back, dropping his glass.

He holds his hand up, warning the others not to get close.

'Is that where the sound is coming from?' Yma asks.

'Amasha?' says Elk. 'Look at this.'

Mesmerised, Amasha goes silently to the structure. She looks in, and her face is briefly lit red from underneath. Then she grips Elk, as if she's going to faint. He puts his arms around her. To Yma, the movement seems so natural, as if they've done it a thousand times before.

'The *garbhanal* …' Amasha murmurs into Elk's chest. She looks as if she is being bathed in monsoon rain, as if she's dancing in her head. 'We've found it.'

'The what?' Yma asks.

Elk gives her a smile, the edges of his mouth so sore and waterless they seem to crack. 'It's the threshold – the Sarkpont.'

The sky becomes dark and, when Yma looks up, she sees a flock of birds circling down onto the rafters, their eyes locked on the family. She can't feel the drugs any more – she feels whole, but her hand hurts.

'Have we found it, Yma?' Cairo asks, dragging at her hand.

'I think so.'

'What about Mahmoud and Nergüi?'

She looks at Mardy.

'Maybe,' she replies quietly. 'Although I don't think you will see them again. Maybe if you come back …'

Elk sighs, leaning his head into Amasha's forehead, touching for the faintest of moments. 'This is it, then. This is what we do.'

'Please,' Splendour cries. 'Please – I don't want to; it smells. And where are Mahmoud and Nergüi?'

'We'll figure it out,' Yma whispers, holding Splendour's hand tightly. 'Haven't we always figured it out?'

There is silence, only the humming from the well and the sound of the birds outside as they land on the shattered roof, flapping and cawing. Elk climbs up and pushes himself into a dive, face first. Amasha watches for a moment, then beckons to the children. 'Come on, darlings, come along.'

The children go shyly towards her, Splendour still crying. Amasha wraps her arms around both of them.

Cairo pulls away. 'Is it going to hurt?'

'Not at all. It will feel like heaven. Face first, always face first. *Pætiyo*, you've done it before, though you don't remember.'

'It's going to hurt,' Splendour squeals, but Amasha kisses them both on the head and cantilevers herself, face forward, into the font, pulling them both in with her. There is a struggle, and squeals from the children, then a slight ripping sound, like the noise of a skin breaking.

Then they are gone and the rest of the family are staring at each other.

'Who's next?' Noor says.

'Knut,' says Forlani.

Together they help Knut forward to the well. He sniffs it, curls up his nose. 'Anything's better than this pain,' he says lightly. 'Just don't give a toss.'

And without anyone helping, he tips himself face forward into the well. Again that strange stretching sound, as if a skin is being broken. The smell of iron and blood and grass.

The rest of them stand at the well in shocked silence. They can't see anything except a smooth surface, almost like viscera, vague images moving beyond it – a kind of surreal red light emanating with the smell.

Forlani licks his lips. 'If he can do, it so can I.'

Sweating, moving painfully, he pushes himself onto the side and drops away from them.

None of them bob back to the surface. Then Hugo, without a word, goes to the well and, without a break in his movement, tips himself over the side and drops from view followed by Tita Lily and Madeira.

Yma and Noor stand next to the well and look down into it. She can see blurry images under the surface, as if the faces of the family are turned up to her. Except maybe it's not them – maybe it's not them at all.

A tear wells up in her eye. She looks at Mardy. And then she looks at Spider. He studies her back, with his blue eyes. He really, really watches her. And then he turns his eyes to Noor. There's a hatred there.

She swallows, lowers her eyes and takes Noor's hands.

'Together?'

He nods. 'Together.' They kneel on opposite sides of the well, looking at each other. 'When I count to three. OK?'

She nods.

'One. Two. Three.'

Yma pushes herself away from the side, colliding with Noor, feeling him take her, feeling her hand graze something – a moment's pain, then nothing: just Noor holding her as they sink. She doesn't breathe, expecting to bob back up to the surface, but the fluid around them is so thick she can't move. At first she struggles, feels Noor struggling next to her, then she feels other limbs, senses the rest of the family next to her. She is coming to the end of her breath and she still can't get to the surface. She opens her mouth to scream and the fluid flows in, goes into her lungs like cream, not making her choke, but filling her with a sense of calm that even the crystals have never brought her close to.

She opens her eyes in shock, sees Noor staring back at her, equally surprised. The light in here is clean and clear, and beyond Noor she sees the others, floating: Madeira blinking in delight, her plaits wallowing in the liquid; and Tita Lily with her hair streaming up above her head like a wedding train. Amasha's sari is billowing around her, while Knut's thick blue hair is swirling like a coronet.

The children are stock-still, arms outstretched, feet pointing down, staring in mute wonder at the fluid that ripples and passes over them like waves in an ocean. The noise is louder, a deep vibrating 'Ohhhhmmmm' sound that makes Amasha close her eyes in bliss. The first sound of the world, she calls that noise; the first sound.

A change in the texture, a rushing noise like a wind. It seems to Yma as if she and the rest of the Dormilones stay still, but a wind comes to them in the fluid, so fast, so reverberating, that their clothes are pushed backwards, their hair, their limbs, even their faces vibrate, the skin is pulled back and the noise intensifies.

Just as she thinks she can't bear it any longer, the sound lessens and steadies to a low beat, the steady, metronomic click of a clock, or a heart. It fills her head, her chest, her limbs until it seems to be one with her – her own pulse, moving endlessly onwards, a force of nature.

Spider is left with Mardy in the darkening church. In his tool belt are many things: awls, knives, ropes – and the chunk of Desert Rose that he's kept for Mardy. He waits for the moment when the others have all gone into the piscina, then goes to the table and puts the Desert Rose down. He folds his arms and studies her.

'Desert Rose,' Mardy says lightly, smiling with her horse's teeth. 'You remembered.'

'And what now? Have we succeeded?'

She puts back her head and squints at him. 'Is that what you thought, drainpipe rat? Is that what you imagined? Which of our dunderhead Scouts gave you that impression? One of those Clermont College Jesuits?'

Spider squares his shoulders, places his hand on the table and leans in. 'Are you going to tell us why we were chosen?' he hisses in a low voice. 'I mean, the kids – what did they do, to be brought here? And where are Mahmoud and Nergüi? Are we going to meet anyone we left on Earth? I'd like to see my mother again.'

Mardy stares at her thick fingernails for a while, humming to herself and pretending to think about it. He sees the tiny bulges in her skin, as if there is something dark there, waiting to come to the surface. And in this moment something becomes crystal-clear to him – something he's known on a deep level for a long time.

'I've worked it out. You're not in control, are you? Not as much as you'd like to be.'

'Oh,' she hisses lightly, fiddling with the buttons on her cardigan with her fat fingers.

'It's fraying along the edges, this place, isn't it? There are mistakes – big mistakes. I'm right, aren't I? And you're afraid.'

Mardy tips forward and looks at the piscina. 'You need to go now. You need to go.'

Spider's heart is thudding. He's right. She needs them as much as they need her. She gets up then, her arms open wide. 'You scum of the *gouttière*. It's not over yet – you still need to prove yourselves.'

Spider turns and watches her go to the piscina. He can't believe what she's just said. She opens her arms and smiles, pointing to the piscina.

'So,' she says, her voice loaded with sugar, 'shall we see what's next?'

About the Author

Mo Hayder left school at fifteen. Gifted with intelligence, determined to shape her own future, she worked as an actress in TV and film, barmaid, security guard, filmmaker, hostess in a Tokyo club, educational administrator, and teacher of English as a foreign language in Asia. She had an MA in film from the American University in Washington, DC, and an MA in creative writing from Bath Spa University, UK.

She wrote eleven crime novels under the name Mo Hayder, and her fifth novel, *Ritual*, was nominated for the Barry Award for Best Crime 2009 and was voted Best Book of 2008 by *Publishers Weekly*. *Gone*, her seventh novel, won the Edgar Allan Poe Award. Two of her books, *The Treatment* and *Ritual*, have been made into films, and her novel *Wolf* was nominated for Best Novel in the 2015 Edgar Awards and is currently being adapted for the BBC.

Prior to her diagnosis with Motor Neurone Disease in December 2020, she had completed *The Book of Sand* under the name Theo Clare, as well as the first drafts of three more books in this series of speculative fiction, from which she took her greatest personal writing satisfaction. She passed away in July 2021 as a result of MND. She lived her life as a creative artist, never afraid to challenge her personal boundaries or those set by the establishment. She leaves behind a husband and daughter, a powerful legacy of books, and an incredible number of people who loved and admired the many facets of her diamond personality.